Praise for

Also by Irene Carr

IRENE CARR was born and brought up on the river in Monkwearmouth, Sunderland, in the 1930s. Her father and brother worked in shipyards in County Durham and her mother was a Sunderland barmaid. *Chrissie's Children* is the stand-alone sequel to *Mary's Child* which is also available as a Coronet paperback.

Chrissie's Children

Irene Carr

CORONET BOOKS
Hodder and Stoughton

Copyright © 1977 by Irene Carr

First published in Great Britain in 1997 by
Hodder and Stoughton
a division of Hodder Headline PLC

Coronet edition 1997

The right of Irene Carr to be identified as the author of
the work has been asserted by them in accordance with the
Copyright, Designs and Patents Act 1988.

10 9 8 7 6 5 4 3

A CIP catalogue record for this title
is available from the British Library.

ISBN 0 340 65435 X

Typeset by Hewer Text Composition Services, Edinburgh
Printed and bound in Great Britain by
Mackays of Chatham plc, Chatham, Kent

Hodder and Stoughton
a division of Hodder Headline PLC
338 Euston Road
London NW1 3BH

CHRISSIE'S CHILDREN

1

Summer 1923. Monkwearmouth in Sunderland.

Chrissie Ballantyne felt fear clutch at her heart. She stood in the shipyard, a slender young woman with her dark eyes narrowed against the morning sunlight, and was cold inside. The din of the riveting hammers beat around her head. The part-built hull of the ship held in the web of staging towered black above her. She sniffed the familiar odours of hot metal, coal smoke, oil and salt air. There was soot clinging already to her day dress of silk taffeta and the clothing of her children as they clustered around her legs. With one hand she held on to her little cloche hat as the wind from the River Wear tried to snatch it from her head.

Her husband lifted his voice against the din, stooped his broad shoulders and bent his head with its shock of black hair so that he spoke into her ear: 'In 1920 there were sixty-seven ships built on this river. This year there'll only be sixteen. That's the way it has gone – and is going. On this stretch of the river alone there's one yard, Blumer's, closed down. The rest – Thompson's, Crown's and us – are fighting to stay alive.' Jack Ballantyne sounded grim, and well he might. This was Ballantyne's yard, he owned it and he was staring ruin in the face.

Chrissie reached out to squeeze his hand and forced a smile. 'We've come through bad times before.' They had, surviving what was called the Great War.

'You're right.' Jack nodded grim agreement and then the fine lines crinkled at the corners of his light blue eyes, startling under the black thatch of hair. 'We're not finished yet.'

Then a foreman up on the staging bawled down, 'Mr Ballantyne!'

Jack clapped his old trilby hat on his head. He wore a boilersuit and the jacket of his suit hung in his office. He was dressed now for climbing about the yard and he started away, heading for the foot of a ladder that would take him up to the foreman. He called back over his shoulder, 'I'll see you later!'

That would be at dinner in the evening. Chrissie had given her instructions to her cook and knew the dinner would be a good one. Now she watched him go, tall and long striding, her husband and lover, father of two of her children. The three of them were waving, and Tom, the eldest, called, "Bye, Daddy!' His voice was lost in the din but Jack turned and waved before setting foot on the ladder, so that was all right.

Tom, just four and a half and dark like Jack, was fascinated by the yard. He loved to be taken there, to stand with his mother as now, but preferably in his father's arms. Jack would carry him all over the skeleton of the ship and down into its darkest depths. Jack himself had grown up in the yard this way and Tom would follow him.

'Go home!' Matthew was just short of four but going to be

tall like Jack. He clung to his mother and demanded again, 'Go home!' He hated the noise and smoke.

'Baa, baa, black sheep,' sang Sophie. The clamour and smoke did not affect her. At two and a half she held on to her mother's skirt with plump little fingers, smiled and beamed her blue eyes coquettishly at every workman who passed – and they, faces grimed and sweat streaked from the yard, found themselves grinning at the blonde toddler.

Chrissie led her children out of the yard, past the stacked lengths of timber and sheet steel, the sacks of rivets. The Rolls-Royce Silver Ghost, bought by Jack's late father in 1909, stood gleaming outside the time office where the workmen clocked on. Benson, the chauffeur, opened the rear door and touched his cap. Then with Chrissie and her brood sitting in the back he drove out of the gate.

Chrissie maintained her outward calm, smiling and talking to Sophie sitting on her knee, Matt and Tom either side of her, but the fear was still there. What if Ballantyne's did not get another order to build a ship and had to close? It would not be the first yard on this river to do so. That would be a terrible blow to Jack, the fourth generation of Ballantynes to build ships in this yard. He would feel responsible in some way for the failure – and for failing the men. Closure would mean poverty and near starvation for the hundreds who worked at Ballantyne's, and their families.

Chrissie stared out of the window, seeing the people in the narrow, cobbled streets, long terraces of houses that crowded close outside the yard. The Rolls slid past the women as they stood gossiping at their doors in their aprons, or scurried to and from the little corner shops. The children, some of the smaller ones naked in the sunshine except for a grubby vest, played on the pavement. This was the summer holiday but they would spend it here. Chrissie knew these people and how they lived. She had grown up in these streets.

'Gerroff, yer little bugger!' the driver of the pole-wagon shouted at Peter Robinson, but he took no notice. He was five years old, with brown hair cropped short, worn and patched shorts and shirt. He ran barefoot over the cobbles in pursuit of the wagon carrying steel plates from the railway station to the yard. They were called pole-wagons because of the long pole, like a huge roof beam some six inches square. It ran from front to rear of the open, flatbed wagon, and extended for another ten feet or so behind it.

A quick and tough five-year-old could catch up with the wagon as the two horses in its team hauled it over the cobbles. Peter caught it, jumped up and got his arms over the swinging pole and rode along on it, legs dangling. Until the driver turned and cracked his whip, when Peter dropped off and trotted away, laughing. He went back to the gate of the yard to wait for another wagon.

'That's the way, bonny lass, get them clean!' Isabel Tennant called out from the washhouse. It was built in one quarter of the back yard. The lavatory and the two coalhouses, one for each family, backed on to the street behind and filled another quarter. The surface of the rest of the yard was cemented and coated with dust except where the only tap dripped into the sink by the back gate. Isabel's daughter, Sarah, played in the grime and looked up and smiled at her mother's call.

She was two and a half, her brown hair tied in two plaits with pieces of ribbon. Her dress was woollen and worn thin because it had been bought for the previous winter. So was her other one but that was in the wash. Sarah was washing, like her mother. Isabel had given her a tin of warm water and some rags. Sarah soaked them and wrung them out – then washed them again, dabbling happily in the water.

She was oblivious to the thumping of the wooden poss-stick as the panting Isabel banged it up and down on the clothes in the tub full of suds. The hot water came from a coal-fired copper in a corner of the washhouse, filling the room with steam. When the clothes were washed and rinsed Isabel fed them through the wooden rollers of the mangle, heaving at the handle, wiping at her brow. She would pause now and again to peer through the steam and across the yard to the terraced house which they shared with the Robsons: the Tennants lived in the two downstairs rooms, and the Robsons upstairs.

Sarah did not notice, but Isabel was always aware of the coughing. Her husband was in bed in the room at the front of the house but she could still hear the coughing that racked him.

'Daddy!' Helen Diaz stepped from the passage into the yard in another street, but still a carbon copy of the Tennants' house. She was also two and a half, with glossy black hair and dark eyes like her mother. Her father was swarthy with a long moustache, lean and narrow faced.

'No!' he snapped at her impatiently. He picked her up and dumped her back in the passage, then snatched the doll from the floor and shoved it at her. 'You stay in here.' Helen's smile slipped away but she continued to stand looking out into the yard, the doll clutched in her arms. It was a cloth doll, made by her mother.

Paco Diaz had once been a seaman but had left his ship when it came from Spain into the river. He had married Lizzie – full name Elizabeth but always called Lizzie – Helen's mother, soon afterwards and worked as a nightwatchman at one of the yards. So he was able to play football during the day with his six-year-old son, whom he called Juan, though he was christened John. He was a handsome child, and Helen could not be called pretty. Helen watched them play together, laughing and talking in Spanish.

Monday was washday, and Lizzie Diaz looked out of the washhouse once, saw her little daughter standing alone and sighed helplessly.

The Rolls carried Chrissie and her children back to the big house in a quiet, tree-lined street in Ashbrooke on the outskirts of the town. It was as she always remembered her first sight of it as a small girl: the tower at its centre lifting high against the sky and the wide front of the house with its ranked tall rectangles of windows ablaze with light. She had never dreamed then that this would become her home, that she would marry Jack Ballantyne.

''Bye, my pets!' She kissed all three of her children and handed them over to their red-cheeked, plump and cheerful nurse. They waved to their mother as she climbed back into the Rolls, then Benson drove her down into the town to the Railway Hotel.

The sight of the hotel lifted her heart. It stood in the High Street in the middle of the town and across the road from the railway station, so its stonework was inevitably darkened by the soot of years. However, its windows were clean and sparkled in the sun, the curtains were bright, crisp and fresh, the brasswork on the two swinging front doors glittered. And it was hers. Chrissie had worked her way up from the back streets of the town to ownership of this hotel before she married Jack Ballantyne. So now she entered it with pride as Benson drove the Rolls away.

'Good morning!' she replied and smiled as she walked through the foyer and was greeted by the receptionist and other staff working there. Then she hung up her hat and sat at her desk, the mail waiting her attention before her. Usually at this time her mind would be buzzing with the things she had to do but now she stared across the room at the fire laid in the grate but not lit in the warmth of the summer.

She told herself that Ballantyne's yard would not close, because that was unthinkable. But these were hard times and there were more ahead. Every day she saw men, dressed in the suits that they usually wore only at weekends, trudging into the railway station, carrying cheap suitcases. They were going south to look for work because their yard had shut and they could not find a job in the town. Their wives would come with them to wave them goodbye, then trudge home alone, to manage as best they could.

Could that happen to her? Chrissie silently vowed that she would hold her family together, come what may. For the sake of the children. And with that resolve she thrust her worries behind her for a time and turned to her work.

The sudden silence tore Sarah Tennant from her play, as a sleeping seaman wakes when the engines of his ship

7

cease turning. She realised her father's coughing had stopped and saw Isabel Tennant run across the yard and into the house. The silence dragged on for long seconds then Sarah heard her mother scream and was herself afraid.

2

Summer 1935

Sarah Tennant woke and her first thoughts were of Fannon. She was just fourteen years old and her fear of Joshua Fannon – squat, fat and leering – was always lurking at the back of her mind. His presence seemed to hang over the house like one of the shipyard cranes that towered above the surrounding streets. Then she remembered that this was not the day the landlord would call for his rent for the two dilapidated rooms in which Sarah and her mother lived.

She relaxed for a moment then remembered how important this day was. She slipped out of the bed she shared with her widowed mother and drew back the worn and faded curtains. The lace curtains behind them were yellow and ragged with age. She stared through them, the cracked linoleum cold on her bare feet. A line of cranes lifted long arms high above the boundary wall of a shipyard, all of them still. That yard had been closed for a year now.

The sky was clear and bright with dawn light. Sarah thought that it would be a fine day. The bairns were home from school – a holiday – and before noon the sun would have softened the tarmacadam of the street. They would pick it out to roll between their palms and make marbles. Sarah smiled, forgetting she was little more than a child herself, small and slight with wide dark eyes in a thin face.

She picked up her clothes from a chair and tiptoed out into the other room, the kitchen and living-room. There was no fire in the blackleaded grate and the coal bucket in the hearth was empty. She washed in a bowl on the kitchen table then breakfasted on bread and margarine with a cup of tea brewed on a gas-ring standing in the hearth. She ate hungrily, despite her excitement and nervousness.

'Sarah?' her mother called.

'Coming, Mam!' Sarah helped Isabel to wash and dress, then shuffle out, coughing and panting, to sit in her armchair by the empty fireplace. Dr Dickinson had said, 'It's consumption. She has to rest,' so Isabel spent her days a prisoner in the old armchair.

Sarah prepared the same breakfast for her mother. As Isabel was eating it Sarah cried, 'Milkman!' She had heard the iron wheels of the two-wheeled milk cart. She snatched up a jug and ran out into the street. The horse stood patiently in the shafts as its driver ladled a half-pint of milk from the churn on the cart and poured it into Sarah's jug. She paid with a penny from the few in her mother's purse.

Sarah washed up the cups and plates then changed into her best cotton dress, made from one that had been her mother's. She looked at the clock on the mantelpiece and saw it was still early, but that was all to the good. She said, 'I'll make a start now.'

Isabel Tennant agreed, 'Aye, get there afore time. Tell the lass behind the desk that you want to see Mrs Ballantyne. When you get to see her, tell her who you are. I remember her when she was Chrissie Carter and she's not one to forget. I worked part time for her years ago, afore I went into the factory. I did that for more money when your dad died, but it was long hours and heavy. If I'd stopped wi' Chrissie I might ha' been all right now.' She stopped then as the coughing racked her again.

'I'll tell her.' Sarah stroked her mother's hair, kissed her cheek and left.

'Coal! Tuppence a stone!' the coalman bellowed, mouth pink in a black-dusted face as his horse-drawn cart turned into the street. Sarah did not pause. There was no money for coal in her house and they could manage without as long as the weather did not turn cold.

She walked the two miles or so to save the tram fare. Once she passed a group of girls playing ball against a wall with the dexterity of professional jugglers and chanting, 'Raspberry, strawberry, marmalade and jam, tell me the name of my young man . . .' Only weeks ago she had played like that. And she was a star pupil at her lessons. Her teacher had sighed when Sarah had turned down the chance to go to grammar school.

Crossing the bridge – 'ganning ower the watter' – she looked up and down the river running in its steep-sided ravine. There were few ships lying alongside the quays and being fitted out, fewer still lying building on the stocks. Sarah knew that this was part of the depression, one of the reasons for the poverty around her, the workmen standing idle at street corners. However, the lack of work in the shipyards did not directly affect her – women were not allowed to work in the yards anyway.

She paused a moment outside the front doors of the Railway Hotel, smoothed down her dress and ran her hands

11

over her hair. She had washed it in rainwater from the butt the night before so that it shone. She took a deep breath and walked in, thin and nervous and straight in the back.

In the Ballantyne house an hour earlier Chrissie put down the letter from Elsie Massingham and swore silently yet again that she would hold this family of hers together. She looked around the oval breakfast table, set in the window at one end of the huge dining-room that ran from front to back of the house. The other, long table that would seat more than a score of people was set back against the wall, its polished surface gleaming and empty save for a bowl of flowers from the garden. Overhead hung the huge chandelier, sparkling with reflected sunlight. She remembered dancing in this room with Jack, just the two of them, the night Matthew was conceived, and later when she and Jack were engaged.

A smile twitched her lips then, remembering. Jack caught that smile as he entered. He was tall and lean in a dark blue suit and white shirt with a starched collar. There were flecks of grey now at the temples in his thick, black hair. He dropped a briefcase, bulging with work he had brought home the previous night, on a vacant chair and asked, 'Penny for them?' But Chrissie pressed her lips together and shook her head, eyes laughing. As he passed behind her chair he touched her shoulder and she shivered and leaned back into his hand for a moment.

He moved over to the sideboard, greeting the boys as he went: 'Morning, Tom, Matt. Where's Sophie?' though he guessed the answer to that.

Tom, a sixteen-year-old copy of his father with the same

black hair and neat in a dark blue suit, but dark eyed, answered, 'Morning, Dad. I think I heard her. I expect she's busy with something in her room, be down shortly,' making an excuse for his sister, as usual.

Jack did not believe him and cocked a cynical eye at Chrissie, but accepted the explanation. 'Hum.' He picked up a hot plate from the sideboard and helped himself to eggs, bacon and sausages from the dishes there. He said again, louder, 'Good morning, Matt!'

His younger son was not quite sixteen, lanky in baggy grey flannel trousers and a white cricket shirt open at the neck. His sandy hair was unruly and growing down to his collar. He turned from staring vacantly out of the window and blinked vague light blue eyes at his father. 'Sorry. Good morning.'

'Dreaming again,' Jack said half affectionately, half irritated, then shook his head and sat down opposite his wife.

Betty Price, the maid, a rosy-cheeked country girl smart in black dress, white apron and cap, bustled in with fresh coffee and toast. She set them on the table then whisked up Chrissie's and the boys' emptied plates and carried them out. Chrissie automatically watched to see it was done properly, as she supervised all the work of the house. She had done it all herself in her time.

Now she handed the letter to Tom, asking him, 'Pass that to your father, please.'

Tom obeyed and Jack took it, brows raised, then read as he ate. Chrissie followed the example of the boys and buttered toast, going over the contents of the letter in her mind. Elsie Massingham had written from California that her husband Phillip had lost every penny he had in the Wall Street crash of 1929 and two years later was sacked from his job as a film director. Since then he had failed to find work. Elsie wrote: 'It seems he antagonised the studio bosses, refusing to abandon his principles and do as he was told.' Now he had suffered a nervous breakdown and run off. He had left a note saying that he would not be a burden and would rather live the life of a tramp.

Chrissie had invested her money in Phillip's company, Massingham Films, when he was a near-penniless, crippled ex-officer. She was desperately sorry for him and his family now. 'I wish we could do something for him, Jack.'

He shook his head and sighed, 'That isn't possible because we don't know where he is. Hollywood has closed its doors to him so he won't be able to work in films. It will be impossible for an Englishman to get any other kind of job. He's one of eleven million unemployed in the States right now. Five thousand banks collapsed and nine million savings accounts went down the drain. There are all kinds of men, lots of them professionals, tramping the streets or riding boxcars on the railways, all looking for work. Hoboes they call them. But –' and he tapped the letter, '– we can send a cheque to his wife.'

Chrissie nodded, 'We'll do that.' It was something, but she left the toast, not wanting it now.

Matt had eaten two slices with marmalade after a plateful of eggs and bacon. He now said, 'You look like a bookie's clerk in that suit, Tom.'

His brother only grinned at the intended insult. He wore the suit because this was the day he was starting work. He had wanted to work in the shipyards almost from the time

who was stooped over the open bonnet of the Ford, tinkering with its engine.

'She comes from the street next to where I was born.'

He grinned at her. 'She'll know about you, then, "Chrissie Carter that was".'

She returned the smile, accepting the truth: people talked. There would obviously be gossip, some of it malicious, about a girl from that neighbourhood who married a Ballantyne. She said primly, 'She won't know all about me.'

'I would hope not.' And they laughed together.

Then Jack said, 'I've got to have another word with Matt. It really is time he made up his mind about a career, had an objective in life. He's just drifting.'

Chrissie defended her son: 'His last school report wasn't bad.'

'It wasn't good, either. The only *good* marks he got were for art. On the last report he did well at literature, but not this time. He told me that was because he wasn't too keen on the books they studied this term. And that's it: he won't apply his mind, just flits from one subject to another as the fancy takes him. And that applies outside of school as well. He likes to fiddle with the car but he doesn't want to be any sort of engineer. He takes no interest in the yard. When I was his age—'

'Jack!' Chrissie laid a hand on his sleeve and stopped him. 'He doesn't take after you. Tom does and he will be going into the yard, no doubt of that. Just be grateful for him.'

'That's true. Strange, though,' Jack mused, 'him being just like a real Ballantyne.' He went on, 'That still doesn't excuse Matt. He will have to earn his living one day.' He halted in his strolling. 'I'll tell you who he's like: my mother. You've seen her picture.'

'There's a resemblance,' Chrissie had to admit it. Hilary Ballantyne was a tall, slender woman, blonde where Matt was sandy haired, but there was no denying the likeness.

'And not just physically,' Jack said grimly. '*She* was a dreamer, never did a hand's turn and walked out on my father and me when I was five years old.' Hilary Ballantyne had run off to the South of France with another man. 'I never missed her. Old Amy Jenkinson, my nurse, was a mother to me, both before and after my real mother left. I don't want Matt turning out like her.'

'Glory be to God!' Chrissie exclaimed. She lifted her gaze to the sky then returned it to Jack. 'He's not yet *sixteen*! He doesn't *have* to know what to do with his life this early just because you and Tom did!' As Jack opened his mouth to argue she shifted her ground and charged, 'You'd do better to have a word with Sophie,' knowing full well that her daughter was Jack's favourite. 'Now, she *does* take after her grandmother, *my* natural mother.'

Jack shrugged. 'I never met her, as you know, but you've told me all about her, how she was a singer and dancer – and the rest.'

'I've told you *some* of it,' said Chrissie grimly, 'but you don't know the half.' Her natural mother had been uncaring, had deserted her as a babe in arms. 'She was known as "Vesta Nightingale – vocals and dance". So far as I know, she still is. *And* she rolled her eyes at every man she met. That's Sophie all over – *and* she knows what she wants to do, unfortunately.'

They glared at each other for a moment then Chrissie's

lips twitched and she laughed. Jack grinned, because this was an old argument and they had said it all before.

Jack said, 'All right, I'll take a stricter line with her.' Chrissie remembered him saying that before, too. He asked, 'Where is she, anyway?'

'She went off to play tennis. She's meeting some of her friends from school at the club, said they'd probably stay on for coffee and a chat afterwards. I said I wanted her in by ten.'

Jack nodded agreement. 'No harm in that.'

Sophie was just one more young girl in a summer dress at the dance, except that hers was a floral silk and more expensive than the cotton frocks around her. She had smuggled it out of the house in her tennis bag along with the cheap high-heeled shoes she had bought, secretly and illicitly, with her allowance and extra shillings she had begged from her father. The lipstick and make-up had been purchased the same way. Her tennis dress was in her bag in the cloakroom.

The dance-hall was a high-vaulted cavern, its floor filled with gliding couples under a blue haze of smoke. They danced to the music of a twelve-piece band in dinner jackets who played on a stage at one end of the hall. Lights sparkled and reflected from a mirrored globe circling above the centre of the floor.

Some of the men wore dark double-breasted suits from Burton's or the Fifty-shilling Tailors – just about a labourer's weekly wage – and others dressed more cheaply, in sports coats and grey flannel trousers. The hands of clerks and draughtsmen among them were pink and clean but those who worked in the yards had calloused hands, bruised or burnt, grey with ingrained dirt no scrubbing would remove.

They made a sober background for the splashes of colour of the girls' dresses. Shop assistants and office workers sat on chairs ranked along the walls and chattered excitedly while young men stood in groups, eyeing the girls, smoking and talking, summoning up the nerve to ask for a dance.

One crossed to Sophie where she stood near the band and asked, 'Would you like to do this one?' She had danced with several already, and eagerly, but now she shook her head impatiently and the young man flushed and strode away.

Sophie did not notice. All her attention was focused on the stage. The band's singer, a woman in her mid-twenties wearing a close-fitting evening dress that fell to her silver slippers, got up from her chair and stepped forward to the microphone. The bandleader, out in front, pointed his baton and she began to sing. 'I Only Have Eyes For You . . .' Sophie sang silently with her, mouthing the words, and imitating the gestures in her mind.

When the singer was done, Sophie sought out the young man she had turned away, telling him, 'Sorry, but I couldn't dance then. I will now.' She opened her arms and the startled youth automatically stepped into them before he could grumble at her previous refusal. But Sophie was back by the stage again when the singer came on for her next number.

She left at a quarter to ten, changing rapidly in the ladies' toilet, racing to catch her tram. She ran, light footed in plimsolls, the last four hundred yards from the tram stop through the wide and tree-lined silent streets of big houses standing in expansive gardens. Her home was one of the biggest and she reached it at a quarter past ten.

She took the six steps up to the front door in two bounds. The main door was open, but the inner door with its big stained-glass panel she opened with her key. As she padded along the hall her mother called from the sitting-room on the left, 'Sophie!'

Sophie sauntered into the spacious sitting-room, with its chesterfield and several armchairs forming islands of furniture on a sea of polished floor. The pictures on the walls were all of ships built in the Ballantyne yard, except for the one that hung over the mantelpiece, a life-sized portrait of Sophie's smiling mother.

Chrissie was not smiling now as she looked around the wing of her armchair and accused, 'You're late.'

Sophie controlled her breathing and apologised meekly. 'Sorry, Mummy. I lost track of the time.'

Jack lowered his paper for a moment and frowned. 'Talking, I suppose.'

Sophie sat on the arm of his chair and leaned against him. 'A bit.'

He grinned at her, then caught Chrissie's eye on him and said sternly, 'When your mother says ten o'clock, that's what she means. Remember another time.'

'Yes, Daddy.' Sophie kissed him and headed towards the door, but diverted to the grand piano that stood by the window. She ran her fingers along the keys then sat down and played, singing softly.

Matt, his lean length stretched along the chesterfield, broke in, 'You're beating that piano to death.' He could

27

play with careless ease, while Tom did so conscientiously but laboriously and Sophie with slap-bang abandon.

Now she laughed and went on her way, softly humming.

She was still singing when Matt passed her open door later on the way to his room. He paused and glanced behind him to make sure no one else could hear, then warned, 'They'll find out one of these days.'

Sophie grinned at him. 'Bet you they don't!' Then as he started to move on, 'Why are you so miserable?'

Matt scowled. 'Oh, the usual thing: Dad wanting to know what I'm going to do with my life, asking when I'm going to pull up my socks, telling me my reports aren't good enough.'

Sophie pointed out simply, 'Well, they aren't.'

'I can't help it. I just get bored.'

She sighed then smiled at him and reached up to ruffle his sandy hair. 'Never mind. Cheer up. *I* think you're great, the cat's whiskers.'

'Just because I cover up for you.' But he was grinning as he went on his way.

Chrissie thought of her daughter that night in the moments before she slept, with Jack already slumbering quietly beside her. Sophie was of an age with the girl who had come to Chrissie for a job that day, but Sophie was taller and in body a young woman. She was far removed from the grim reality of Sarah's life, having been brought up in this big, comfortable house, so different from that where Sarah lived, and where Chrissie was born and raised . . .

* * *

'Will he be all right?' Margaret Hackett asked anxiously that evening. She was a drab, thin woman in her early forties with faded good looks, a clean apron over her old dress.

'Why d'you worry about him?' Her son, Peter Robinson, answered her question with another. Peter had kept his father's name when Margaret married Bert Hackett. He was seventeen now, inches taller than her, still thin, but strong. He wore a patched jacket and trousers handed down from his stepfather. Peter continued bitterly, 'He wouldn't worry over you.'

They stood in the kitchen-cum-living-room, one of the two rooms they rented on the ground floor of an old terraced house. The fire was not lit but the fireplace was blackleaded, and the brass fender and fire irons – tongs, poker and shovel – gleamed. The oil cloth spread on the table was washed clean. This was also the bedroom for Peter and his six-year-old half-brother, Billy Hackett; they shared a bed that folded down out of the old sideboard that stood against one wall. Bert Hackett and Margaret slept in the other room.

Peter and his mother looked out through the window into the back yard, watching Bert Hackett staggering across from the outside lavatory. He hitched his braces over his shoulders as he came into the room and peered at them owlishly. He said thickly, voice slurred, 'Right, I'm ready. Let's away or the bloody ship will sail without me. Fetch me bag, you,' he threw at Peter as he fumbled his arms into his jacket and staggered out of the door into the passage.

Peter did not answer him but hoisted the big kitbag on to his shoulder. It held Hackett's spare clothes, blankets and 'donkey's breakfast' – the mattress, at one time straw filled, that would go inside his bunk. Peter told his mother gently, 'No need to fret. I'll see he gets aboard all right.' She smiled at him, although the corners of her mouth turned down as he turned and tramped away down the passage.

Margaret Hackett slumped down into her chair, the smile gone. She recalled miserably how she had married Hackett in 1928 to give her growing son a stepfather to replace the real one he had hardly known – Frank Robinson had died of pneumonia when Peter was three years old. But Hackett had made her life hell, given her another child, Billy, and a succession of miscarriages. Now she believed she was pregnant again. She wept.

Peter strode up the street, thinking that his mother seemed better these days. That was probably because she could look forward to weeks or months of freedom from Hackett, depending on how long this voyage lasted. And she wasn't bruised now. That had stopped a few months ago when Hackett had started to beat her for the hundredth time and Peter's anger had exploded into equal violence. He had fought his stepfather out of the house and into the yard while the neighbours watched and his mother covered her face with her apron and wept, until Peter grabbed a coal shovel and felled Hackett.

Now he overtook the lurching man, walked with him to the tram and sat by him as it swayed, rattled and clanged across the bridge. It was fully dark now, and the lights on the ships shed yellow pools on the oily black surface of the river below. They got down from the tram and Peter shouldered the bag again and guided the weaving Hackett through the dark wilderness of the dock. They wound through black canyons between sheds, trudged beneath cranes and circled huge bollards. Peter held the bag on one shoulder and yanked at Hackett with his free hand to keep the drunken man on course. Even so, at one point, stumbling through a dark alley they fell on a pile of coal and emerged filthy and coughing on dust.

They finally came to Hackett's ship. Peter steered him up the gangway, urged him forward to the fo'c'sle and set him on the ladder. Hackett missed the last few rungs and fell to the deck, but without injury. The men already sleeping in the bunks set around the fo'c'sle woke and swore: 'Keep quiet! Noisy bastard!' Peter dragged out the 'donkey's breakfast', spread it on an empty bunk and shoved Hackett into it.

He climbed back up the ladder and went ashore, his duty done. A load had been lifted from his shoulders, and not just the kitbag. As he walked home he thought, Good riddance. But there was still bitterness because he and his mother needed the money that Hackett made – what little he gave them. Peter was unemployed, only making a shilling or two from odd jobs and they were few.

And winter was coming . . .

'Wondering whether to gan in, lad?' One of the men in the river of hundreds streaming through the gates of the shipyard on the Tyne threw the question at Tom. This was the first morning after his leaving home and he stood in the road, smart in his suit, with the crowd sweeping around him. He stared at the yard, the sheds visible through the open gates, the huge bulk of the half-completed vessel standing inside the staging, towering above the walls. The joker threw back at him as he went on with the crowd, 'Toss a brick up! If it comes down, gan home; if it stops up, come in!'

Tom had heard that one before and laughed. His laughter came easily because he was excited and proud, and had looked forward to this day for a long time. He was going to be a shipyard worker, and earning – not much, but he would be paid and that was enough. He grinned and joined the throng, then walked in through the gates to clock on.

When he came out that evening his ears rang from the din of the riveting hammers. He was weary but happy, and walked back to his lodgings content.

But then, he could not see into the future.

Joshua Fannon, pot bellied, greasy haired and in his forties, was thinking of Sarah as he washed up the breakfast dishes in the untidy kitchen. Meggie, his wife, insisted he should clean it, as she demanded he do all the other work about the house. He obeyed, but in slovenly fashion, and she berated him endlessly.

'You've got to get them Herbert Street rents today!' Meggie bellowed at him from where she still lay, mountainous, in bed.

'Aye, I know.' He answered her meekly but whispered, 'Ye daft cow!' He would not forget the Herbert Street rents because that lass Sarah Tennant lived there.

Meggie bawled again, 'And I want them all, mind! Tak' no excuses!'

'I'll get them,' he promised. He had no thought of rebellion. On their wedding night some ten years ago he had tried to claim his conjugal rights and she had scared him off with a red-hot poker drawn from the fire.

He was still frightened and the marriage had never been consummated.

He had proposed to her because of her money: she had rents from a number of houses left to her by her father, a builder. Joshua had looked forward to a life of ease. Meggie was as big as himself, with boot-button little eyes in a doughy face, but she had posed as compliant and willing. Only after the wedding had she become harsh and domineering. She wanted a husband as an appendage, because other women had one, and she needed a servant, someone to collect her rents and do any work that was needed about the house. Now she stayed in bed until noon every day, when Joshua brought in their lunch from the fish and chip shop.

'Get me a bit o' haddock!' Her shriek followed him as he set off down the passage, pulling on the old raincoat with big pockets that he wore to collect the rents. The passage was uncarpeted, just the bare boards swept clean. Joshua took turns with Mrs Bennet to sweep it. The Bennets, man and wife, lived in the two rooms upstairs. Despite her money, Meggie would not have a house to herself, nor would she buy carpet for the passage because the Bennets would not pay a share.

In Herbert Street Fannon took the few shillings and coppers from Isabel Tennant, counted them and dropped the money in his raincoat pocket. He used his cheap fountain pen to enter the sum in the rent book and handed the book back to Sarah's mother. He asked, 'Where's your lass, then?'

Isabel smiled. 'Sarah's got a job.'

'Has she?' Fannon was unimpressed. His gaze wandered around the cramped little room, assessing. He saw that the grate and coal bucket were empty and the curtains, face turned to the world, were frayed. He could read the signs of dire poverty and he knew the kind of wages a young girl could earn.

He promised, 'I'll see you next week.' And the week after that. The Tennants would find the rent for a little longer but soon the ends would refuse to meet, at first by only coppers, but the gap would widen. A day would come when Sarah would not have the rent and she would need help from him. She would not accept the . . . arrangement . . . easily – he had seen her unspoken dislike whenever she met him – but to keep a roof over her mother's head . . .

4

Winter 1935

On a bitterly cold night Bert Hackett staggered out of a bar in Hamburg and blinked his eyes against the darkness and the driving rain. He hiccupped, swore and stumbled across the cobbled street, heading for his ship. She lay moored to a buoy out in the basin and he looked for the boat that would take him back to her. He had left it tied up at the foot of a flight of stone steps running down from the quay. He squinted blearily against the rain then grunted as he saw the head of the steps and lurched over to them.

He paused then, peering down and trying to focus his eyes. The stairs fell steeply into blackness, relieved only by the glint of yellow light from a distant lamp. It reflected from the wet steps, their surfaces seeming to shiver as rain splashed on them. He thought he could make out the boat and started down, one hand groping along the wall slimy with weed, booted foot feeling for the tread.

He was close to the surface of the water before he saw there was no boat at the foot of these steps. He mumbled an oath and turned away from the wall, intending to climb back to the quay and look elsewhere, but the steps were narrower than he thought. He set one foot down in space and then he was falling. He plunged in face first, foul water driven into his mouth by the force of his fall.

He sank, rose briefly, buoyed up by the air in his clothes, but then sank again, dragged down by the weight of his sea-boots. In the second that his head was above water he started to draw a whooping breath but at the last he sucked in more water than air and went under choking. He still struggled to the surface once again with the strength of desperation. His fingers found the wall and scrabbled like claws at its weed-hung surface. He tore away handfuls of the slime but found no purchase, no hold that would take his weight. That weight was increasing now as the air went out of his clothes and water flooded in to take its place, wrapping him in its freezing embrace. So he sank for the last time. He tried to scream for help, but his lungs filled with water, drowning his cries and himself.

Margaret Hackett received a letter from the shipowners: '. . . regret to inform you . . .' Peter went with her to the shipping office in Tatham Street where she collected the meagre balance of pay that Hackett had not been able to booze away in some foreign port.

Peter realised that he was now the breadwinner of the family. He tramped around the shipyards again in the bitter cold, following the dreary trail he had beaten often before. He went to a different yard each day and set out from home before half past seven, because that was when the yards started. He wanted to be at the gate before the foremen arrived to clock on. He stood in the crowd of men and boys hungry for work and chanted the enquiry like an incantation or a prayer: 'D'ye want any men, mister?' And time after time he was turned away: 'Sorry, son.' That was mostly said with regret or sympathy, the refuser subconsciously thinking, There but for the grace of God go I, because anybody could be laid off.

At Ballantyne's yard Peter offered up his plea to a foreman called Gallagher, muscular but beer bellied, with a veined nose and narrow eyes that glared out of a red face. He shoved Peter aside and jeered, 'Get out o' my way! If there was a job going I'd want a man, not a skinny lad! Now bugger off!'

Peter started forward, fists clenched, ready to avenge the insult, but another man was coming up behind Gallagher, bigger and broader, with a cropped head, bent nose and scarred face. He put a hand on Peter's chest and sent him staggering to the ground. The hungry crowd growled its disapproval, and Peter was scrambling up again, outraged, when a stranger stepped between him and the other two. He held Peter back and snapped at the big man, 'That's enough, McNally. You should pick on somebody your own height and weight.'

He was a man into his fifties, slight and a head shorter, but McNally did not shove him. He muttered sullenly, 'He should keep his lip buttoned up, Joe,' and slouched off after Gallagher.

The little man turned on Peter, who was still bristling. Peter demanded, 'What did you shove your nose in for? Who d'you think you are?'

The other held on to him and said mildly, 'I'm Joe Nolan.'

Memory stirred in Peter of talk he had heard. He said, 'You used to be a boxer.'

Nolan's reply was an ironic 'Aye.'

Peter eyed him with new respect. He looked a quiet, inoffensive man, with thinning ginger hair and a face not scarred, a nose not bent. Peter said, 'You were a champion, a professional, fighting for money.'

Nolan shrugged. 'I was a champion around here and I made some money, but somebody else finished up wi' it.' He was not complaining, just stating a fact. He went on drily, 'You're either brave or barmy, wanting to have a go at McNally. He's a nasty bit o' work, a bare-knuckle fighter, and he's half killed a few men at that game.'

'Aye? Never mind, I'll see my day with him.' Brave talk, but Peter took pause as another thought struck him. One day Gallagher might have a job to give and Peter still need it. He had his mother and little half-brother to think of.

The little man saw that Peter's anger had cooled and let him go, saying, 'You'll need to learn to control a temper like that or it'll get you into trouble when you're older. Ever thought of boxing?' When Peter shook his head Nolan went on, 'I run a class for a few lads in the club.' Peter opened his mouth to refuse, but Nolan could read his mind as he had read others, and got in first: 'We've got all the gear needed at the club so none o' you lads have to bring anything.'

That was different. Peter said, 'Aye? Well, I'll think about it.'

Nolan settled for that because he was sure the lad would be there. Peter sauntered off, having had his first encounter with two mortal enemies.

One morning, a week before Christmas 1935, Sophie left her room in the Ballantyne house and ran lightly up the stairs of the tower. She stopped at the open door of the room at the top and peeped in. It was simply furnished, with two leather armchairs before the fire, a thick rug on the polished floor and pictures of Ballantyne ships on the walls, and smelt of leather and polish. A desk was set under the window so that anyone who worked there could look up from their papers and out over the trees and the town beyond, to the distant river and the sea. Years ago a ship's captain had called it the 'crow's nest'.

Sophie's father was collecting papers from his desk where he had worked the evening before and shuffling them into a briefcase. He looked up as Sophie tapped on the door and entered. He grinned and teased, 'You're up early. I thought you were on holiday.'

'I am. But I have to ask a favour.' Sophie took his arm and rubbed her face against it. 'I need some money.'

Jack buckled the straps on the case. 'You've had your pocket money for this week.'

Sophie nodded. 'Yes, thank you. But this is an awkward time of year, Daddy. I've been to a lot of parties and to the pictures, and there are all sorts of little things that add up. I don't want you to *give* me anything and I'm not asking for a *loan*. Only, if you could advance me a couple of bob from next week's pocket money I could go out, instead of hanging about the house all of the holiday.'

Jack lectured her on economy and the value of money all the way down the stairs, but at the door he fished in his pocket and handed her a florin. 'And that *is* an advance. So don't expect all your pocket money next week.'

'Thank you, Daddy. You're a sweetie.' Sophie kissed him and waved as he climbed into the Ford beside Chrissie and it rolled away down the drive.

Matt had brought the car round to the front door. Now he said, 'Well, you got it like you said you would, but how will you manage next week?'

Sophie grinned at him. 'I'll ask for another advance.'

Matt shook his head admiringly. 'You cheeky monkey.'

She ran upstairs, laughing.

Jack dropped Chrissie at the Railway Hotel then drove over the bridge and through the last narrow, terraced streets of houses to Ballantyne's yard. This was the festive season but the weather was not made for rejoicing. A cold sea wind sweeping in up the river brought with it a fine, driving rain that sluiced down the windscreen of the Ford. In the last hundred yards he passed a youth, head down as he plodded into the wind, towing a bogey with a length of rope. It was no more than an orange box mounted on four wheels from an old pram. Jack saw some of these every day and took no notice of this one. He drove on through the gate into the yard and parked the Ford outside the office block. He unfolded his tall figure from behind the wheel and stepped out.

One of his foremen, his rank marked by the trilby hat he wore, smirked and put a finger to the hat in salute. 'Morning, Mr Ballantyne.'

Jack recognised Gallagher, red faced and burly, and was not sure about him. He got the work done by the men under him, but Jack thought there was a fawning insincerity about Gallagher. However, you could not sack a man for that, let alone the mere suspicion that it existed. Jack replied, 'Good morning,' and strode on into his office.

*　　*　　*

Peter Robinson trudged on, towing the bogey along the street. His patched jacket was buttoned up against the wind which still cut through him. He wished he had an overcoat.

His mother had suffered a miscarriage after hearing of the death of her husband. Peter had no regrets about the loss of Hackett – except for the money he sent, little as it had been, as there was no work to be had.

The bogey was filled with bundles of firewood. He had begged some empty boxes from a market stall, chopped them up and tied the sticks in bundles with string. He hoped to get a penny for each bundle, or a ha'penny at any rate, and he had to sell them all before the week was out. If Peter could sell all the firewood he would have a few shillings to buy a piece of pork to roast for the Christmas dinner, and maybe a few luxuries like an orange or a bar of chocolate for young Billy's stocking. He was doomed to disappointment.

He knocked on the hundredth door and asked the old woman who opened it, 'D'ye want any firewood, missus?' He sold none at all.

'*Aqui!*' Paco Diaz came out of the bedroom carrying his shoes in one hand and beckoned his daughter where she sat reading a book in a chair by the fire. He had come home from his job as nightwatchman, eaten a huge breakfast and slept for an hour or so. He had catnapped frequently during his night on duty, as always, and now was refreshed.

Helen was fifteen years old now, quiet and thin, her black hair scraped back tightly into plaits. She put the book down quickly and went to him. 'Yes, Dad?'

He looked past Helen to her mother, Lizzie, busy ironing the first of a pile of washing on one end of the kitchen table, and told her, 'We go to buy new clothes for Juan. You will dress, please.' Now he turned his gaze on Helen: 'You will iron. Then cook dinner. But first—' he held out the shoes – 'clean these.'

'Juan' – Helen's eighteen-year-old brother John – worked nightshifts on a maintenance gang in the yard where his father was watchman: Paco had got him the job. John had inherited his father's colouring and stance, dark and haughty. Now he was washing in an enamel bowl set on the other end of the kitchen table from where his mother was ironing. He reached for the towel and said, 'Clean my shoes as well.'

Helen was about to object but Paco said, '*Si,*' and her mother caught her eye, warning her.

The girl shut her mouth and took the shoes. 'Yes, Dad.' She smiled at him but he was already turning away to talk to John, ignoring the females. Elizabeth put the iron back on the fire to heat, put her arm around Helen and squeezed. 'There's a good lass.' Then she whispered, 'He loves you.' She lied because she wanted Helen to believe it – and Helen believed it because she wanted to.

Paco had always wanted a son but not a daughter. John had been one of twins, but his twin sister, Helen, had died within days despite the efforts of the nurses. It was because of those efforts that Lizzie determined that her own daughter would be a nurse. Paco scarcely mourned the death of the child because he was totally absorbed in his son. His celebrations were muted when another girl was born three years later, but she was the daughter Lizzie yearned for.

Because this child seemed to be a replacement for the one she had lost, she also named this little girl Helen.

Lizzie loved her husband as strongly now as she had when she first fell for the handsome young Spaniard. She was not blind to his faults, but was prepared to ignore them or live with them to keep him.

'He loves you.' Lizzie had said it and Helen accepted that it was true despite evidence to the contrary over the years. She told herself that it was just that her father was . . . different. She boasted to the other girls, 'My father says this' or 'My father does that.' There was something romantic about him being a Spaniard and her having a family in Spain. She knew there was nothing romantic about herself.

She would boast to the other girls, 'Look! Those are my aunties, uncles, cousins . . .' She showed the photographs, posed studio portraits of black-haired women in flounced skirts, lace and shawls, men in tightly fitting suits staring into the camera with wide, dark eyes. Helen yearned to meet those distant relatives, but her father had only once saved enough money to go back to Spain for a holiday. He took Juan with him and left his wife and daughter behind. Helen had wept in her bed that night – and hugged him when he came home. He would cause her to weep again.

Helen cleaned the shoes then took up the iron and set to work. The rest of her family left the house to board a tram and cross the bridge into the town. When the pile of ironing was done she turned to cooking. She made a meat pie from some leftovers, peeled potatoes and prepared a panful of cabbage. All the while she worked she kept her schoolbook propped up beside her so she could read a line or two in snatches.

Helen had never needed encouragement to study. When she had passed the examination for entrance to the grammar school, Paco Diaz, predictably, was against her going, but for once Elizabeth stood up to him and won her fight. Her mother urged her, 'You want to get a good education so you can be a nurse when you grow up.' It was Elizabeth's dream that her daughter would one day become a nursing sister, member of a respected profession. It was a dream Helen shared – although secretly the dream did not stop there.

The pie was cooked and Helen took it out of the blackleaded oven alongside the fire and set it aside to cool. She left the pans of vegetables in the hearth, ready for her mother to put on the fire to cook when she returned. A glance at the clock on the mantelpiece told her she would just be in time. She shrugged into her coat as she hurried along the passage and out into the street, into the biting wind and driving rain. She followed the trail of the others 'ower the watter' into the town.

'Have you been running?' Sophie Ballantyne grinned at Helen.

She panted, 'No, but I had to hurry. I thought I might miss you.' She had walked across the bridge, deciding to save her tram fare for later.

'I nearly went off with a lad a minute back,' Sophie teased. Helen wondered if there might be a grain of truth in that, knowing Sophie. She took Helen's arm. 'Come on, we'll get in out of this rain.'

The window of Eade's music shop in Fawcett Street was filled with instruments: trumpets, trombones, accordions . . . there was also a display of sheet music and gramophone records. The last two were on sale at the back of the shop and Sophie had come to see them. The girls spent a happy hour browsing through the sheets. Sophie was known there and they listened to records played by the youth behind the counter at her request. She finally bought a record and sheet music '*Anything Goes*'.

'Come back to the house,' said Sophie. They took a tram, each paying her own fare, and then walked to the Ballantyne home. After three years of friendship Helen was no longer overawed by the size of the house and its staff of servants. She and Sophie had met on their first day at the grammar school, sitting side by side because their names fell together alphabetically. They were different, but went together like two halves of the same coin.

'Let's have this one,' said Sophie.

'And this,' added Helen.

They sat on the bed up in Sophie's room and wound her gramophone, played the records that were stacked up by the dozen. Sophie's wardrobe doors stood wide open as she had left them that morning, showing the dresses hanging ranked inside. Sophie sang and practised stances and gestures, lifting her skirt with one hand, watching herself in the mirror.

'Don't look like that,' ordered Sophie as Helen pursed her lips in disapproval. Sophie pouted, mimicking, and Helen had to laugh.

'You really ought to study for another career,' Helen chided. She knew Sophie was determined to be a singer, but did not take her seriously. She did not believe this girl who had grown up alongside her for three years could be an entertainer like those who appeared on the stage of the

Empire Theatre in the town. Helen had only been there once, to a pantomime. She had thought it a world of magic, but not *real*. Now, nursing, that was a worthwhile profession, demanding dedication and commanding respect.

'Now we're into the New Year things might look up.' Jack said it with more hope than confidence. He struggled with the stud on his winged collar and grunted with satisfaction as it slid into place, then he tweaked his black tie into a neat bow.

Chrissie smoothed the printed velvet evening dress over her haunches and picked up her stole to cover her bare shoulders. 'Who'll be there tonight?'

'All people you know.' Jack slipped his dinner jacket off its hanger and worked his wide shoulders into it. He went on, 'Except one. That's Tourville, Randolph Tourville. He's boss of an oil company. He's up this end of the country because he has a tanker building on the Tyne. Davenport's invited him because Tourville does a lot of business with Davenport's bank. He thinks he might get him to do some more with one of the builders on *this* river, but he's wrong.'

Chrissie picked a shred of white cotton from his jacket and told him, 'Don't be pessimistic.'

Jack grinned. 'I'm not. I just know Randolph. He's a devil for the women and he never changes his mind. He's happy with the ships he gets from the Tyne and he won't move.' He slid his arms around her and kissed her. 'You're gorgeous.'

Chrissie detached his hands and said firmly, 'We're going out for the evening.'

They sat down to dinner a full score, all couples except

for Tourville, the bachelor. The men were in business, most of them shipbuilders like Jack Ballantyne, and their host was Davenport the banker, chubby and urbane. Chrissie was the only businesswoman. Tourville was partnered by Davenport's daughter, pretty, unattached and in her twenties, obviously smitten by him.

He was a man who looked taller than he was and walked with a self-confident, straight-backed strut. Handsome in a square-jawed, hard-eyed way, he could grin to show strong, white teeth. Chrissie thought that in anger that mouth could probably also close like a trap.

No places were marked, except that the chairs at the head and foot of the long table were left for Davenport, the host, and his wife. Tourville sat directly opposite Chrissie.

Conversation was general. Davenport twice steered it gently round to ships and the need for orders on the river. Tourville equally gently turned it away. The third time Davenport attempted this, halfway though the meal, the oilman looked the banker in the eye and told him with a smile, 'I always go to the Tyne for ships and always will.' The message was clear and Davenport got it. He did not try again.

Chrissie glanced at Jack and he lowered the lid of one eye in a wink that said, 'I told you so.' He addressed Tourville: 'I looked over one of your other interests a week or so ago.'

The oilman's brows lifted a fraction. 'What would that be?'

'A Tourville film. I believe you are a major shareholder as well as managing director.'

Tourville laughed. 'I hold most of the shares, it's true,

47

although it's not so much an interest as a distraction. Tourville Films Ltd makes the films, but when I go to the studios it's as a spectator. I like backing a man and an idea, and that's all I do: put up the money. The films are made by a lot of other people.'

Davenport put in, 'That's a bit of a gamble, though. Suppose people don't like the film and don't pay to see it?'

Tourville gave him the tolerant smile of the wealthy man who could afford to lose. 'I find it profitable. And more fun than backing horses.'

A little later Chrissie realised that while Tourville was talking in turn to his neighbour on either side, one of them being Davenport's infatuated daughter, he was always watching Chrissie. He saw the dawning of that realisation and smiled at her. She felt the flush rise to her face and bent her head over her plate, although she was no longer hungry.

At the end of the evening, when they were all about to take their leave, Davenport shook Tourville's hand, admitting defeat. 'So you don't expect to find anything you want here?'

Chrissie was aware of Randolph Tourville's eyes on her again as he replied, 'You never know,' and she knew he was attracted to her.

She slept badly that night and it was days before she could put the man out of her mind.

Sarah Tennant hurried, almost running, along Herbert Street, passing through a succession of pools of yellow light cast by the streetlamps. The wind brought the rain in from the sea, but she had a winter coat now – secondhand, well worn and too big, but warm. She carried two baskets of shopping, bought in the covered market just before the stalls closed, when they sold off stock cheaply.

She paused as she pushed open the front door and stepped into the passage. One low-powered bulb shed a meagre light and filled the corners with shadows. The cheap linoleum covering the floor was slick with water and mud, and reflected the light dully. Sarah set down the baskets, wiped rain from her face and tossed back her wet hair. As she picked up the baskets again, Joshua Fannon stepped out of the shadows and waddled heavily along the passage to meet her. He wheezed, 'I've been waiting for you.'

Sarah held the baskets in front of her like a shield between her and Fannon. She used them to hold him off and pushed past him, hurrying on to the end of the passage and the door into the Tennants' kitchen. Once inside she put down the baskets, took the rent book from a drawer and told her mother, sitting by the fire, 'I'm just going to pay the rent.'

She found Fannon had retreated to the far end of the passage again and now waited by the front door. Sarah went to him, took her purse from her damp pocket and counted out the six shillings and sixpence. Fannon took it, entered the amount in the book and initialled it with his fountain pen. Sarah reached out for the book but he held it against his chest. 'You got behind wi' the rent last winter.'

'It's up to date now.' Sarah held out her hand. 'Give me the book, please.'

Fannon ignored that, and gripped her arm with a damp hand, warning, 'If that happens again you might need a friend to keep a roof over your heads.' He smiled, face oily with sweat. 'And nothing's lost that's given to a friend.'

He tried to fondle her, but then a door opened upstairs and a neighbour clattered out on to the landing. Fannon's attention was distracted for a moment. Sarah seized her chance and the rent book, tore away from him and ran back into the kitchen.

Fannon swore as the door slammed behind her. He lumbered out of the house and set off along the street, buttoning his raincoat.

When he got home he found a familiar scene. Meggie was slumped and snoring, mouth sagging open, in her armchair by the fire. An empty bottle and a half-empty glass stood on the floor beside her and the room stank of gin.

Fannon cursed her under his breath as he spilled the money he had collected out of the pockets of his raincoat on to the table. He muttered, 'You can check it yourself and bank it, you cow.' She always did. Joshua Fannon knew there had to be a bank book in the house but he had never been able to find it. He went to the fire and warmed his hands – and himself at the thought of Sarah. He only had to wait his time.

Sarah stared into her almost empty purse. The shopping and the rent had taken the last of her mother's savings and nearly all the wages paid to Sarah that afternoon. A young girl was paid less than a grown woman, and the law said she could not be allowed to work overtime, that the number of her working hours was restricted. Sarah faced the fact that she and her mother needed more money.

She knew only one way to make it.

5

February 1936

A month later, on a day of grey sky and driving rain, Chrissie took the train to Yorkshire and Jack's old school. Her dark eyes apprehensive, she sat in the headmaster's study with its photographs of cricket XIs and rugger XVs and listened to the Head: '. . . Good of you to come . . .' That was purely courtesy: he had sent for her. Or one of them, and Jack could not leave the yard because he was awaiting the visit of a Brazilian millionaire, hoping for an order from him to build a ship. Chrissie had left the running of the Railway Hotel to Dinsdale Arkley and come to face the music.

The Head's message was not new, it had been spelled out in successive term end reports, but now it was more forceful: Matt was not keeping up. Chrissie sat in the aroma of chalk dust and leather and listened to the droning of the Head against the background of a slow-ticking longcase clock, its pendulum swinging inside its glass door. A cane, long and whippy, stood in a corner.

'He reads a great deal and draws well . . . Only works enough to keep out of immediate trouble . . . A rebel, might be a very good wing three-quarter but—' and shocked now '– he doesn't *try* . . . didn't want to play for the school First

Fifteen this afternoon, I had to *order* him . . . Not a good advertisement for the school.'

Chrissie listened to the accusations and sighed inside herself for her son, Oh, Matt, my baby.

Chrissie promised the Head, 'I'll talk to him, take him into the town for tea, if that is all right?' It was a request made out of courtesy.

The Head acknowledged it, 'By all means.' He then went on, 'We do not want to lose him, he is a good boy and his morals and manners are not in question, but he is not learning here.' He paused, then summed up: 'He is *drifting*.' Chrissie had heard that before, from Jack.

She walked out into the afternoon with the Head and put up her umbrella against the drizzle. The crowding boys hastily made room for them on the duckboards laid along the side of the pitch and Chrissie, huddled in her long winter overcoat, watched the game and her son. Her feet, in their neat, black glacé court shoes that had cost her two guineas, grew steadily colder. She told herself she should have worn wellingtons, as she would usually when she went to a match, as she had when she was first married and watched Jack play.

Matt had been changing, pulling his jersey over his head and reaching for his boots, when his captain came to stand over him, asking, 'Are you sure you're all right to play?'

Matt had looked up as he tugged on laces, ''Course I am. Why?'

'Well, you said you couldn't turn out.'

Matt had explained patiently, 'I said I didn't want to play, not that I couldn't.' He had been pulled in because the two boys who were first choice and reserve for the position had both been injured. Matt had moved on from reading the adventures of The Saint and Bulldog Drummond and was now deep into Hugh Walpole and Thackeray, and did not want to leave them to play football. His captain had not understood that at all and went away baffled and outraged.

Chrissie understood the game well enough to realise after only a few minutes that her son's heart was not in it. The ball was greasy with mud so it was not surprising that he dropped a pass or two, but he looked awkward and ill at ease. Matt was tall for a winger and now seemed clumsy, all arms and legs. Chrissie thought with a pang of sympathy that he looked miserable.

He was. And bad tempered. He had not wanted to be out here, freezing on the wing, a spectator except when he failed to hold a pass. Then his peers on the touchline groaned, 'Oh, come on, Ballantyne!'

At half-time they were losing eight points to nil. His captain trudged through the mud to where Matt stood alone sucking on a slice of lemon and told him, 'You've got to buck up and get into the game.'

Matt glared at him and snapped, 'I can't get into it if I don't get the bloody ball!'

'You're a wash-out.' The captain glared at him and walked away.

Matt turned his back on his team and found himself facing the crowd on the touchline. His captain, his team and the gang over there could think what they liked. He didn't care. Then he saw his mother, standing under an umbrella in the thick of the crowd where she would hear all the jibes they hurled at him.

She saw his start of recognition, waved and smiled. Then it was time to restart the game.

He lined up with the others, and now the situation had changed. He didn't care what they thought about him, but he wouldn't have them running him down in the presence of his mother. He would show them. So when his opposite number took a pass and raced down the wing, Matt felled him with a crunching tackle that left the boy winded. Matt started yelling at his forwards, urging them on, and calling for the ball. But he did not get it. It was passed out to the other wing with monotonous regularity, and with equal regularity somebody in the centre failed to hold it and the movement broke down.

The game raged up and down the field, and with ten minutes to go one of the opposition broke through the defence, sidestepped the full-back and made for the line. Matt chased and caught him, bringing him down only feet short of scoring. The touchline crowd cheered him then, but he was oblivious to it. The scrum was formed and the ball was won by the opposing side. Matt watched it bobble through the booted feet churning the mud and he caught the glance the other team's scrum-half threw at the winger facing Matt, so when the ball came out Matt was already running. He cut between the scrum-half and the winger as the former passed to the latter, intercepted the ball and snatched it out of the air – then he was running.

The opposing fly-half charged across and Matt fooled him with a change of pace that left him toiling along behind. The awkwardness was gone and he was running flat out now, graceful and balanced. He covered the length of the field, swerved around the full-back and scored under the posts. His captain kicked the goal.

They restarted with only five minutes to play. Four minutes later the ball was passed out along the line of three-quarters. Matt guessed what would happen, abandoned his position and ran across the field, looping behind the line. When the ball was dropped he swooped on it and scooped it up one-handed on the halfway line. He outran two men, swerved and jinked past two more and hurled himself over to score under the posts again. Again his captain kicked the easy goal. They had won. Matt looked across to the touchline and saw his mother jumping up and down excitedly. He laughed, happy now.

Chrissie gave him a substantial high tea in the restaurant of the Red Lion. She told him why she was there, eyeing him severely, and then asked, apprehensive, ready to wince herself: 'Do they beat you?'

He blinked at her. 'What?'

'The headmaster has a cane in his study, a wicked-looking thing.'

Matt laughed, 'No! The old boy is dead set against that sort of thing. We think he keeps it there for show, in case some parents think he isn't strict enough.'

'Oh!' Chrissie was relieved at that, anyway. 'Well, your father will be pleased when I tell him about the game, but as to the rest . . .'

Matt's thin face lengthened as he became serious. 'The Head read you the lesson, didn't he?' He sighed, 'Look, Mother, I don't deliberately laze about and skip work. It's just that I keep finding other things I'd rather do. But I promise you, I will try.' He meant it.

Chrissie slipped a half-crown into his hand as she climbed into the train.

'I'll try,' Peter Robinson had told his mother when he set out before dawn. He hauled his bogey down to the shore and collected sea coal from the high tide line. He hawked the coal around the streets then went back to collect more. He finally dragged the bogey home empty when it was past sunset. The lamplighter was going around the streets with his long pole, a loop on the end, switching on the lights. Peter was weary but happy, with a few shillings in his pocket.

Men were spilling out of the yards that still had work, finished for the day, a sea of bobbing caps. As Peter passed Ballantyne's he saw Billy Hackett, his seven-year-old half-brother, begging at the gate: 'Got any bait left, mister, please?' 'Bait' was the sandwich lunch a workman took to the yard.

Peter seized Billy by the scruff of his neck, but gently. He remembered when he had begged for food in the same way when he was Billy's age. He still ticked off the boy: 'Your mother would cry her eyes out if she saw you doing that, and if I catch you at it again you'll get belted.'

Billy didn't believe that, although he saw Peter was serious in his warning, and went with him, protesting, 'I'm hungry.'

'You're always hungry.' Peter ruffled Billy's hair, already cut short so it stood up like a clothes brush. Then he saw Gallagher and McNally in the crowd coming out of the yard. He hesitated, then remembered what Joe Nolan had said and chose discretion. He steered Billy on to the other side of the road and down a side street.

Billy demanded, 'Where are we going?'

Peter told him, 'To get some fish and chips.'

'Great!'

Peter bought two 'tuppenny lots' – a penny fish and a pennyworth of chips in each. He and Billy took them home to Margaret Hackett and shared them out between the three of them, filling up with bread and margarine.

Peter went to bed content. He would go picking coal again next day.

Chrissie had to change trains at Durham. She was in no hurry for her dinner after high tea with Matt, so she left the station and walked down the hill into the ancient town. Tommy Johnson, Dinsdale Arkley's predecessor as manager of her hotel, lived in Durham now. He had moved to a little house near the station after he retired. Chrissie took the opportunity to visit an old friend.

Tommy and his wife made her welcome and wanted to feed her again but Chrissie laughingly refused the food they urged on her and settled for a cup of tea. She spent a pleasant hour with them, talking of old times: how she had first met Tommy when she was a young barmaid, and later bought the hotel. Tommy said, 'You saved my life then. That's no exaggeration. The feller that owned the place was going to sell up and it was a certainty the one that wanted to buy it would have sacked me. I'd never have got another job like that at my age and the worry would ha' killed me.' His wife put her arms around Chrissie and kissed her.

It was late in the evening when Chrissie walked up the hill to the station. A stocky, broad-shouldered man carrying a small suitcase preceded her. As they came to the foot of the last steep bank another man stepped out of the shadows and appealed to the stocky man, 'Carry your case up to the station, sir?'

The stocky man brushed past him and said, not unkindly, 'No, lad, I can manage this meself. Mebbe better than you can,' because the other appeared sunken cheeked and hollow eyed in the harsh light from the streetlamps, and walked with a limp.

Chrissie stared at the disappointed man for a long second, not wanting to believe the evidence of her eyes, thinking she must be mistaken. Then he glanced her way and she saw him flinch with shock as he recognised her. Chrissie said, 'Hello, Phillip.'

Phillip Massingham started to turn away but Chrissie caught his arm and held him. The arm felt thin as a stick in her grasp. For some seconds they were silent. Chrissie did not know where to start. She said, 'What are you doing here?' then stopped, because the answer was obvious. He was trying to earn a few coppers by carrying the cases of passengers up the long haul to the station. She amended: 'I mean, I thought you were in America. Elsie wrote to me . . .'

Phillip tried to turn away and avoided her gaze. He muttered, 'I suppose she told you I'd made a mess of things and run out on her.'

'*No!*' Chrissie tugged him around to face her again. 'She said you'd been ill and very noble, gone off so you wouldn't be a burden. I don't think it was noble. I think it was bloody silly. So – ' she drew a breath – 'how did you get here?'

He still would not look at her, but he answered, in jerky sentences as if the words were forced out of him, 'There's millions on the road over there. A lot die alongside the railroad tracks. Or in the hobo jungles, places where they sleep on the outside of towns, under a bridge or a tree. I was on my own and the States was a foreign country to me. I wanted to come home. A skipper of a ship let me work my passage and put me ashore at Glasgow. After that I walked or got lifts, heading south, but I've been here for three weeks. I remembered the people around here were kind to me before – years ago, when I met you. So I stayed, I thought I'd build up my strength.' He had paused after every muttered sentence and there was a longer pause now. Then: 'I had nowhere to go anyway . . .' He petered out and stood silent, patient, beaten.

Chrissie swallowed then linked her arm through his and urged him into shambling motion, heading up the hill. 'Come on. I'm not letting you go now I've found you – and by a miracle.'

He went along with her, unquestioning except when she bought his ticket at the booking office and he asked, 'Where are we going?'

Chrissie had foreseen this and answered, 'To find you a bed for the night.'

He tried to pull away then, saying, 'I don't want to go to your home.'

'You're not. Don't worry.' Chrissie had guessed he would prefer anonymity to the Ballantyne house with its curious adolescents.

She took him to the Railway Hotel, installed him in a room and had a meal sent up on a tray. While he was eating that she took a taxi home and brought back a set of Jack's pyjamas and a dressing gown. Back at the hotel she took away Phillip's clothes and threw them out.

Next day Jack went with her to buy some new ones for Massingham. 'Poor devil,' he said. 'Wonder how long it will take for him to get back on his feet again?'

'I don't know,' Chrissie answered. 'He needs a long rest and feeding up.'

Jack nodded, recalling Phillip's gaunt face. 'And some work, some aim in life. That's just as important for a man like him.'

Chrissie thought she knew the answer to that, but she waited a week, putting off the moment, before she finally took the plunge and telephoned long distance to London. After she had got past two layers of secretaries: 'This is Chrissie Ballantyne. Do you remember me, Mr Tourville?'

His deep voice came down the crackling wire. 'I remember you well.' Chrissie could picture his smile, confident. 'Very well . . .'

She stumbled on, 'When we met you mentioned your interest in the film industry. Have you heard of a man called Phillip Massingham?'

There was silence for only a second then Tourville said, 'Massingham Films.'

'That was his company.'

'He got an offer from the States, sold out and went over there. That was over ten years ago.'

'Yes, but he's back in this country now.' Chrissie took a breath and asked, 'Can you get him a job?'

Another silence, longer this time, then Tourville said, 'I remember the work he did over here and I've seen some of the films he made in the States, too. But the last was three or four years ago and it's what he can do now that matters.'

'I'm sure he does good work.' Chrissie tried to sound certain, prayed she was right.

Tourville chuckled, then: 'For you, I'll give him a try. Where do I find him?'

'You can write to him here.' Chrissie gave him the address of the hotel then added, 'I'm very grateful. If ever I can do anything for you . . .'

Silence, then another chuckle and, 'I may take you up on that.'

6

March 1936

The club was only two or three streets from where Sarah Tennant lived, a few minutes' fast walking through the rain. She hesitated for a moment at the foot of the steps leading up to the big double doors. They flapped continually as working men in cloth caps and scarves shouldered in and out. Nervousness made Sarah swallow but she told herself that she could not give up now she had got this far. She took a breath, climbed the steps and pushed in through the doors.

An elderly man sat at a small table in the hallway, a glass of beer before him. He rose to his feet as Sarah entered, and challenged the slight, dark-haired, dark-eyed girl: 'Now then, lass, what d'you want in here?' But his friendly grin took the edge off the words.

Sarah answered, 'I wondered if they were needing some help behind the bar.'

He shook his grey head. 'Not as I've heard, but you'll find the steward down the passage there, in his office.'

Sarah followed the direction of his pointing finger. There were two doors at the end of the passage and one of them opened as she came to it. The man who stepped out was hardly taller than herself. She asked, 'Excuse me, but are you the steward, please?' Then she saw over his shoulder that the room he had come from was not an office. It was big, with a bare wooden floor, and several young men were skipping and shadow-boxing. She could just see one corner of a roped boxing-ring.

The little man smiled and said, 'No, lass. I'm Joe Nolan, the boxing trainer. The steward is in there.' He nodded at the opposite door.

'I'm sorry.' Sarah turned away, blushing with embarrassment.

As Joe Nolan walked off up the passage he laughed and called back to her, 'Never mind, lass!'

Sarah knocked at the door and a voice bellowed, 'Come in!' The steward's office was a small cubby-hole and the steward almost filled it. A big, burly man with a wide, red face and hard blue eyes, he stood behind his desk, glared coldly at Sarah and rumbled, 'Aye?'

Sarah whispered, 'I wondered if you wanted . . .'

He cut her off, bawling, 'Can't hear you! Deafened! Guns in Flanders!' He tapped one ear with a thick finger.

'I'm sorry.' Then Sarah realised he would not hear that, either. She raised her voice. 'I'm sorry! I wondered if you wanted any help in the club? I mean, part time, at night?'

His glare was unwavering and he shook his head. 'You're too young to wait on. I can't have a bairn like you pulling pints, it's against the law.'

Sarah kept trying: 'I can do cleaning. I'm really strong.'

Still he glared. Sarah decided she had failed, and was about to turn away when he guffawed, his wide, red face splitting in a grin. 'I can see that. You're a regular Samson.'

Then the grin slipped away as quickly as it had come. He said tersely, 'Can you wash glasses without breaking half o' them?'

Sarah answered eagerly, 'Aye, I can.'

He grumbled, 'If that's true you'll be the first. Can you start now?' He had sacked his regular washer-up the previous night after she had dropped a tray full of glasses after too many illicit nips of port. He saw Sarah nodding quickly and said, 'Right you are, then. I'll give you two and six a week.'

Two shillings and sixpence! Sarah knew she and her mother could survive with that extra money. She took off her coat and put on the apron she had brought with her, in hope. She washed glasses in a little room behind the bar from seven till ten, then hurried home.

At first she was filled with elation because now she and her mother would be able to make ends meet, but then her worries began to crowd in on her again. She was afraid of Fannon and afraid to tell her mother because it would upset her. Sarah knew she had to get away from Fannon somehow.

When she arrived home and opened the front door she heard her mother coughing. It was a sound Sarah had lived with for months, but she had not grown accustomed to it. It seemed to be tearing her mother apart. The doctor had given her medicine but had said there was nothing more he could do. He had taken Sarah aside and told her, 'Call me if she gets worse.' Sarah wondered how much worse her mother could get, and was afraid for her.

*　　*　　*

'Have you got the letter from Tourville?' Chrissie smiled up at Phillip Massingham as they stood by the open door of the train.

He tapped his breast pocket. 'In here. I wouldn't forget that.' It was just a month since Chrissie had brought him back to the hotel. Now he wore a tailormade suit, one of two bought for him by Chrissie, along with a complete outfit of other clothes, including the overcoat laid on his seat in the carriage. There was flesh on his bones, colour in his cheeks and he stood straight. He said, 'I won't forget what you've done for me.'

'Now don't start that again.' Chrissie knew he was nervous. 'And don't worry. They're expecting you at the studios and you have a good reputation in the business in this country.'

He nodded, acknowledging that. 'I didn't think I'd ever work in films again, let alone as a director.'

The guard's whistle shrilled. Chrissie shoved Phillip towards the train and he climbed up into the carriage. She closed the door behind him, and as he leaned out of the window she told him, 'You can do it.'

The train pulled away and he answered firmly, 'Yes, I can.'

Later that day Sophie poked her bobbed, blonde head around the door of her mother's office in the Railway Hotel, smiled and asked, 'Got a minute, Mummy?'

Chrissie looked up from the menus for the following week that Jock Kincaid had submitted for her approval. 'A minute? Fine. But what else?' The challenge was stern but Sophie knew it was good humoured. She entered and Tom followed her.

Chrissie's brows lifted. 'What are you doing here?' Tom was a rare visitor to the hotel. He worked in Newcastle during the week and on Saturday mornings – and there was no reason for him to go to the hotel this Saturday afternoon during his precious free time. He wore a tweed sports coat and grey flannel trousers, a newly fashionable, collar-attached shirt and a tie.

'I came in with Sophie.' He grinned at Chrissie. 'Or she came in with me. It turned out she didn't have any money for the tram.'

'Ah.' That summed up Chrissie's appreciation of the situation.

Sophie went on to confirm it, hitching herself up to sit on the desk by her mother, long legs swinging. 'I spent an awful lot of money at Christmas, on presents and – and things, and that left a sort of vacuum that's sucked up my allowance since then—'

Chrissie cut in cynically, 'And your father is away for the weekend.'

Sophie skated around that: 'Well, there's been so much to do, and everything seems to cost more these days than it used to, and I'm growing.' She paused to take a breath.

Chrissie recognised words taken out of her mouth that her daughter had heard and cannily noted for use later: costs, and growing? That much was true: Sophie was turned fifteen now and becoming a woman before her mother's eyes – physically. However, there was more to growing up than that, and Sophie still had a long way to go. Chrissie pointed out, 'You don't buy your clothes out of your allowance.'

'No,' Sophie conceded, 'but I think I eat and drink more when I'm out now.' She laid a hand on her mother's and suggested, 'If you could lend me half a crown, just till I get my next allowance . . .'

Chrissie lifted the hand away. 'I happen to know that allowance of yours is mortgaged for the next month.' Sophie had asked for half-a-crown – two shillings and sixpence – so . . . Chrissie picked up her handbag from beside the desk and took out her purse. 'Two shillings.' She laid the florin on the desk. 'No more. And don't come back tomorrow, or batten on to your father as soon as he gets back.'

'No, Mummy, I won't. Thank you.' Sophie scooped up the coin, slid off the desk and danced across the room.

Tom smiled as he watched her gyrate out of the door and Chrissie asked him, 'Are you managing to make ends meet?' although she knew the answer.

'I've got money to spare after I've paid for my digs and I'm even saving some,' Tom assured her with pride.

Chrissie prompted, 'And still enjoying it?' knowing that answer, too.

It came pat and sincere: 'Marvellous!' Tom's enthusiasm shone out of his face. 'To see the ship growing a little bit every day, *and* knowing what you've put in yourself, even if it's only a small drawing you've done in the drawing office, it's, it's . . .' He stopped then, lost for words.

Chrissie supplied one, teasing: 'Marvellous!' Tom laughed and Chrissie told him, 'Now off you go and let me get my work done.' She was still smiling when the door closed behind him.

Tom found Sophie waiting out in the foyer, talking to a girl in an apron, her hair bound up in a kerchief. Sophie was taller, and the other girl was thin faced, slighter. Sophie turned as Tom came up. 'There you are.' Then to the girl,

'Have you met my brother? Tom, this is Sarah Tennant, one of Mr Kincaid's staff.'

Tom said, polite, 'Hello.'

'Hello.' Sarah had met Sophie many times because she was often in the hotel visiting her mother, and usually called into the kitchen for a cup of tea or glass of milk. She would talk to Jock Kincaid and the other kitchen staff and they would laugh – and shake their heads over her when she had gone. 'She's a little madam, that one.'

Now Sophie, knowing Sarah's shyness, teased, 'He's handsome, isn't he?' and grinned to see the colour flood into Sarah's face.

Tom did not notice her blushing. His casual glance had registered a quiet girl, two or three years younger than himself, and he thought of her as a schoolgirl. He did not blush and told his sister, 'You do talk rubbish. Look, I have to go now, must get the paint I want.' He lifted a hand in a parting salute and made for the door.

Sophie watched him go, then turned back to Sarah. She saw the blush still there and stopped grinning. She squeezed Sarah's arm and apologised. 'I'm sorry. Just a joke.'

'That's all right.' Sarah pretended she had not been embarrassed and asked, 'Does he paint a lot?'

'No! Not him. Matt—' she lifted a hand high above her head – 'my other brother, the tall skinny one, he is the artist in the family. Tom only wants the paint for his plane. He makes models of aircraft and paints them like real ones.'

Sarah said, 'Oh, I see,' though she was not sure that she did. Then she excused herself. 'Mr Kincaid sent me out to the dining-room with a message and he'll be wondering where I've got to.' She made her way back to the kitchen, but flushed again when she thought that Tom Ballantyne *was* handsome.

'We're going to the pictures!' Helen Diaz protested. She and Sophie had arranged to see Ginger Rogers and Fred Astaire in *Roberta*.

Sophie soothed her, 'Yes, we will. I just want to have a quick look in here,' and she tugged Helen into Eade's, the music shop.

The 'quick look' dragged on for ten minutes as Sophie listened to records and perused sheet music, until Helen presented her ultimatum: 'I'm going now.'

Sophie caught her eye, saw Helen meant what she said and agreed, 'All right.' She bought a record and music then pulled a face at the coppers she received in change.

Helen asked with foreboding, 'What's the matter?' and then answered her own question with an accusation. 'You've spent the money you wanted for the pictures!'

Sophie led the way out of the shop and turned towards the cinema on the corner. Helen asked, 'Are you going to ask your mother again?'

Sophie shook her head. 'She told me not to try.'

'Well, what are you going to do?'

'Just leave it to me.' Sophie stopped outside the Regal cinema, ostensibly studying the stills mounted on a sandwich board in the foyer, but her gaze roved. She saw the two youths, yard workers out on a Saturday to spend their pay, as they sauntered into the foyer. Both wore double-breasted blue suits, collars and ties. She caught the eye of one of them, held it a moment then shyly looked away, but she was aware that they had stopped and had their heads together in muttered plotting.

Helen, unaware, pressed her, 'What are you going to do?'

Sophie replied, 'I'm doing it,' as the youths swaggered over.

One of them said, 'Aye, aye.'

Helen refused to look at him but Sophie did and repeated, 'Aye, aye.'

Encouraged, he asked, 'Going in?'

Sophie sighed, shook her head and smiled at him, rueful. 'No money.'

The second youth shoved forward to put in, 'Come in wi' us – our treat.'

'Oh, we couldn't,' Sophie protested, but weakly.

'Go on!' they both urged.

She hesitated, glanced at the red-faced Helen, and then as if seeing some signal there, said, 'Well, all right.'

Helen was helpless, overtaken by an unfamiliar situation. She had looked to Sophie for a lead and now did not know what to do, so she went along. After the tickets were bought and before they plunged into the darkness, Sophie warned their consorts, 'No funny business in here, mind.'

'No,' they agreed, quickly but insincerely.

Sophie watched the film, enjoyed it and kept the young man's caresses within bounds. Once, intent on the screen, she told him, 'Keep still. I want to see this bit.' She was watching the stance and gestures of the singer. Once she brushed his hand from her leg and hissed, 'I said no funny business in here!' He accepted that.

Meanwhile Helen sat two seats away, stiff with shyness

and nerves, and held the hot hands of the other young man between her own.

As they came out into the foyer Sophie's young man said, 'What about a drink, then?'

Helen opened her mouth to utter a shocked refusal but Sophie got in first and said quickly, 'Good idea, but we'll just be a minute.' She took Helen off and left the two youths waiting.

In the passage leading to the ladies' Helen objected, 'We can't go into a pub!'

'We're not.' Sophie led on past the ladies' and round a corner to the emergency exit. She pushed down the bar and the door opened into the street. A little crowd of a half-dozen youngsters, without the entrance money and waiting for a friend to open the door from inside, immediately rushed in. Sophie and Helen shouldered through them and hurried away.

Sophie said happily, 'Great picture, wasn't it?' When her friend did not answer, she glanced at her and asked, 'What's the matter?'

Helen did not look at her. 'Those chaps.'

'What about them?'

'I didn't like them. I didn't *know* them! I didn't like—' She stopped.

Sophie said, 'Well, you've just got to keep them in order.'

Helen said, 'And it wasn't fair. On them, I mean, letting them pay for us and think that . . .' She stopped again.

Sophie shrugged. 'I didn't ask them to take us in – they offered. And I didn't promise anything. Isn't that true?'

Helen had to admit that it was, although she was still

unhappy when they parted to board their respective trams. Sophie was more puzzled than concerned by her friend's attitude but she soon shrugged that off. She was humming the songs from the film before she got off the tram. Then she sang them, panting, as she ran home.

On the other side of the river Sarah Tennant ran all the way to the house of Dr Dickinson and hammered on his door. When he opened it she gasped out, 'Please, Doctor, it's me mam!'

7

April 1936

'They want me to play in a match for the county schoolboys.'
Matt, home from school, grimaced and dropped the letter
on the breakfast table. 'Blow that!'

Jack, his breakfast finished, looked up from *The Times*
and scowled, irritated. 'It's usually considered to be an
honour.'

Chrissie concentrated on pouring tea then passed the cup
and saucer to Sophie, but was wary.

Matt had already turned down an invitation to play
for the local club. Now he grumbled, 'I don't *have*
to play. Sometimes I don't *want* to play. I want to
please myself, not turn out whenever somebody else
wants me to.'

Chrissie saw the anger on Jack's face and put in quickly,
'All right, Matt, that's enough.'

Sophie, ready for school in gym slip – another three days
before the end of term for her – muttered, 'I think Matt's
right. Why should he—'

Chrissie rapped, 'And that's enough from you.'

Sophie had not finished but she caught her mother's eye
and was silent. Jack shook his head in exasperation, then

picked up his coffee cup and returned to reading. Chrissie relaxed.

Jack set down his empty cup and folded the paper. He said quietly, 'Hitler is in the news again. I don't like the way things are going.' He had voiced that worry before outside his home and no one had echoed it. He knew he was in a minority.

Chrissie knew it, too, and that most people read Hitler's speeches and shrugged. She said, 'I don't like it, either.'

Jack went on, 'We ought to have acted when he marched his soldiers into the Rhineland a month ago. The French should have thrown him out and we should have supported them.'

Matt's voice rose in incredulity. 'You mean a war? But you were nearly killed in the last one! There are men in this town who lost arms or legs, and hundreds of war widows! There must be better ways of settling differences!'

Jack said flatly, 'If they'll let you.'

Matt waved that away with a flap of his hand. 'Anyway, Hitler and Mussolini are a comic turn – prancing about and saluting like Caesar!'

Jack persisted, brows coming together in a black line, 'We have to take them seriously.'

Matt shook his head. 'Well, I'm not. And I won't fight. I don't want to kill anybody and I don't want bits of me blown off.'

Sophie cheered. 'Hurray! Good for you, Matt!'

Jack shoved back his chair and snapped at Matt, 'I'll talk to you this evening.' He stalked out of the room and along the hall, heading for the stairs, the tower room and the papers he had worked on the previous night.

Chrissie flared at Sophie, 'Keep your mouth shut!' She saw her rage reflected in the shock on her daughter's face. As Sophie put a hand to her mouth, Chrissie turned on Matt: 'And *you*! That was a disgraceful outburst! I'll thank you to apologise to your father!' Matt shoved up out of his chair and started out of the room, and Chrissie demanded, 'Where are you going?'

'Out!' Matt tossed the reply over his shoulder without pausing or turning his head, then he was gone.

Chrissie drove Jack to Ballantyne's yard in the Ford. He said, 'I know I shouldn't have lost my temper, but—'

'I don't blame you,' Chrissie cut in. 'I did too.' She sighed. 'The pair of them worry me sick.'

Jack said wrily, 'Well, now we can go to work and worry about something else,' and he kissed her.

'Jack!' Chrissie was scandalised. 'We're driving through the town!' Then she realised she was giggling and he was grinning.

'That's better,' Jack said.

Chrissie set him down at the gates of the yard and drove back to the Railway Hotel. She had barely settled at her desk, her mind still recalling the angry scenes over breakfast, trying to put them behind her, when Sarah Tennant tapped at the open door of her office. Chrissie managed to smile at her, then saw that the thin, pale face was drawn, the soft brown eyes red with weeping. 'What is it, Sarah?'

Sarah had worked at the hotel for almost a year now. She had proved to be quick to learn and hard working, cheerful and willing. She was not cheerful now. Her voice husky, she asked, 'Can I have some time off, please, Mrs Ballantyne?

I mean, could I have one or two days of my holiday now and I'll work them in the summer?' Then she explained, 'You see, my mam's died and I have to see to the funeral.'

Chrissie thought, Oh, dear God. She had been Sarah's age when she arranged the funeral of Bessie Milburn, who had been more of a mother to her than her own. She went to Sarah and put her arm around the girl. 'Come and sit down. When did it happen?'

Chrissie listened, wiped the tears and heard of the coughing that went on night and day. Sarah said simply, 'It was the consumption, you see. The ambulanceman said Mam coughed her lung up on the way to the hospital. She was dead when she got there.' She shivered.

Chrissie drove Sarah to the undertaker's. The girl knew what to do and had obviously helped her mother on similar occasions. From there they went on to the two rooms she had shared with her late mother. There were sympathetic neighbours to welcome the girl, but before Chrissie left she took the girl aside and asked, confirming, 'Will you be living here on your own now?'

'Yes, Mrs Ballantyne.'

'If you like, I'll find room for you at the hotel and you can live in. You don't have to make your mind up now . . .' Chrissie left the offer hanging but guessed from Sarah's face what the answer would be.

The young girl was in no position to make a dispassionate decision. She had watched her mother's steady decline through the winter. Isabel Tennant had spent all winter in that back kitchen, looking out on a yard, black roofs and smoking chimneys. There was not a blade of grass to be seen, let alone a flower. And coughing, coughing.

Sarah had shut her eyes to the obvious, afraid of it, and was still shocked by her mother's death. Her thoughts were in turmoil. She grieved for her mother and she had taken no thought for the future; it was too soon for that. Emotions made the decision for her. Later she would see that she would no longer have to find the rent – nor face Fannon to pay it – but now she could not think of staying here without her mother, would look for her every time she walked in at the door.

So Sarah said, 'I'd like to do that, please, Mrs Ballantyne,' and managed to smile for the first time that day. Chrissie hugged her.

When Sophie cycled home from school she had Helen Diaz for company, come along to borrow a book needed for homework. As they turned into the drive of the Ballantyne house, Sophie braked, back wheel sliding on the gravel, and Helen stopped alongside her.

'Here comes Matt.' Sophie pointed and Helen saw him trudging up the pavement under the trees that spread their branches over the road. Sophie laughed. 'I wouldn't be in his shoes.'

Helen asked, 'Why?' and Sophie told her of the row at breakfast that morning. Helen was not amused as Sophie seemed to be, and said, 'He ought to have some idea of what career he wants.' She thought Matt was lucky to have his opportunities. She made no secret of her intention to become a nurse, though she told no one of her greater ambition.

Matt came up scowling and growled, 'What's so funny?'

Sophie's grin stayed in place as she answered, 'Mother was wild. You'll catch it tonight. And serve you right.'

Matt kept on walking past them. 'I don't care.'

'Yes, you do. And I took your side, remember? But how could you walk out the way you did? That was daft!'

Matt paused and turned to grumble, 'Dad keeps on at me about going into the yard, or studying for this, that or the other. I don't *know* what I want to do. It's all right for Tom; he loves the yard, always has, couldn't wait to get into one, and he's counting the days until he can start work with Dad. It's all right for you; you're a girl and nobody minds what you do as long as you grow out of this barmy idea to go on the stage.' That wiped the grin from Sophie's face. 'But I don't want to go into the yard. I don't *want* to do anything much. And I'm fed up with this place.' He walked on up the drive.

The two girls followed, pushing their bikes, Sophie fuming over his remark about her 'barmy idea'. Helen realised that he had looked through her as if she didn't exist.

Chrissie sought out Matt in his room when she got home that evening and spoke her mind, finishing, 'Don't you dare answer me like that again!'

Matt muttered, 'I'm sorry. I didn't mean to upset you,' and he was miserable because he had hurt her. 'I just get fed up – with school and people wanting me to do this and that.' He shrugged, still glumly rebellious.

Chrissie said, 'Your father's not a fool and if you listen to him you'll learn a lot. Now will you apologise to him?'

Matt sighed. 'I'll tell him I'm sorry.'

So Chrissie waylaid Jack when he returned from the yard

and pleaded Matt's case: 'He is sorry. He's young and he just doesn't *know*, Jack.'

Jack grumbled but listened and later told Matt, 'Before you start airing your views on world politics you need to study some of the people involved. *I* don't want another war; the last one was bad enough.' Matt apologised and they all sat down to dinner. It was an uneasy truce.

Next morning Sarah opened the door to the dealer. He was in his fifties, wearing a greasy jacket and a shirt fastened at the neck with a brass collar-stud, but no collar. His grey flannels had a hole in the knee and his toes poked out of his plimsolls. He looked over the two rooms with their few sticks of furniture, all of it cheap and old. He came from the next street, knew Sarah and her mother and Sarah knew him, so he made her a fair offer: 'I'll give you twenty-two and six for the lot.'

Sarah took the crumpled pound note and the half-crown from him and he called in his mate who waited outside by the horse and cart. Together they loaded the furniture on to the cart, rolled up the mats made out of clippings of rags and the old and cracked linoleum, and took all of those as well. Then they climbed up on top of the load and the horse hauled it away. Sarah was left with two rooms empty but for a bucket, an iron-hard block of carbolic soap and a scrubbing brush. Her mother had told her, 'Always leave a place as you'd like to find it.'

The key was in the pocket of her apron. When she was finished she would take it upstairs and leave it with her neighbours. They were out now but she would shove the key under their door and they would give it to Fannon.

Her own possessions, all she wanted to keep from this place, she had taken away the night before. She had also cleaned out the fireplace and hearth, and for hot water had lit a fire under the boiler in the washhouse across the back yard. Now she dipped the bucket in, hauled it out nearly full and started in the bedroom.

When Sarah had scrubbed out the bedroom and most of the kitchen, she climbed wearily to her feet. It was time to throw away the dirty, soapy water and take one last bucketful from the boiler. She picked up the bucket, turned to the door and saw Fannon standing there. She wondered how long he had been watching her as he was now, wet lips drawn back in a smirk that showed yellow teeth. And she remembered she was alone in the house.

Fannon moved towards her and she took a step back. He reached out for her, looming over her, and she retreated another pace, panic gripping her as one of his hands seized her shoulder. 'Just a bit o' fun, lass. I'll make it worth your while . . .' he started, then the contents of the bucket hit him full in the face. He recoiled, gasping and spluttering, wiping at his eyes as the scummy water ran down from his hair to drip off his chin. He swore, blinking, reaching out again, but then Sarah jammed the empty bucket over his head, scurried round him and out into the passage.

She pulled the door shut behind her and fumbled for the key in her apron pocket. She slotted it in the lock and turned it. She heard the *bang!* and *clank-clank* as Fannon threw the bucket aside, then he rattled the door and hammered on it with his fists. 'Open this door or I'll . . .' he bellowed, but by that time she had run down the passage and was out in the street, his threats fading into unintelligible bawls, sounding like some distant bull.

Jack came home for lunch silent and abstracted. Chrissie sat opposite him at the oval table and asked, 'Something wrong?'

He sighed. 'The Greek contract we were negotiating fell through. We had a letter from them this morning.'

Chrissie said, 'Oh! That's bad news,' and knew it was very bad.

They fell silent a while as Betty Price, the fresh-faced maid, entered, pushing a loaded trolley. She served them with chops and set the tureen of vegetables on the table. Chrissie said, 'Thank you,' and the girl left.

Jack went on, 'It's mostly bad news these days. Last year – 1935 – was the best since 1930: we built eight ships on this river, totalling 31,000 tons. But ten years ago we were averaging over *131,000* tons! That's how good this "best year" is.' He paused and eyed Chrissie grimly, then finished, 'If we don't get a contract for another ship we won't be able to keep the yard open through next winter. We'll have to lay everybody off.'

'*Everybody!*' Chrissie said with her face creased as if it hurt, and it did. She knew what that meant to the men and their families who made their living from building ships. It meant the dole and the Relief, ragged clothes and empty bellies.

Jack said heavily, 'There's still time to find another contract, but it's getting short.'

He looked up as Matt wandered into the dining-room and slumped into a chair at the oval table, his long legs stretched out. Chrissie said absently, still shaken by Jack's news, 'Matt, you have oil on your face.'

'I've been working on the car.' He held up his hands. 'I did wash.'

Jack glanced at him and said brusquely, 'Well, clean your face as well, there's a good chap.'

Matt grumbled, 'What's the point? There's no one here but us.' Sophie ate lunch at school.

Chrissie intervened quickly. 'Please, Matt.'

'Oh, all right.' He sighed and slouched out. When he returned he muttered, 'Chops again?' and helped himself from the trolley. As he did so, he said, 'I think this chap Churchill is a warmonger. He says we should fight Hitler.'

Jack answered curtly, 'He's been down this road before. I think he knows what he's talking about.'

A shriek came distantly from the back of the house, followed by the crash of breaking glass or china. Chrissie jumped up from her chair and hurried out. That kind of sound coming from a kitchen always rang alarm bells for her.

She found the cook and Betty Price mopping up a broken dish and a steamed pudding that had spread across the floor. The cook wailed, 'Sorry, Mrs Ballantyne! I was lifting it out o' the pan wi' the clout and it shot out o' me hands!'

Chrissie saw the pan on the gas cooker that had replaced the old, black kitchen range. She said, 'No one hurt, then?' When they confirmed this she sighed her relief. She had worried that the shriek came from someone scalded having known too many such accidents when she had worked in kitchens. 'Never mind. We'll have some fruit for dessert.'

She left to return to her lunch and the cook muttered,

'"Never mind," she says? I was looking forward to having a bit o' that pudden meself.'

Betty Price commiserated, 'Me an' all,' then added, 'There's a row goin' on in there, atmosphere you could cut wi' a knife.'

As Chrissie approached the door to the dining-room it flew open and Matt charged out. He paused to shout back at Jack, 'You treat me like a kid!' then almost ran along the hall on long legs, slamming the front door behind him.

Chrissie looked at Jack and he glared back at her. She did not speak and after a moment his glare faded and became a frown of irritation. He growled, 'He came out with some more of his half-baked claptrap, about warmongers like Churchill – and me.'

'*You!*'

Jack nodded wryly. 'That's right. It seems I want a war to make business for the yard.'

Chrissie bit her lip. 'Oh, Jack. That's awful. I'm sorry.' She went to him and put her arm around him.

He gripped her hand. 'I suppose I blew up because there's an element of truth in it. I don't want a war – God forbid! – but it would bring orders for ships and he's right about that.'

Chrissie kissed him. 'He's wrong to accuse you of hoping for a war and he knows he is wrong. He'll come back and apologise. He'll be sorry.'

Matt was sorry already. He strode aimlessly along the road under the trees and wondered, How could I say that? He had missed his lunch but didn't care about that because he knew he would be fed whenever he showed his face in the kitchen. The cook doted on him.

* * *

Peter Robinson was still waiting for lunch. He had gone down to the seashore early that morning, collected a load of driftwood that filled the bogey and hauled it back to his home. In the back yard he chopped the wood into sticks and bound them in bundles with odd lengths of string. Then he set out to haul them around the streets looking for buyers. He now knew it was no use offering them in Monkwearmouth where he lived because people there couldn't afford to buy, or they found their own firewood where they could. He towed the bogey back to the sea-front houses of Roker and Scaburn where some people had money to spend. However, that still did not mean they would buy.

At the end of an hour he had not sold a stick and the bread and margarine he had eaten for breakfast was only a distant memory. He found some comfort in the knowledge that there was food in the house for his mother, while Billy, his half-brother, was given a free midday meal of broth at St Peter's Mission Hall in Dame Dorothy Street. It was another hour before he made enough to buy a sandwich in a pork shop. The butcher dipped the two halves of the bun in the gravy and then forked the sliced pork in between them while Peter watched hungrily. It took the edge off that hunger. He could have eaten another and he had just enough to buy it, but he was determined to go home that night with more than just the price of a pork sandwich. He set out again, towing the bogey.

Ursula Whittle was tall, thin, nervous and just turned thirty. She peered out at the world through tortoiseshell-rimmed spectacles. This was her first term at Sophie's school, her first teaching job, and she was afraid she was going to lose it. She had been warned a month ago that her enforcement of discipline was inadequate. She had tried, but she liked the girls, wanted them to like her, and found that hard to reconcile with discipline. This morning she had received another warning – and been given the job of supervising the entire school through the lunch break.

Her once wealthy father had died of a heart attack when his business foundered and he lost everything in the depression. The shock left her mother deranged, and she had lingered on, vaguely smiling and ineffectual. Ursula looked after her through those last years and through the last of the money, paid out on her father's insurance policy. When her mother died Ursula was left alone and penniless. She had got the job at the school because a governor was an old friend of her father. She knew she was lucky to have it and would not get another. If she lost it she was doomed to a poverty she had never known but knew of. She was desperate.

So she hastened across the quad, filled with girls from eleven to eighteen, talking and playing. Then she set out to patrol the playing fields where more of the girls practised hockey or rounders. Ursula was almost running herself, her head turning all the while, trying to be everywhere and see everything. She was panting and feeling dizzy. Then as she passed a belt of trees and shrubs that walled off one end of the playing fields she saw and heard a sudden rustling in the bushes. She forced her way in to investigate and found a small clearing.

'Sophie!' She was almost sure of the name, but there were so many girls and all looked alike in their uniform, so she added, 'Isn't it?'

'Yes, miss.' Sophie climbed to her feet and brushed down her gym slip. The youth from the boys' school on the other side of the copse scrambled to his feet and ran.

Ursula shouted after him, 'Stop! Stop!' but he took no notice and in seconds was lost beyond the trees. She demanded of Sophie 'Who was that?'

'I don't know, miss,' Sophie answered with wide-eyed innocence. 'I just found him in here when I came to look for some nature study specimens.' That was almost true. She had been seeking leaves when she saw the youth on the playing fields on the other side of the wood, and had called to him . . .

Ursula did not believe her, and had the damning evidence of her own eyes. She said, trying to be stern, but squeaking, 'This is a *very* serious matter. You'll go before the headmistress this afternoon. Come along now.' She ushered Sophie out of the copse ahead of her.

Sophie also knew this was a serious matter. There had been cases before, and all had ended in expulsion. Then she would have to face her father – and her mother. That would be the worst. The sky had darkened as if to match the cloud hanging over her. Thunder rumbled and as she trailed across the field ahead of Ursula Whittle the first fat raindrops began to fall. So she was driven into the school hall along with all the other girls seeking shelter.

There were five hundred of them. Their voices, echoing in the high-ceilinged hall, drowned the sound of the storm outside. Crowded together and excited they ran amok, playing hastily devised games, scuttling in and out of the rows of chairs, leaping over them, kicking them aside. Ursula stood on the stage and ordered, 'Sit down! Find your usual places in assembly and *sit down!* None of them heeded her, her words lost in the din. The clock on the wall told her that the headmistress and other teachers would return in fifteen minutes. If they found this chaos then she would be dismissed.

Sophie saw an opportunity. There was the piano on the stage. In front of her was an audience. Did she dare? She was a crash-bang pianist, and the chord she struck made Ursula Whittle jump and produced one moment of silence while the five hundred girls gaped at the stage. Sophie sang 'Stormy Weather' and they giggled and booed – but then they listened. And when she finished the song and went straight into another, they still listened. Her voice was a powerful contralto, husky and adult. She held them, their heads nodding in time, humming and rocking to the music, until the bell clanged for afternoon school.

Ursula Whittle had sidled off to the side of the stage. She returned now as Sophie closed the lid of the piano and stood up. Ursula lectured her, 'That might have become a very serious matter. You must be more careful where you go to collect specimens. Promise me you won't go there again.' It was meant to be a severe warning but it came out weakly, gratefully, because Ursula knew she had been rescued.

'Yes, Miss Whittle,' Sophie answered meekly, knowing she, too, had been saved. She was still grinning when Helen Diaz put an arm around her.

'That was marvellous!' Helen said with admiration – and surprise, because she still could not believe that it had been her friend performing on stage. 'You can really do it.' Sophie nodded, laughing.

Not everyone was as enthusiastic. Pamela Ogilvy was

the only daughter of a director of a shipbuilding firm. She was in Sophie's form and never understood why Sophie Ballantyne befriended Helen Diaz rather than herself. She had not joined in the applause, and dismissed Sophie's performance as 'exhibitionist'. However, she did not say so aloud, and she smiled at Sophie in passing. Sophie did not notice and Pamela sniffed and walked on.

Unaware of this, Helen opened an exercise book and took out a sheaf of leaves, carefully picked and pressed. 'Here you are.'

'What?' Sophie was still excited.

'I got these in the park for this afternoon's lesson, some for me, these for you. I told you I would. You said you had some homework you wanted to catch up on.'

Sophie smiled. 'That's right. I did.'

Helen admonished her. 'You shouldn't leave your homework till lunchtime.'

'I've promised not to do it again,' Sophie said, as she secretly thought, In another place, at another time . . .

She lived through those fifteen minutes on stage again and again through the afternoon, thinking, So it's as easy as that.

Sophie was still singing when she arrived home and found her mother using the telephone in the hall. Chrissie set down the receiver tight lipped. Sophie glanced through to the sitting-room and asked, 'Where's Matt?' She had to tell someone about her performance in the hall and dared not tell her mother.

Chrissie answered grimly, 'You may well ask. He left a note. I've just phoned your father with the news.' She handed the sheet, torn from a sketching pad, to Sophie, who read, in Matt's neat script, 'Gone to Finchale. Cook fitted me up with supplies. Back in a few days.'

Chrissie snapped, 'It's no laughing matter.'

Sophie tried to stop grinning and agreed, 'What a cheek, sloping off like that. Of course, he's Cook's blue-eyed boy. She'll have seen him all right for grub.'

'She did – and claims she assumed he had permission to go off.' Chrissie suspected the truth of that, knowing the cook's fondness for Matt.

Sophie soothed, 'Still, he's been away like that a few times now.'

Jack said the same when he returned that evening: 'Well, he's done it before.'

Chrissie pointed out angrily, 'Not without asking our permission first.'

Jack shrugged. He had spent an afternoon dealing with problems at the yard and that had taken the edge off his original anger. 'He said too much earlier, so he's got out of the way. He'll come home in his own good time and I'll have a word with him then.'

Chrissie said unhappily, 'He worries me, Jack. I want him to be happy.'

'So do I. And I hope he is now.'

Finchale Priory lay some six miles away. Matt got down from the slow train at the little station, shrugged into his pack and walked the country mile to the priory. It lay by the river in its steep-sided valley. He found a clearing where he had camped before, a hundred yards from the ruined priory and close by the river. There he set up his little tent, cooked his supper of sausages and potatoes on his fire and ate it by the light of the flames. Then he unrolled his groundsheet and blankets. He lay peering out of the open door of the tent, blinking at the embers glowing in the darkness, listening to the run of the river beyond. In minutes he was asleep.

In the days that followed he would wake thinking of the row before he left home and the one that awaited him on his return. Then he would become involved in the small chores of the day – washing up and cooking – and afterwards take his pad and pencils and go sketching, or sink into one of the books he had brought with him, or go roaming the countryside, long striding, for hours.

He missed Tom. They had grown up together, different but close, playing, fighting, scheming, arguing – and uniting to look after Sophie. They had gone to the same school with less than a year between them. Now they met only at weekends when Tom came home. Matt didn't want to complain to Tom or ask his advice – though he had in the past and would again. He just wanted his brother there. However, that was not possible. He reminded himself that they would be camping together in France in the summer and was more cheerful. Meanwhile tomorrow could wait; he would let life take its course.

He returned home at the end of a week, in time for dinner, and was made welcome. He did not have a prepared speech, but after dinner he just spoke his mind: 'I'm sorry, Mother, Dad, but I just had to get away. I like to read, sketch, play rugby – but when I feel like it, not doing a period on this, another on that, according to a timetable. I don't want to go to school at all but I know I need a certificate, a piece of paper to be able to get a job. The trouble is, I just don't know what job I want.'

Jack glanced ruefully, exasperated, at Chrissie. 'Which leaves us where we were before. What are we going to do with him?'

Chrissie did not care, was only glad to have her boy back.

Pamela Ogilvy was blonde, and big for her age. She had heard of Matt's running away and thought him romantic. She waylaid him as he left the house with Sophie and Helen, who had called to see Sophie. Pamela met them at the gate, smiled at all of them, but a little more at Matt than at the rest. Her eyes were still on him when she addressed Sophie: 'I wondered if you could tell me one or two things about this trip.'

Matt asked, 'What trip?' and thought she was a pretty girl.

Pamela still smiled at him. 'We're going to Germany this summer.' She was aware of Helen listening and added, 'Well, some of us are – about a dozen or so actually.'

Matt said, 'That sounds great.'

Sophie glanced from Pamela to Matt and back again, then asked, 'What did you want to know?'

Helen Diaz started to walk away. 'I'm going home.' She was not going to Germany and Pamela knew this.

Sophie had read the situation and said quickly, 'I'll see you as far as the tram. Come on, Pamela.'

Matt said, 'I'll walk with you.'

Sophie cut in, 'Dad said the car wasn't running properly. He was going to ask you to mend it.'

'Not running properly?' Matt halted, puzzled. 'What d'you mean?'

Sophie called back to him, 'That's all I know – except that you need to keep on the right side of him after this last week. Come *on*, Pamela!'

So Pamela had to go, while Matt made his way back to the house wondering, Not running properly? I'll have to ask Dad . . .

When he did, Jack Ballantyne answered him, 'Must be some mistake. The car's ticking over like a clock, nothing wrong with it.'

Later, when Matt challenged Sophie, she replied cheerfully, 'I was keeping you out of trouble. You've been in enough without getting off with Pamela. She'd put you through the mangle.'

Riled, Matt answered, 'You can stop interfering in my affairs.'

Sophie walked into her room and paused only to tell him, 'Somebody has to look after you. I'd have thought you'd be glad I was prepared to do it because lots wouldn't.' Then she closed the door in his face.

Joshua Fannon came home from the pub early because he had spent all his own money and had only the rents he had collected that day. The coins chinked in the pockets of the old raincoat buttoned tight over his belly, but he dared not spend them. He smelt the gas when he opened the door and heard the hissing.

'What the hell . . .' He shoved the door wide and stepped into the kitchen. The gas lamp was not lit because the room was still twilit on this spring evening. He saw his wife,

Meggie, lying fat and loose in her armchair by the fireplace as usual, though the grate held no fire, only dead ashes. A half-empty bottle of gin and a glass stood by her chair, again as usual. In the hearth was a teapot and a gas-ring with a kettle perched on top of it. The hissing came from there.

Fannon swore. 'Ye daft cow!' He guessed that Meggie had turned on the gas to boil a kettle for tea but, in her drunken stupor, failed to light it. He lumbered across the room, belly wobbling, and bent to turn off the gas, then froze there with his hand on the tap. Meggie was a very bad colour and breathing harshly. He rose slowly, wheezing, then moved quickly to close the door with barely a click. Stepping carefully and light on his feet, he went to the gas meter in a cupboard on one side of the fireplace, dug down into his raincoat pocket and brought out a handful of change. He picked out the pennies, bent down and fed them into the meter one by one. As each rattled down inside, a nerve twitched in his cheek. He was sweating and watching Meggie but she showed no sign of waking. As he rose he knew the gas would flow for several hours.

He left the house quietly, and as he had entered it, by the back door and the back lane. No one saw him go. The rooms upstairs were empty and would be until his neighbours came home after the pubs shut at ten.

He went on to the Pear Tree and the barman greeted him. 'Aye, aye, Josh!'

Fannon answered, 'Give us a pint,' and as the man pulled it Fannon went on, 'I've just left the Frigate. There's a rare crowd in there tonight.' That was true.

The barman said, 'Is there?'

'Aye.' Fannon pulled out the money from his raincoat

pocket. He could spend the rents now. 'Have one for yourself.'

'Ta, Josh.' The barman lifted his glass in salute and drank.

Fannon stood at the bar through the rest of the evening. He had time to think about what he had done on the spur of the moment and now he realised he had committed murder. If he was found out he would be hanged. He sweated with fear and drank feverishly, talked to anyone who would listen. He was one of the last to leave the Pear Tree when it closed. Then he stood outside because he could not go home, talking with a group of late leavers.

His neighbour found him there, the man hurrying up, panting, to lay a hand on his shoulder. 'I've got some bad news for you, Josh.'

Fannon mourned in public and recovered his confidence as the death was accepted as an accident. He celebrated in private. The bank book was found by the coroner's assistant, secreted in a pocket on Meggie Fannon's vest, and he returned it to Fannon. There were legal procedures to go through because Meggie left no will, but nor did she have any other kin and eventually Joshua found himself a man of property with money in the bank.

He had not planned for this day as long as he had yearned for it, but he was not unprepared, either. He decided he would not be idle but would use his inheritance to build a bigger fortune by uniting his capital with his experience. He would become a bookie. He would not stand on street corners to take the bets and risk being chased by the pollis. He would pay somebody else to do that while he sat in comfort, checking the gambling slips and money as they were brought to him, and grew rich.

It was beyond his fearful imagining that he could be involved again in the plotting of murder – but in time, he would.

Sophie did not know that, nor did she know him, and slept peaccfully in her bed.

8

Summer 1936

The Bavarian *bierkeller* was crowded, dimly lit and smoky.
The four girls, all made up and trying to look older than
their fifteen or sixteen years, had secured a table near the
little dance floor and the band. They had set out in a spirit
of bravado, led by Sophie, who told them, 'The old girl
will be sound asleep by eleven.' She was referring to their
headmistress. 'She won't know anything about it.' So they
had crept past her door, run down the stairs and out of
the hotel. Now it was past midnight. They sipped beer and
tried to keep up their act as blasé young adults, tried also to
ignore the ogling of the handsome young men at the tables
around them.

Pamela Ogilvy collected most of the glances. She was
tall, and her full figure and long, blonde hair attracted the
men. She was aware of their glances, and while nervous of
returning them she blushed and basked in the admiration.

Sophie returned any of the looks that came her way,
grinned and shook her head when one of the youths came
to speak to her. Pamela asked, jealous, 'What did he say?'
The other two girls leaned forward to hear.

Sophie shrugged. 'I don't know. Couldn't hear with all

the noise. Probably what they all say.' Now the band had stopped playing and were leaving the little stage to take a few minutes' break. Sophie watched them go. Only a pianist was left.

Pamela suggested, provoking, 'Why don't you get up and sing, Sophie?' The others laughed.

So did Sophie. 'All right.' Then she was on her feet and edging between the tables, crossing the floor and climbing on to the stage. Her painfully acquired German deserted her then, but the little man at the piano knew more than enough English to understand what she wanted. He started to play the introduction and Sophie turned to face the crowd. Everyone in the *bierkeller* knew this was one of the English girls. And was she about to sing? There were cheers, jeers, catcalls and laughter.

Sophie stepped forward, and paused with her weight on one long leg, the other slightly bent, hands on hips. High heels added two inches to her height while the poor lighting carved hollows in her cheeks, putting ten years on her age. She pitched her voice even lower than usual to match the song and the act – a take-off of Marlene Dietrich. And the crowd were watching, listening to, another striking blonde. They were silent as she sang. When she finished they bawled their appreciation and hammered on the tables.

They easily persuaded her to sing again and she held them until the band returned, then sang all the way back to the hotel. Pamela Ogilvy said little.

Helen Diaz spent some of her summer holiday training with the St John's Ambulance Brigade. She had joined at eleven as a cadet, with her mother's urging ('It will help you when you go to be a nurse'). She worked enthusiastically and was proud of her white cap and grey dress, with the Service Star and single stripe on her sleeve that showed she had proved efficient in First Aid and Home Nursing.

Some of her time was spent helping her mother, cooking and scrubbing. On washday she lit the boiler in the washhouse, pounded the washing in the tub with the poss-stick and heaved on the handle of the mangle as her mother fed the clothes into the wooden rollers. If the weather was fine the clothes were pegged on the line in the yard. On a day of rain they were hung on the clothes horse – and Paco Diaz cursed Helen as he shoved them aside because they hid the fire: 'Fool! Take them away!'

Chrissie returned from two weeks' walking in the Scottish Highlands with Jack and met Sarah Tennant in the kitchen of the Railway Hotel. 'What did you do in your holiday, Sarah?'

The girl looked up from the pile of potatoes she was peeling and smiled. 'I spent nearly every day on the beach.' She had walked across the bridge over the Wear and down to the sea front, carrying a basket containing her towel, bathing costume and a packet of sandwiches. When it rained she stayed in her room and read. Every evening she reported to the club for her part-time job of washing glasses. Sarah was living frugally and saving.

Chrissie asked, 'Did you enjoy yourself?'

'I had a lovely time,' Sarah replied, and meant it.

Matt and Tom had been camping in France, wrangling and laughing, talking far into the night by their fire. Sarah would pass both of them with smiles now if she met them in the hotel when they came to see their mother, but she was still shy. To them she was just a rather skinny girl who worked in the kitchen, deserving their courtesy and respect but having no common interest.

When Tom went back to work he was in overalls because he would be spending a year working on the ship itself rather than in the office. Like many of the other men, he took with him his 'bait', sandwiches for his midday meal, prepared by his landlady and wrapped in a red and white spotted handkerchief. His can with its wire handle, and lid that served as a cup, held tea leaves, sugar and a dollop of condensed milk, ready for wetting.

Jack told Chrissie proudly, 'I hear he is doing very well.'

Then there was Matt. He had received a School Leaving Certificate, albeit not a good one, but had not found a job. Chrissie pressed, 'I think we ought to give him one more year.'

'He doesn't want to go back to school,' Jack pointed out, 'and there's a doubt as to whether they would take him. The Head suggested as much when you saw him, remember?'

Chrissie agreed, but insisted, 'His reports said he had a talent for art.'

Jack qualified that: 'He likes sketching.'

'Well, then, there is a good art school in the town, so why not send him there for a year? He might develop a real interest.'

Jack said unhappily, 'I doubt it. I would hope so, but I doubt it.'

Chrissie wanted more time for this boy of hers, hoping

he would find his way eventually, but she, too, was uncertain.

They put it to Matt, his sandy hair tousled and black oil streaked across his brow. The three of them sat in the spacious sitting-room one evening, with its pictures of Ballantyne ships, while Sophie was upstairs in her room with Helen Diaz, playing records.

Jack said, 'We'll give you a year at art school to see if you have the talent or interest to make a career in that line. But in August next year you'll be eighteen. If you haven't made up your mind what you want out of life by then, you go to work in the yard. I'm not supporting you after that.'

Chrissie hated the ultimatum but accepted it, remembering how she had to work as a young girl. She urged Matt, 'Whatever you really want to do, we'll back you.' Jack had not meant to go that far – he liked to know what he was getting into before he committed himself – but he grunted agreement.

Matt was silent for a moment, on the edge of revolt, but he told himself he could only argue against, he could not argue for anything, and he did not want another row. He said, 'Well, that's fair, I suppose.'

He went off for a walk in the dusk and found Sophie walking down to the tram stop with Helen Diaz. He told Sophie the verdict, omitting to acknowledge Helen in his abstraction.

Sophie said, 'You're lucky to get the year. Some fathers would have taken you straight into the yard whether you liked it or not.'

Matt grumbled, 'I can't see me being an artist for the rest of my life.'

Helen, annoyed at being ignored, said, 'There are plenty of young chaps around this town that would jump at the chance of a year at art school – or a job at Ballantyne's yard.'

Matt blinked at her, startled, then snapped, 'I don't see that it's any of your business.'

Helen was red faced and angry, but her tram came clanking and rumbling at that moment. She climbed up into its lit interior and was driven away, wishing she had slapped his face.

Later that week Pamela Ogilvy sought out Sophie at school to tell her, 'I was talking to Matt last night . . .' She paused to gauge the effect of that.

Sophie knew Matt had 'bumped into' Pamela: he had told her. Sophie suspected it had been no accident and that Pamela had arranged it. Now she only smiled and said, 'I talk to him all the time.'

Needled, Pamela said, 'Don't you think he should be going into his father's yard instead of taking this art course?'

Helen Diaz was standing by, and before Sophie could answer, she snapped, 'What has it got to do with you? It's his life.'

Pamela was startled into silence for a moment but then recovered to say primly, 'It's my business because I don't want to see him waste his time messing about with little pictures when he could be following a career. He's a gentleman's son – but you wouldn't know anything about their standards.'

Helen flinched as if struck and Sophie shoved in front of her. She told Pamela, 'You're a stuck-up cow,' then she grabbed Helen's arm and hurried her away.

*   *   *

On a fine summer's afternoon Lizzie Diaz walked down Church Street on her way home, a basket of shopping on her arm. In the warmth of the summer she just wore an old cardigan over a thin cotton dress. As soon as she got home she would put on her pinny to keep the dress clean. The streets on her right around Society Lane, narrow and cobbled, were being demolished. The cramped little houses, huddled together in rows, were empty, their former tenants moved to the new estates being built far away on the outskirts of the town. Lizzie saw the workmen knocking down a house a hundred yards or more away, saw also the children playing in and out of the empty houses close by. But her mind was on her own child, Helen.

She was well content with the girl, who was gaining good reports at the grammar school and was set on following the course her mother had advised. Lizzie was sure that one day her daughter would be a nurse, a sister, maybe even a matron. It was a fine career, respected in the community. If she had not married Paco . . . And Paco was the trouble. To him his son, Juan – though the boy's friends all called him John – was the most important person in the family after himself. Juan came first in his father's thoughts and always had, to the almost total exclusion of his daughter. Lizzie flinched as a child shrieked and then laughed somewhere in among the old buildings. She wished those bairns wouldn't play in there.

Paco Diaz treated Helen as little better than a servant for him and his son, as he had treated Lizzie; and she, meek, gentle and loving had accepted the situation for herself. However, now she sensed danger ahead because Helen had a mind of her own and was becoming rebellious. The girl had not defied her father – yet – but she had complained to her mother about the work heaped on the pair of them while Juan did nothing in the house. Lizzie worried over it, wanted to stand up for her daughter but was afraid to confront the man she had married and loved.

The shriek came again, this time followed not by laughter but a sudden rumbling crash. Lizzie saw the children, dirty faces frightened and shocked, running out of a gap in the old walls. She called to one of them, 'What's wrong?'

The boy stopped beside her and the others gathered around. He panted, 'The ceiling fell in and Freddy Williams was underneath it.'

Lizzie whispered, 'Oh, my God!' then she ordered them, 'Go and fetch the men. Tell them we might want an ambulance. Run, now!' They did, racing down the road towards the workmen.

Lizzie ran too, into the gap from which they had come, stumbling over the litter of rubble – stones, brick and lumps of rotten timber. She could see where the ceiling had come down because a pall of dust still hung in the air inside the shell of one house. The side walls still stood, holding up the roof, but the front and back had collapsed and what had been the ceiling of the ground-floor room, and the floor of the room above, had fallen in. There was a pile of debris almost as high as Lizzie, great chunks of plaster still adhering to the laths it had been spread on, with broken rafters poking out at odd angles. And somewhere under it all was little Freddy Williams.

She could hear him, a plaintive, frightened, small voice mewing from under the pile: 'Mam! *Mam!*'

'It's all right, bonny lad!' Lizzie called to him. 'I'm coming to get you out! Just lie still!' She began digging into the wreckage, tearing at the laths that in turn tore her fingers. When she strained to lift and shove lengths of the rotten timber that had been the rafters she left bloody imprints on the dirty wood. Her flowered cotton dress was torn and filthy, her cardigan ripped in a dozen places, but she found the boy.

First she uncovered a leg, a bare foot shoved into old plimsolls with holes in uppers and soles, scratched, bruised and dirty skin. Then shorts that had been patched in the seat, followed by a jersey worn into holes through which showed a shirt washed thin. Lizzie lifted one more baulk of timber, held it propped up with her shoulder as she balanced on the pile of rubble and tossed aside the last of the plaster that covered little Freddy. She grabbed him by the waistband of his shorts and hauled him out of the hole in which he lay. He scrambled to his feet and Lizzie told him, 'Go and find your mammy.'

She saw him start, running out through the gap in the wall, then she tried to throw off the timber pressing on her shoulder. As she did so she slipped on the rubble and fell, the timber falling on top of her. It was no heavier than other lengths she had thrown aside but she was tiring now. She fumbled to lift it, awkward because of her position, lying on her side. Then she heard a creaking and groaning, looked up and saw the roof sagging. Its beams had been holding the two side walls apart, but now the roof collapsed and the side walls fell inwards. Lizzie saw the whole mass dropping towards her and screamed, screamed again, then was silent. The dust rose in a much bigger cloud this time, standing above the other houses for long minutes before the wind dispersed it.

* * *

Peter Robinson was one of the many who ran to the scene and helped to clear away the rubble. He saw the crushed body as it was uncovered and recognised it as that of a woman from the street next to his. It was gently lifted out by a score of hands and he stood back, shaken and shocked, as it was carried past. He could not know that he was soon to witness another violent death.

Paco Diaz arranged the funeral with the help of the neighbours. Some of them advised that he order horses to pull the hearse and carriages, being traditionally more in keeping with such a solemn occasion, but he settled on a black motor hearse because that was cheaper. Afterwards there was the usual tea with boiled ham and some discussion as to how much compensation would be paid – but not in the hearing of the family. Paco never told anyone how much he received.

Helen was pale and hardly uttered a word for a week. Her mother had been taken from her without warning. Helen had kissed her in the morning as she left for school and never saw her again. They would not let her look at Lizzie in her coffin because even the undertaker's art could not conceal the battering she had received from the tons of timber and brickwork.

On the morning after the funeral Paco sat back from his empty plate, having eaten the breakfast Helen had cooked for him on the fire. He wiped his mouth on the back of his hand then told her, 'Now you must look after the house and everything. Fetch some paper and write what I say.' He had never tried to write English. When Helen brought a sheet of paper, pen and ink bottle, he dictated: 'Dear miss, now

I am alone I must have the daughter to keep the house so she finish school today.'

Helen pleaded with him while the ink dried on the pen and the paper, with the letter only half done. She told him how important it was for her to get her School Certificate and then go on to be a nurse, told him it was her mother's wish. He only shook his head, implacable and uncaring. 'No, no. School no good for girl. Other girls can be nurse but I need you here. This is woman's place.'

Juan, still eating, put in, 'That's right. Same as we have to work. Cleaning and cooking is a woman's job.'

'No more talk,' said Paco. 'Write the letter,' and he lifted his hand. Helen dipped pen in ink, finished the letter in a shaky copperplate and gave it to her father to sign.

She took the letter to school, gave it to her headmistress and returned home. She had not seen Sophie or any of the other girls and could not have trusted herself to say farewell without bursting into tears. But she cried when she got back to the empty house, cried for what she had lost – her mother and her hopes and ambitions – and for what lay ahead of her: virtual slavery as the servant of the two men.

Then she dried her eyes and started work.

Next morning Chrissie drove Jack to work in the Ford. He was on his way to the Balkans to try to obtain a contract for a ship to be built in the yard. His case was in the car but he had to pick up some papers from his office. As Chrissie steered the Ford across the bridge and turned down the road to the yard, Jack said, 'This civil war in Spain is a bad business.' The war had broken out only weeks before with Franco leading a revolt against the Spanish government.

Chrissie nodded agreement. 'There was a report in the paper this morning of nearly two thousand being executed by Franco's men.'

Jack said flatly, 'Franco and Hitler are two of a kind.'

Chrissie braked the Ford at a T-junction to let a lorry loaded with coal pass by. The lorry was grinding along slowly and as Chrissie eased the car forward she saw a youth running some fifty yards behind the lorry. He wore a collarless shirt, its sleeves rolled up above the elbows, and patched dungarees. He was carrying a shovel. Then Chrissie swung the car in through the open gates of the Ballantyne yard and he was lost from sight.

Peter Robinson had borrowed the shovel and was following the lorry to find where its driver was going to deliver his load of coal. Peter hoped then to earn a shilling by shovelling the load into the buyer's coalhouse. The lorry slowed, turned into a cobbled back lane then halted at one of the back gates that ran down either side. The driver switched off his engine and got down from the cab. As he did so the back gate opened and a stocky man, stripped down to a vest and trousers with braces dangling, came out into the lane. He had brawny arms and held a shovel in one big hand.

Peter, resting on his own shovel while he caught his breath, saw that he was out of luck. This man was ready to unload his own coal. The back of the lorry tilted, the load poured out raising a cloud of black dust and the stocky man started shovelling it through the hatch into his coalhouse. Peter turned and walked away.

Across the street was the fence of Ballantyne's yard. His yearning for work drew him to peer through a crack in the fence, looking enviously at a world where men had regular jobs and pay.

It was a small, secluded corner of that world. He could see the stern of a partly built ship, the steel gleaming with fresh paint and dotted with neat lines of rivet heads. Few men were working there. Gallagher, the burly, florid foreman, and McNally, his big crony with the scarred face, stood close to the fence. Another man was perched at the top of a ladder that leaned against some staging erected along the ship's side. Peter knew him: Harry Henderson, timid and nervous, with a worn-out wife and three small and usually near-naked children. Harry turned his head now to shout, 'This doesn't look too safe.'

His voice came thinly, almost drowned under the hammering and clangour of the yard. Peter wondered what Harry was on about. He withdrew his eye from the crack to wipe it because the draught was causing it to water. He heard Gallagher shout back, more clearly because he was closer, 'That's all right! Get on with it – or I'll find somebody that will!' McNally laughed raucously.

Peter set his eye to the crack again and saw why Harry Henderson had complained. The staging had, at first sight, appeared to be wide enough for a man to walk, provided he had a good head for heights, being thirty or forty feet above the ground, but now Peter saw that it consisted of only a single plank less than a foot wide.

Harry Henderson had taken in that scarcely veiled threat from Gallagher and, desperate to keep his job, set his feet on the plank. He hesitated, peering down at the drop beneath his feet. Gallagher shouted again, 'We want that gear down here for another job! Now *get on wi' it!*

Harry moved one foot, then another. Peter saw that Harry had been set the task of sending down a block and tackle and coil of rope hanging from the staging at the far end of the plank. He edged towards it, one foot sliding ahead of the other, arms outstretched to balance him.

The gull seemed to appear from nowhere. Suddenly it was there, swooping past Harry's head with a flap of its wide wings and a shrill cry, which was echoed by Harry, startled, as he threw up onc hand to fend it off. As he recoiled from it, he stepped backwards into empty air. Harry Henderson's arms windmilled wildly and then he was falling, shrieking all the way down until he landed on head and shoulders and the cry was cut short.

The men working on the ship further along its side could not see the staging from which Harry fell as it was hidden by the curve of the stern. Nor had they heard his shriek and fall, lost in the din of the yard. Peter saw him lying there, still, saw Gallagher and McNally run to him, kneel over Harry's body, then rise. McNally climbed the ladder and walked the plank without fear or doubt, at home up there. He used the block and tackle to haul up more planks, one by one, as Gallagher fastened them on below. He laid them on the staging so there was a walkway over two feet wide. Then he descended the ladder, joined Gallagher and they ran off up the yard.

Peter had stood frozen with shock, but now he began to think, and quickly. Then he, too, ran.

9

Jack was in his office, handing over to James Irving, his manager, and picking up the papers he wanted, when his white-faced chief clerk brought the news that a man had fallen from some staging and been killed. Jack said heavily, 'Oh, dear God.' Chrissie stood at his side, her hands to her face. After a shocked moment, he told his manager, 'I want a full report and names of witnesses. Someone must tell his widow or his mother. One or two of his friends should go along.' There would be an inquest, compensation to be settled and paid. Jack knew the man by sight, could put his face to the name, knew him to be a good worker.

He sighed and looked at his watch. 'I have to go to catch my train.'

Irving, in his forties, competent and experienced, said sympathetically, 'Of course, I'll see to everything here. And good luck.' He, as much as anyone, knew how important it was that Jack should obtain a contract. The existence of the yard and his job, like hundreds of others, depended on it.

Jack and Chrissie went down to the Ford where it stood outside the offices. As they stepped out into the open they saw Gallagher only a few yards away. A youth ran in between the gates, set wide to let out the Ford. Sweat ran in beads down his face and his shirt was stuck to his back.

He carried a shovel and Chrissie recognised him from less than an hour earlier. He halted in front of Gallagher and panted, 'I hear you're short of a man now.'

Gallagher gaped, for once taken aback. Jack Ballantyne glared, outraged, and demanded, 'How dare you? The man's only been dead a few minutes! Have you no sense of decency, no respect?'

It was Peter's turn to be taken by surprise because he had not seen Jack and Chrissie come out of the offices, all his attention being on Gallagher, but he recovered quickly and answered, 'Aye, Mr Ballantyne.' He recognised the yard's owner and his wife. 'And I'm sorry. But I've got a widowed mother and a little brother and we're living on a pound a week from the Relief. I need a job to feed them. That's all I'm asking for, Mr Ballantyne; a job.'

Chrissie turned her head so only Jack could see her face and murmured, 'We would have found one for Matt, and I think this lad's desperate.'

Jack looked past her and asked, 'What's your name?'

'Peter Robinson.' He met Jack's glare, unashamed, hungry and hoping, but honest.

Jack's gaze shifted to Gallagher and he told him, 'Take him on.'

Gallagher swallowed his anger and answered, 'As you say, Mr Ballantyne.'

Peter said quickly, 'Thank you, Mr Ballantyne.'

Jack climbed into the car and Chrissie slid in behind the wheel. She set off to drive him to the station. He sat in silence for some minutes as they wound through the streets, and Chrissie did not disturb him, knowing he was upset by the accident. Then as they were crossing the bridge he glanced down at the river and the yards that lined its banks and said, 'I don't like that chap.'

Chrissie protested, 'Be fair, you've only just taken the lad on.'

Jack shook his head. 'Not him. I'm talking about the foreman, Gallagher. He knows his job and gets the work done, but there's something about him . . .' He shrugged. 'It's just a feeling I have. Maybe it's only imagination and I'm being unfair.'

Soon they were at the station, and Chrissie stood on the platform, waving as the train pulled away with Jack leaning out of the window of a first-class carriage. She managed a smile and called after him, 'Good luck!'

Back at the yard, Gallagher had turned away from Peter with a jerk of the head, indicating he should follow. Peter did, and when they were some yards from the other men Gallagher stopped, confronted him and snarled, 'You'll wish you'd never shoved your ugly mug inside that gate!'

Peter held his ground as Gallagher thrust his face close. 'Will I?'

'Aye, you will.' Gallagher was furious because he had cronies lined up for jobs in his gang and would have given Harry Henderson's place to one of them.

Peter did not know that and opened his mouth to say, 'I won't fall like Harry did,' but then he said nothing. If Gallagher thought Peter had seen the 'accident', and he and McNally covering up their guilt, then Peter's own life would be at risk. He had intended to use blackmail if he had to, in order to get the job, but Jack Ballantyne's intervention had rendered it unnecessary. He saw now that it would have been a fatal mistake because Gallagher would have shut Peter's mouth. Besides, Peter was sure that Ballantyne's yard would have insurance to cover its workers against compensation claims, but if Peter told a coroner that Gallagher had caused the death of Harry Henderson, then Harry's widow could only look to Gallagher for compensation – and she would get nothing.

So he held his tongue and Gallagher said reluctantly, 'Start in the morning.' Then he warned, 'And you'd better work or you'll be out quicker than you got in.'

Peter made no answer to that, either, only turned and walked away. As he left the yard he swore to himself, 'You'll not get rid o' me, Gallagher!' He would work till he dropped but he would keep this job. If Gallagher tried any dirty tricks he would find Peter Robinson ready. Peter knew he had to keep his secret and watch his back.

Jock Kincaid picked up a wickedly long, sharp knife and rumbled, 'Sarah! I've just been talking to Mrs Ballantyne about you.' She was stooped over the big white sink, washing a huge pile of vegetables, fingers busy and deft. He grinned as he saw her smile fade to be replaced by apprehension. 'Dinnae worry. I've not said a bad word, but get away up to her office as soon as you've finished wi' that lot.'

Sarah went on with her work, partly relieved but still worried, wondering uneasily why Chrissie wanted to see her. She spun the job out now, trying to delay the interview, afraid of what might be in store for her.

This was a Sunday but Sarah worked on Sundays and had a day off in the week. Chrissie's presence in the hotel came as no surprise. She often called in for an hour or two to check with Dinsdale Arkley, her manager, that everything was all right.

Sarah went to Chrissie's office and found it empty, the door left wide open, and guessed that Mrs Ballantyne had just gone out for a minute. Sarah waited in the doorway and noticed the model aircraft. It sat on the blotter in the middle of the desk, a flying boat, its silver paint reflecting the sunlight from the window. Sarah was drawn to it, curious. She tiptoed to the desk and stooped over it.

'Hello!' The voice came from behind her and Sarah jerked back, startled, then turned and saw Tom Ballantyne. He had been to church that morning and wore his best dark grey suit. He said proudly, 'Looking at my Sikorsky?'

Sarah shook her head. 'No. I was waiting for Mrs Ballantyne. She wanted to see me.'

'Oh.' Tom, abashed, said, 'Well, I wanted to see her but I can't find her. Expect she'll be back soon, though.'

Sarah saw his disappointment and guessed the reason. She asked, 'What is a Sikorsky?' though she had guessed that, too.

Tom brightened and stepped past her to lift the flying boat from the desk. 'This is a Sikorsky S42. It came out in 1934. Four engines—' and he pointed to them, ranged along the wings – 'and a range of three thousand miles. You could fly across the Atlantic in this. Carries thirty-two passengers. Well, not *this* one—' and he grinned – 'but a *real* one.'

Sarah reached out a hand, red and roughened by the kitchen work, to run one slim finger along the hull of the aircraft. 'It's lovely. It feels smooth as silk. Did you make it?' She knew he had.

'That's right. It's sanding it down that gives it that finish. You have to use a very fine sandpaper.'

'Ah!' said Chrissie behind them. She entered and walked round them to her chair, seated herself at her desk. 'There you are, Sarah. Tom – what are you doing here?'

He said, 'I came to show you this, now I've finished it.' He held out the model.

Chrissie said briskly, 'I want to see it, would love to, but I must talk to Sarah first because Mr Kincaid will be missing her. Show it to Dinsdale Arkley and then bring it back to me in about ten minutes.'

'Righto,' said Tom, and called, 'Cheerio,' to Sarah as he left the office and closed the door.

Chrissie pointed to the chair in front of her desk and said, 'Sit down, Sarah.' When the girl had perched on the edge of the chair, she went on, 'I've been keeping an eye on you, and I was impressed by the school report you brought in when you first arrived. Also I've talked to Mr Kincaid and he speaks well of you. Now, you know Mrs Featherstone?'

Sarah did, a dark and lively, bustling little woman. 'Yes, Mrs Ballantyne. The housekeeper.'

'That's right. She tells me that one of her girls has handed in her notice and will be leaving at the end of next week. I'd like you to take over her job as a chambermaid. The hours will be a little different but no longer and the money will be better. Would you like to do that?'

Sarah would. 'Yes, please, Mrs Ballantyne.'

Chrissie smiled at the girl's relief and obvious delight. 'All right, then. You'd better get back to Mr Kincaid and let him know your decision. He knew I was going to offer the job to you and he won't be annoyed. I've talked to

Mrs Featherstone, too. She wants you, will have a word with you later and you'll start with her a week tomorrow.'

Sarah left in a happy haze; she had taken her first step up the ladder, if she never took another. And she couldn't help thinking how nice Tom Ballantyne was.

Chrissie was content. She had decided Sarah deserved a promotion, and that was only in the short term. In the long term she had grander ideas for the girl because she saw something of herself in Sarah. She knew she would easily get a replacement for her in the kitchen.

On Monday she did, and also talked with Mrs Featherstone again. The housekeeper welcomed the idea of Sarah joining her: 'Mr Kincaid thinks the world of her.'

Chrissie laughed. 'He made that clear.'

That morning there was a letter from Phillip Massingham. Chrissie realised that four months had passed since she put him on the train to London. He said that he was happy in his work, in the throes of directing a short film, and his wife was on the way back from the USA to join him.

Chrissie hesitated a long time but finally telephoned Randolph Tourville. After passing interrogations by a switchboard operator and then a starch-voiced secretary, she heard his voice, deep and confident. She told him the news she had received from Phillip.

Tourville answered, 'Yes, I know he's doing very well. I've heard reports.'

Chrissie thought that he would, took a breath and said, 'I phoned to tell you and also to say how grateful I am that you gave him this chance to get back on his feet.'

'Not at all. I hate to see talent going to waste. I prefer to have it working – for me.'

Chrissie could picture his confident grin. Then Tourville's voice dropped a tone as he went on, 'You must let me know if you ever come down to London.'

Chrissie could hear his deep chuckle as she said quickly, 'Goodbye,' and hung up, her face hot.

An hour later she waved from the platform as the train took Sophie off to London with a dozen other girls. They were bound for a tour of the capital's sights and museums. Ursula Whittle, nervous and worried, was in charge of them. Sophie teased her mother: 'Bet you wish you were coming.'

Chrissie remembered Tourville's invitation – wondered if it was an invitation – to what? She retorted, embarrassed, 'Don't be silly.'

Sophie still smiled at her, but was puzzled as the train pulled away.

As Chrissie crossed the road from the station her gaze rested speculatively on the Wiley building that stood only twenty or thirty yards from the hotel. Wiley's, an old family firm, had been a shop selling better-class goods. Its founder, Old Wiley, had grown up in the trade and had thrived at the turn of the century, but his sons had neither his drive nor his ability. They failed to run the shop profitably and refused to pay a manager who could. They milked it to support their extravagance and finally went bankrupt in 1932. Nobody else had been prepared to take the place on in those years of crushing depression and Chrissie could understand that. The business would not pay. But it was a fine, spacious, solid building . . .

Next day Matt also left for London with a group of students

from the art college who were to visit the galleries in and around the capital. He bade farewell to Chrissie and his family before he left home, refusing to be accompanied to the station 'like some kid'.

When he had gone Chrissie assessed the work she had on hand at the hotel and contemplated a week at home without Jack or any of the children. It would be very lonely. She decided to stay at the hotel until one or more of them came home, and instructed the staff at the house accordingly. She took a few things down to the hotel in a taxi, leaving the Ford in its garage at home as there was no car park at the hotel. Then she settled at her desk. She told herself she was as happy as she could ever be without Jack, but failed to convince herself. She was miserable without the man she loved.

When the girls arrived in London, King's Cross station was clamorous with the tramp of hundreds of hurrying feet and the hissing of a dozen huge steam locomotives. It smelt of dust and coal smoke. Sophie plucked at Ursula's sleeve. 'The taxis are through this way, Miss Whittle.' She pointed through the arch.

'Oh, I see,' answered the flustered teacher. 'Come on, then.'

Sophie restrained her. 'We'd better wait for Sheila. She's looking for her mac.' When Sheila climbed out of the train with her raincoat Sophie looked over the group and reported, 'I *think* we're all here now.'

Ursula took the hint, counted them and saw all were present. She realised she might have lost one of her charges in a strange city immediately after getting off the train. Sophie murmured, 'There's a porter, Miss Whittle. If we give him a shilling he'll take all our luggage and get us into taxis.' And he did.

Sophie helped in other ways. Ursula and most of the other girls had never been to London before, while Sophie had, so on their second evening she allowed Sophie to talk her into a visit to a cinema near their quiet hotel in South Kensington.

The main film was *Broadway Melody of 1936*, with Eleanor Powell, the dancing star. They had to queue, and after they had waited for half an hour a man in a shiny, shabby suit, a muffler wrapped around his neck, stood in the gutter by the queue and started to sing in a cracked baritone. He wore four medals on a bar pinned to the left breast of his jacket and held out a greasy old cap. He was a man of forty or so but his shaggy hair was grey at the temples and so was the stubble on his chin.

He did not sing very well, wavering uncertainly on some notes, voice cracking on others. After the first few seconds most of the people in the queue ignored him and went on with reading their newspapers or talking. Ursula Whittle hesitated, not wanting to push herself forward, but finally left her place in the line to drop a penny in the cap and scurry back again, pink cheeked. The man broke into his song to say hoarsely, 'Thank ye,' then he sang on.

Sophie waited until he had finished then stepped out and said, 'I'll have a go and you take the cap round.'

He stared at her and said blankly, 'What?' but Sophie gave him a gentle shove on his way and started to sing, 'It's Only A Paper Moon'. Her voice rang clear and true above the noise of the traffic in the street. Talk stopped, heads turned, papers were lowered. Sophie sang for ten minutes, until the crowds streamed out of the cinema and the queue began to file in.

The man came back to her then with a cap full of pennies. They rattled as his hands shook with excitement. 'Here y'are, girl. Shall we split it half 'n' half?' He grimaced. 'Though you earned the most of it to tell the truth.'

Sophie shook her head. 'No, you keep it. It's your pitch. And I enjoyed it.' That was the truth. She was flushed, and as excited as he, but because of performing, not the money. She tried to be blasé. 'Better than just standing there, bored stiff.' Then she ran to join Ursula and the others.

Sarah Tennant was stooped over a huge sink filled with glasses, working one of her evenings at the club. She would be able to save a little money from her pay as a chambermaid besides what she was paid at the club. She hummed softly, happily, to herself, thinking that one day she would have a place of her own. The door swung open and the steward glared at her then asked, 'All right, lass?'

'Aye, thanks.' Sarah smiled at him. She had come to know him and found that he expected her to do her job but that the glare hid a kind heart.

Now he growled, 'You're doing all right. Stick in, lass.'

'I will.' Sarah could see past him to the hall outside and saw a youth turn in at the door of the boxing gym. She recognised him because she had often seen him there. Then the steward backed out and the door closed.

In the gym Peter Robinson stripped to the waist and held out his hands to Joe Nolan. As Joe wrapped the bandages on them and shoved on a pair of gloves,

Peter told him, 'I've got a job. Ballantyne's have given me a start.'

Joe grinned at him, hearing the pride and excitement in the young man's voice. 'That's grand news. It's a good firm to work for. Depends on your foreman, mind. Who is he?'

Peter pulled a face. 'Gallagher.'

'Oh, aye?' Joe tied a lace. 'You want to watch him.'

'I know. And I will.' Peter trotted over to the punchbag and started belting it. He could see Gallagher's face on the bag, at the receiving end of the punches, but the training, the hard work and the sweating under Joe Nolan's constant urging, eased the anger and the hatred out of him. Afterwards he walked home to his bed and slept without a dream.

Peter woke in the night to the clanging of fire bells and saw a red glow in the sky on the southern side of the river where the centre of the town lay.

10

The hellish, rapid alarm-clock ringing of the hotel fire alarm woke Chrissie. She rolled out of bed, grabbed her dressing gown from a chair and opened her door. The passage outside was dimly lit throughout the night and she saw other doors opening and guests appearing. There was a strong smell of smoke. She called, 'Down the stairs and outside, please, everyone!' She saw them set out, checked the other rooms on that floor then followed them.

On the ground floor Chrissie found the foyer full of smoke and felt the heat of the fire, though she still could not see any flames. She groped her way through the smoke towards the front doors, coughing and choking, weeping like the other blundering figures around her. A figure appeared before her and as she reached out a hand to it she saw it was Dinsdale Arkley. He was wrapped in an old overcoat and shepherding the guests out into the street, assisted by barrel-bodied Walter Gibson, the night porter.

Chrissie held on to Arkley and asked, coughing, 'What about the top floor?' Arkley's room was up there with those of the rest of the staff.

He answered, 'I've cleared that and they're all out.'

'Where is the fire?' Chrissie asked, although she had already guessed the answer.

It came as expected, from Walter Gibson: 'In the kitchen, Mrs Ballantyne – or back of the hotel, anyway. I'd gone round and collected all the shoes and I was sitting in me little cuddy—' that was his small workroom '—cleaning them. Then I thought I could smell smoke. I walked back to the kitchen, went to open the door and soon as I did the flames were jumping out at me. So I slammed the door quick and set the alarm off, telephoned the fire brigade.'

'And here they are,' Arkley shouted above the clanging of the bells as the first engine arrived, closely followed by a second. Firemen jumped down and began unrolling hoses. Chrissie groped her way across the foyer again to reception, found the register and went to rejoin Arkley and Walter Gibson. As she reached them there came a muffled explosion. She felt a hot breath searing her back and the smoke-filled foyer was lit by a red glare.

Arkley shouted, 'The kitchen wall's gone!' and he and Walter hauled Chrissie out into the street.

They picked their way across the tramlines and the snaking hoses to the other side of the road and the entrance to the railway station. There all the others from the hotel were huddled together in dressing gowns or bathrobes, one or two of the men in shirts and trousers, a shocked and dishevelled group.

Chrissie called, 'Will you answer your names, please?' She began to read from the register by the shifting glare from the fire that now flamed from every window of her hotel. When she was satisfied that all her guests were safe she counted off her staff and confirmed that none of them was missing either. Then, at last, she heaved a sigh of relief. She caught the eye of young Sarah Tennant, her lips parted in horror, hair tousled as she had run from her bed. Chrissie smiled at her reassuringly. Then she turned around, her smile slipping away, and watched all she had worked for over the past twenty years and more reduced to a pile of steaming, smoking, blackened rubble.

Later the fire chief would tell her, 'It was an old building and tinder dry. It might have been an electrical fault – I don't know. If it had happened during the day somebody would ha' seen it and we'd ha' caught it in time. But in the night, it had a chance to get a hold and there was no stopping it.'

Chrissie turned her back on the fire again. She found rooms for the guests in other hotels and boarding houses and had them ferried there in taxis. Most of her staff who lived in went back to their families to put a roof over their heads. Chrissie took Sarah and another of the maids to her own home where there were rooms standing empty that had once been used by servants no longer needed.

She was weary but she thrust aside the temptation of her bed. She bathed, dressed, breakfasted on toast and strong coffee then drove down into the town in the Ford.

She parked it in a side street near the station and walked down to the bridge over the Wear. She stood there for some time, looking down at the ships in the river or building in the yards, listening to the clamour that meant men were at work and earning for their families. She thought about Jack, at this moment striving to find work for the men of the Ballantyne yard. She would not heap her troubles on him, nor on her children.

After a while she walked back into the centre of the town and entered the office of an estate agent. The clerk who greeted her did not recognise her, but one of the partners, happening to come out of his office, greeted her. 'Good morning, Mrs Ballantyne. What an awful business, last night's fire . . .' Chrissie accepted his condolences and waited until he came to: '. . . and if there is anything we can do?'

'I think there might be,' she said, and went with him into his office.

Later she hurried back to the High Street and looked at all that was left of her hotel. The roof and the other floors had fallen in, leaving only an empty shell of four walls open to the sky. Windows and doorways were just gaping, blackened holes. She knew it would take six months to a year to rebuild. Add to that cost the loss of trade that she had built up over the years and it came to a mammoth sum, far exceeding the insurance cover. Her gaze shifted.

'It's a right mess,' Dinsdale Arkley said heavily. He stood beside her. He had gone home to his seventy-five-year-old mother on the other side of the river and had just come over on a tram. He was haggard and depressed after the fire and a sleepless night. He was facing the fact that he had lost his job and knew he would be lucky to find another. He was very conscious suddenly of his artificial leg, the result of a wound in the Great War. There was little work for a one-legged man. He said, 'I came over to see if there was anything I could do, but . . .' He broke off there and shook his head. Then he said, 'Hello, lass.'

Chrissie turned and saw that Sarah Tennant stood a respectful yard or two behind them.

Sarah replied, 'Hello, Mr Arkley – Mrs Ballantyne.' Still addressing Chrissie, 'Thank you for the clothes. Betty Price said you'd told her I could have them.' Sarah had accepted them with some hesitation, but was still uncertain, because the dresses and other things, down to the shoes, were much better quality than she had ever worn, would ever have bought.

Chrissie smiled at her and removed the last doubts. 'You're welcome. They'll do until you can get to the shops, but keep them anyway, if you like. Sophie has grown out of them and they seem to fit you all right.' While the two girls were of an age, Sophie was the taller by a good two inches. Chrissie added, 'I'd have thought you would have stayed in bed this morning, after a broken night.'

Sarah shook her head. 'I'm used to waking at the usual time.' She could have turned over and slept again, only . . . 'I wondered if I could do anything to help, but . . .' She echoed Arkley's words and, like him, her voice trailed away despondently. Overnight she had lost her home and her job. The job would not be easy to replace and God only knew where she would live. She would have to find a room somewhere, or lodgings, and that would soon eat away her small savings.

Chrissie guessed what was running through their minds and said, 'I intend to keep everyone on, for the moment, anyway.' And she hoped it would not be at a loss for long. 'You can keep that room, Sarah, until we see what we're doing.' She saw relief in both their faces.

Arkley said, 'What will we be doing?' His gaze was drawn again to the empty, soot-fouled walls of what had been the Railway Hotel, pocked with holes that had been windows, like the eyeless sockets in a skull.

Chrissie said, 'Well, let's see. They say two heads are better than one, so three should be better still. Come on, the pair of you.'

She led them to the old Wiley building that was almost next door and took from her handbag the keys she had been given by the estate agent. He had offered, eagerly, 'I'll come and show you round,' but Chrissie had firmly refused, preferring to take a first look herself. Now she unlocked the front door and walked in.

Arkley limped in after her and said, 'Dear Lord! What a state!' When Wiley's had closed down the creditors had ripped out everything that could be removed and sold. The ground floor now was just that, an empty floor covered with litter, scarred where the display stands had been. One of the pillars that held up the rest of the building still held a dusty mirror that reflected Chrissie and the other two as they picked their way through the debris of splintered woodwork, old newspapers and the occasional empty beer bottle – these last left by the workmen who tore the heart out of the place.

In the centre stood the main staircase. That had been left in its old glory. The carpet on the treads was worn and dirty but the curving banisters and handrails of a lustrous, polished, dark timber still gleamed through their coating of dust. Arkley said grudgingly, 'That looks a good job.' Chrissie nodded and went on, her eyes everywhere, assessing, picturing. So they climbed the stairs to the first, then the second and third floors, finding the same emptiness, all lit by pale light coming through the tall windows with their dust and cobwebs.

Finally they walked out of the back of the building into a yard at the rear. The gates leading out into a back street were shut. Chrissie remembered seeing them, still bearing the name 'Wiley's' in faded and peeling paint. By the gate was an old stable building, once used for the horses that had pulled Wiley's delivery vans, later as a garage for their motorised pantechnicons. Chrissie found more keys on the ring given to her. They opened the garage doors and another that gave on to a staircase leading to a flat over the garage. It was small, consisting only of a bed-sitting-room with two doors, at one end leading to a kitchen, at the other to a lavatory. Both garage and flat were stripped of everything but dust and litter.

Outside in the High Street again, Chrissie locked the front door then stood back on the pavement to stare up at the Wiley building. She was busily recasting a lot of old plans, nurtured over months, to meet this new crisis – or opportunity. She saw the others waiting, watching her, and laughed at them.

'Sorry! I was dreaming. Now, I'll tell you what I want you to do: work out how you would turn this place into the Railway Hotel.'

Arkley could not believe what he had heard and that Chrissie could laugh at such a time. He exclaimed, 'This place?'

Chrissie nodded. She could guess what he was thinking, but he did not know how the excitement of this new challenge was gripping her. 'I'll call a meeting as soon as I'm ready to compare notes.'

She left them then, almost running, to seek an architect and a builder.

At the end of the week Matt and Sophie returned from London, and Tom from his job at Newcastle. They were ready to console their mother but found it was not needed.

'Thank you,' said Chrissie when they offered their help, 'but this is a job for professionals.' She hugged them, grateful and proud, then turned to Arkley and Sarah.

They produced sketches of how they thought the new hotel should look. At first the sketches were small and simple, almost childish, but soon they became much bigger and detailed. Arkley, Sarah and Chrissie would pore over them, and Chrissie's own sketches, spread out on the silkily polished surface of the table that ran the length of the dining-room in the Ballantyne house. The architect stood at Chrissie's elbow making notes and suggestions, issuing tactful warnings as to the practicality of constructional details: 'I don't think you can do that, Mrs Ballantyne.'

'Why not?'

He grinned. 'If we take that pillar away as you suggest then the building will collapse because it's one of those bearing the load of the upper floors.'

Chrissie laughed. 'We don't want that! All right, we'll cover it with mirrors on all four sides and put a bench seat around it so people can sit with their backs to it.'

When Jack returned from the Balkans one evening a few days later he found her excited and exciting. She was waiting for him on the station platform. She waved as she saw him leaning out of a window and ran into his arms as he stepped from the train. He kissed her, then held her off to look at her. Despite the poor lighting in the station he could see the high colour in her cheeks, her dark eyes sparkling. It brought a smile from him. 'You're a sight for sore eyes.'

Chrissie thought he looked tired and fed up, guessed that the trip had been a failure, and that Jack had come home more worried than when he had left. She laughed up at him. 'I'm just glad to see you home.' That was true, but not all of the truth.

They climbed into the Ford and drove out of the station with Chrissie at the wheel. Jack exclaimed, 'My God!' He had seen the boarded-up shell of the Railway Hotel, like a haunted house in the yellow light of the streetlamps. He put a hand to his head, appalled.

Chrissie said drily, 'Yes, indeed.' She swung the Ford through the gap between the pavement and a tram. 'It happened just a few nights after you left. We woke up to find the place on fire . . .' She told him all about it as she drove home.

The children claimed him then through dinner, plying him with questions about his trip. Jack casually dismissed the fact that he had not secured a contract to build another ship: 'We'll have to look elsewhere, that's all.' He was cheerful and amusing.

Later in the sitting-room Jack sprawled in his chair and Chrissie sat on the rug, leaning on his long legs. They were alone, the embers of a dying fire in the hearth. She told him about her plans and how they were proceeding. He listened, asked questions, looked increasingly concerned and finally asked, 'What about the money for all this? Where is it coming from?'

'The insurance on the Railway Hotel.'

'But what about the cost of rebuilding that?'

Chrissie shrugged. 'It will have to wait – for a year or ten years if necessary – until I can raise the cash. The main thing now is to get back into business and I plan to do that in three months. That way we won't lose the clientele we've built up over the years.'

Jack was silent a moment, then said low voiced, 'I wondered why you were so excited when I saw you first tonight. It was this new hotel business.'

Chrissie shook her head. 'I was full of it all through the day but not when I came for you.' Chrissie got up from the rug and stood over him, saying softly, 'I've missed you, Jack. Come to bed and I'll show you how much.'

Helen Diaz was frightened but steeled herself for the task. She rehearsed her speech from the early morning when she washed the front doorstep and whitened it with the 'stepstone'. It was her father's payday, and she waited until her brother had gone out with his friends for an evening round of the local pubs. As Paco Diaz pushed away his empty plate after finishing his supper, Helen asked, 'Can I have some more money, please, Dad?'

Paco scowled at her. 'What for you want more money? I have give you the housekeeping money. Is enough.'

That would have silenced Helen a few months ago when she was at school and her mother was alive to hush her, but now she was nearly sixteen, running a home and she had buried her mother. She stood her ground, though her stomach churned with fright, and insisted, 'I want some money of my own. I'm not a child. I need to buy clothes and I want to go out now and then. I think it's only fair.'

Paco shrugged that off. 'I don't think so.' He reached for the evening paper, the discussion finished as far as he was concerned.

But Helen was not finished. 'I want five shillings a week. I think that's the least I should have for looking after this place. I could make a lot more than that if I got a job outside.'

'Five shilling!' Paco slammed down the paper. 'Five shilling! Is impossible.'

'No, it isn't. You can always find ten bob to lend to Juan when he's broke on a Monday, so you can find it for me.'

'I tell you, no!' her father shouted, shoving up out of his chair and lifting his hand.

Helen retreated as far as the kitchen door and held it open ready to flee into the passage. As he strode towards her she stood fast there and warned him, 'If you try to lay a finger on me I'll scream for the neighbours and the pollis.'

That stopped him dead. Paco had never been completely sure of his rights as a citizen in this country where he was still a visitor – he had never become naturalised. The word 'pollis' was to him full of menace, threatening arrest and possibly deportation. And then there were the neighbours. Paco liked to think he was a respected figure in his neighbourhood, head of his family, man of the house. But if his young daughter shrieked for help and proclaimed his tightfistedness . . . For once he was uncertain how to deal with her.

Helen saw it, wanted to make up the row, hug him and tell him she loved him, but knew that would do her no good. She had to obtain his respect before she could hope for his love. Now she said, more quietly but still firmly, 'I'm going to have that money if I have to take it out of the housekeeping. I earn it, I need it and I deserve it as much as Juan.'

Paco gave in. 'A'right.'

Helen persisted, determined to establish the principle, 'Now. And every payday.'

'*A'right!*' he shouted, and dug into his trousers pocket.

He pulled out two half-crowns and threw them at her feet.

Helen bent and picked them up. 'Thank you.' She closed the door behind her and walked off down the passage. Her hands were shaking and her knees wobbled. She wondered if it was worth it for five shillings.

A month later she was glad she had fought as she had. Sophie Ballantyne came seeking her, asking, 'Come over and see the new place they're working on,' and because of the money Paco threw at her every payday Helen had a new dress. She had bought it at Binns, the big department store in Fawcett Street, for three shillings and sixpence. The two girls walked across the bridge into the town and found the old Wiley's building full of workmen. They had to pick their way through gangs of men building new dividing walls, others plastering walls already completed, electricians running out miles of wiring, plumbers putting in more miles of piping.

They were stopped more than once by busy men in overalls demanding, 'Here! Where do you two lasses think you're going?'

Sophie would answer, 'To see my mother, Mrs Ballantyne. Isn't she here?'

Then they were grudgingly allowed to go on. 'Aye, she's up on the second floor. But mind how you go. This is no place for lasses like you.' Then the men would watch them, Sophie looking older than her nearly-sixteen years, sauntering long legged.

Helen hissed at her, 'Stop it! They're all looking at you!'

Sophie only tightened her lips to keep the giggles in and went on posing.

Chrissie repeated the men's warnings when the girls ran her to earth. She was in consultation with the architect and the builder whose men were carrying out the work, their heads bent over plans. Chrissie eyed the girls with disapproval. 'This is no place for you.'

Sophie answered cheerfully, 'I just wanted to see and I brought Helen along.'

'Well, you've seen. Now stand here till I've finished and you can go out with me. *Don't* wander off on your own. Buildings like this can be dangerous if you don't know what you're doing.'

Chrissie turned back to the architect and builder but as she resumed their conversation she could see Sophie out of the corner of her eye. After some minutes she broke off again with a word of apology to the two men: 'Excuse me a moment.'

She stepped over to where Sophie was strolling back and forth, smiling at the men who were working near by. Helen stood gazing into the distance, pink cheeked. Chrissie seized Sophie by the arm, spun her round and hissed, 'Stop that!'

Sophie protested, 'Stop what?'

'You know very well.'

'It's only a bit of fun,' Sophie complained at her mother's vice-like grip. 'And you're hurting me.'

'I'll hurt you a damn sight more if I have to. It may be a game to you but other people might want to play differently. Now behave yourself.'

Sophie looked into her mother's eyes and obeyed.

That night Chrissie recited the incident to Jack and

sighed, 'She's acting just like her grandmother – my mother.'

Jack asked, 'Do you know where she is now?'

'The last I heard she was in London.' Then she added, 'And I hope to God she stays there.'

11

September 1936

A month later the old Wiley's building, changed almost
out of recognition, opened as the new Ballantyne Hotel.
Matt took Pamela Ogilvy along to the celebration opening
and wore his best dark blue, double-breasted suit on his
mother's instructions. He explained as he ushered Pamela
in through the swing doors, 'There are two bars, a residents'
lounge, reception and offices on this ground floor. Then
upstairs there's a dining-room, function room and kitchen.
And on top of that there are two floors of bedrooms.' Then
he realised his pride in his mother had led him into boasting
and he stopped abruptly and asked instead, 'Fancy a drink?'
There was a buffet for the invited guests, local dignitaries
and press.

Pamela asked, 'Can I have a gin?'

Matt stared at her. 'Are you kidding?'

Pamela tossed her head. 'I've had gin before.'

'Maybe you have but you won't get it from me.' Matt
grinned at her. 'Dinsdale Arkley's running this bar and
he won't serve me with beer, let alone gin. How about
a lemonade?'

Pamela grumbled, 'Oh, all right.' Left to herself she stared around at the spacious foyer with its deep carpet, the magnificent staircase leading up to the dining-room, trying to calculate the worth of it all. When Matt returned, edging through the throng with two glasses of lemonade, she asked him, 'Why don't you go into the hotel business?'

Matt laughed at the idea. 'Not on your life. Anyway, I'm studying to be an artist.'

'I don't think it's funny.' Pamela's wealthy father had made a number of jibes about her starving in a garret if she kept up her acquaintance with Matt.

Matt still grinned. 'I do. Me, run a hotel? I wouldn't know where to start.'

Pamela gave up for the time being and sulkily sipped her lemonade.

Chrissie saw the tousled head of her younger son in the crowd and noticed how he resembled Jack in height and breadth of shoulder, though he still had a few inches and years to grow. She also recognised the girl with him and sighed. Matt seemed to look for trouble.

Tom, talking now with Jack, while an inch or two shorter than Matt, was more like Jack in character, decisive and clear minded as to where he was going. She wondered if this was just an extraordinary coincidence or imitation, the most sincere form of flattery – albeit unwittingly.

Sophie and Helen Diaz suddenly appeared out of the crush, Helen in her cotton frock and Sophie wearing a 'junior miss' dress that had cost three times as much. She carried a folded raincoat over her arm and smiled at her mother. 'We're just off. Going to the pictures.'

Helen blinked, startled, because Sophie had not mentioned any proposed visit to the cinema.

Chrissie said, 'Well, don't be late.' As she watched them go she thought sadly that her daughter was not flattering *her* by imitation. Sophie was not like her at all.

Some of the guests came to thank Chrissie on leaving and she laughed and joked easily with them, elated by the success of this opening. She had pushed through the refurbishing – nay, the transformation of the old Wiley building into the Ballantyne Hotel – in record time. All her guests had been favourably impressed and the resulting publicity would be good. She had been showered with congratulations all evening and was suffused by a warm glow of success.

Then she saw Jack edging through the crowd towards her and she remembered he was leaving again this evening, this time for France, still seeking a contract for another ship. She knew he was worried, was always worried these days about the survival of Ballantyne's yard. She started to move to meet him but then the architect and the builder got in her way. They were celebrating and wanted her to join them. She laughingly tried to put them aside but had to stay to be introduced to their wives and accept their congratulations, too. She saw Jack raise a hand to wave to her, unsmiling, then he turned and walked away. The last she saw of him was his broad back disappearing through the door.

As soon as she could detach herself from the laughing group she hurried out of the hotel, dodged between trams to cross the street to the station and ran down the stairs to the platform. She was only in time to see the last carriages of his train pull away. Chrissie walked back to her hotel despondently.

*　　*　　*

'Where are we going?' Helen put the question as she followed Sophie up the curving stairs to the top deck of the tram.

Sophie only answered, 'You'll see.' The conductor yanked on the cord that looped along the ceiling above his head. It rang the bell by the driver who set the tram moving. The conductor came along the aisle, swaying to the motion. The girls paid their pennies and took the tickets he punched and handed to them. Sophie went on, 'I had to say we were off to the pictures. Mum doesn't mind me going there so long as I'm not too late home. I will be tonight, though, so when I get in I'll tell her I stayed talking to you.'

Helen protested, 'I'm not telling lies to back you up.'

'I'm not asking you to. I doubt if she'll check up on me, anyway.'

'Why can't you just tell the truth?'

'Because Mum would be dead set against it.'

'Against what?'

'Singing.'

'*Singing!* What sort of singing?'

But Sophie only replied again, 'You'll see.'

The tram rolled across the bridge, turned down towards the sea and the two girls got off at Church Street then walked down the hill towards the river. They came to a pub called the Frigate, and Sophie recalled her mother telling her that she had worked there as housekeeper some thirty years ago – when she was just Sophie's age now.

Sophie led the way down its passage to the ladies' toilet. She went into one of the cubicles while Helen waited outside. When Sophie emerged Helen saw what the raincoat had been hiding. Now Sophie wore a new pair of high-heeled court shoes she had bought herself and kept hidden from her mother. They had replaced a pair similarly bought and secreted a year ago. Her dress was not the 'junior miss' she had worn to that evening's function but one that belonged to her mother – as did her sheer silk stockings. Now she applied lipstick and powder and asked, 'How do I look?'

Helen answered, startled now besides being worried, 'All right, but what . . .'

'Come on, then, or we'll be late.' Sophie led on again, out of the Frigate and through the lamp-lit streets to the club. Helen followed, but when they came to the club she stopped. Sophie paused on the steps to urge her, 'Don't hang about. Let's get in.'

Helen shook her head firmly. 'Not likely. I live just down the street. There'll be all kinds of people in there that know me. If I went in there tonight me dad would hear about it tomorrow and I'd get a belting.'

Sophie stared at her, at first disbelieving. 'Would you?'

'Aye, I would. I don't know what you're up to, but . . .'

Sophie glanced at her watch and said quickly, 'I've got to go in now. I'll let you know how I get on.' She hesitated, nervous at entering this male stronghold. She needed someone . . . A young man in worn and baggy grey flannels, a collarless shirt and darned woollen pullover started up the steps. He was barely taller than Sophie on her high heels but broad in the shoulder and deep chested. Sophie put out a hand to catch his sleeve. 'Excuse me.'

He paused and asked shyly, 'Aye?' This blonde, blue-eyed girl, or rather young woman, was poised, attractive, well dressed. The girl with her looked a year or more younger.

Sophie gave him a wide smile. 'There was an advert in

the *Echo* about a talent contest in here tonight. Do you know who I have to see to go in for it?'

Peter Robinson said, 'Aye – well, I think I do. It'll be the entertainments secretary, I suppose. Do you want me to show you?'

'Yes, please.'

Peter held the door open for her and Sophie passed through. Helen stared after her for a moment then sighed, shook her head and walked home, wondering.

'This is the entertainments secretary.' Peter introduced Sophie 'This – er – lady wants to go in for the talent competition.' He stepped back then, reluctantly, and said, 'I've got to meet a feller.' Joe Nolan was waiting for him in the gym. 'I hope I'll see you later on.'

'I hope so.' Sophie smiled at him, then she was left with the entertainments secretary, a short, thickset man with a wide, flat face and a pair of Woolworth's spectacles perched on the end of his nose. He held a pen in fingers that looked like a bunch of bananas and asked, 'What name is it, lass?'

'Sophie . . .' She paused then for a moment, panicking. She hadn't thought of this. Impossible to use her own name, so . . .

The secretary prompted, 'Sophie . . .?'.

'Nightingale,' and wondered if he would recognise that one, if he remembered her grandmother, Vesta Nightingale.

He did not. He wrote down the name carefully, his tongue following the pen: 'Sophie Night-in-gale.' Then he asked, 'And what d'you do?'

'I sing.'

He wrote that down, too, then told Sophie, 'Righto, lass.

See Billy – he's the piano man on the stage – then get yourself a drink and find a seat.'

The hall looked enormous to Sophie and was already nearly full of members and their wives. Billy was short, fat and had a stool with a cushion on it to lift him high enough to play the scarred upright piano. He was playing when Sophie climbed up the steps at the side and stepped on to the stage. She bent to say, 'The entertainments secretary said I should see you.'

'In the competition?' he asked.

'Yes, I'm a singer.'

'What are you singing?'

Sophie laid her music on the empty stand before him and Billy played on with one hand while lifting a pint glass of beer from the top of the piano. He drank a quarter of the contents then replaced the glass. He gave the music a cursory glance then grinned at her. 'Right y'are, I know that one. I'll be ready when you are.'

Sophie smiled weakly and got down from the stage, away from the stares from scores of curious eyes. She found a seat close by the steps and tried to look poised and used to this business. A woman hurrying past with an empty tray checked in her waddling stride and asked, 'Can I get you owt, pet?'

She looked kindly, and old enough to be Sophie's grandmother. Sophie clutched at this little bit of friendship and said, 'I'd like a lemonade, please.' Then she worried if she would have enough to pay for it. She did, just, when the waitress brought it on a tray filled with pints of beer. Sophie sipped it and told herself it would have to last.

The contest got under way, the secretary pulling names

out of a hat, and as each name was called its owner climbed on to the stage and gave his or her performance. There were comedians, an accordionist, two baritones and a tenor. There was one other girl singer, announced as Mollie Gates. She was in her mid-twenties and obviously known already, because she was applauded as she came to the stage and waved to friends in the audience, confident and smiling. She sang and Sophie watched and listened, immersed in the performances. She thought coolly that this girl was good, but she herself was better.

Then came the moment when the secretary announced, 'Sophie Nightingale!' and she was climbing the steps on legs that seemed to wobble, then teetering across the stage on her high heels to stand at the microphone. Billy played the opening chords and she took a breath, then turned to him to say, 'That's too high.'

Billy stopped his playing, fingered a key then started again, eyebrows raised in a question. Sophie nodded gratefully and he winked at her. Sophie faced the stares from the packed hall, but she had prepared herself for this. She picked out a face at the back of the room and saw without surprise that it was the young man who had brought her into the club, now standing by the long bar. Sophie sang to him.

Peter Robinson had just finished his training under Joe Nolan's tutelage. He listened open mouthed as the girl on stage sang. He thought that she seemed to be singing to him, then told himself that it was just his imagination. But she was *good*!

He did not notice a slight, dark-haired girl only a yard away from him.

Sarah Tennant had come through to the bar with a tray

of clean glasses. The singing caught her attention first and then she froze as she saw the girl on stage. She whispered to herself, 'Oh, my God! Miss Sophie! And in her mother's dress!' She had seen Chrissie wearing it only a few days before. But then she watched and listened.

Sophie relished the applause as she took her bow, and it accompanied her back to her seat. She waited, excited, until the secretary consulted the judges scattered around the room and then announced, 'The winner is . . . Mollie Gates.' There was polite applause but also a rumbling of discontent. The secretary peered out at them unhappily and went on, 'The runner-up is Sophie Nightingale.' That was greeted with cheers and hammering on tables. 'Now I'll call on the winner to give us an encore.'

Mollie Gates obliged and was again politely applauded. Sophie waited until she had left the stage and then quickly took her place, whispered in Billy's ear and faced her audience. Billy began to play and the secretary came hurrying over. 'Here! Now then, lass, it's only the winner that gives an encore.' But Sophie was already singing: 'It's A Sin To Tell A Lie' and the crowd cheered her on, then fell silent and listened, and cheered her again at the end. The secretary retired sheepishly, muttering, 'Young lasses think they can do as they like . . .' Mollie Gates was red faced and furious.

Sophie thanked Billy and left the stage knowing she had won a moral victory. Then she put a hand to her mouth as she saw Sarah Tennant watching from behind the bar. Their eyes met then Sarah turned away and went out through a door.

Sophie collected her prize of ten shillings from the

secretary and then made for the bar. Peter Robinson met her there and said, somewhat awed, 'You were great. You should have won. All the fellers round here thought so.' He jerked his head sideways at the men lined up along the bar.

Sophie laughed, the excitement still flushing her cheeks. She pressed the folded ten-shilling note into his hand, surreptitiously to preserve his male dignity, and asked, 'Will you get that changed for me? Buy us a drink apiece.'

'Aye.' Peter was glad to take the money. Nearly all his small wage as a labourer was swallowed by the upkeep of the two rooms that made up the family home, and supporting his mother and brother. 'Wait here.' He pushed his way through to the bar.

Sophie glanced around her, and did not see the face she sought, but then the waitress who had brought her lemonade came out of the crowd round the bar carrying a tray of drinks. Sophie asked her, 'Can you tell me where I'll find a girl called Sarah Tennant? I saw her behind the bar a minute ago but she isn't there now.'

'Sarah will be washing glasses at the back – in the little room there.' The motherly woman pointed. 'Go through that door to the passage, then in the door on the right and you'll find her.'

Sophie found Sarah working over a huge sink of soapy water filled with glasses. She said, 'I didn't know you worked here.'

Sarah sighed and admitted, 'I'm not supposed to. The law says I should only work a certain number of hours and I put them in at the hotel. I do this to make a bit of extra money.' She appealed to Sophie: 'You won't let on to Mrs Ballantyne, will you?'

'No.' Sophie looked around the bare little room, walls dripping with condensation from the steaming sink. 'How long do you work in here?'

'Seven till ten, six nights a week.'

'Doing this all the time?'

'Sometimes in the week when business is slack and there aren't many glasses I do a bit of cleaning or odd jobs like that.'

And that's after a day's work at the hotel, Sophie thought. She said, 'I won't tell Mother – provided you don't. Will you keep quiet about me singing here tonight?'

'Oh, yes, Miss Sophie,' Sarah agreed willingly.

Sophie squeezed her arm and said, 'Righto, then.'

She returned to the bar and found Peter waiting with a lemonade and a half-pint of beer, looking about for her. She apologised. 'Sorry. I thought I'd be back before you were.'

He said quickly, 'That's all right,' then he furtively pressed her change into her hand. They sat down at a table and he said, 'I haven't seen you in here before.'

Sophie grinned at him. 'I haven't been in here before. I suppose you're a regular.'

'Oh, aye. Not in this bar, mind.' He could only afford an occasional beer.

'Where, then?'

With that encouragement he told her about the boxing club and Joe Nolan. Then when Sophie pressed him he told her about his job. 'I work at Ballantyne's. To tell you the truth I was taken on by the old man himself – Mr Ballantyne.'

149

Sophie's lips twitched, wondering how her father would react to being the 'old man'. 'Really?'

'Aye. I was asking the foreman for a job – he's a feller called Gallagher, a right—' He stopped then. 'Well, anyway, Gallagher wasn't having any of it but Ballantyne came out of the office and said, "Take him on."' He told her of the hardships of the work and the rough humour, of the differing characters in the gang in which he worked. 'They're a good set o' lads, bar Gallagher and McNally.'

Sophie asked, 'Do you all hate those two?'

'No. It's just me. Some o' the other fellers don't like them although they all get along in the yard. But I know something they don't.'

'What's that?'

He wouldn't tell her, knowing that if Gallagher found out his secret he would try to shut Peter's mouth. Peter remembered Harry Henderson's still and twisted body where it had fallen from the staging.

Sophie was attracted by this young man, who was not handsome nor well dressed but had an open, honest face that was sombre now.

He shrugged and grinned, embarrassed, and tried to change the subject. 'Never mind. Where do you work?'

Sophie sidestepped the question. 'Over the bridge.' That was barely true – so far as she worked at all it was in her school on the other side of the river. However, it implied she had a job somewhere in the town and Peter took it to mean just that, as she knew he would. She glanced at her watch and stood up. 'I'll have to be getting home.'

Peter said, 'That's a nice watch.' He stared at it on her wrist. No working girl could afford a watch like that.

Sophie said quickly, 'My father gave it to me last Christmas.' That was true.

Peter grinned. 'He must have had a winner up or got a club out.' They were the only sources of large sums of money so far as he knew: a win on the horses or a five-pound or ten-pound voucher obtained from a store, spent there and repaid with interest spread over several months.

Sophie understood about the horses but was baffled by the reference to a club. When her parents made a purchase they paid cash or had it charged to their account at the shop. She smiled brightly and said, 'That's right.' Sophie moved towards the door and Peter went with her.

He offered, 'I'll see you home.'

'No! Thanks, but it's away over the water.' She saw his disappointment and didn't want to leave anyway but knew she had to. 'Could you come as far as the tram?'

Outside the streets glittered wetly in the light of the lamps. Sophie pulled on her raincoat, bulky with her other clothes crammed into the pockets. She and Peter hurried through the dark streets, some still cobbled, others black tarmacadam. The wind off the sea drove a fine drizzle at their backs. They came to the Wheatsheaf, a pub that stood on a junction where three tram routes met, and Peter said, 'Stand in here.' He pulled her into a shop doorway where they were out of the worst of the rain. 'What tram do you want?'

Sophie replied, still evasive, 'Any that goes over the bridge.'

'Where do you live, then?'

Sophie could not answer that, sensed that if he found out who she was he would break off the young and fragile relationship. She did not want that. She was still excited by her success that night and the whole adventure. She saw her tram come rocking around the bend in the road, clanking over the maze of points. A shift of the wind sent the rain driving into their shelter and their faces. Sophie stopped Peter's questions by throwing her arms around his neck and kissing him on the mouth. Then she broke away and ran for her tram.

Peter followed her for a few strides, but the tram was already moving again, Sophie swinging up on to the platform beside the conductor. Peter saw her face turned towards him, laughing, and saw her wave a hand, heard her call, 'See you here next week! Eight o'clock!'

'Aye!' he shouted, then walked home jauntily.

'Goodnight, Sarah.' Chrissie Ballantyne said it quietly but startled the girl as she entered the hotel by the back door.

'Oh! Goodnight, Mrs Ballantyne.' Sarah flushed as she shook the rain from her hair, embarrassed at being found entering so late. She headed for the stairs that would take her to her room, praying that Mrs Ballantyne would not ask where she had been.

Chrissie did not. She guessed that Sarah had been working somewhere, remembered how she herself had worked when she was Sarah's age. Besides, she reasoned, she was not the child's guardian. Having said that, however, she would keep an eye on the girl and if it looked as though she was doing too much, then that would be the time to spell out the law.

Chrissie had dined at her new Ballantyne Hotel and worked late there, partly as there was work to be done but mainly because Jack was still away and would be for another week or more. Before she left that evening Chrissie walked through the building, savouring again the pride in completing it in such a short time, looking it over lovingly. So she had happened to be around when Sarah Tennant returned.

Now she went on to the yard at the back and climbed into the driving seat of the Ford. The wipers swept the rain from the windscreen as she drove home to the Ballantyne house in Ashbrooke. There she found Sophie, scrubbed clean of make-up and curled up in bed, listening dreamy eyed to music on her radio and recalling her triumph on stage – and Peter Robinson.

Chrissie smiled and said, 'Hello.'

Sophie waggled long fingers at her. 'Hello, Mummy.' Then the fingers went back to tapping out the beat.

Chrissie asked, 'Was it a good picture?'

Sophie remembered the excuse she had given earlier, that she was going to the cinema. Now she said neutrally, 'Mm!'

Chrissie could not help comparing Sophie's childhood with that of her own. 'When I was your age I was a housekeeper, cooking and cleaning, at the Frigate,' she mused. Before that, at fourteen, she had cooked and cleaned for a household of eight working men.

Sophie's lips twitched but she answered solemnly, 'Yes, Mummy. I've heard of it. Over in Monkwearmouth, isn't it?' She recalled the startled look on Helen's face that evening in the Frigate when she saw Sophie in the dress she had borrowed from her mother's wardrobe, but she kept her face straight and went on, 'You've told me all about that before, Mummy. It's history.'

Chrissie thought that young Sarah Tennant had worked

since she was fourteen and cared for her ailing mother, while Sophie was only interested in her music and dreamed of being a singer, like her grandmother, Vesta Nightingale. Chrissie had received love and care not from Vesta Nightingale, her natural mother, but from Mary Carter, who had adopted her when she was abandoned by Vesta. And it was Mary's upbringing that had set Chrissie on the path in life that would lead her to success and a happy marriage with Jack Ballantyne. Chrissie was determined to give the same love and care to her own children – but now was not the time to labour the point. She sighed. 'Goodnight.'

'Goodnight.' This time Sophie blew a kiss from her long fingers and Chrissie went away somewhat comforted.

She slept alone and not well. Jack had not written for a week and they had parted coldly.

12

Jack Ballantyne had difficulty keeping his eyes off Angélique. Her dark eyes had cast him smouldering looks all through dinner. Her jet-black hair was expensively coiffed, her body expensively clothed. The silk gown was cut low to show off her full breasts and fitted her haunches like a second skin. The skirt flared out but its fullness still clung and moulded itself to the long, slender legs. She knew the effect she was having and smiled.

Her husband did not seem to notice. He was a shipowner, with nearly a dozen vessels in his fleet, and Jack was trying to sell him another. Jean-François sat gaunt and drawn at the head of the table, a frail old shadow of the lusty man Jack had once known. His young wife of barely two years was seated at its foot. Jack sat halfway down the long table and tried to share his gaze equally between them. The three servants, all elderly men, moved soft-footed and silent around the room and Jack never saw a change of expression on any of their faces. Jack remembered all of them from his previous visits, but he had not met Angélique before.

The house stood between Cannes and Nice on the Côte d'Azur, because Jean-François had substantial interests in both places. It was palatial, built on a hillside, and this huge dining-room looked out over the Mediterranean.

Dinner was over and the servants cleared the table. Jean-François never talked business during a meal but now he said, 'I am tempted to give you the contract for old times' sake.' Ballantyne's yard had built several ships for him. Then he went on, 'But our own French yards need the work and they are cheaper.'

Jack knew why they were cheaper: because of the subsidies they were paid they were always able to undercut his price. He said nothing of that – had learnt never to complain when bargaining – and Jean-François knew of the subsidies anyway. Instead Jack smiled easily and said, 'Of course I appreciate that, but there is also the question of workmanship. Ballantyne's can match anyone in the world there. And then there's delivery. We can guarantee . . .' As he talked, one of the servants re-entered the room and murmured into Jean-François' ear. He nodded and held up a bony finger, its joints misshapen. The servant stepped back a pace and waited behind his master's chair.

Jean-François let Jack make his points and finish, then nodded his appreciation of the arguments put forward and said, 'I will sleep on it. Now I have a visitor.' He nodded and the servant left the room. Jean-François inclined his head again, this time to his wife, and suggested, 'Perhaps you would like to entertain Jacques with coffee and cognac on the terrace. Henri Dupuis has come up with some papers I asked for. I'll see him in here.'

The servant returned then, ushering in a man in his thirties wearing a neat, dark business suit and carrying a briefcase. Jean-François introduced him: 'Henri's father was my lawyer and good friend for many years. Now his father has died and Henri has taken over the task.'

Henri smiled a wide smile, thin moustache over thin lips. 'No burden; a pleasure.' He turned the smile on Angélique. 'Madame.' She only nodded, and did not glance his way.

She was already rising, one of the servants snatching away her chair. 'Shall we, M'sieur Ballantyne?'

Jack followed her out to the terrace where they were served with coffee. He refused cognac at first, wanting to keep a clear head for one last attempt to obtain Jean-François' signature on a contract on the morrow. Angélique pouted and complained, 'Must I drink alone?' so he accepted the glass and they talked, looking out over the sea far below. She questioned him about his wife and then summarised his answers: 'So your wife has three nearly grown-up children and she is a woman of business. But what business is she up to now, while you are away?' Jack smiled politely and she laughed, held out her glass for the servant behind her to refill. It was her third.

A staircase at each end of the terrace led to another terrace above. The bedrooms up there also looked out to the sea. Jack's was one of them and now he saw the lights go on in another. That was Jean-François' room and he saw the shipowner's bent frame moving against the lights before a servant drew the curtains.

Angélique had seen this, too. She drawled, 'We live very quietly here. My husband, as you know, is an old man. The house is full of old men, even the chef is over sixty. I have my maid, of course.' Her eyes slid to Jack as she murmured, 'I've sent her to bed.' She sipped her cognac then said, 'He is interested only in ships. But not yours.' She laughed.

Jack said, 'I think he will be interested,' although he thought nothing of the sort. 'He said he would sleep on it.'

Angélique laughed again, unpleasantly, and waved a hand dismissively at the servant, who had stood like a statue in the shadows, blank faced and eyes distant, ignored. Now he turned and walked silently away. Angélique gulped another mouthful of cognac and said thickly, 'He will sleep, yes. You understand, I am just a chatelaine, a housekeeper for him. He retires early, his servants put him to bed and he takes sleeping pills.' Jack knew it was to kill the pain of arthritis that made all Jean-François' waking hours a torment. His wife went on, 'He will be unconscious now. And I think it is time we retired.' She drained her glass and stood up, smoothing the thin dress down her body, licking her wet lips that were curved in a smile of invitation and hunger. She said, 'Do not concern yourself for your ship. I will speak to him. He listens to me.'

Jack saw that the lights were out in Jean-François' room, and elsewhere in the house, except on this terrace on which he stood, and one faint glow that marked Angélique's room on the terrace above. All the servants had vanished. He and the woman were alone.

Jack followed her as she slowly climbed the stairs, knowing that she knew he was watching her body, and that he could not help it. The french windows opening on to her room stood open and she turned into it. Jack caught a glimpse of the single small light by the big bed, saw that there was no maid and that Angélique was alone, standing before the light so he could see her body through the dress.

'Good morning, Sarah!' Sophie smiled brightly. 'Have you met my big brother, Tom?' She was passing through the foyer of the Ballantyne Hotel with Tom, who had come home from Newcastle for the weekend. She had spoken tongue in cheek, knowing full well that the two had met before, and seen each other, although only in passing, on several of Tom's weekend visits. Sarah, stepping out of the lift with a sackful of linen, busy servicing her rooms on the floor above, knew she was teasing. Sarah also knew that Sophie had guessed that Sarah was fond of her brother, and blushed accordingly.

Only Tom did not see what was going on and answered politely, 'We've met. Hello, Sarah.' He thought she was a nice enough kid. A bit shy, though, turning red like that every time she met someone. He asked, 'Is Mrs Ballantyne about?'

Sarah answered, 'I think she's in her office,' then she hurried away.

Tom and Sophie found Chrissie there. She asked, 'What are you two up to?'

'I've come into town to buy some books and thought I'd look in and see you,' Tom replied. 'You'd gone out before I got up this morning.'

Sophie said, 'I've come in to do some shopping as well.'

Chrissie said, 'Oh, yes?' and waited, but Sophie did not ask for a loan. Chrissie wondered about that, not knowing that Sophie still had in her purse most of the ten shillings she had won. She said, 'I'm glad to see you're managing your allowance better.'

Sophie only smiled, but Tom had looked more closely at Chrissie and now asked, 'Are you worried about something, Mother?'

Chrissie blinked at him, startled, and instinctively denied it. 'No! Why?'

'You're looking tired.'

Sophie glanced from one to the other, surprised that Tom had seen something she had missed, but now she said, 'That's right, Mummy. You look worn out.'

Chrissie had not slept well and knew why, but she lied, 'I'm not worried. It's just that I've been working pretty hard since the old place burned down to get this hotel opened. I'll have to take things a little easier now – and I should be able to.' Secretly she thought, If only I had some word from Jack.

Jack and Jean-François had breakfasted on the terrace, just the two of them, then repaired to Jean-François' study at his suggestion: 'One does not speak of everything in front of the servants, though I have few secrets from them.' Jack's suitcase had been taken down to the car by one of the servants and the big Renault waited now for him. Jack was tired, had seen the dawn come up. He thought that Jean-François looked even worse than he had done at dinner the night before. The morning light showed the deep grooves that pain had carved into his face and heightened its bloodless, yellow tinge.

Jean-François said, 'You have a saying in England: "No fool like an old fool." Yes?' When Jack nodded, he went on, 'Angélique told you she would persuade me to give you a contract to build a ship. She makes that kind of offer to every man who comes here. Most of them grab it. You did not.'

Jack shoved up in his chair, angry. Last night he had said, 'Goodnight, madame,' then walked on to his own room, closed the french doors behind him and jammed them shut with a chair. But how . . .

Jean-François held up a knobby, skeletal hand. 'I did not spy on you. There was no need because Angélique is transparent. Her bad temper when I looked in on her this morning told its tale. At other times, with other men, she has quietly gloated.' He shook his head. 'An old fool. She is beautiful, of course, and I thought she loved me, because she wanted me to think that, but once we were married . . .' He took a breath and for the first time he smiled. 'But I must not burden you with my problems. What time is your train? You will be happy to be going home.'

When the Renault carrying Jack drove away, Jean-François waved from the terrace.

Chrissie woke at midnight to see a towering figure standing over her. Then Jack shed the last of his clothes and slid in beside her. His arms around her and his body on hers he told her, 'I got the contract with Jean-François,' then he closed her mouth with his.

It was a premature celebration.

13

December 1936

'We'll have to swim for it!' Peter shouted as the rollers crashed against the sea-wall and exploded in spray. The spray drove in on the wind across the wide promenade, mixing with the fine rain that was falling, and ran down their faces so they could smell and taste the salt sea.

'We'll have to run!' Sophie countered as she grabbed Peter's hand.

He broke into a lope alongside her, but demanded, 'Why? There'll be another tram in a minute.'

'I have to catch this one. I've got to get home by ten.' He understood that. It was common for girls to have to be home by that time or earlier.

Peter had been courting Sophie for some months now. She would meet him at the Wheatsheaf corner where she had waved to him at the end of their first meeting. Then they would go walking, often down the long road to the sea and then along the promenade. Sometimes it strained Sophie's patience, as she would have prefered to go for a coffee somewhere but she was fond of him.

They took the steps up from the promenade two at a time, crossed the road and ran along past the Italian ice-cream parlour and the other shops and cafés they never entered because Peter did not have money to spare for ice-cream or coffee. There were few people about on this midweek winter's night, though the cafés would be full at the weekend. The few in there now peered out through windows misted with steam at the young man and the girl running hand in hand.

They jumped aboard the tram, panting and laughing, as it started to pull away, and climbed to the top deck. When the conductor came for their fares Sophie asked, as usual, for 'Fawcett Street, please.'

Peter said, 'Make that two.'

Sophie glanced at him, startled, because she had persuaded him right from the start of their courtship that they would part at the Wheatsheaf: 'It's too far for you to have to come back when you need to get up for work the next morning.' Up to now she had not met him at weekends.

He saw that glance, and as he took the tickets from the conductor he said, 'I just want to make sure you get back all right. We've got some dark nights now we're into the winter. I've felt a bit guilty letting you go home on your own this last month.'

Sophie thought of trying to dissuade him, then decided she probably could not. Besides, it might lead to an argument and Peter's bewilderment – and curiosity. She did not want him probing into her background, so she remained silent but thought rapidly – and came up with an answer. They got down from the tram together in Fawcett Street and Sophie led Peter round the corner into the High Street then across the road to the Ballantyne Hotel, where she knew her mother was working late that night. She stopped outside the swing doors and said, 'Here we are.'

Peter stared, impressed. 'You live in here?' He looked through the glass of the doors into the spacious foyer, thickly carpeted, with the grand staircase beyond. 'By, lass, you've got a good place to work.' He automatically assumed that Sophie was a member of the staff 'living in'.

She was grateful that she did not have to voice the lie. A quick glance around told her that neither her mother nor anyone in the hotel who knew her was watching. She leaned forward and kissed Peter. 'Goodnight. See you next week?'

'Aye.' His gaze followed her as she crossed the foyer and he saw the girl behind the reception desk smile at her and say something. He did not hear the words: 'Hello, Miss Sophie.' He waited until she had disappeared into the recesses of the hotel and then started on his way home. He turned up his jacket collar against the rain that was falling more heavily now and walked across the bridge to save the penny tram fare, whistling softly all the way.

The record shop was full on Saturday morning. Sophie sifted through sheet music for sale, humming to the record being played. She broke off to say, 'We were soaked on Wednesday night.'

Helen Diaz asked, 'You and Peter?' She was privy to the *affaire* and had made a threesome on occasion, reluctant despite Sophie's insistence but relaxing in the face of Peter's welcoming grin.

Once he had said to her, 'You're a bit younger than Sophie, aren't you?'

She had answered, straight faced, 'A bit.' In fact it was just a week.

Now Sophie nodded. 'We walked along the sea front. It rained all night. He's a bloody nuisance sometimes.' She got a disapproving stare from Helen because of both the language and the sentiment, but went on absently as she selected a sheet of music and searched in her purse. 'There are times when I want to go somewhere but he can't afford it so I pretend I don't care. He won't let me pay for him, he's so bloody proud.'

Helen snapped angrily, 'He's a nice chap!'

Now Sophie looked at her, startled. 'I know that.'

'Then how can you talk about him that way?'

'Because it's true. I didn't want to go out that night but I'd promised, so I went. I would have loved to have gone in and had a cup of coffee somewhere instead of squelching along with my shoes full of water, but I knew he didn't have the money and I wouldn't embarrass him by asking. I'm fond of him and I like talking to him and . . . you know . . . but that's all. I'm not in love.'

Helen was silenced for a moment, then she asked, 'No? But what about him?' and walked out.

Sophie hurriedly paid for the sheet of music and a record and dashed after Helen but could not see her in the Saturday crowds filling Fawcett Street. She walked back to the hotel disconsolately, telling herself that Helen was wrong, that there was no harm in what was to Sophie a casual *affaire*.

As she pushed through the swing doors she followed a woman in a fur coat who crossed the foyer on high heels with a long-legged, hip-swinging stride. She paused at the reception desk and asked, 'Can you show me in to Mrs Ballantyne, darling?'

The receptionist blinked at her but Sophie said from behind, 'I'm just going in to see her. I'll take you.'

The woman swung around on one heel, the open fur coat swirling to show a clinging, close-fitting rayon dress beneath and wafting a wave of expensive perfume towards Sophie. She now saw that this was not a young woman and that the heavy make-up only concealed from a distance the fine lines at the corners of her eyes. But that did not matter. There was a style and flamboyance about her that Sophie had not seen before. The woman was dark haired and her wide mouth smiled at Sophie. 'That's kind of you, darling.'

Sophie returned the smile and said, 'Her office is through here.' She led the way, pausing only to tap at the open door, and as Chrissie looked up from her desk Sophie announced, 'There's a lady here to see you, Mother.'

Chrissie's welcoming smile dissolved and turned into a face of stone. The woman brushed past Sophie to enter the room, but turned her head, again with that wide smile, to say, 'Mother? Then you must be Sophie.'

'Yes, I am.' She looked from one to the other, puzzled.

Chrissie said, without expression, 'This is your grandmother, Martha Tate.'

Martha settled in an armchair before Chrissie's desk, crossed long legs in sheer silk stockings and pulled off kid gloves. 'You'll have heard of me as Vesta Nightingale.'

Sophie put her hands to her face and breathed, 'Oh, yes!'

Now Martha smiled at Chrissie. 'It's been a long time.'

Chrissie thought her mother had changed little. She looked

a little older, although the make-up hid most of the signs, and a little harder, but she had always been hard. This was the woman who had abandoned Chrissie as a child, only came to her for money or help, cared only for men and her own pleasures. Chrissie said, 'It has,' thinking, Not long enough. She asked abruptly, 'What do you want?'

Martha took a silver cigarette case from her bag, extracted a Players with scarlet-tipped fingers and lit it with a silver lighter. She blew smoke and explained, 'I've got a week at the Empire here. I thought you could put me up.'

Chrissie saw Sophie lower herself into a chair by the door, her eyes fixed on Martha's face. 'Sophie, will you run along to the kitchen and fetch some tea for all of us, please?'

'Oh, yes.' Sophie smiled at Martha and hurried out.

'Actually, darling, I'm not too keen on tea at the moment. I see you've got a drink there . . .' Martha's gaze flicked to the bottle-filled cocktail cabinet against one wall.

Chrissie replied, 'Help yourself,' but Martha was already crossing to the cabinet with that hip-swivelling stride. She poured gin into a tumbler and added a token splash of tonic. Taking a gulp from the brimming glass to save it from spilling, she returned to her seat.

She smiled at her daughter. 'That's a bonny lass you've got there. She does you credit.'

Chrissie warmed to that praise and said, 'She's a good girl.' She hoped she was right.

Martha said, 'She's your daughter so I'm sure she is. You always had your head screwed on the right way. You deserve everything you've got now.'

'Thank you.'

Martha tapped ash from her cigarette and asked, 'So I

suppose you can let me have a room here on reasonable terms? Usually I'd go to the Palace with the rest of them on the bill . . .' The Palace was the biggest hotel in the town where most of the 'theatricals' stayed. 'There's not so much work around these days. The cinemas are killing the old variety halls, so I have to economise a bit.'

Chrissie hesitated, weakening, and told herself that what was past was past and if her mother had fallen on hard times . . . Martha Tate, dressed to the nines and steadily drinking gin, was scarcely an object of pity, but . . . Chrissie said doubtfully, 'I expect we can find a room.'

'Lovely.' Martha's smile stretched wider. 'I'll square up with you in the New Year when business picks up.' Chrissie knew what that promise was worth. Martha, relaxing now, helped herself to more gin and settled in her chair again. She glanced at the framed photographs on Chrissie's desk. 'That's Sophie, of course, and that's the chap you married – you knew what you were doing there. That one looks like his father.'

Chrissie supplied, 'Matthew.'

Martha reached out a hand to the last photo, picked it up and examined it. 'And this is Tom?'

'That's right.'

'I wouldn't have believed it possible. He looks more like his father than the other one, but from what I've heard he was somebody else's mistake.' Martha swallowed gin and drew on the cigarette, blew smoke and pushed the photo back on to the desk.

Chrissie flinched, and held her tongue somehow until the first flush of anger had gone – but it left behind cold rage.

She slid from behind the desk, stalked to the door and flung it open. 'Get out!'

Martha Tate stared at her, red lips parted and trickling smoke. 'What?'

'Get *out*!' Chrissie shouted.

Martha's head jerked back as if slapped. In genuine bewilderment she asked, 'What's got into you now? You said you'd put me up . . .'

'Not here or anywhere, any time! Now get out of here and out of my life! I swear to God I'll drag you out by the scruff of your neck if I have to!' She meant it, and Martha Tate saw that she did, so she rose and flounced from the room. Chrissie watched her walk, still swaying but hurrying now, along the passage and across the foyer. Then she became aware that Sophie stood open mouthed behind her in the passage, a tray loaded with tea things in her hands. Chrissie said, 'Put that on my desk.'

Sophie shoved the tray at her. Chrissie saw there were tears in her daughter's eyes and now Sophie said, her voice breaking, 'How could you turn your own mother away?' Then she turned and ran.

Chrissie called after her, 'Come back! You don't understand!' Sophie kept on, rounded a corner in the passage and disappeared. Chrissie set the tray on the desk with shaking hands then sat down, laid her head on her arms and wept.

After a time she looked up to blink through her tears at Tom's photograph. He had come home from school in tears some years ago. A child had overheard his parents talking about the Ballantynes, venting their jealousy and spite. He had taunted Tom with being a bastard. Tom had fought him but the boy had still insisted the story was true.

Chrissie had told Tom his antecedents in front of Sophie and Matt. 'Your mother was a good friend of mine and your father was a brave man who was killed in the war. I'd promised your mother I would look after you if anything happened to her and when she died we adopted you.' Then she had told them, 'Your father and I had all three of you because we wanted you, but while we took a chance on Sophie and Matt we knew what we were getting in Tom.'

Then Jack had put in, 'It's not a secret but there's nothing to talk about. Tom is the eldest and your brother as he has always been and that's all there is to it.'

Chrissie put away her work and took the untouched, cold tea back to the kitchen. She drove home, looked for Sophie and found her in her room, curled up on the bed. She was listening to the wireless playing dance music, a girl singing.

Chrissie switched off the set and said, 'I want to talk to you.' Sophie glared at her rebelliously but Chrissie went on, 'I'm not going to tell you all about your grandmother, though I could go on all night, but the reason I turned her away today was because she made an unpleasant remark about Tom not being my child – in fact, that he was illegitimate. I couldn't forgive that.'

Sophie shifted uneasily. 'Maybe she was just making a joke in bad taste. None of us is perfect.'

'It was in bad taste but it was no joke.'

Sophie complained, 'I still don't think you should have thrown her out like that. I've never had a chance to get to know her. I thought she could tell me about her life on the stage. She's been all over this country and America, hasn't she?'

Chrissie admitted, 'She does have talent but I think she's wasted it. I don't think you would learn anything good from her.'

'It looks as though I won't have the chance to find out for myself. Is that why you did it? Because you don't want me to be a singer like her?'

Was it? Chrissie hesitated, for a moment uncertain, and Sophie jumped on that: 'So that was it! I think that's mean!'

Chrissie shook her head, the brief doubt gone. 'It's true I don't want that sort of life for you, but I turned my own mother away because of what she's done to me in the past and would do to me again. And that's the truth.'

Sophie said with distaste, 'I think that's awful.'

Chrissie's patience ran out and her bruised emotions spoke: 'I think you should wait until you grow up and know what you are talking about before you judge me,' and she left Sophie staring after her mutinously.

On the Monday night Sophie sat in the 'gods' at the Empire, the cheapest seats right up under the roof, squashed shoulder to shoulder among the others who had paid their coppers to climb the interminable stairs. From up there Vesta Nightingale looked like a child's doll singing and pirouetting in the beam of the spotlight. Sophie did not care. She was seeing her own grandmother performing on stage in front of a packed house. She came on immediately after the interval, when people were still making their way back from the bar in a clatter of talk and banging seats. Her voice was gin-coarsened, but Sophie did not realise this. Nor did she see the flabbiness of the lifted arms, the wrinkles at the neck, because distance and make-up hid these. This was her grandmother, *the* 'Vesta Nightingale – dance and vocals'.

Sophie stood up as soon as Vesta left the stage to scattered applause, and made her way out, squeezing past people's knees and ignoring their grumbling: 'Come on, lass! We've just got sat down!' Outside the theatre she ran around to the stage door and told the man guarding it, 'I've come to see Vesta Nightingale. I'm a friend of hers.'

He nodded. 'Oh, aye. She's expecting you.'

Sophie was taken aback at that but followed his directions and found Martha Tate in her tiny, smoke-filled dressing-room. She slouched in a straight-backed chair balanced on its back legs, her feet on the little table. She wore a robe that had fallen open to show her long legs up to her knickers and held a cigarette in one hand, a glass of colourless liquid in the other. When she saw Sophie she set the chair down with a crash and dropped her feet to the floor. She pulled the robe around her and snapped, 'Christ! What the hell are you doing here?'

Sophie blinked at this reception. Nervous already, now she said shyly, 'I came to watch you. I was up in the gods. You were *marvellous*!'

Martha Tate smiled. 'They loved me, didn't they? They always did – do. And you came to see me all on your own?'

Sophie groped for words, 'Yes, well – besides, I wanted to say sorry about the other day. When Mother – you know – I don't think she should have . . . done what she did.'

Martha waved the hand that held the cigarette, realised it was there and stubbed it out in an ashtray. 'Don't worry about that, darling. I've had plenty of kicks in the teeth in my life. You've just got to keep your chin up. The show must go on.' She gulped gin, saw Sophie looking at the glass and explained, 'For my heart. Nothing much wrong with it, but it's a hard life on the boards. You give your life to your public out there. My doctor said a drop of this now and again would relax me, rest the heart.'

Sophie nodded her understanding, and started to say eagerly, 'I want to be a—'

Martha cut in, asking, 'Does your mother know you're here?'

'No.' Sophie blushed, embarrassed at her mother being brought into the conversation again, and because she had told Chrissie that she was going to the cinema with Helen Diaz.

Martha saw that embarrassment and sympathised. 'She wouldn't have let you come? Never mind. I know how she feels and I don't blame her. Mind you, she's never seen my side of it. It broke my heart when I had to give her up, but how could I look after a little baby when I was moving all the time?' She did not mention that she had obtained a hundred pounds through blackmail, lying as to the identity of Chrissie's father, and had given up her child to the first woman who asked for her.

She wiped away a nonexistent tear and said chokily, 'And she grew away from me after she married that feller in the big house. Sorry, darling! That's your father. But I'm sure you have a lovely home there.' She sighed. 'Not like my young days. I really had to sing for my supper.'

That gave Sophie another chance and she jumped at it, saying quickly, 'I want to be a singer.' She waited for Martha to ask to hear her.

But Vesta Nightingale, the professional, said absently, 'That's nice.' She glanced at a clock on the wall and stood up hurriedly. 'It's been lovely talking to you but I have to make a change now. Come and see me again, won't you?'

'Yes, I will. I'll come every—' Sophie was urged towards the door, Martha's hand in her back.

'Do that, darling. Here . . .' Martha fumbled in the pocket of the robe, pulled something from it and shoved it into Sophie's hand. 'Couple of complimentary tickets for a midweek night. Enjoy the show. Goodnight.' The door closed on her smile.

As Sophie danced away, clutching the tickets, she passed a middle-aged man in an overcoat which hung open over his paunch. A cigar stuck out of his fat, red, round face. His shoulder caught Sophie, sending her staggering, but he waddled on without a word of apology and instead gave her a glare. Nothing could upset Sophie now, however. She had talked with her grandmother, Vesta Nightingale, and was invited to meet her again. As she passed the man guarding the stage door she waved the tickets at him and called, 'I'll be back!'

Meanwhile the fat man had tramped into Vesta Nightingale's dressing-room without knocking and demanded, 'What the 'ell's going on 'ere? That stage door keeper just told me your friend had already come in. Who is he? Where is he?' He glared around the room that was little bigger than a cupboard.

Martha patted his cheek and let her robe fall open, saw

his eyes hungry on her and soothed him, 'It was the lass you must ha' passed on your way in. She turned up out of the blue to see me and he thought she was the guest I told him I expected. That's all I told him: "I've got a friend coming to see me, George." See?'

He wiped a fat hand over his red face and mumbled, 'Ah! Well, that's different.'

She kissed him and pushed his bulk down into the chair. 'You sit there, Wilf. I've got to make a change and if you're a good boy you can watch. Then later on, when I've finished here, we can have a drink and a bite to eat – and so on.'

He smirked at her. 'Aye. And so on.'

Then they both laughed.

The tickets were for the night Sophie was due to meet Peter Robinson, so instead of walking with him along the sea front in the rain she took him to the Empire. The seats were in the circle and Peter gazed wide eyed at opulence such as he had never seen. The soft carpets underfoot, the luxuriously padded seats, the orchestra and the lights – the whole show was a world removed from the sixpenny seat in a small local cinema.

When he had asked how she came by the tickets, Sophie told him, 'One of the chaps in the show is staying at the hotel. He left a few tickets for the staff.' That was true – but those tickets had gone to the staff and were for another night. Sarah Tennant was given one of them and had sat enthralled through the performance.

After Vesta Nightingale took her bow and left the stage, Sophie asked, 'Wasn't she good?'

Peter answered cautiously in face of her enthusiasm, 'All right. A bit brassy, though.'

She did not say much to him for the rest of the show and left him at the hotel with a curt 'Goodnight.' She would not tell him of her relationship with Vesta Nightingale, nor take him to the dressing-room to meet her. Vesta was Sophie's secret.

She went to the Empire every night for the rest of the week, wheedling the money out of her father. She watched, rapt and dreaming dreams. After the last performance on Saturday night Sophie asked Martha, 'Can I write to you?'

Martha patted her cheek with a beringed hand. 'Course you can, pet. And let me know how you get on with your singing. It would be nice to have another artiste in the family.' She glanced at the clock and hedged, 'I haven't got digs yet but you can drop me a line at the Empire in Newcastle. My agent has got me a month or more in panto: *Aladdin*. Now I have to pack because we'll be travelling tomorrow.' She eased Sophie through the door and sent her on her way with a pat on the back that was half a shove: ''Bye, 'bye, love.'

On her way out Sophie passed a fat, red-faced man in an overcoat. She thought vaguely that his face was familiar but did not recognise the man she had seen earlier in the week. She was too excited by the encouragement she had received from Martha: 'It would be nice to have another artiste in the family.'

Sophie wrote to Martha several times a week in the month that followed, without getting a reply. She read the reviews of *Aladdin* in the *Sunderland Echo* and in the *Newcastle Journal*. She was surprised and disappointed when Vesta

Nightingale was not mentioned but told herself that critics were notoriously biased.

She stopped seeing Peter, another biased critic. Sophie had kept on meeting him at the Wheatsheaf corner though he now believed she lived in the Ballantyne Hotel, but there came a night when she told him, 'I can't meet you next week. I'm busy.'

Peter answered glumly, 'Working overtime?' He could understand that because you worked whenever you got the chance.

Sophie let him believe it and nodded, but then he asked, 'When will I see you again?'

Sophie searched for an answer but only found, 'I'll send you a postcard.'

Peter reluctantly accepted that.

Sophie still met Helen for visits to the cinema. Then one night Helen asked, 'Have you seen that Peter Robinson lately?' When Sophie shook her head, Helen went on, 'I thought you hadn't.'

Helen had seen Peter hanging around the Ballantyne Hotel, had guessed why and avoided him. One wet night, when she had been hurrying, head bent against the rain, he had stepped out of the station forecourt, across the road from the hotel. He caught at her arm and Helen yelped, startled. He released her quickly. 'Sorry.'

'Never mind.' Helen forced a laugh, guessing what was coming. 'You didn't hurt me, just scared me the way you jumped out.'

He muttered again, 'Sorry. Look, have you seen Sophie lately?'

'Not much. I think she's been busy. Work, you know.'

Helen looked round at the hotel as if searching for Sophie, but in fact avoiding his eyes because she was a reluctant and poor liar.

'Aye, well, if you see her, tell her I was asking after her.' The rain ran down Peter's face, plastering his hair to his skull. Helen had promised to tell her.

Now she said to Sophie, 'He's been standing outside the hotel, watching for you.'

Sophie sighed. 'I know. I've seen him.' She pulled a face, 'I've been ducking out of the back door to avoid him.'

Helen, remembering and resenting how Sophie had lied to Peter, snapped, 'You're not being fair to that chap.'

Sophie shrugged, uninterested. 'All right, I'll chuck him.'

'Just like that?'

'I told you it wasn't a big love affair. Remember?'

'I remember that, and telling you he might feel differently.'

'Well, I can't help that now.'

Helen shook her head despairingly. 'Sometimes you can be a right little bitch.'

Sophie reacted angrily. 'And sometimes you can poke your nose in where it's not wanted.'

So they went their separate ways. Sophie avoided Helen, not wanting to face that accusing stare and having to make excuses. Helen was just too busy looking after her home to seek out Sophie.

When the letter came at last it was little more than a note. Sophie found it beside her plate at breakfast, saw the Newcastle postmark and exclaimed, 'It's from Gran!'

Her mother had seen the postmark and sat tight lipped, but did not condemn or forbid, guessing that Sophie would only construe that as trying to turn her away from Martha. Chrissie reasoned that Martha Tate out of sight would soon be out of mind. She cold-bloodedly calculated that her mother would not waste time, paper and stamps on her grandchild and that this letter was just an attempt to annoy Chrissie.

She was right about the motive, and the letter, a single, pink, scented sheet, did little more than give the address of rooms in Newcastle where Martha would be staying for a while. She said, in an erratic scrawl, 'I have got some work lined up locally for when this panto finishes. Love . . .'

However, the letters, albeit only a single sheet each time, continued. One arrived every week and Sophie took them upstairs to read. Often there was a brief enquiry, like: 'I hope you are getting along all right with your singing. I wasn't much older than you when I went on the stage.'

It was in March that Sophie stopped avoiding Peter. She needed his help no longer – and she had to play fair with him. She walked up to him where he wandered along the pavement opposite the Ballantyne Hotel but then lost her nerve and only asked, 'Will you come to a dance with me on Saturday? I'll pay for my own ticket.' She insisted on that and he gave in, just glad to see her again. At the dance he found her silent. She seemed intent on watching and listening to the band and the one singer, a young man with a nasal tenor voice. Peter put up with that, too. The hall was not a big one, nor was the band. There were just seven instrumentalists, the tenor and the leader at the front, conducting. Their dinner jackets were shiny with wear and their hands, except those of the leader, were rough and broken nailed, showing the signs of manual work. Peter thought they looked to be only part-time musicians.

The leader was a man of forty with a thin moustache and a 'fiddler's haircut', long and combed back from a central parting. When he announced a short interval, Sophie emerged from her apparent abstraction, took a breath and spoke the piece she had prepared and rehearsed – and postponed as long as she could. 'I don't want to hurt you, Peter, but I think you want to be too serious. I think we'd better stop seeing each other.'

He stared at her, bewildered, and asked, 'What?' Sophie repeated her little speech as the floor cleared around them. Now he recalled how he had not seen her for some weeks, her silence. He said, 'You've got somebody else.'

Sophie had not expected that, and was dumb for a second, then she shook her head. 'No! Nobody else. I just don't want anybody – yet.'

He didn't believe her, couldn't believe that she would do this to him, but then faced the fact that she had, and that she meant what she said. His hurt came out in anger then and he told her, 'That's all right wi' me, lass. There's plenty o' fish in the sea.' He turned and walked away, leaving her alone.

Sophie watched him go, hurt that she had hurt him. Then she turned and walked across the wide, empty floor to the stage and the band who were climbing down for their break. She pulled at the leader's sleeve. 'Excuse me.'

14

'You are a woman now. You must look to yourself.' Helen could almost hear the words of Paco Diaz as she watched the train pull out of Monkwearmouth station. Her father and brother were aboard it, bound for Newcastle to catch the night train to London and then a ship to Spain. They were going to join the Republican Army and the fight against Franco. She was left on the echoing platform with its cones of yellow light and the smell of smoke, soot, steam and hot metal.

Helen walked home in the quiet of the evening, the silent shipyards shut for the night. She would be walking everywhere now because every penny was precious: 'You must look to yourself.' And was she a woman? At sixteen? And home? There would be no home. Paco had left her no money, saying, 'Close down the house and keep what you get for the furniture. Find some work and lodgings.' Helen knew the furniture would fetch little, and to get a job and find lodgings would not be easy, but she thought she knew a way . . .

She was into Monkwearmouth and walking up Church Street when she glimpsed a couple sauntering down the hill towards her. She recognised Matt Ballantyne as they passed under a streetlamp, and saw that the girl clinging to his arm was the blonde Pamela Ogilvy. They turned into the Frigate, the public house on the corner. Matt had not seen Helen, but then she told herself that he never had done.

Back at the house, spread out on the kitchen table were the newspapers with the reports that had finally broken up Helen's world. She glanced at them now, the big headlines shouting that the German Condor Legion had bombed the little Spanish town of Guernica. Paco and his son, Juan, had devoured all the earlier news of the fighting in the Civil War in Spain since its outbreak in the previous July. Paco had muttered vaguely about going to fight against Franco and Juan had more noisily agreed. But Helen had taken that to be just talk. She and Juan had been born here. She had never been to Spain in her life. Why should she or her family be involved in this war?

The bombing of Guernica changed that. Her father and brother had gone and now she was alone. 'You must look to yourself.' A small fire burned in the grate, just enough to take the chill off the house and boil a kettle. Helen swept up the newspapers from the table and fed them into the fire. She watched the flames roar up the chimney and wiped at the tears that would not stop.

The sitting-room of the Frigate was lined with leather-covered benches. The round-topped wooden tables gleamed with polish and a spittoon filled with sawdust sat under each table. Pamela whispered, 'Here.' She pushed the half-crown into Matt's hand. 'Buy some more.'

Matt said, 'Well . . .' He looked up at the clock above the door to the bar, doubtful.

Pamela urged, 'Go on! There's plenty of time. It's only eight o'clock.' This had been her idea. She had asked Matt, 'Can't we go to a pub, somewhere we're not known?' They were both underage, though Matt at nearly eighteen could pass for a year or two older with his height and breadth of shoulder.

Matt asked, 'Are you all right?' because Pamela had downed two gins and orange.

'I'm fine.' She smiled at him, rubbing his hand. 'Go on, big boy.'

Matt swallowed his doubts and gave in. It was easy. Pamela was an attractive girl and he liked the envious glances he got from some other males. He lifted a hand and the woman waiting on in the sitting-room came with her tray and took his order. 'Gill o' beer and a gin and orange, please.' They had another round later and left just after nine because Pamela said, 'Mam says I have to be in by ten.'

Once outside Pamela clung to Matt and giggled. He found he had to hold her steady or she would waver from side to side of the pavement. He worried that she might fall asleep in the tram but instead she became more alive. Normally talkative, now she was silent as she held his hand. She clung to him as they walked the last quarter-mile to her home in the warmth of a spring night.

As they walked up the drive they could see chinks of light at the sides of the curtained windows. Matt said, 'I'll see you later, then.' He did not want to leave Pamela but neither did he want to meet her father.

From what Matt had heard, Pamela's father was a pompous bore.

But Pamela still held his hand, and pulled him on. 'Round here.' She led him down the side of the house to the garden at the rear and a summer house that stood there. She shoved the door open, and the moonlight filtering through the windows showed that it held a lawnmower and some other tools used by the Ogilvys' gardener. There were also a stack of basket chairs and a pile of cushions that chanced to form a couch.

Pamela closed the door, sank down on to the cushions and drew Matt down with her.

Helen Diaz sold off the furniture and shut up the house as she had been told. All she took with her were her own clothes in one cheap suitcase and her few mementoes of her mother. Among these was her birth certificate, and that of the sister who had died before she was born and been given the same name of Helen.

It was this one she produced when applying for a post as a student nurse because it showed her as being over eighteen. That and her record with the St John's Ambulance Brigade saw her installed in the nurses' home.

On her first night there she went to her bed happier than she had been for a long time. Her heart still ached for the father and brother who had left her, but she would settle for being a nurse and she knew her mother would be content.

Her only regret was that she no longer had a friend to share her happiness. She had not seen Sophie Ballantyne since their quarrel over Peter Robinson.

*　　*　　*

Some three months later, in June, the afternoon sunshine beamed like a spotlight through the window of Chrissie's office in the Ballantyne Hotel. It reflected from the dark, polished surface of her desk and lit up the notes laid out neatly across it. She looked them over again, partly to confirm the extent of Sophie's sinning, partly to control her temper. All the notes were written on plain stationery, her home address at the head, and all in a passable imitation of Chrissie's own writing. The excuses were varied: a cold, a visit to the dentist, a sprained ankle, etc. . . . All appeared to have been signed by Chrissie.

She pushed them away, sat back in her chair and looked across her desk at Ursula Whittle. Ursula had knocked at the door a few minutes ago and asked nervously, 'Can I talk to you about Sophie, Mrs Ballantyne?' And then, 'Did you write these letters?'

Now Chrissie said crisply, 'I did not. They are forgeries.'

Ursula sighed. 'Oh, dear. I was afraid you would say that.'

Chrissie poked at the note on the top with one slim finger, 'This is dated the end of March. I take it that's when this business started?'

Ursula nodded. 'Her attendance record was good until then.'

'And the increase in absences made you suspicious.'

Ursula blinked unhappily. 'Well, no. To tell the truth I never doubted they were true until I had to go into town one afternoon and I saw Sophie going into a dance hall. The next day she brought a note saying you had kept her at home with a stomach upset.'

Chrissie said grimly, 'I see. Well, I would be grateful if you would leave me to deal with this. Is Sophie at school today?'

'No,' Ursula admitted, 'and I'd be glad to leave this to you. I haven't told the headmistress yet. I know I should, but something like this is an expulsion offence and I can't think Sophie deserves that. She must have had a good reason for acting as she has.'

'I'm sure she had a reason.' Chrissie collected the notes and locked them in her drawer. 'Whether it was a good one is another matter. Where is this dance hall?'

When Chrissie left the hotel a few minutes later she found the weather changing to match her mood. The storm clouds were gathering low and black as she drove round to the dance hall. It stood in a neighbourhood of terraced houses and small shops, a shabby red-brick building stained nearly black by soot from the chimneys around it. The double doors were open but blocked by a sandwich board bearing a chalked notice:

Tony DeVere and the Caballeros
Tea Dance 3 p.m. 6d.

The first drops of rain fell, splashing big as florins on the dusty pavement. Chrissie edged past the board to reach the paybox where a man in shirtsleeves and braces sat reading the *Sporting Man*. She took a sixpence from her purse and pushed it through the hole in the glass. 'One, please.'

The man lowered the paper to gape at her. He warned her, 'It's only half past two. They won't be playing till three.'

'Are the band in there?'

'Some o' them, but . . .'

'Then I'll go in and wait.' Chrissie took the small ticket he slid through to her and marched on.

The hall inside was dim, with curtains drawn over the windows against the last of the sunshine that still leaked around the edges in narrow shafts. There was a light over the stage on which stood a drum kit, piano and four chairs set round a small card table. Three men sat on chairs playing cards. Their heads turned as Chrissie's high heels tap-tapped across the dance floor.

She halted below the stage. 'I'm looking for a friend of mine: Sophie.' She noticed that the men were all in their thirties or forties and held the cards in hands roughened by manual work.

One of them said, 'Sophie Nightingale, you mean?'

Chrissie swallowed, then, 'That's right.'

'Are you in the business an' all, then? Looking for a job?'

Chrissie blinked at him. 'A job?' Then prevaricating, 'I might be.'

'You'll need to sing better than Sophie, and that'll take some doing. Tony will hang on to her for as long as he can, but he might send you on to somebody else that wants a singer.'

Chrissie asked again, 'Where is she?'

'Tony's having a word with her.' He jerked a thumb, gesturing towards a door at the back of the stage.

Chrissie climbed on to the stage, using the steps at the side. In so doing she moved out of the dimness into the light and she saw the men's faces change. They glanced at each other. As she crossed to the door they watched her, suspicious of this slender woman, now seen to be well dressed and so out of place there. She harked back to the days of her youth and grinned at them. 'I suppose you're all working the night shift tonight.'

They relaxed as she spoke their language, showed she knew the economics of their lives. Their spokesman laughed. 'Aye, we're all working the neet. Making a bit extra this afternoon. It's easier than hewing coal.'

Chrissie paused at the door, tapped on a scarred panel then shoved it open and walked in. Half of the room formed an office, with a small desk at one side and an old settee with sagging springs on the other. Sophie was seated on the settee with a man old enough to be her father. He was dark and thin, with a pencil line of moustache, his long hair oiled and slicked back from a central parting. His arm was around Sophie's shoulders and she was holding his free hand in both of hers. As Chrissie burst in on them he shoved up on to his feet, glared at her and demanded, 'What the hell do you want?'

Chrissie crooked a beckoning finger at Sophie. 'Come on.'

Sophie stood up, smoothing her dress down over her hips, objecting, 'I don't want—'

Chrissie recognised the dress as one of her own and raised her voice over Sophie's to demand, 'Come *on!*'

Tony took a pace towards her and started, 'I don't know who you are but—'

Chrissie rapped, 'I'm her mother and I'm here to take her back to school.'

Tony swung on Sophie. 'Is that right? This is your mother?'

Then he turned back to Chrissie, the significance of what she had said sinking in. *'School!'*

Chrissie nodded. 'That's right. She's only sixteen.'

'Good God!' Tony took a quick shuffling sideways stride away from Sophie. 'I haven't touched her,' he defended himself.

'You're lucky, then.' Chrissie reached forward and grabbed Sophie's arm, hustling her towards the door.

Sophie tried to resist and pulled back. 'You don't understand! I've got a job here! A regular job! Tea dances once or twice a week, evening dates Thursday, Friday and Saturday! This is what I want to do!'

Chrissie refused to enter a tug of war but threatened, 'You're coming home with me! Now! And I swear to God I'll call the police if I have to!'

That shook Tony DeVere into life. He rammed a hand into the middle of Sophie's back and told her, 'You did have a job here but not any more. Get out and take your mother with you.'

Sophie turned her head, still resisting, and appealed to him, 'What about all those things you just said about me? How I was one of the best band singers you'd ever heard? And we were going to London and you would fix me up with one of the bands there?'

Tony winced and his eyes fell before Chrissie's glare. 'You can forget all that. Just now you're more trouble than you're worth. Now get away to hell out of here.' He yanked open the door and shoved her out of the office. As Chrissie went to follow her he muttered, 'Mind you, Mrs Whoever-you-are, that lass of yours does have real talent, a lot of it.'

Chrissie snapped, 'You can tell that to your wife. I bet she'd be interested!'

He glowered after her and hurled low-voiced curses at her retreating back as she ran across the dance floor in pursuit of the fleeing Sophie.

She caught her daughter at the entrance to the hall, where Sophie was struggling to get through a crowd sheltering from the rain that was falling in torrents now. She didn't resist when Chrissie seized her arm again and marched her to the waiting car. They did not speak on the drive home. Chrissie was too angry, Sophie too miserable. She walked into the house and up to her room without saying a word.

Chrissie waited an hour for her anger to subside a little, then went to find Sophie, who had changed into a skirt and blouse of her own. Chrissie's dress was on a hanger by the door. The gramophone was playing, and Sophie lay on her bed, hands behind her head, sullen.

Chrissie said, 'I've seen the notes you wrote to cover your absence from school. Are you sorry?'

'I'm sorry I *had* to do it, not sorry I did it.'

Chrissie tried to reason with her. 'I won't let you waste your life—'

Sophie broke in, 'I wouldn't be wasting it. And it *is* my life! I'm going to be a singer, no matter what you say. You can stop me now but you can't keep me here for ever.' Then she began to cry. Chrissie went to her, comforted her, and both said they loved each other. But still, at the end, Sophie said, 'I *will* be a singer.'

Chrissie left her then and descended the stairs. She sat down on the last of them and cried again.

*   *   *

In Newcastle Tom, neat in his blue suit, returned to his lodgings after his day's work to find his landlady sitting on the bottom stairs, her head in her hands. As he entered by the front door she looked up and said weakly, 'I'm sorry, Tom, but I had a funny turn. Just a touch o' dizziness and headache. I get it now and again but it goes off. I'll have to go and see the doctor one o' these days.'

But she never did.

Sophie thought about it for some weeks, but when she finally decided to act she did so in a hurry, before she could lose her nerve and change her mind. It was in August, during the last days of the summer holidays, that she crammed her most precious possessions into a single suitcase. She carried it, tiptoeing, down the stairs while the staff were eating lunch in the kitchen. Then she lugged it along under the trees that lined the road, changing it from hand to hand to ease its dragging weight.

When the tram stopped she shoved the case up on to the platform beside the driver, who reached a hand down to take it from her, then she ran around to the passenger entrance at the rear. Getting off in Fawcett Street, she used the side entrance to the station so she could not be seen by her mother in the Ballantyne Hotel.

She left the suitcase in the station at the left luggage office, then took another tram across the bridge to Monkwearmouth. There she looked for Helen Diaz, only to find strangers in the rooms where Helen had lived. The woman told her, 'She left an address . . .' so Sophie crossed the bridge again in yet another tram and asked for Helen at the nurses' home.

They fell into each other's arms. There was no need for

apologies. They were friends again and that was sufficient. Then Helen explained how her father had left her and how, lowering her voice, she had used her dead sister's birth certificate to become a nurse.

Sophie told her, 'I'm going away.'

'A holiday, you mean?' Helen questioned, still smiling.

'For good.' Sophie was not smiling.

'Oh, no.' Helen was serious now and listened sadly as Sophie told how she had joined the band as a singer, forged the notes and been found out.

'I know what I want to do. The only way I can do it is to leave home, so I'm going.'

'Are you sure?' Helen shook her head in dismay. 'It's a big step. I know I couldn't have left Dad, in spite of the way he treated me, and he wouldn't hear of me going into nursing. I just couldn't.' Then she remembered something else and asked, 'What about Peter?'

'I broke it off.'

'How did he take it?'

'He said there were more fish in the sea.' Sophie added unhappily, 'But I think he was upset, and you were right, he was more serious than I was.' She looked at her watch. 'I've got to go now.'

'Where are you going?'

'Promise not to tell Mummy if she asks?'

'All right.'

So Sophie gave her the address, they embraced once again, and Sophie hurried away. Helen watched her go, feeling the tears come to her eyes. She had found her friend again but immediately lost her.

* * *

Chrissie found the note on the table in the hall when she returned home from the hotel in the evening. It was addressed: 'Mummy'. It read, 'I love you and Daddy dearly but I want to run my own life. Don't worry about me. I'll write.'

Chrissie thought, Don't worry? Good God!

She ran out to the car and drove down into the town. She was too early at the dance hall again. The man who had been in the paybox was cleaning the entrance with a bucket and a mop. He told her, 'There's none o' the band here yet and won't be for another half-hour.'

Chrissie had to wait, sitting in the car, her stomach churning and anger mounting. Thirty minutes later Tony DeVere sauntered along the pavement, an open raincoat over his dinner jacket. In the daylight it was stained and shiny with age. He was whistling cheerfully, but that died away when Chrissie threw open the car door and stepped out in front of him.

She demanded, 'Where is she?'

Tony answered quickly, 'Not wi' me.'

'Where?'

'How should I know?'

'If you won't tell me you can tell the police.' Chrissie turned back to the car but he reached out a hand to pull at her sleeve. She faced him. 'Let go of me!'

The look in her eyes was enough. He snatched back his hand as if he'd burned his fingers. 'No need for the pollis. I'm telling you the truth. She came to see me a few days ago. I didn't want anything to do with her but she said she wanted an intro to a band in Newcastle and I gave her one.'

He didn't say that he had done so to spite Chrissie, but she guessed as much.

Chrissie drove home, ran up the stairs to Sophie's room and found it in a state of chaos. It was obvious that she had left in a hurry. Chrissie sifted through the clothes, the books and papers, looked into the drawers and in one of them found the bundle of letters Martha Tate had written to Sophie. Chrissie made a note of the address on the latest and replaced the bundle. Then she tidied the room, working with furious energy, and left it neat as a new pin. She told herself wrily that her old skills had not deserted her.

Jack came home that evening tired. He was stunned and disbelieving when she gave him the news, then hurt and enraged when it sank in that his daughter on whom he doted had run away. He was all for setting out that night to find her and bring her back but Chrissie would not have that: 'I'll go tomorrow, on my own. I think this is something I should do.' He was finally persuaded. Neither of them slept well.

Chrissie found the address in Newcastle the next day. It was one in the middle of a long terrace of narrow-fronted houses, separated from the pavement by small gardens. Children played a game of rounders in the middle of the street. They stood back and stared curiously as she drove slowly through. So did a few women who stood in their aprons, curlers in their hair, gossiping at their front doors.

Chrissie parked the Ford outside the door she wanted, crossed the pavement and put a finger on the bell push. She heard it ringing deep in the house and then there came a shuffling of feet inside and the door opened.

'Aye?' The woman was fat, wore a soiled apron over a

greasy black dress and slippers on her feet. Her watery brown eyes wandered over Chrissie and took in the smart costume, the neat court shoes and kid gloves that marked her out of place there.

Chrissie asked, 'I'm looking for Vesta Nightingale. Doesn't she live here?'

'Oh, aye. Come in.' The woman turned and waddled back along the passage, feet shuffling in the slippers. She stopped at the foot of the stairs and shouted, 'Vesta! *Vesta*! Somebody to see you!'

A voice came faintly from overhead: 'What?'

'Somebody to see you!' The watery eyes wavered to Chrissie again. 'A lady!'

'Righto, darling.' There were sounds of movement on the floor above.

The fat woman stood aside. 'Go on up.' Chrissie climbed stairs that creaked under her, conscious of the woman below watching her back, turned at the half-landing and went on to the top. She was out of sight of the woman below now but knew she was still there, listening.

There were two doors on the landing where she stood. The voice came from behind the nearer: 'Who is it?'

'Chrissie.'

'Bloody hell!' Now the door opened and Martha Tate emerged. She had not bothered to prepare herself for the public, as the visitor was only her daughter. Like the women in the street she wore curlers in her hair. She was fastening a worn, imitation silk négligé, beneath which showed a cotton nightdress. Her face was bare of make-up, the skin pallid and blotchy. 'I might ha' known you'd turn up,' she grumbled. 'You'd better come in here.' She led the way to the second door, opened it to let Chrissie through then followed, closing it behind her.

She folded her arms then. 'Not that you're welcome, not after the way you treated me the last time we met, but I'm not talking to you with that fat old cow flapping her ears downstairs. Now, what d'you want? Though I can probably guess.'

Chrissie had taken in the room in one sweeping glance as she entered. There was a dead fire in the grate and a half-empty bucket of coal standing in the hearth. A table covered with a flowered oilcloth, cracked and peeling in places, stood in the centre of the room, four straight-backed chairs around it. There were two armchairs at one side of the fire, a small couch on the other. All the furniture was old and well worn, as was the linoleum on the floor and the rectangle of carpet before the fire. The window looked out on the street and the net curtains were yellow with age, grubby from the coal fire. Sophie's suitcase stood by the couch.

Chrissie thought, Furnished rooms with use of kitchen and the tin bath hanging outside in the yard. Probably ten shillings a week rent. She said, 'I want to see Sophie.'

Martha glanced at the clock on the mantelpiece. 'She'll be here soon. Said she'd bring something back for our dinners.'

'I don't want this life for her.'

Martha smiled, lips tight, then said, 'Depends what she wants, doesn't it?'

'Sophie is still only sixteen.'

'That's old enough in this business. What were you up to when you were sixteen? You weren't at some posh school, I'll lay a bet on that.'

At sixteen Chrissie had been running Lance Morgan's house for him and helping out in his pub. She thought now that it was not a bad life; she had been happy most of the time. 'That's not the point.'

The front door opened and closed and then they heard feet ascending the stairs. Martha listened, head cocked on one side, still smiling thinly at Chrissie. She called, 'We're in here, darling.'

Sophie entered, paused in the doorway watching her mother and said, 'I saw the car, knew you were here.' Her gaze switched to Martha. 'I got some chops, potatoes and veg.' She put a loaded brown paper carrier bag on the table and a handful of coins. 'There's your change.'

Martha complained, 'You should ha' got some fish and chips and saved me having to cook.'

'I'll cook them.' Sophie went on quickly, 'I've got a job.'

'With the band?'

Sophie shook her head then defended her failure. 'He has two singers already and he can't take on another one.'

'So where's the job?'

'Woolworth's.'

'That'll do till Solly finds you something.' Martha crossed to one of the armchairs and sat down, grinned up at Chrissie. 'Solly Rosenberg's my agent. He got me all this work in the clubs when the panto finished. He'll fix up Sophie, you'll see.'

'I don't want her fixed up.' Chrissie turned on Sophie 'I've come to take you home. Your father is very upset. So am I.'

Sophie shook her head. 'I'm not coming. You might force me to go back but you won't keep me there. I'm going to be a singer.'

Chrissie looked from one to the other: Martha gloating and triumphant, Sophie cockily determined. She saw something of her own ambition and drive in her daughter, and knew Sophie had spoken the truth, that she could not keep her at home against her will. Chrissie asked herself, what could she do? And then supplied the answer: do nothing.

She said, 'Your home will be there when you come to your senses,' and walked out, turning her back on her mother, who now gaped disbelievingly, and passing her daughter who blinked in uneasy surprise. She ran down the stairs, strode quickly along the passage and into the street. She was in the Ford again before she could change her mind. For a long moment then she hesitated, but finally shook her head and drove away.

Jack was incredulous then angry. 'You didn't bring her back? Are you out of your mind? You left that child with your mother after all you've said about *her*?'

Chrissie had had time on the drive home to let her own anger die and so recover from her distress, and she had stopped for a while to cry. Now she answered calmly, 'She's not the adult she thinks she is, but she's not a child, either. I was thrown out in the world long before her age. It's better for her to find out about my mother for herself. Sophie knows where we are when she needs us.'

But she cried again that night, and wondered if Sophie could be right.

Chrissie drove down into town to the hotel that Sunday to catch up on her desk work. Tom put his head around her door in the evening as she bent over her papers. Tall and dark, as time went on he looked more and more like Jack.

Chrissie marvelled at the resemblance as he said softly, 'So long, Mother.'

She thought, not for the first time, Thank God for Tom. She warned him, 'Take care.' Shipyards were dangerous places.

'I will.' Then he was gone, striding off up the passage, on his way to catch the train to Newcastle. He had to clock in at the yard early the next morning.

Sarah Tennant, working at a trolley of bedlinen and hidden behind the grand staircase, saw him go and smiled. Their paths had not crossed and she had not seen him for six months or more. He did not see her now.

When he opened the front door of his lodgings with the key his landlady had given him he found her son, Robbie, standing in the hall. Tom had met him a few times when Robbie had called to see his mother, bringing his wife and children with him. He was a thickset man who worked in one of the yards on the Tyne. Now he said, 'Sorry, Tom, but me mother was taken bad on Saturday. She had a stroke and she's in the hospital. They say she has to take it easy, so when she's a bit better and they let her out she's coming to live with us.'

Tom murmured his condolences and said, 'Will you tell her I was asking after her and give her my thanks? She was good to me.'

'Aye, I'll do that.' Robbie nodded his agreement then went on, 'It was a bit short notice but we asked around and we've found some people that'll take you in. It's not far away, either, so you'll still be handy for the yard. If you'll pack up any things you've got upstairs I'll give you a hand to shift them round there.'

He was as good as his word and carried one suitcase while Tom humped the other. Tom's new lodgings were only a couple of streets away in a house similar to that which he had left. The woman who answered the door was tightly corseted and big bosomed, her hair permanently waved. She wore a fixed smile as Robbie introduced her: 'This is Mrs Simmons.' They exchanged greetings then Robbie shook Tom's hand and strode away.

Tom went on into the hall and put down his cases. Mrs Simmons said, 'Come into the parlour and I'll make you a cup of tea.' She ushered him into the front room off the hall and said, 'This is Mr Simmons.' He stood up from his armchair, a balding man with a drooping moustache. The jacket of his dark blue Sunday suit was unbuttoned to show his waistcoat with its watch and chain, but he wore carpet slippers on his feet. His wife went on, 'And this is our Dolly. Her proper name is Dorothy but you call her Dolly like we do.'

Her daughter looked to be Tom's age and he found out later she was just two months past eighteen, nearly as old as himself. She was taller than her mother but her hair was also permed and her bust well developed. She would grow more like her mother in time, but now was pretty. She smiled at Tom, shy but assessing.

Her mother said, 'Now I'll get you that cup o' tea and a bite o' supper – and Dolly can show you your room. She's just next door to you.'

15

October 1937

After Peter was rebuffed by Sophie he told himself he didn't care – for six long months. When he finally weakened it was still only so far as to return to haunting the High Street outside the Ballantyne Hotel, where he believed she worked and lived. He did not see her, nor Helen Diaz, though he looked out for her, too. But he caught glimpses of Sarah Tennant in the foyer on several occasions. He knew her as the girl who worked some evenings in the club where he trained for boxing. Before the break-up with Sophie he had often exchanged a cheerful greeting with Sarah if he met her on those evenings and had once said, 'You work in the Ballantyne Hotel with Sophie, then.'

Sarah had not been prepared for that but guessed that Sophie had told Peter she worked there to keep her true identity secret. Sarah had tactfully replied, 'Yes, I work at the Ballantyne.'

Joe Nolan was pleased with Peter's progress and spent a lot of time with him. One night after a training session he told Peter, 'You've got the makings of a champion, lad, if you want to go that way.'

Peter, sweating and breathing hard, stared at him in surprise. 'Me? A champion?'

Joe nodded. 'I reckon so. O' course, you've got a long way to go. You've only put the gloves on with the lads in here so we don't know how you'd get on in a competitive bout against a stranger, but those same lads have performed against some stiff competition. I think you've got the ability and the strength, all you need now is a bit more of the know-how. And the hunger.'

'Hunger?' Peter rubbed at his face with a towel and grinned wrily. 'I've had some of that.'

'I mean the hunger to win, to be the best. If you haven't got that you'll never be a champion, because it gets harder the further you go. So I'm not going to push you into anything. Make up your own mind, then let me know how you feel about it.'

'Righto, Joe.' But Peter's attention was elsewhere now. The door of the gym had opened to admit two more of Joe's 'lads' and Peter looked past them. Sarah Tennant happened to walk by in the passage outside at that point and Peter finally decided to act. 'I'll be seeing you, then, Joe,' he said, and he changed into his street clothes and hurried out.

He found Sarah in the little room behind the bar, busily sawing bread into slices for sandwiches. He said, 'Hello. Busy?'

'Always busy in here,' Sarah laughed.

'Aye.' He hesitated a moment, shy, then blurted out, 'I wondered if Sophie was all right, wondered if mebbe she was poorly, because I haven't seen her for a while.'

'Oh.' Sarah sawed at the bread, thinking quickly. Should she tell him the truth as far as she knew it, that Sophie was the daughter of the owner of the Ballantyne Hotel? But then she answered, 'She's gone away, must have been a month or two ago. I heard Mrs Ballantyne telling somebody.' That last was true enough: Chrissie had publicly said that Sophie had gone away to work, though she had not gone into details. Sarah said, 'I don't know where she's gone.'

Peter repeated numbly, 'Gone away.'

Sarah saw his despondency and tried to cheer him. 'I expect she was upset at leaving, and she didn't want to hurt you so she couldn't bear to tell you . . . Or maybe she didn't have your address.'

Peter said miserably, 'She hadn't. She'd never been there.' She had left him without a word. In his heart he had hoped that they would meet again and take up where they had left off, that the break-up had been no more than a quarrel along the way, but now it seemed there was a finality about it. She had gone away.

He left the club and wandered about the streets, alone and unhappy, crossing the bridge into the town. He paused outside the Ballantyne Hotel out of habit, then mentally shook himself and slouched on. There was no point in waiting there because she had gone.

That week there was a travelling fair on the Garrison Field at the end of the High Street. He walked in past the huge steam-traction engine that pounded away, driving the generator that supplied the power for the strings of coloured lights, the whirling, dipping and soaring merry-go-rounds. He meandered among the stalls and amusements until he came to the crowd surrounding the boxing booth. He stood on the fringe, watching and listening.

There were three boxers on the stage outside the

booth, robes knotted over their boxing kit: a heavyweight, middleweight and lightweight. The proprietor of the booth stood at the front, shouting into a megaphone, touting for contenders. He had already found a heavyweight and a lightweight. They stood up there, too, blinking under the lights and grinning uneasily. The voice sounded metallic through the megaphone: 'Five pounds for anybody who can go the distance with Dave Bolger here! Five pounds!' The voice was becoming impatient, irritated. 'You don't have to lay him out or win on points, for Gawd's sake! Just *stay* with him!'

A man in front of Peter muttered, 'The feller that got in with him last night is still in hospital,' and heads nodded around him.

The man with the megaphone must have guessed at the crowd's thoughts. He taunted desperately, 'I thought you were a game lot here! Surely one o' you has the guts to have a go!'

Another voice spoke behind Peter, jeering, 'Are you thinking of having a go, kid?'

Peter turned and saw McNally, scarred and head cropped, grinning at him; Gallagher, the red-faced, narrow-eyed foreman stood by his side. Both of them smelt of beer, and had obviously been going the round of the pubs. Peter had soon managed to swop from Gallagher's to another gang, but they all still worked in Ballantyne's shipyard, and saw each other several times a day. Gallagher's and McNally's hatred was also still obvious. Their grins now were not friendly but sneering.

Peter demanded curtly, 'Why don't you take him on?'

McNally shook his bullet head then nodded it at the stage.

'He wouldn't have me. I'm a light heavyweight, a bit too big for his boy. That's not why he wouldn't let me in with his boy, but it's the reason he'd use.'

Gallagher grumbled, 'The fact is that he knows McNally, so he won't take him on. Wouldn't have him last night. Took a mug instead, that wound up wi' a broken jaw and concussion.'

McNally said, 'It's a pity. I could do with a fiver.' Then, 'Tell you what, kidder, I'll bet you a quid you couldn't last the first round wi' him.'

Gallagher chuckled. 'I'll lay a quid he daren't get in the ring with him.'

All Peter's misery and frustration was now transmuted into anger and he snapped back, 'You're on, both o' you!' He swung back to face the stage and shouted against the blaring megaphone, 'Here! I'll fight him!'

He started to shove his way through the crowd and the megaphone voice ceased its tinny clamour for a moment as its holder peered at the young man prepared to chance his arm against Dave Bolger. Then it bellowed, 'This looks a likely lad! Come on up here, my son!'

Peter clambered up on to the stage and stood by Dave Bolger. He eyed Peter and grinned confidently. The proprietor glanced from one to the other, weighing up both, and nodded. He lifted the megaphone again: 'It looks like a right good match to me! Let's get on wi' it!'

Peter had time to cool off. The megaphone man was something of a psychologist, as he had to be, and suspected that if Bolger destroyed Peter as he had the man on the previous night, then his other two volunteers might change their minds. So he put them on first and Peter saw the lightweight retire after two rounds and the heavyweight knocked out in the first.

'Two to them so far.' The jeering voice again. 'You'll make it three – if you get in.' Gallagher had worked his way through the audience in the packed booth with the help of McNally's elbowing and now stood behind Peter.

Peter shut his ears to the taunts, swallowed his nervousness and climbed into the ring as the proprietor beckoned. He stripped to the waist and listened as an elderly 'second' shoved gloves on to his hands and tied their laces. The megaphone brayed, 'This next bout is at middleweight, three rounds of three minutes each round . . .' The megaphone was lowered for the question, 'What's your name, lad?'

'Peter Robinson.' Now he was watching Bolger and trying to remember all Joe Nolan had taught him, but failing to recall any of that instruction.

The voice was announcing, '. . . and the local champion, battling Peter Robinson!'

Peter knew that was rubbish. He wasn't a champion. Bolger knew it and was laughing behind his gloves so the crowd could not see, but Peter could. Gallagher and McNally guffawed, mouths wide to show yellow teeth. They were all laughing at him.

He fought with a cold rage and a skill that first startled Bolger, then frustrated and finally subdued him. In the last minute of the last round Peter could have finished him but hesitated, reluctant to hit a man who could no longer defend himself. The booth proprietor did not hesitate and the round finished some twenty seconds early to save Bolger.

Peter collected his five pounds from the proprietor and two more from Gallagher and McNally. McNally did not speak and neither did Peter, but Gallagher asked, 'Does anybody else know you can fight like that?'

Peter answered curtly, 'Only Joe Nolan and the lads down at the club.'

He set off for home seven pounds richer but no happier.

As they watched his departing back with rage and hatred, Gallagher said to McNally, 'We could use him.'

'He won't have owt to do wi' us,' McNally spat. 'That's if he has any sense. He knows we'll do for him first chance we get.'

'I didn't mean he could work *with* us. I meant *for* us.'

'How?'

Gallagher told him.

The next day Gallagher and McNally called on Joshua Fannon in the house where Meggie Fannon had died. It was changed now: there was new furniture and carpets on the floor, and velvet cloth covered the table where Fannon added up his rents as a landlord and the bets he took as a bookmaker, worked out what he had to pay the winners. When he opened the door to them that evening there was nothing on the table but the plate that had held his fish and chips, and a half-empty glass of stout.

He greeted them warily and with false bonhomie because he knew Gallagher as a hard man and McNally as a bruiser. 'Now then, lads, what can I do for you?'

McNally's eyes focused on the cupboard by the fire, its door half-open to show the bottles of various kinds inside. 'You could give us a drink for a start. How about a drop o' whisky?'

Fannon said heartily, 'Aye, we'll all have one, eh?' and he got out the bottle.

When they sat around the table and the glasses had been filled and sampled, Gallagher said, 'I've got an idea that could make us all some money.'

'Oh, aye?' Now Fannon was interested, but still wary.

'Have you ever thought of setting up some fights?'

Fannon shook his head so that his jowls wobbled. 'I don't know owt about that business.'

Gallagher assured him, 'You won't have to. I'll find the fighters and the places. All you'll have to do will be to put up a purse and make a book.'

Fannon shifted uneasily. In fact, he was not entirely ignorant of the business of fighting. 'Can you make any money that way?'

Gallagher conceded, 'Not much, if you're particular, but suppose you were managing a fighter yourself and you knew when he was going to lose . . .' He paused and Fannon's eyes drifted to McNally. Gallagher said, 'No, not him.'

'Who, then?'

'A lad called Peter Robinson.'

'I've never heard of him.'

'Neither has anybody else, but he's good.'

'And he'll agree to . . .' He stopped because McNally was shaking his head and grinning.

Gallagher said, 'No, he won't agree to lie down, but he won't have to.'

And then he explained.

Peter Robinson sat in the doctor's surgery with its examination couch and screen and smell of disinfectant. He held his cap on his knee as Dr Dickinson, greying and with long years in that practice, told him gently, 'Your mother's heart is very weak. In fact it's only operating at a third of what its strength should be. That's why she is so grey, easily tired and short of breath. On top of that she's run down.'

Peter twisted the cap in his hands. 'What should I do? Does she have to go to hospital?' He knew she would hate that.

Dickinson shook his head, 'No.' He could have added, 'The hospital can't do anything for her,' but he had decided Peter was worried enough. 'No. She can stay at home but she needs building up with good food – milk, eggs and fruit – and she must rest for a while. No stairs, no housework, just rest for a few weeks until she picks up a bit. Do you understand?' He asked because some men did not, considering housework was not work at all – and anyway it was a woman's job.

Peter nodded, afraid for his mother. 'I'll do all o' that. Young Billy can give me a hand.' Little Billy Hackett would soon be eight years old.

So they were busy that Friday evening. Despite Margaret Hackett's protest, Peter insisted she sat in her chair by the fire while he and Billy cleaned the fire irons for the weekend. There were two sets, one steel and the other brass, each consisting of poker, tongs and shovel. The steel ones were used, regularly, and were cleaned with emery paper. The brass ones were for decoration, laid out in the hearth inside the brass-railed fender, and these were cleaned with metal polish.

Peter and Billy had almost finished when the knock came at the kitchen door, and Billy opened it to show Joshua

Fannon smirking fatly. Fannon said, 'I'm looking for Peter Robinson.'

Peter knew him as landlord of some of the houses in the streets around, and as a bookie. He came over from the table where the fire irons were laid on sheets of newspaper. 'I'm Peter Robinson.'

Fannon asked, 'Can we have a talk?' He jerked his head at the empty passage behind him.

Peter pushed Billy gently towards the table and the fire irons. 'You get on wi' that lot. I'll only be a minute or two.' He stepped out into the passage and shut the door behind him. 'Now, what did you want me for?' He eyed Fannon with dislike.

Fannon's eyes flickered away from Peter's gaze. 'The feller that ran the boxing booth – the one in the Garrison Field – told me about a Peter Robinson that beat one of his lads. Was that you?'

Peter nodded. 'It was. What about it?'

'Ah! Well.' The fat man licked lips already wet. 'I could put you in the way of making some money.' A door opened on the floor above and a neighbour came out on to the landing and peered curiously at the two men below. Fannon muttered, 'Tell you what: if you're interested, come to the Frigate and have a drink. I'll tell you all about it there.'

Peter was interested. His labourer's pay from the shipyard was barely enough to keep the three of them, and now Margaret Hackett needed a more expensive diet. He said, 'I'll get my coat.' As he took his jacket from a hook on the back of the door he ruffled Billy's hair. 'You can knock off now. I'm going out for a bit but I'll finish it when I get back.' Then he warned his mother with mock severity, 'You stay in that chair. Billy will tell me if you get out of it.'

Later, in the Frigate, he told Fannon, 'I'll do it.'

Three weeks later, hidden away in a dark gully between two deserted engine sheds down by the river, he fought his first bloody and bruising bare-knuckle contest by the light of two paraffin lanterns. His opponent was a seasoned fighter from Hartlepool called Brannigan. At the end Peter could see the other man was out on his feet, so he stood back and looked appealingly at the referee, who waved impatiently at Peter to fight on. Peter hit Brannigan again, more a shove than a punch, but it laid him on his back and he was counted out.

As Peter pulled on his shirt he saw Gallagher and McNally standing by Fannon, who – so Peter understood – had set up the fight. Peter faced the three of them but addressed the bookie: 'You didn't tell me these two were in this with you.'

'They aren't in it with me,' Fannon replied. 'Except that I need them on account o' carrying a lot o' money about, like I do at these fights. They work for me just the same as you do, that's all.'

Peter answered, eyeing the two, 'Just you keep them away from me.'

Now McNally jeered, 'You should ha' finished him quick instead o' waiting for the ref.' Peter ignored that and McNally got Gallagher's elbow jammed in his ribs.

Fannon said with an oily smirk, 'Here y'are, lad.' He gave Peter a pound note, his payment for winning the bout.

'Thanks.' Peter tucked it into his trousers pocket, shrugged into his jacket and walked away.

When he was out of earshot McNally complained, 'What was that dig in the ribs for? He should ha' laid Brannigan out when he was wide open, but he hasn't got the belly for the job.'

'You're too soon,' Gallagher told him. 'I'm going to want you to get him riled, but not yet. He needs a few more wins under his belt first so he'll have plenty o' fellers willing to back him when the time comes – plenty o' backers, plenty o' money.'

'Ah!' Now McNally saw the point. The three grinned at each other.

Gallagher said, 'You'll get your chance at him soon enough.'

McNally gloated, 'I'm looking forward to knocking his head off.' So they left him alone.

Peter fought every two or three weeks after that, and every time Gallagher and McNally were there, and acting as if they were no more than the employees Fannon claimed they were, serving as bodyguards and helping to organise the clandestine fights. In fact Gallagher was the moving spirit, but he never spoke to Peter. Fannon was Gallagher's mouthpiece.

Pamela Ogilvy led Matt, hand clutching hand, into the summer house. There was a moon, and by its light Matt spread his raincoat over the couch made of cushions. Pamela whispered, 'I expect you'll be starting at the yard soon.'

Matt grumbled, 'You've said that every week for the past month,' but it was said mildly because he had fallen for Pamela since that first night in the summer house.

Pamela prattled on, 'I'm sure you'll like it after you've

settled in. You'll be an assistant manager for your father in no time.' Mrs Pamela Ballantyne. She thought it had a ring to it. Or would it be Mrs Matthew Ballantyne? But no matter; one would do as well as another.

'No, I won't. I'm bloody sure I won't,' Matt said with some force.

It shocked Pamela into contradicting him: 'My father says you will.' He had delivered his judgment: 'Young Matt will soon buckle down to it. He'll see where his bread is buttered.' Pamela bit her lip now but the words had been said.

Matt retorted, 'He doesn't know anything about it.' Then it sank in what Pamela had let slip and he accused her, 'But he does know, doesn't he? When I told you what my father said – that I had a year to make good at the art college and if I didn't then I would have to go into the yard – that was just between you and me, nobody else.'

They were still standing by the couch and now Pamela put her arm around him and tugged him towards it. 'I only told my dad.'

Matt resisted and suggested astutely, 'And your mother.'

Pamela admitted, failing to move him, 'Well, yes, she was there. But I'm sure they wouldn't tell anyone.'

'I'm not.'

Pamela sighed, growing impatient. 'What does it matter who knows? You'll have to go into the yard anyway. All the other chaps we know are studying for careers or already working at them. And you say yourself that you won't make an artist. Only last night you said, "I can't do that for a living."'

Matt might have said that a lot of 'chaps' they didn't know, young men living in the narrow streets down by the river, did not have jobs, let alone a career. He knew this and was afraid he might become one of them, but still insisted, 'I'm not spending my life in the yard, either.'

'Then what are you going to do? I was talking to Charlie Baines and he said his dad had got him a job in the bank. He'll be a manager one day.' Matt voiced his opinion of Charlie Baines, a burly, hugely confident, fleshy-faced youth. Pamela said stiffly, 'We can do without that language, thank you.' But Matt only glowered mutinously, snatched up his raincoat and stalked out of the summer house.

'Matt!' Pamela called after him.

He only turned his head to answer, 'I'll be seeing you.'

Pamela started to run after him, then calculated that was the wrong tactic. 'Suit yourself. You'll be sorry.'

She was right and he was sorry already, but stubbornly tramped home. It was only when he went to hang up his raincoat in the hall that he realised his gloves were not in the pocket and that they must have fallen out in the summer house. He was not perturbed because it provided him with an excuse to go back to Pamela's home.

He went there the next night after dinner, but hesitated before the front door. He wondered if Pamela would answer the bell when he rang it? Suppose her father came instead? Matt did not want to ask him for the gloves left in the summer house – or explain how they came to be there – so he decided to seek them himself and then try to see Pamela. He walked around the side of the house, careful to stay off the gravel and treading silently on the grass. He pushed the door wide and the moonlight entered ahead of him, shaped by the doorway into a long rectangle of pale light. It showed him Pamela's face, eyes wide and lips parted. Then the head of the young man with her turned and Matt saw the broad face and thick lips of Charlie Baines.

Matt stood still on the threshold, gaping and shocked. Then Charlie scrambled to his feet, fumbling at his clothing, and Matt's shock turned to fury. It was a wild blow because he had only the training of a few hours with the games master at school and the experience of the usual playground fights, but he was enraged and Charlie was equally ignorant of defence. After only a few seconds he was lying on the cushions again with his face in his hands. Matt shouted at him, 'Get up!' Charlie did not move, too dazed to hear or understand. Pamela had screamed once and now was whimpering.

Matt blundered away. Now he knew how the cushions in the summer house happened to form a couch. He had not been the first. He knew he had hurt Charlie and terrified Pamela. He walked home exulting but went to bed heartbroken.

A few days later he saw Charlie, face bruised, with Pamela. They looked happy and did not see him. He remembered what Sophie had said long ago, that Pamela would put him 'through the mangle'. He lost interest in the art college. Instead of attending he took to wandering about the town or along the sea front with a book in his pocket. He would find a sheltered spot and read to his heart's content.

Two weeks after breaking with Pamela he saw her again with a boy who was a stranger to him. This time he could grin.

Then he met Jimmy Younger. It was a meeting that changed the course of Matt's life and almost ended it.

* * *

Jimmy Younger was ten years old and dreamed of being another Raich Carter, the Sunderland football star. He was kicking his ball about near the home of a schoolfriend in Charles Street, near the river. Jimmy's own home was in a wealthier part of the town. This was a street where the long terraces of houses had steps up to their front doors like wedges of cheese – one end thicker than the other – because the street ran down steeply towards the river.

As Jimmy and his friend played, a lorry swung into the kerb and parked there. Its driver got down and headed for an office where he had business. Just then Jimmy booted the ball and held his breath as it missed the windscreen of the lorry by inches, then vanished through the open window of the driver's door into the cab. Jimmy let out the held breath in a sigh of relief that no damage was done and called to the driver, 'Can I have my ball back, please, mister?'

The driver, already late, threw him a harried glance and told him, 'Aye. Get in and fetch it. And *don't* put it in there again!' Then he disappeared into the office.

Jimmy climbed on to the running board, opened the door of the lorry and stepped into the cab. The ball had fallen into the well on the passenger's side and lay by the door. Jimmy trampled across the seats to get it and the door swung shut behind him with a solid *clunk*! Then as he stood on the handbrake he released it. He felt the lorry jerk but took no notice because he was intent on reaching down into the well and grabbing the ball. It was only when he straightened up and turned to tramp back across the seats that he realised the lorry was moving. Parked on the steep incline, once the handbrake was released it started to roll downhill.

His friend cried out, 'Jimmy! *Jimmy!* It's *moving*!' The

warning had come too late. Jimmy fell against the steering wheel and clung to it, terrified, the ball dropping into the well again, forgotten. His clinging to the wheel kept the lorry from swerving off the road and smashing into the houses that lined it, but did nothing to slow it down. It accelerated rapidly. Jimmy shrieked in panic and glimpsed a tall, thin youth with a mop of sandy hair gaping at him from the pavement. Then the lorry had flashed past and the youth was gone.

Matt had seen the big vehicle start to roll and stared in horrified disbelief as he realised there was only one small boy in the cab. The shriek and his brief sight of the boy's face, open mouthed and wide eyed with fear, spurred him into action. He ran after the lorry and reached for the door handle but missed. Instead he caught hold of the steel framing of the open window. Pain tore at his fingers from a rough edge and he was forced to let go. He tried again and this time seized the handle and swung up on to the running board. As he yanked the door open he looked ahead and saw the street ran down to a T-junction and the lorry was headed for a brick wall.

He half fell into the cab and shoved in on top of the boy. He snatched at the wheel with one hand while he hauled on the handbrake with the other as the boy screamed and cried. That was nowhere near enough to halt the runaway but slowed it sufficiently to be able to swing around the corner at the bottom of the hill. The lorry rocked over on to the wheels on one side and for a second Matt thought it would capsize. He saw the wall frighteningly close as he and the boy were tossed about inside the cab. The boy clung to Matt, who hung on to the wheel. Then the lorry slammed down on to all four wheels again with a crash that shook the teeth in their heads.

It still careered on but Matt managed to shove the boy to one side so he could plant his boot on the footbrake. He stamped on it hard, long legs and long body rigid with strain. The lorry skidded, first one way then the other, then crashed broadside against a streetlamp and came to rest. For some seconds there was comparative silence. Matt and the boy sat in the cab, Matt pale as he suddenly realised how close he had come to death, and little Jimmy weeping. Then the street came to life.

Housewives ran out from their doors, and men, either old or unemployed, ran from the groups on the street corners. The first to arrive was the driver, his chest pumping from his run, white faced as Matt in his fear. He fell up against the side of the cab and gasped out, 'Are ye hurt?' He was reassured by Matt's nod of the head, but seeing the boy, cursed him feebly: 'Ye little bugger!' Then he turned away and vomited from his reaction.

A woman, large but quick footed, in a flowered apron and ancient slippers, took the driver's place and demanded of Matt, 'Are ye all right, hinny?'

A neighbour of hers, thin as a rake with hair in curlers, accused Matt sourly, 'Ye shouldn't be driving this thing wi' that bairn beside ye. Yer not much mair than a bairn yersel.'

The driver straightened up from his retching to say weakly, 'Give over, woman. If it hadn't been for that lad somebody wad ha' been killed. He risked his life to turn that lorry away from the wall and stop it.'

A policeman had arrived, pacing steadily, and a shining

black Morris 10 motor car had stopped and its driver had got out. He and the policeman both heard the lorry driver's defence of Matt. They listened as he went on to tell how he had seen Matt leap aboard the runaway to prevent a fearful crash and to save the boy's life. The policeman wrote it all down slowly in his notebook.

When the lorry driver finished there was a murmur of applause. Matt decided it was time he got away and started to climb down from the cab. The large woman peered past him at the boy and declared, 'That lad should go to the hospital.'

The thin woman, with a sudden change of heart, put in, 'And the young feller. He's bleeding.'

Matt found it was true. He had torn his hand reaching for the door handle and now it dripped red. As he wrapped his handkerchief around it the driver of the Morris 10 volunteered, 'I'll take them to the hospital. I'm a commercial traveller and I have to make a call up that way.'

The policeman had finished writing down the lorry driver's account, and now he said, 'I'll just have your names and addresses first.'

Matt murmured his details so only the policeman could hear. He glanced up from his notebook at the name 'Ballantyne' but made no comment. The boy said, 'Jimmy Younger . . .' Matt didn't hear the rest because the commercial traveller urged him into the car. The boy's name was familiar to Matt for some reason he could not remember, but then Jimmy, grimy face streaked with tears, joined him in the car and it pulled away.

At the hospital they took the boy away and a nurse cleaned and dressed Matt's hand. As he was about to leave the swing doors of the casualty ward flapped open as a man in a suit and tie threw them wide and strode in. Matt stepped aside to let him pass. Matt saw the suit was well cut and from a good tailor – he had learnt that much from his father. The newcomer walked with his back very straight, the self-confident stride of a man who has got on in the world, used to responsibility and organising. He glanced around, immediately singled out the sister in charge and headed for her. He asked, politely though brusque, 'I hear you've got Jimmy Younger in here?'

Matt pushed at the still-flapping doors and passed through into the corridor outside. He was about to turn right towards the exit when he glanced to his left and hesitated. Was it? he wondered. The face was familiar, but the uniform and the girl inside it . . . He said tentatively, 'Hello.'

Helen Diaz, in crisp blue dress, starched white apron and cap, stopped in her hurried walk and stared at him. 'Matt! What are you doing here?'

He couldn't take his eyes off her. 'Oh, getting this dressed.' He held up his hand in its new white bandage, but still looked at Helen. He realised he was not really surprised by the uniform. She looked the part, fitted in there, and gave off an impression of confidence and efficiency.

Helen said, 'Good God! What have you done?'

He shrugged, dismissing the hand. 'It's just skinned. The nurse in there said I can take this lot off the day after tomorrow and it should be just about better.' He thought that it was not the uniform, but Helen herself. She looked older, and it was going on for a year since he had seen her. She was no longer the skinny, pallid schoolgirl. This was an assured young woman.

Helen thought that Matt had changed, but searched for the reason. It was not just that he had grown taller still and now topped six feet, and was broader and heavier. Then it came to her that the change was in the way he looked at her and for a moment she glanced away. When her gaze returned to him she found his eyes waiting to meet hers, and they both laughed shyly.

They talked for a minute or two and she told him how her father and brother had left and so she had become a nurse. She did not tell him how she used her sister's birth certificate to gain entry. As they chatted she cautiously kept watch on the corridor, because as a student nurse she was a dogsbody and very much on probation. She had been sent on an errand, so she said, 'I've got to get on.'

She moved to pass him but Matt caught her arm. 'Just a sec. What about coming out with me?'

'What?' Helen was not ready for that much change in him. She drew back in surprise, but not far because he held her.

Matt said, 'I'll meet you outside here. When?'

'You will *not*! They don't like men hanging around outside waiting for nurses.' She did not want her colleagues watching her from the windows.

He pressed, 'Where, then?'

'Excuse me, but are you the chap who brought in the boy just now, the one that was in the lorry that crashed?'

Matt turned his head to see the man who had burst into the casualty ward. 'I brought him in, yes,' and turning back to Helen: 'Where?'

'Where?' she repeated, head whirling now, trying to think.

Then a rendezvous familiar in the town popped into her mind: 'Mackie's clock.'

'Am I interrupting?' The man looked from one to the other.

Helen said quickly, 'Oh, no.'

He smiled. 'Thank you.' Then to Matt, 'I'm George Younger, the boy's father.'

Matt turned again and saw Younger holding out his hand. Matt took it in his bandaged paw but still held on to Helen with the other hand. He winced as the man squeezed. 'Matt Ballantyne.' Then to Helen, 'When?'

'Sorry!' Younger released Matt's hand. 'That must be painful.' Then he added, 'I'm very grateful.'

'That's all right. I'm glad I could help.' Matt wished he would go away, and demanded of Helen again, 'When? Tonight? About six?'

'No! Tomorrow night.' The postponement was for no reason but to give her time. She saw another figure at the end of the corridor. Was it Sister? 'Six o'clock, then.' She finally pulled free and hastened off down the corridor away from the approaching figure.

Matt watched her go, with regret but elation. Then he found he was still half-turned to Younger and apparently listening courteously to the man's speech of gratitude, though Matt realised with guilt that he did not remember a word. Younger was saying, '. . . so if ever I can do anything for you, son, just say the word.' He paused then, waiting.

Matt's memory stirred as it had earlier, but this time it made the connection. George Younger? There was a chain of garages called Younger's. He said hesitantly, 'I need a job. So if you were wanting anybody . . .' He tailed off into embarrassed silence.

Younger thought, You and thousands more, lad. But he asked, 'What are you doing now, signing on?'

'I'm at the art college.'

Younger sighed within. 'So you'll be wanting a clerical job.'

'No. More mechanical. I know a bit about cars, I've worked on them.'

'Oh, aye?' Younger had heard that one before, many a time, and it had turned out the fellers couldn't change a wheel. As it happened, though, he needed another man to replace an old employee who was just about to retire. 'I can use an odd-job man to do a bit of sweeping up and cleaning, a few simple jobs on the cars, learn from the mechanics as you go along and move up a bit. What do you think?'

Matt grabbed the offer. 'I'll take it.'

Younger said, 'Start tomorrow at my garage on the Durham Road.' He began to turn away but now a name jolted his memory in turn. He said, 'Ballantyne? Any relation to the shipbuilders?'

Matt admitted, 'Jack Ballantyne is my father.'

That startled Younger, though he kept his face blank. He wondered, Why the hell does Jack Ballantyne's son want to work as an odd-job man? But he shrugged mentally, deciding it was none of his business. 'I'll see you in the morning.'

That evening Jack Ballantyne said, 'This sounds to me as if you are still drifting. I think this is just a way of getting out of starting at the yard.'

Matt admitted that to himself. He had no intention of

working in a garage for the rest of his life, but he said stubbornly, 'I'll be working.'

Chrissie pleaded for him, 'At least he'll be gaining experience of some sort and keeping himself while he makes up his mind.' She still had faith that Matt would succeed – somehow – though she was not able to produce any evidence to support that faith.

George Younger had called on Chrissie and Jack and told them how Matt had saved his son, so Jack set his doubts aside and grinned at his son with pride. 'I wish you the best of luck with it, then.'

Chrissie sighed with relief.

So did Matt, because he had been uncertain whether his father might somehow have stopped him from taking up the job.

He was jubilant when he met Helen the following evening. 'I've got a job!' he said, and went on to tell her about it.

'I thought you were at art school.'

'I was, but I just wasn't good enough. Oh, I can draw a bit, and I like it, but spend my life at it?' He shook his head. 'I was just wasting other people's time. I didn't want to go on doing that. Would you work at something you didn't like?'

Helen had been listening, disapproving. 'Lots of people have to.'

'I know they do, but would *you* want to?'

Helen hesitated, then admitted, 'No,' because she was on the way to attaining her ambition, to become a nurse. That was not completely true, though: nursing was to some extent a compromise, because she had really wanted to become a doctor. She knew that was a dream impossible of fulfilment for she had neither the brains nor the money to go to medical school, and its impossibility meant she had told no one. However, she sympathised with Matt's point of view now. She did not consider that she might be becoming biased.

Matt invited her to the cinema and she refused. They walked instead, out along the sea front.

Helen was not allowed to wear uniform outside the hospital. Her dress was an old one, but the tweed swagger coat with a pleated back that she wore over it was new and had cost her twenty-five shillings, most of her savings. Matt did not notice it, but Helen, on the other hand, saw that he needed a haircut, his grey flannel trousers bore a smudge of engine oil and his sports coat – borrowed illegally from Jack's wardrobe – was loose on him. He was so tall and ungainly and she couldn't help smiling at him. They talked a lot, and though neither could remember much of it next day, they thought it a memorable evening all the same.

Matt said as they parted, 'When will I see you again?'

Helen replied, 'I'll think about it and let you know,' and he had to be content with that.

He put his head around the door of the sitting-room when he got home and his mother looked up from the book she was reading to greet him with a smile. 'Hello, Matt. What have you been up to?'

'I went for a walk.' Then he added casually, 'I met Helen Diaz – Sophie's friend, remember?' He went on to tell her how Helen had been deserted by her father and was now a student nurse living in the nurses' home.

Chrissie was not deceived by that casual pose, and she remembered the girl very well.

A day or two later Chrissie called in at the hospital and

sought out Helen to tell her, 'Think of our home as yours. Come and stay whenever you like. We'd love to see you.' She left before Helen burst into tears – and drove home wondering what her own daughter, Sophie, was doing.

16

November 1937

Now they were into another winter. The clouds hung heavy and dark above Newcastle and although it was close to noon there were lights burning in many of the houses. Sophie trudged miserably, head down into the rain, carrying a heavy shopping basket. It drove almost horizontally along the street, borne on the wind coming off the Tyne and smelling of smoke and the sea. The umbrella she held before her face kept off some of the rain but blew inside out every few seconds. When she shoved open the front door and stumbled into the passage she was dripping as if she had crawled out of the river itself, her blonde hair hanging darkened and damp against her neck. She swore under her breath and shook the worst of the rain off the umbrella, holding it outside the door. Then she closed both umbrella and door, wiped her feet and walked along the passage. As she mounted the stairs she was conscious of the moist eyes of the fat landlady watching her from the door of her kitchen at the back of the house. Sophie mouthed silently, 'Nosey old witch.'

Once inside the sitting-room she put the shopping basket on the table, hung up her coat on a nail in the back of the door and stood before the small fire drying the hem of her dress. But not for long. Hunger sent her to take a loaf of bread from the basket and cut it into slices. Then she toasted it on a fork before the glowing coals. The food in the basket would be the first she had eaten that day.

The door of the bedroom next door opened and Martha Tate stepped out on to the landing, blinked around then wandered into the sitting-room to stand over Sophie. She clutched a garish, imitation silk robe about her. 'Hello, pet. Making a bit o' breakfast?'

Sophie replied shortly, 'Lunch.' She had missed breakfast because there had been no food in the house when she woke. That was a regular occurrence.

'I'll have a cup o' tea and a slice with you.' Martha sank into an armchair and slid off her slippers, stretched her toes out to the coals and yawned. 'Then I think I'll go back to bed for another hour or two.'

She had been in bed when Sophie returned at midnight. Sophie had a job singing with a band now and last night's dance across the Tyne in Gateshead had not finished till close on eleven, just in time for the patrons to catch the last buses and trams. She had stolen up the stairs carrying her shoes because their landlady complained about any noise at night. The door of the bedroom had been closed but Sophie had heard the mutter of voices, one of them hoarse and male. She had heard him leave as she lay on her own bed on the couch in the sitting-room. That, too, was a regular occurrence.

'You have this one.' Sophie unpacked the carrier bag to get at the butter, spread it on the slice of toast and gave it to Martha on a plate. Then she made a pot of tea.

'I'll go out and get some grub later on,' Martha promised and crunched toast. 'I've got some money next door.' Sophie knew where it came from – and guessed where it would go. She glanced at the table in one corner and saw the bottles standing on it were all empty.

Martha drank tea thirstily, licked her lips, then her eyes slid round to the corner table and she saw the empty bottles. 'Well, I think I'll get dressed and go out now.' She rose to her feet, clutching the robe with one hand and pushing at her tangled hair with the other. Sophie wondered what the men would think if they could see her now, her lined face bare of make-up. On the stage she looked half her age, but that was in truth – what? Chrissie knew her own mother, Martha's daughter, was forty-three. So Martha was . . .

Martha asked, 'How's your job with Bobby going?'

'Fine,' Sophie lied.

Martha leered, 'You be careful. Some o' these fellers . . .' She winked a bloodshot eye. 'If he puts his hand on your leg, you tell him where he gets off.'

'I will.'

That night he did – and she did, then smacked his face into the bargain. 'You're sacked!' he shouted at her, holding a hand to his jaw.

She snapped back at him, 'I'm resigning!' and walked out of the dressing-room. Then she wondered, What now? She had given up the job at Woolworth's when she went to sing with the Bobby Delville band. She had saved only a pound or two because Martha frequently borrowed money and only infrequently paid it back. Sophie knew she had to get another job because her grandmother could not – would not – support her, and that would not be easy.

She walked back to her lodgings to save the fare. The rain had stopped but a bitterly cold wind roared up the Tyne from the sea and cut through her clothes as she fought her way against it, crossing the bridge to Newcastle.

On a fine morning a few days later, the receptionist at the Ballantyne Hotel telephoned Chrissie in her office. 'There's a gentleman called to see you. Mr Rosenberg. He says he doesn't have an appointment but he'd be grateful if you could spare him a minute. He's come from Newcastle.'

Chrissie wondered if it was a commercial traveller wanting to sell her something for the hotel. She said, 'I have a minute or two so send him along. But first ask the kitchen to send up coffee for two, please.'

He turned out to be a good ten years older than herself but a darkly handsome, dapper man in a well-cut, well-pressed suit and polished shoes. His smile was wide and his handshake firm. 'Solly Rosenberg.'

'Sit down, please.' Chrissie gestured to the chair before her desk and offered, 'Coffee?'

'Thank you,' he said then he got down to business without wasting time, and Chrissie warmed to him. 'I'm a theatrical agent, Mrs Ballantyne. I act for Vesta Nightingale, and some few weeks ago she asked me if I could find work for her granddaughter, Sophie Nightingale.' He broke off there as he saw Chrissie stiffen behind the desk and freeze in the action of handing him a cup of coffee. 'I understand she is your daughter.'

Chrissie said tautly, 'She is.'

Solly nodded and took the cup from her. 'Thank you. Well, I fixed her up with a job, singing with Bobby Delville's band

– not easy because she had very little experience to offer, but I did it. That seemed fine, up to a point.'

He stopped to sip coffee then went on, 'You understand, as far as I knew the band was respectable and so were the venues. I had some reservations about other aspects of your daughter's life but I'll get round to them later. Now, a couple of days ago she came to see me and said she'd walked out on the job with Bobby Delville. She wouldn't go into details but I suspect he misbehaved himself. She asked me to find her another job. I think I could do that because she was a success with Bobby. *He* phoned me to say he was sorry and could I persuade her to go back. I told him I wouldn't.' When Solly stopped this time he looked ill at ease.

Chrissie prompted, 'So . . .?'

He went on unhappily, 'I said I was not happy about other aspects of your daughter's life. Well, I'm talking about Vesta Nightingale. I know the lady is your mother, but frankly, I think Sophie would be better off out of her influence. I've acted for Vesta Nightingale for more years than I care to remember. She was a real talent. But in her private life . . .' He shook his head.

Chrissie said, 'I understand. I'll go and see Sophie.' She was silent for a full minute, thinking. Solly waited for her, and was beginning to worry at that long-drawn-out silence. Then she broke it to say, 'I wonder if you would help me?'

'If I can,' he promised quickly.

It was a half-hour and several telephone calls later when a relieved Solly Rosenberg stood up. Chrissie rose, too, saying, 'And thank you for taking the trouble to come and tell me.'

He smiled at her. 'I like the girl. And she, too, has a real talent. I would hate to see that wasted like—' He checked himself there and held out his hand, then gave Chrissie one more useful item of information before he left: 'Vesta is performing at a club tonight and she will be out of their lodgings from about seven until well after ten.'

So Chrissie met her daughter on the landing that evening and Sophie greeted her with the words, 'Grandma is out. She won't be back till late.'

'I know. I came to see you.' Chrissie kept her smile in place though she saw that Sophie was thinner and there were shadows under the girl's eyes. She followed her daughter into the sitting-room and sat down in one of the lumpy armchairs. Sophie sat opposite, stared at her defiantly and waited. Chrissie said, 'I came to make you an offer.'

Suspicion was now added to defiance as Sophie asked, 'What sort of an offer?'

'Why don't you come home to live, find some work around Sunderland, and study for a trade during the day?'

'You mean I could sing in the evenings? Be a professional singer in the evenings?'

'That's right.'

'But you don't want me to be a singer.'

'True, but this way you wouldn't be wasting *all* your time.' Chrissie leaned forward. 'Look, Sophie, you might make a success of being a – a theatrical, but a lot of people try and fail. If you have an alternative skill you can still earn a living and get some satisfaction out of it. I think that is the best way forward for you,' she said with sincerity.

Sophie wavered, but questioned, 'What made you change

your mind? You didn't want me to be a singer at all, any time, anywhere.'

'I haven't changed my mind, but I miss you.' That came from the heart. 'Come home, Sophie.' Chrissie waited as Sophie looked around the room. Sophie recalled how eagerly she had come here and the picture she had nurtured of her grandmother, then of the weeks between, the drinking and the borrowing, lying sleepless on the couch and hearing the men in the room next door.

Sophie left a note for Martha Tate, thanking her for her help but saying that she was going home to work locally in Sunderland.

Seated in the Ford she told Chrissie, 'I'm going to be a singer. Don't think I'm giving up. And I'll tell you now, my agent has already fixed me up with some dates in Sunderland and round about. He came to tell me just an hour or so ago.'

Chrissie said happily, 'That's a bit of luck. I'm pleased for you.' Solly Rosenberg had arranged those dates earlier in Chrissie's office, using her telephone. 'Sing, then.'

Sophie sang all the way home, where Jack Ballantyne wrapped his arms around both of them.

So Chrissie had all her family at home for Christmas and they saw in the New Year of 1938 together.

Two weeks later Tom Ballantyne smiled shyly around the table at his lodgings. 'Thank you very much for the tea, Mrs Simmons. It was kind of you to remember my birthday.'

Violet Simmons simpered and flapped a hand in denial. 'Why no! You're welcome. You're just like one of the family now. Isn't he, Dennis?'

Her husband dutifully agreed. 'Aye. That's right, Mr Ballantyne.'

'Call me Tom.' He had asked them to before, but they persisted in giving him his full title, except, that is, for Dolly. She addressed him as Tom.

He was well pleased with his new lodgings. The food was good and generous, his room was comfortable and he was treated as an honoured guest. Now they had given him a special high tea to mark his birthday and cards to add to those he had received from home. Also he had been given a pay rise at his work in the yard because of the anniversary. He was happy.

Now Violet Simmons stood up and ordered, 'Help me to clear away the tea things, Dennis. And you two young ones, why don't you go out to the pictures as it's Tom's birthday? Here . . .' She rummaged in a drawer for her purse and took out a florin she had put there for the purpose. 'My treat.' She pressed it into Tom's hand, ignored his laughing protests and herded him and Dolly towards the door.

At the cinema Dolly found them a seat at the back and they sat close together in the warm darkness.

17

February 1938

The ship was launched in Ballantyne's yard on a blustery afternoon in March, the wind setting the lines of bunting dancing. The bottle of champagne shattered on the bow of the ship and the crowd of invited spectators and workers gathered around burst into a roar of cheering. The ship began to move slowly down the slipway. It gathered momentum, and as its near ten thousand tons rammed into the river, it displaced a huge wave which rolled away from the ship to break over the sides of the quays on both sides of the Wear. The banks of the river were also crowded with spectators who had applauded the launching, and now they shrieked and laughed, and ran from the wave that washed on to the quay towards them, threatening to fill their boots.

Chrissie stood by Jack on the flag-draped platform with the privileged guests. She clutched her bouquet and cheered with the rest. The ship had been launched by Madame Benoit, whose husband was Jean-François' manager. The shipowner was not well enough to attend the launching and had sent the Benoits instead.

Chrissie had asked, 'Why didn't he ask his wife to do it?' and Jack had recounted what he knew of Jean-François' marriage. Chrissie had bitten her lip, shrewdly guessing the temptation offered to Jack, and had kissed him. She wanted to kiss him now but knew she had to show more decorum as the wife of Mr Ballantyne.

She and Jack had entertained the Benoits, Monsieur Benoit lean and courteous, Madame plump and chic, and were sending them home bearing good wishes to Jean-François. He had ordered another tanker from the yard and Chrissie was happier than she had been for a long time.

Sophie swallowed her nervousness again and again but it always returned. Her mouth was dry. She was used to all these symptoms now and knew she would perform when the time came, but that did not help much in this waiting period. She wore a new dress that had cost her fifteen shillings and clung to the curves of her slender body. She knew she looked attractive and had seen the admiring glances turned her way, but reminded herself there were others in the contest, too.

The talent contest was being held in a big public house in the middle of the town. The venue was the lounge bar, long and narrow with a small stage at one end, just big enough for the pianist and a performer. The floor of the lounge was packed with small tables set close together. The chairs crowded about them were all occupied. There were some three hundred people or more in the audience. At a table near the entrance sat three men. Their glances were not admiring. They leered and muttered among themselves. Sophie avoided their eyes and concentrated on what she had to do.

She won the contest, to a storm of applause, which she

received flushing and laughing. Looking out over the heads of the crowd, her eyes found one face. Peter Robinson stood in the doorway, smiling, hands raised, applauding. She wondered how long he had been there, and without thinking lifted her hand and waved to him. He saw that and his smile slipped away. He turned and walked out of her sight.

'Thank you!' Sophie collected her prize of two guineas, picked up her coat and left the hall. Out on the pavement she looked for Peter Robinson but could not see him. The street was busy, thronged with people. Trams clanged and rattled up and down with an occasional car hooting its way through. On a nearby corner the Salvation Army band boomed and blared brassily. Sophie sighed and decided it was just as well she had not caught up with Peter. She had intended to ask him how he was, as a friend, but now she admitted that would have been a mistake. Peter would not be satisfied with friendship. She would only have reopened an affair that she had closed at the cost of some pain to both of them.

She turned away from the din into the alley that ran along the blank side wall of the pub. This was a short cut to the stop where she could catch her tram. The alley was dark because the only light had gone out, but that did not deter her. She was used to walking at night without fear.

She had scarcely taken a dozen paces into the gloom when heavy and hurried footsteps sounded behind her and a hand seized her arm and swung her against the wall. One of the three men she had noticed earlier pressed against her. He was a head and shoulders taller than she, hair shorn down to his skull, muscular and heavy. McNally shoved his face close to hers and breathed, 'You're a bonny lass.' Then his free hand went exploring. Sophie screamed, then realised with horror that no one would hear her above the din of the street and the band. She fought and for a second McNally drew back his face, startled. He hissed, 'Shut up! I'll not hurt ye if—'

Then someone grabbed his shoulders, spun him around and hurled him aside. Caught unprepared, his legs tangled and he fell. Sophie saw Peter had taken his place. It was he who now gripped her arm and hurried her on along the alley to its end. Sophie saw her tram rattling and swaying towards her stop and Peter pushed her in that direction. 'Go on! Get away home!' Shaken, she obeyed, but when she reached the stop she remembered the other man and looked back to see if Peter was safe. She saw the big man burst out of the alley and now the other two men were with him. She froze, one foot on the step of the tram.

Gallagher grabbed McNally and swung in front of him before he could reach Peter. McNally raged, 'Get the hell outa my way! I'll kill the bastard!'

Gallagher snapped at him, 'Shut your row! If you start a fight here somebody will shout for the pollis and the pair o' you will land up inside!' He glared at Peter, who was also standing ready with his fists up.

Fannon, sweating and waddling, said, 'Aye, there's a pollis up the street there now.'

Both he and Gallagher stood in McNally's path, forcing the angry man to pause. Gallagher soothed him, whispering, 'I told you I'd give you your chance at him. Now's the time.' He turned his head to speak to Peter, challenging, 'He wants to take you on. Fannon here will fix it up. What about it?'

Peter spoke to Fannon. 'Aye. I'll fight him. Where you like and when you like.' He saw he was not about to be attacked now, lowered his hands and turned away.

Sophie had not heard the exchange, but now saw him go. A voice said irritably, 'Are you gettin' on or not?' She realised the conductor was standing on the platform by her, waiting impatiently, his hand lifted to the bell cord, ready to send the tram away.

'Sorry.' Sophie stepped aboard and found a seat inside. Her hands trembled when she took out her purse to pay for her ticket. She closed her eyes and relived those awful moments in the alley. She did not want to think what would have happened if Peter had not been there. And she had not given him a word of thanks.

'That was a lovely picture.' Dolly Simmons clung tightly to Tom's arm as they came out of the cinema. He had not gone to the launching because he had to work in the yard on the Tyne. He was disappointed but philosophical: 'I've seen launches before and I'll see a lot more.'

Dolly had not been interested, except that it meant he had been able to escort her to the cinema. Tom took her on one night of every week now. Dolly would have liked to have gone more often but Tom attended evening classes or studied in his room on the other evenings. So Dolly would go out on her own: 'I'm off to see Mavis, Mam.' She worked with Mavis, serving behind the counter of a cake shop.

Now she said, 'I think that Deanna Durbin is a lovely singer.' She prattled on about the films they had seen and Tom listened. She was a pretty girl and he had become fond of her. When they reached her front door she lowered her voice. 'The lights are out. They've gone to bed.'

Tom replied softly, 'No need to wake them. I've got my key.' The house was silent. When he closed the door behind them they stood in the pitch darkness of the hall. They paused a moment, breath held, and heard the ticking of the clock on the mantelpiece in the parlour. Dolly groped for and found Tom's hand, squeezed it, then led him to the foot of the stairs and up. On the landing she drew him past her parents' room and his own and so to her door. She turned to him then and slipped her arms around his neck, stood on her toes and kissed him. For a moment he was surprised by her intensity, the pressure of her body on his, then he returned the kiss. Now she was pressed back against her door and it gave to that pressure, swung silently open. They staggered, she falling backwards and taking him with her, as if in a clumsy dance. Then her legs were against the bed and she was falling.

Tom saved her and they swayed for a moment. She reached out one hand to close the door and whispering, lied, 'You can stay for just five minutes.'

18

March 1938

Sophie lied, 'I'm just going into the town.'

Tom stood at her open door, handsome in dark blue blazer and grey trousers, and asked, 'You've finished packing?'

'All done.' Sophie jerked her thumb at the two suitcases by her bed. Solly Rosenberg had found her a month's work singing with a band in Yorkshire, starting in Leeds. Chrissie had raised no objection, no longer sure if she was right to stand in the way of Sophie's ambition.

Tom said, 'I'll come with you.' He was home for the weekend and this was Saturday night.

Sophie tried to dissuade him. 'Don't you want to go to the pictures?'

'I go one night in the week; that's enough. I'll just keep you company.'

That was a nuisance, but Tom was one of the two brothers Sophie adored, and she reluctantly agreed. 'Come on, then.' She pulled on the tweed coat she had bought for two guineas on the strength of the Yorkshire booking.

When they were out of the house and walking down the road to catch their tram, Tom enlarged shyly, 'I go to the pictures every week with Dolly.'

Sophie questioned, 'Dolly?'

'The girl in my digs, Mr and Mrs Simmons' daughter. She's about my age.'

'Well, well, well, well, *well!*' teased Sophie. 'You little devil, our Thomas. Taking girls to the pictures now. What next?'

He grinned, able to take this from her. 'You can cut that out.'

Sophie did, because she had other business. 'Listen, Tom, I'm not just going into the town. Somebody did me a favour the other day and I have to thank him. I think I can find him at the club. You might find one or two people know me, because I've done some singing there.' Then she told him about winning the talent contest and also how Peter Robinson had saved her from McNally. She found it hard not to shiver when she recounted that episode and Tom bristled. 'But I don't want Mother to know about this. She's letting me go out to sing, but if she heard about that she would want to stop me again. So keep quiet, please.'

Tom grumbled, still outraged, but agreed.

At the club Sophie revised her opinion of Tom. 'You'll be some use after all.' She pointed at the door of the gym. 'I daren't go in there, so you can. I want to see Peter Robinson if he's there. If he isn't, ask if Joe Nolan can come out for a word.'

Tom shoved through the door into the gym. At that moment another door opened and Sarah Tennant stepped out into the passage. Sophie greeted her. 'Hello, Sarah. You're still working here, then?'

Sarah smiled and nodded. 'When I'm not at night school.'

Now Tom emerged from the gym and stopped dead, staring at Sarah. She said shyly, 'Hello.'

Sophie asked, 'Did you see him?'

Tom started, glanced at her and asked, 'What?' then, remembering his errand, he reported, 'Joe Nolan is there and he'll be out in a minute.' And then to Sarah, 'Hello.'

Sophie explained, 'Sarah works here sometimes in the evenings because she isn't allowed to work overtime at the hotel.'

'I am now,' Sarah put in. 'That only applied when I was under sixteen. But the steward here was good to me so I still work a shift two or three nights a week and save the money.'

Tom said, 'I didn't know.' And he had not known how Sarah had changed. Though Sarah had seen him often when he called at the hotel to visit his mother, she had stayed quietly in the background and he had not seen her for over a year. In that time she had grown and the top of her head came up to his shoulder now. She was just turned seventeen and though still shy she had acquired an assurance while working with Chrissie Ballantyne. Tom stared at this stranger and Sophie watched him thoughtfully.

Then the door of the gym flapped open and Joe Nolan joined the little group in the passage. He addressed Sophie brusquely. 'You're the lass looking for Peter?'

'That's right. I—'

Joe cut her off. 'If you'll tell me where he can find you I'll give him a message.'

But Sophie wouldn't settle for that. 'I need to see him now, tonight. I'm going away for a month and I have to see him before I go.'

'Well, you can't.'

'Why not?'

'Because it's no place for a young lass like yourself.'

Sophie flared. 'I think I can make up my own mind about that. What is he up to?'

Joe knew determination when he saw it. He admitted reluctantly, 'He's fighting. Bare-knuckle fighting. It's illegal.' Sophie had not known that it still went on. Joe continued, 'I want nothing to do with it.'

Sophie protested, 'But you taught him to fight.'

Joe smiled sourly. 'I taught him to box. He was born a fighter.'

She was shaken by Joe's disapproval but nevertheless she persisted, 'I want to see him – tonight.'

Joe sighed. 'All right.' He jerked a thumb at Tom. 'Who's this?'

'My brother.'

Joe asked Tom, 'Have you been listening?' When Tom nodded Joe said, 'Then you'll be a witness that I'm doing this because your lass here would have it. I don't want her father down here blaming me.' Tom nodded again and shifted uneasily, aware that if anything happened to Sophie, Jack would be asking questions of Tom himself.

'Come on, then,' Joe said, and led them out of the club and down to the river, threading the dark streets for ten minutes or more. Soon they came to an alley that formed a black gulf between two big sheds. There was a circle of yellow lamplight halfway down the alley and a man standing at its entrance. He was the look-out, posted there to keep watch and give warning if the pollis appeared. He wore working clothes that were grimy with coal and oil. His hands were jammed in his trousers pockets, his shoulders hunched and jacket collar turned up against the cold wind that whistled between the sheds, bringing a fine rain in from the sea. He called, 'Here! Where d'ye think you're going?'

Joe Nolan did not check in his stride, only snapped back, 'Down to see the scrapping. What d'ye want? A ticket?'

The man grinned with recognition. 'I didn't see it was you, Joe. Gan on in.'

Joe was already leading Tom and Sophie deeper into the gulf, and the look-out's words were submerged by the shouting from the crowd ahead. The men in the crowd were comfortably dressed against the bitter chill of the night and the drizzling rain that had turned the ground in the makeshift ring into slippery mud. As the fighters, both stripped to the waist, danced, ducked, punched and panted they sucked in great lungfuls of air, which in that ring smelt of coal smoke and soot, whisky and beer, sweat and linament.

The spectators were well fed, many smoking cigars and with their motor cars parked not far away. They were there because they could afford it, and they were devotees of bare-knuckle contests. They had paid Fannon because he had set up the fight and they betted with him. He had the money stuffed in the bulging pockets of his raincoat, buttoned tight over his belly.

Sophie knew nothing of this, was only aware that the shouting died as she came to the fringe of the crowd. Joe Nolan stopped then and told her, 'Look, lass, you don't want to see . . .'

'Yes, I do!'

Joe growled irritably and shoved into the crowd, elbowing his way, and the men there, knowing him, parted to let him through. Sophie followed on his heels, hearing the raucous breathing and the butcher's-block thudding of fists on flesh, smelling the oil and smoke on the clothes of the crowd, the sweat. She was sickened and wondered what awaited her. Then she was peering into the ring. She recognised with shock that one of the fighters was the big crop-headed man who had seized her in the alley. And the other . . .

It was the biggest crowd Gallagher, though ostensibly Fannon, had gathered for a fight. Peter now had a string of successes behind him and McNally had a reputation locally as a bruiser. Gallagher had also dropped hints that rapidly became circulating rumours, that McNally was growing old and was now too slow to take on the rising young star. So they had come to see a new champion crowned – and to make money by backing him. Gallagher had been preparing the ground for this bout for months. Fannon had taken bets in handfuls of notes and coins, most of it on Peter Robinson. Fannon, Gallagher and McNally were looking forward to making a killing – in more ways than one.

McNally had come primed to destroy Peter and had tried his hardest, but Peter had learned a lot from Joe Nolan and more later in the ring of experience since Gallagher had been arranging fights for him – though Peter thought that was Fannon's work. Peter had boxed his man for fifteen minutes. He moved quickly but carefully on the treacherous ground, because a slip could leave him open to McNally's big fists. He watched his opponent to the exclusion of all else and did not see the open-mouthed, shouting faces around him. One moment they were lost in semi-darkness, the next lit yellow as the wind swung the oil lamp on the wall. He heard them only as an animal-like growl around him. He had anticipated and countered all McNally's dirty tricks and worn him down.

McNally was half a head taller and two stones heavier but he was tiring now. Peter had taken some punishment but he was still strong.

He blocked a punch from McNally that lacked strength, and replied with a blow below the bigger man's heart that had him grunting and folding in pain. McNally's hands lowered and Peter saw his chance. His fist conncted with McNally's jaw and he spun then fell face down in the dirt and mud of the alley. The bellowing of the crowd was stilled.

Peter felt savage satisfaction, the slights and insults of months and years avenged. Then he remembered the money: he would collect ten pounds from Fannon for this fight, a fortune! He sucked in great breaths of air now, filling his chest, and ran a hand with bloody, skinned knuckles across his face, wiping away the sweat, smearing the gore.

And so Sophie saw him, naked to the waist and running with sweat, his body blotched with bruises and stained by the blood fallen from his face and his opponent's. In that one split second her mind photographed the scene: the circle of sweating faces, the fat man in the tight raincoat, and the narrow-eyed, muscular man by his side, both of them glaring hatred at Peter.

Peter stared at her white face in the crowd, saw the eyes wide and lips parted in shock. Joe Nolan stepped in front of her, grim faced, and spoke to Peter. 'See us back at the club when you've cleaned yourself up.' Then he turned and pushed his way out of the crowd, herding Tom and Sophie before him.

When they were clear of the press he said brusquely,

'Well, you've seen him. Satisfied?' He glanced at Sophie. She did not reply but her drawn face was answer enough. She was trying to reconcile the Peter she knew with the fighting machine she had seen this night – and failing. Joe grunted and led her and Tom back to the club.

The crowd left behind them was shifting now, some who had betted on McNally drifting away up the alley, grumbling at the money they had lost. Most of the men now gathered around Fannon to collect their winnings. His face was a sickly green and shone oily with sweat in the light from the lamps hung on the shed wall. He squeaked again and again, 'You'll get your money! Just let me pay you one at a time! You'll get your money!' Gallagher stood by his side, holding off the more importunate.

Peter took a towel and his shirt and jacket from the man who had acted as his second, and who was now impatient to collect his own winnings and said hurriedly, 'You fought a great fight, young 'un.' Then he elbowed his way into the crowd.

Peter followed him. His heart was still thumping from the battle, his mind still filled with that picture of Sophie's face, but he wanted his money. That was, after all, the reason he had fought. So he pushed to the front and stood before Fannon, held out his hand. Fannon licked his lips then said, voice hollow with insincerity, 'Good lad. You earned every penny. Here y'are.' The crowd went quiet as he dipped into the pocket of his raincoat and drew out the pound notes, counted them into Peter's outstretched hand: '. . . eight, nine, ten.'

Gallagher said nothing but his glare was evil.

Peter crammed the notes into his trousers pocket and

eased out of the crowd. As he towelled his face and body then donned his shirt, he saw that McNally had been revived and was now leaning with his back against the wall of a shed under a lamp. Peter did not go to him because this had been no sporting contest. He turned away and walked out of the alley, pulling on his jacket as he went.

Soon afterwards, washed and in a clean shirt, he strode up to the club, never realising that he was hurrying. He found Joe Nolan sitting at a table with Sophie and Tom in the room where women were allowed. One or two sat with their husbands, sipping at glasses of port or stout. Tom had looked around surreptitiously to see if Sarah was there but she was working in the room behind the bar.

Peter joined them, glancing at Sophie, reminding himself that this girl had sent him on his way a year ago. He sat on a stool pulled out from under the table and asked Joe, 'What did you want to see me about?'

'I didn't.' Joe gestured with a jerk of his head towards Sophie. 'This lass does. You know how I feel about tonight's business,' and with that he stood up, nodded 'Goodnight' to Sophie and Tom and walked out.

Peter looked at Tom but spoke to Sophie: 'Who's this?'

'Tom, my brother.'

Peter nodded to him then turned on Sophie. 'Joe had no call bringing you to the fight.'

'He didn't want to. I made him.'

'Why?' Then before she could answer he added, 'It was none of your business. Nothing I do is any of your business.'

Sophie faced his hostility and put a hand on Tom's arm as he started to rise from his seat. 'All right, Tom.' Then to

Peter: 'I wanted to see you urgently because I'm going away for a few weeks. Joe told me you were fighting but I didn't realise what it would be like. I wish you wouldn't do it.' She had been afraid he was hurt, was still afraid for him.

He said, hiding his disappointment behind a poker face, 'Is that why you wanted to see me?'

'No. I came to thank you for helping me the other night when that drunk was . . . being a nuisance.'

Peter shrugged. 'I settled with McNally tonight.'

'McNally?' The name nudged a memory and Sophie frowned, thinking back. 'You told me about him. He works with you, and there was another man . . .' She paused, trying to remember.

Peter supplied the answer: 'The foreman, Gallagher.' He added drily, 'He was there tonight, the red-faced, slit-eyed feller.'

Now Sophie remembered. 'Yes, Gallagher. Was he next to a fat man in a raincoat?' She could recall the scene clearly, every detail, every face, and she shuddered inside.

Peter said, 'Aye. The fat feller was Josh Fannon. He's a bookie and he sets up the fights.'

Sophie said, 'McNally was the drunk the other night.' Now she was angry. 'I didn't want you fighting on my account! I'm grateful for what you did but don't use me as an excuse.'

'I didn't,' Peter said grimly. 'McNally wanted it. And we both wanted the money.'

The money. Sophie knew he was poor and would have a need for the money but she could not accept the method he had chosen to obtain it, unless there was no other open to him. But even then . . . She asked Tom, 'Will you wait outside? I'll only be a minute or two.' When he had gone she told Peter, 'I wish you wouldn't fight, but it's none of my business, as you say, because there's nothing for us. I want to be a singer, up there under the lights and in front of the band. I won't be tied to anybody.'

Peter said heavily, 'Aye, I know.' He stood up with her and watched her walk away. He had hoped through a long year, but nothing had changed. The ten pound notes were still in his pocket but he felt he had won nothing.

Sophie did not sleep well and travelled south on Sunday.

A few days later Tom was thinking guiltily of Sarah, guiltily because of his fondness for Dolly Simmons. He was walking back to his lodgings from his night school in Newcastle and turned into his street, which was dark and deserted at this time of night. His footsteps echoed hollowly on the pavement. He was only a score of yards away from his lodgings when a looming figure stepped out of the doorway of a closed and shuttered shop. Tom moved aside to pass him, then all went black and the next thing he knew he was sprawled in the gutter, his head ringing and jaw aching. The other man stooped over him and asked hoarsely, 'Know who I am?'

Tom saw he was a stocky young man, broader and heavier and probably a year or two older than himself. Dazed, he mumbled, 'No.'

'Fred Dagg. They call me Dagger. You've been going out wi' my lass, Dolly, takin' her to the pictures. You keep away from her or you'll get a bloody sight more.' Then Dagger strode away.

Tom hauled himself to his feet, holding on to the big

padlock fastening the wooden shutters of the shop. He clutched it and waited as his head spun, while surprise and shock gave way to anger. That cleared his head and he shoved away from his temporary support, looking for his attacker, but the street was empty and silent once more. Now he could narrow down his pain to two areas: his jaw, where Dagger had hit him, and the back of his head. He felt gingerly at the latter and found a large lump that was tender to his touch. So that was why he had been laid unconscious for a few seconds: he must have been punched on the jaw then banged the back of his head on falling. He walked on, anger smouldering.

Tom let himself into his lodgings and was met in the hall by Dolly. 'Hello, Tom. Would you like a cup of tea and a bite of supper?'

He feigned tiredness with a yawn. 'No, thanks. Think I'll get an early night.'

'All right.' She gave him a weak smile.

There had been an awkwardness between them since Dolly had taken him into her room. It seemed to Tom that Dolly was ill at ease – and he was regretting the *affaire* but now he said, 'I've just met a chap called Fred Dagg. He said you were his girl.'

Dolly's face reddened and she shook her head. 'No, I had – finished with him.' She turned away quickly, darted into the kitchen and closed the door behind her.

In his room Tom used a hand mirror and that on his dresser to examine the bump on the back of his head. It had stopped bleeding and was hidden from sight by his hair, though it felt the size of an egg. His anger still simmered. Dagger had taken him by surprise but he would not be caught again. Next time he would put Dagger on his back.

It was in that week that George Younger sought out Matt in the garage where he worked. George found him with his head under the open bonnet of a lorry and tapped his shoulder. Matt turned, saw him and pulled his head out. 'Yes, Mr Younger?'

The garage owner asked, 'How long have you been with us now?'

'Four months.' Matt was apprehensive. Was Younger going to say, 'Well, you've had your chance and you aren't up to the job'?

However, Younger grinned and said, 'I didn't think you'd stick it. I've never employed a bloody artist before, but you've made out pretty well. I've got a place at Darlington that's short handed now because a man's gone sick. I want to keep his job open for him because he's been with me a good long time and he's a rare worker. I don't want to take another feller on but I can't leave them struggling with a man short. Will you go there and work for a few weeks till he's better? I'll give you a quid a week towards your digs.'

Matt did not want to go but he was grateful for the job he had and wanted to keep it. 'Yes, I'll do it.'

He told Helen Diaz that night as they walked along the sea front. 'It'll only be for a few weeks.'

Helen was silent for a moment on hearing of this new blow. She had received mixed tidings that day in the shape of a letter from her father in Spain. He had said that he now appreciated how good a daughter she had been over the years and how badly he had treated her. 'I am sorry. When this terrible war is over and we return, I will make it up to you.' She had wept with joy but then began to worry for him and her brother more than ever.

Now she rallied, smiled at Matt and teased him, 'Why should that make any difference to me?' Then she laughed as she saw the corners of his mouth turn down. She squeezed his hand. ''Course I'll miss you. And be careful down there.'

Matt grinned. 'It's Darlington. They're not exactly foreigners there.'

'It's nearly into Yorkshire. Same thing.'

He laughed at her. They laughed a lot together. He knew he would miss her, but he was happy.

Ballantyne's yard was closed and silent. The nightwatchman opened the gate to let Chrissie drive the Ford in and told her, 'Mr Ballantyne is down the yard.' She parked by the offices and walked down the slope to where the part-built tanker lay on the stocks inside the cage of the staging. She found Jack standing in its shadow, his tall figure almost hidden in the gloom, hands dug deep in his trousers pockets and shoulders hunched. Chrissie slid an arm through his, scenting trouble, and asked, 'What are you doing down here? Everyone else has gone home.'

He turned to her and she saw his face was drawn. He answered, 'I had a letter from France. Jean-François is dead. His widow inherited the business and she has cancelled the contract. We won't get another penny.'

Chrissie bit her lip, shocked into silence for long seconds. Then she asked, 'But can she do that? Is it legal?'

Jack said wearily, 'No, it isn't and she can't. Her firm

is contracted to buy the ship. But it will take months, if not years, to fight it through the courts. We can finish the ship but then we'll have to sell it. And if we don't, we go bust.'

Chrissie knew that would mean ruin for him – and for her. He would not only lose his fortune but his heart would be broken. And then there were the others, the hundreds of men who worked in the yard and the families who depended on them. She fought to hold back the tears and blinked up at the shell of the hull above her. It stood black against the night sky like the skeleton of some prehistoric monster.

Jack said bitterly, 'At least we know how to name her. We can call her the *White Elephant.*'

19

April 1938

Sophie worked four weeks in Leeds and York, then on the night she finished her contracted shows she received a telegram from Solly Rosenberg: 'Have got you audition Michael Beaumont . . .' It went on to give details of time and place, but Sophie was already dancing around the cramped little dressing-room she shared with another girl. Michael Beaumont's was one of the biggest bands in the North-east, with a national reputation. After a time she stopped laughing and cavorting and cold reality set in. She reminded herself that all she had got was an audition. She had to prove herself good enough to get the job. She wanted it so badly she was sure she would not sleep that night. But she did.

The audition was in a dance hall in Newcastle. She caught an early train from Leeds, deposited her case in the left-luggage office at Newcastle and took a taxi to the hall to be sure she was there on time. She was thirty minutes early and spent most of them pacing around the block. When she rounded the corner on her final circuit she saw Solly Rosenberg waiting on the steps, his car standing at the kerb.

He glanced at the watch on his wrist. 'Just in time. Michael doesn't like to be kept waiting.' Sophie had spent almost her last penny on a printed silk suit that showed off her small waist and long legs. Her blonde hair shone and she was flushed with excitement. Solly studied her a moment then shook his head in admiration. 'You're a cool one. Any of the other singers I know would have been here half an hour ago.'

Sophie tried to look cool and followed him in. The hall was windowless and empty, a desert of darkened, open floor with black-shadowed corners. The only light illumined the stage at the far end. It was set with music stands and chairs, a drum kit and a piano. A man sat at the keyboard and another stood beside him. Both were in shirtsleeves. They broke off their conversation and turned to watch as Sophie and Solly walked across the desert. Solly said, low voiced, 'Take no notice of *anything* the rest of us do, just do your act.' They halted below the stage and Solly said, 'Morning, Michael. This is Sophie Nightingale.'

Michael Beaumont was the man standing at the piano, tall and slender, with dark hair greying at the temples. Despite this he looked younger than his fifty years. He reached down to shake Sophie's hand. 'Come on up. The band finished rehearsal so I sent them off for a break, but Charlie here will accompany you.' Charlie was the pianist, short and tubby, bald and grinning. Sophie gave him her music and went to the microphone. Michael Beaumont and Solly Rosenberg now sat in chairs below the stage.

Sophie sang three numbers. At the end of the first of them she saw Michael Beaumont lean towards Solly to speak to him. They talked together, not looking at Sophie, as she sang the other songs. She did not falter, remembering Solly's instruction: 'Take no notice . . .' but it required an effort of will because she was certain Beaumont had heard enough and she had not got the job. She was right, up to a point. When she finished he turned to face her, stood up and said, 'Very nice.'

Sophie replied, 'Thank you,' and thought that at least he was polite.

He and Solly joined her on the stage. Sophie saw her agent was smiling and wondered what that meant. Michael Beaumont said, 'We've agreed you should start next Monday at five pounds a week. Is that all right with you?'

Sophie swallowed. All right? A labourer in the yards was getting only half that amount. She squeaked, 'Oh, yes.' Solly winked at her. She floated across the floor as they left.

Outside Solly opened the door of his car and asked, 'Can I drop you anywhere?'

'At the station, please.' Sophie wanted to break the news at home.

Peter Robinson was walking quickly through one of the sheds at Ballantyne's yard when he heard voices coming from behind a stack of crates. He peered behind the stack and saw a group of half a dozen young men using a crate as a table and absorbed in a game of pontoon for ha'pennies. One looked round and asked, 'Want a hand, Peter?'

'No, I'm busy.' Then he turned as he heard a footfall behind him and found himself face to face with Gallagher, McNally scowling at his shoulder.

Gallagher demanded, 'What's going on here?' He tried to move forward to see into the little hiding place but Peter was in his way. There was scrambling behind him and Gallagher swore, 'Get outa my bloody way!' He shoved Peter aside and charged around the corner. The space behind the stack of crates was now deserted. There was no money to be seen but the well-thumbed cards were scattered across the top of the improvised table.

Gallagher swung round on Peter and demanded, 'Who were they?' The gamblers were all known to Peter. Some of them were married with young children. Men were being laid off at Ballantyne's because a buyer had not been found for the ship on the stocks and another contract was not forthcoming. When Peter said nothing Gallagher grinned evilly and said with satisfaction, 'You're covering up for them. Right! You're sacked!'

Peter felt as if he had been kicked in the stomach. He knew there was nothing he could do. He had seen the gamblers, there was no denying that, and McNally was a witness. Nor could he use his knowledge of their virtual murder of Harry Henderson. It was too late for that. Any such accusation would sound like a charge drummed up out of spite because of his sacking.

He was out of a job again.

The next morning was cold but he left the house early, riding the old bicycle he had bought from the money he had made fighting. Now it would be a source of income. He pedalled out to the colliery tip and the day started well when he managed to grasp the tail of a passing lorry with one hand while steering with the other. It towed him along at a spanking twenty miles an hour, almost to the colliery. When he let go of the lorry his hand was numb and blue with the cold.

The colliery tip was where the shale separated from the

coal was dumped. Inevitably some coal, though not much, was left among the shale, and men out of work could comb through with a short coal-rake and ferret out the little black nuggets.

By the late afternoon Peter had filled three sacks. One he slid through the frame of the bike, another he laid across the seat and the third balanced on the handlebars. He started back into the town, pushing the bike and leaning over it to hold all of its precarious load in place. Now he had to find a buyer.

Sophie, wrapped in her warm tweed coat against the cold, had walked out along the sea front for miles, breathing the salt air. She was savouring a few days of relaxation before starting work with the Beaumont band. Or relishing the anticipation, because she was looking forward to the job. A singer with the Beaumont band! She laughed from the sheer joy of it.

She could have caught a tram to take her home but instead diverted to pass by the Ballantyne yard. As she approached the gates she saw the Rolls steal out. Her father was at the wheel, using it this day because the Ford was being serviced. Sophie broke into a light-footed run, waved and shouted, 'Daddy!' Jack stopped and rolled down his window. As she came up she called, 'Can I beg a lift, Daddy?'

He laughed, leaned over and opened the door on the passenger side. Sophie walked around the long bonnet and climbed in. The Rolls moved quietly away, picking up speed.

Peter Robinson watched it go. He was grimy with coaldust that was streaked where little runnels of sweat had trickled down from his hair. He sprawled over his bike, embracing its load. Sophie had run up from behind him, passed within yards, and he had heard every word of her exchange with her father. He had thought she lived and worked at the Ballantyne Hotel. Now he knew differently, and who she was. It took time to sink in, while the Rolls turned a far corner and was lost to his sight. He still stood hunched over the bike. Then, finally, he wiped a hand over his face, smearing sweat and coaldust and heaved the bike forward again.

He could forget her.

At the boxing club that night he hammered away furiously at the bag, venting his anger and hurt. Joe Nolan stood watching with an old friend of his who now said, 'I like the look of that lad, Joe.'

Joe nodded. 'Aye, he's got a lot of talent, a lot of promise. So had you, mind. You were one o' the best around here.' Joe's gaze was still on Peter as he went on, 'He told me tonight he's just got the sack. Any chance of you finding him a job? I can tell you he's a worker.'

The other man rubbed his jaw with a tattooed hand. 'He'd be better off staying ashore. It's a dog's life at sea.'

Tom used his key to let himself in, glancing at his watch as he did so. He was a good half-hour late coming home from the yard because he had stayed to finish a job – not for the first time – and this was the night he usually took Dolly to the cinema. He saw that if he hurried through his tea they would just make the start of the film.

As he stepped into the hall he was confronted by Mrs Simmons, glaring with lips pressed tight. She opened them thinly to order, 'Mr Simmons wants a word with you, young man. In here.' She pointed to the parlour. In fact it was Mrs Simmons who did most of the talking. At the end of it Tom, caught unprepared and shaken, asked, 'Can I talk to Dolly, please?'

'No!' Mrs Simmons snapped. 'You'll not see her or talk to her till you put a ring on her finger or face her in court.'

Tom rapped back angrily, 'There'll be no need for that!' He stalked out of the house and strode down the street. He had to get out and walk, and try to think.

As he came abreast of the shop, open still at this hour, Dagger stepped out of its doorway, but Tom had seen him in the light from the shop and was not taken by surprise this time. He cocked his fists, hungry for revenge. Dagger did the same, ducking and weaving as he threatened, 'I warned you about takin' out my lass. Now you're goin' to get it.'

Tom answered, 'Try if you like. She's not your girl. I asked her and she said she'd finished with you. And – and we're going to get married.'

Dagger stood still. 'I don't believe you.' Then on a note of rising rage, 'You're a bloody liar!'

'I'm not. We're getting married next month.'

Dagger's hand came down as his anger drained away. He said again, 'I don't believe you,' but it was said without conviction. His shoulders slumped.

Tom said, 'I don't care what you think. Now get out of my way,' and he shoved past Dagger and walked on. He strode around the streets for the rest of the night but only reached one decision. He and Matt had always shared secrets and troubles, so he caught an early workmen's train to Sunderland and was outside Younger's garage when Matt, returned from Darlington, turned up for work.

Matt stared at his brother and demanded, 'What are you doing here?' Then, taking in Tom's pale face and dishevelled appearance, Matt said with a brother's candour, 'You're a mess.' But the comment was tinged with concern. He realised this was not the usual neat and cheerful Tom and asked, 'What's wrong?'

Tom told him and Matt listened. He was not used to his brother asking for advice – the boot was usually on the other foot – and would have had difficulty giving it now because these were deep and strange waters to him, too. However, Tom made it easy for him, not asking, 'What should I do?' but rather, 'What would you do?'

Matt could answer that: 'Tell Mother.'

When Tom knocked at the open door of Chrissie's office she looked up and echoed Matt's words, surprised: 'What are you doing here?'

Tom tried to postpone the evil moment. 'I've got the day off.'

Chrissie asked, 'How? What's wrong with you?' People only had days off for sickness or a funeral, and Tom was pallid, with dark circles around his eyes.

'I'm all right. It's just that I've worked a lot of extra time lately.'

Chrissie was not satisfied. She pushed aside the papers on her desk and declared, 'There's something wrong. What is it?'

Tom admitted, 'Well, yes, I wanted to see you and Dad.' He took a breath. 'I'm going to get married.'

'What!' Chrissie stared at him for a long moment, stunned. Then she asked, 'Who do you intend to marry? This is the first I've heard of a girl, let alone an engagement or a wedding!'

Tom laboured through his explanation, Chrissie listened, and when he thought he had finished she said, 'Don't go and tell your father. But tell me *everything* now. From the beginning.'

Tom started again, hesitantly, 'Well, one night we came home from the pictures . . .' Chrissie coaxed him through it, first with the weariness of having heard it all before, then wondering, and finally suspicious.

She asked, 'And how many times have you slept with this girl? Once? When?' Finally Chrissie asked, 'Do you love her?'

Tom shifted awkwardly. 'Well, I'm fond of her. And I want to marry her. I want to do the right thing.'

Chrissie sighed, gathered up her papers and put them away in a drawer. She snatched her coat and handbag from the rack and told Dinsdale Arkley, 'I'm off to Newcastle with Tom. I'll see you tomorrow.'

'Righto, Mrs Ballantyne.'

Chrissie drove the Ford to Newcastle with Tom by her side and followed his directions to the cake shop. She parked a few yards away, out of sight from the shop, and saw there was a small café just a few yards further on. She got out of the car and walked past the shop and saw two girls serving behind the counter with a middle-aged woman. Then she looked in the window of the café, saw that it stayed open late and returned to her seat. 'There's a fair-haired girl and a dark one. Dolly is the fair one?'

'Yes.'

Then they waited.

When the lights of the shop were lowered Chrissie gripped the handle on the door of the Ford. She said, 'You stay here,' and stepped out into the road. The girls came out of the shop, the middle-aged woman following them and switching off the last light.

Chrissie was facing Dolly as the girl turned to walk away, and told her, smiling, 'It's Dolly, isn't it? I'm Tom's mother.' She held out her hand and automatically the girl took it. Chrissie held it, saying, 'I'm just going to have some tea. Come and join me – please? We have a lot to talk about.' And she led Dolly to the café.

Inside she settled the girl at a corner table and sat down opposite her on one of the scarred wooden chairs, pulling off her gloves. A motherly body wearing a wraparound printed cotton apron and slippers, her hair in a net, bustled up and asked, 'What would you like? We do a nice pie and peas.'

Chrissie glanced at Dolly then answered with a smile, 'I think tea for two would be fine.'

'Right y'are, pet.' She retired behind the counter, poured dark brown tea from a large urn into two thick cups and added milk from a jug. She set them on the table and pointed to the bowl already there. 'Help yourself to sugar.'

Chrissie broke the silence she had deliberately allowed to stretch out. 'Thank you.' Then as the motherly body disappeared through a bead curtain into a back room she said, 'Now, you've seen your doctor, of course?' She looked the question and when Dolly nodded, went on, 'And I'm sure he's very good, but—' Chrissie broke off to take her diary from her handbag and open it, poised the pencil. 'Just to be on the safe side I'll make an appointment for you with an obstetrician. He's marvellous, one of the best, and he'll be able to tell us a lot about the baby and whether there might be any problems, how far along it is and when it's due. When is it due, by the way?'

Chrissie wrote down the date as Dolly blurted it out, frightened by this threat of an all-knowing specialist. Chrissie stared at the neat figures, pencil tapping on the oilcloth-covered table, letting the silence hang again. Then she looked up at Dolly and said simply, 'So who is the father? Because it can't be Tom.'

Dolly's head was lowered now, looking at the table. Chrissie prompted, 'Another boyfriend?' After a moment Dolly nodded. Chrissie reached a hand across the table to lift the girl's chin and saw her blinking back tears. Chrissie asked softly, 'Did he deny it? Is that why you said it was Tom?'

Dolly shook her head. 'He doesn't know. It wasn't my idea. My mam said I should get Tom to take me out and I liked him but I was still seeing my proper chap, though Mam had told me to finish with him. She never liked Fred, wouldn't have him in the house. Then, when I found out I was in trouble, Mam called me all kinds of names like she does and frightened me. She said I should let Tom . . . you know?' When Chrissie nodded she went on, 'So I did. He's a nice lad – it was easy to pretend . . . But I knew it was wrong, I knew I was nothing special to him.'

Chrissie said, 'I think you were a bit special to him. He was fond of you.' Then Dolly cried and Chrissie consoled her. She offered to take the girl home. 'I'm going there to collect Tom's things.'

Dolly wiped her eyes and refused. 'I'll walk around for a bit and wait till my dad gets home from work. He'll stick up for me.'

So Chrissie drove to Tom's lodgings, told Mrs Simmons why she had come and the details of her conversation with Dolly. She packed Tom's belongings into his case and carried them out of the house as Dolly's mother shed tears of rage and frustration.

In the Ford, driving home through the rain that was falling now, Chrissie said to Tom, 'You'll have to live at home until we find some new lodgings for you. That means you'll have to travel to work every day, but you'll have to put up with it.' Then she read him a lesson on the facts of life, beginning, 'That girl may have offered herself but that was no reason why you should take advantage of her. She might have been in love with you – though she wasn't – but you certainly were not in love with her . . .' He got out of the car in a chastened mood. Chrissie put her arm around his neck to pull down his head and kiss him. She said, 'Just remember.'

On that rainy evening Matthew Ballantyne met Helen Diaz under Mackie's clock. Their raincoats glistened wetly and Helen wore a kerchief on her head, tied under her chin. She smiled and Matt thought she was very pretty. He ran a hand through his sandy hair, now black with the rain, and told her, 'Mr Younger wants me to go to Darlington again for a month.' He had worked there for three weeks until the regular mechanic returned after illness. Now they wanted Matt again because they had more work than they could handle. 'I don't want to go but I think I should.' He was grateful to George Younger for giving him the job that kept him out of the shipyard, but he did not want to spend a day away from Helen, let alone a month.

Helen squeezed his hand but only answered, as if she had

not heard, 'A chap came to see me at the infirmary today. He was with Dad and Juan out in Spain. He couldn't tell me much because I was at work, but he said he would be in the back room at the Frigate tonight. Come on.' They ran across the road to catch a tram which took them across the bridge to Monkwearmouth, and then walked down Church Street through the rain to the pub.

There were few people in the sitting-room at the back of the Frigate and Helen said quickly, 'There he is.' She led Matt across the room to a little round table. The man sitting there stood up as they approached, and Helen introduced them. 'Hullo, Dick. This is Matt Ballantyne. Matt, this is Dick Webster.'

Dick was lean and thin faced, burned brown by the sun. He held out his left hand – the right was wrapped in a white bandage. He waved it with a sardonic grin. 'Souvenir of sunny Spain. It's good as new but still a bit tender so I don't want it mangled.'

They all sat down around the table and Matt ordered a round of drinks from the barmaid waiting on in the back room. Then Dick Webster explained how he had gone to fight in Spain with the International Brigade, been wounded and then met Helen's father and brother. 'There was a crowd of us wounded being repatriated, waiting in this station for a train. Another one came in filled with a regiment going up the line. Your dad and brother were on it. They looked pretty fit. We got talking because they were just about the only ones on that train who knew any English. When they heard I was coming back to this part of the world for some leave they asked me to look you up.'

Helen asked, 'They hadn't been hurt, then?'

Webster shook his head. 'Not a scratch.' Then he apologised. 'Sorry it took me so long to get to you but I was given the job of trying to recruit a few men – sort of paying for my passage home – so I've spent the last three weeks travelling about the country talking to anybody who would listen.' He grimaced. 'Not with much success though.'

Helen sat back, relieved but still worried, and sipped a little of her lemonade. Matt asked the soldier, 'Did you say "leave"?'

'That's right.'

'You're going back, then?'

'Day after tomorrow.'

'Why?'

Webster had answered the question before and did so now without hesitation. 'Because I believe Franco should be stopped. Because two other dictators, Hitler and Mussolini, are supporting him and using the war to try out tactics and armaments. Because I think we will be at war with Hitler one of these days.' Matt had heard this from his father and refused to accept it but now he sat silent and thoughtful.

Helen didn't care about politics. She asked, trying to imagine a picture into which she could fit her father and brother, 'What is it like out there?'

Webster said cautiously, not wanting to upset her, 'Well, it's a war. Fighting now and again, some people hurt or killed, but a lot of the time it's boring and all the time it's dirty.'

'What was it like when you were wounded?'

Webster shifted awkwardly, not ready for that question. 'Not funny. I was hit by shrapnel. That hurt like hell but the worst part was having to wait God knows how long for an ambulance to take me back to a dressing station and another long wait before anybody had time to see to me. They're very short handed in that line.'

Matt said, mildly curious, 'I've never been to Spain. Is it summer there now?'

Webster grinned and relaxed. 'No, but it's warmer . . .'

They talked about the country and its people and culture for some time. It was only when the conversation ran out that Helen suddenly said into the silence, 'You said you were recruiting.'

'That's right,' and Webster joked, jerking a thumb towards Matt, 'Is that why you brought him along?'

Helen did not laugh. 'Will you take me? I'm a nurse.'

The two men stared at her, then Matt exploded, 'That's silly!'

Webster countered, 'No, it isn't. They could use her.' He addressed Helen: 'You should think hard about it, though. It wouldn't be like a hospital here, it might not be a proper hospital at all. I don't know what you would be paid or even if you would be—'

Helen broke in then, 'I want to go. My father and brother are out there.'

Webster pointed out, 'You probably wouldn't be anywhere near them, would never see them.'

'I know that, but if anything happened to them, if they were hurt and not properly looked after, then I would never forgive myself for not *trying* to be there. Take me.'

Matt, fearing for her, fearing he was going to lose her, argued, 'You can't go out there! You need a passport, a visa—'

Webster cut in, 'I can fix that. There's a Spanish ship in the Tyne. I'm joining her tomorrow night and taking a

273

couple of dozen lads with me. They've all got passports but I reckon the skipper will take another passenger on the quiet for me.'

Matt said again, helplessly, 'You can't go out there on your own.' And so the argument went on.

He returned home at the end of the evening, plodding through the rain with shoulders hunched. The lit windows of the house did nothing to cheer him. He found his parents in the sitting-room and told them with forced brightness, 'I'm off tomorrow. Mr Younger has asked me to go to Darlington again.' They discussed arrangements, his mother ticking off on her fingers what she would pack for him and promising, 'I'll give you a lift as far as the station with your case.'

Matt said, 'I'm going from the garage.'

Chrissie shrugged. 'They're giving you a lift through, then. All right, I'll drop you there.'

His father said, 'It's not the career I had in mind for you but if that is what you want more than anything . . .' He stopped there, hoping for a denial, a change of heart.

But Matt said, 'This is what I want to do.'

Chrissie was just glad he had a job and an aim in life, however transient.

Matt hardly slept at all and when he kissed his mother as she set him down at Younger's garage he could have wept. He trudged in carrying his suitcase, handed in his notice to George Younger and a letter to a mechanic he had worked with, asking him, 'Will you post this on Friday for me?'

Then he jumped on a tram that took him to the station and caught a train to Newcastle.

20

May 1938

The big hands reached out of the alley close by the shipyard gate and grabbed Tom by the lapels of his jacket. They yanked him out of the crowd of men pouring from the yard then hauled him around and banged him against the wall. One or two of the hurrying men stared but went on their way, minding their own business. If two young chaps had a fight that was up to them and common enough. Tom gasped with the shock of it and then began to fight, but even as he pulled back his fist, Dagger, big in overalls that strained across his wide chest, appealed, 'Hang on! I'm not starting owt!' He let go of the jacket and stepped back, then complained, 'I've had a hell of a job finding you. I've waited outside of here all this week and never seen you.'

Tom had worked late every night until now, but he decided that was none of Dagger's business, and kept his fists up. 'I've had enough of you. What do you want, anyway?' he demanded.

Now Dagger looked uncomfortable. He said, 'Dolly came to see me and told me all about it. The bairn she's having isn't yours. It was her mother's idea to say it was. Mrs Simmons doesn't think much o' me 'cause she knew I would get the sack as soon as I finished me time.' That happened to lots of youths when they completed their apprenticeships, there being no work for them and the employers unable to keep them on at a man's wage. 'Dolly's ma thought if she saddled you wi' it the least she would get was a tidy sum to keep her quiet.'

Dagger shook his head and muttered, 'Old bitch.' Then he went on, 'But as I said, it's not yours; it's mine.' He tapped that wide chest with a thick finger. 'I'm the father. And me and Dolly are getting married. I got the sack like Ma Simmons expected but I've got a job down south now. Me and Dolly are getting married and that's where we're going, where that old bitch can't get at us and make trouble.'

He relaxed, at ease now he had had his say. 'So I just wanted to let you know and say I was sorry about that night I got hold o' you. I'd just got the wrong end o' the stick, that's all.' He held out his hand.

Tom shook it. 'Congratulations and best wishes. I hope the two of you will be very happy.'

Dagger grinned. 'I think me and Dolly will be all right. I've got what I want and I won't let old Ma Simmons nor anybody else spoil it for me. Happy? I'm happy now.'

So was Tom, and he whistled all the way back to his new lodgings.

The next Saturday he loitered in the foyer of the Ballantyne Hotel for almost two hours before he could meet Sarah Tennant and say with feigned surprise, 'Hello! On your way out?'

Sarah smiled up at him, genuinely surprised and shy. 'I was just going for a walk.'

'So am I. Thought I'd stretch my legs. I'll keep you

company.' Tom offered his arm and Sarah took it. Chrissie came out of her office just too late to see them go.

She was leaving early but only to go on to Ballantyne's yard where Jack was working in his office. He was clearing his desk before leaving on the sleeper that night, on his way to Holland to try to find a buyer for the *White Elephant*, the unfinished tanker still on the stocks. Chrissie took a picnic meal with her in the Ford and they ate it sitting at Jack's desk. Then she helped him finish his paperwork as night fell.

Jack sat back in his chair, stretched his long arms and said, 'That's the lot.' He glanced at his watch. 'There's not long before my train goes. Just time to go home and pick up my case.' He was silent a moment, watching Chrissie as she shuffled the last sheaf of papers into neat order. She stopped, smiling at him, and the coals burning in the big fireplace settled, crunching and firing sparks up the chimney. Jack said softly, 'I wish I wasn't going.'

Jack and Chrissie drove home to collect Jack's case. The house appeared empty because the staff had long since gone off duty and none of the children was at home. 'Look at the time!' Chrissie said. 'I'll drive you to the station.' As they passed through the hall, she saw a letter lying on the small table there. She picked it up and slipped it into the pocket of her coat and ran out to the car. Jack caught his train but only just, running down the stairs to the platform as the doors banged shut, jumping aboard as the guard's whistle shrilled. Chrissie only had time to kiss him and say breathlessly, 'Take care and good luck.' Then he was carried away and she was left alone.

She had parked the Ford outside the station and as she

came up from the platform she decided to look in at the hotel. Pushing through the swing doors she remembered the letter and took it out. It was only then that she saw it was addressed to 'Mr & Mrs Ballantyne' and the writing was Matt's. She ripped open the envelope as she crossed the foyer and took out the sheet inside. Then she began to read and stopped dead at the door to her office. She whispered, 'Oh my God!'

Chrissie read the letter from her son again and again, not wanting to believe its message but slowly accepting. When she looked up she saw Tom and Sarah Tennant come in through the swing doors. They were laughing together and looking into each other's eyes. Even in her anguish she could see there was something between them.

21

Chrissie got a message to Jack aboard the packet bound for Holland before it sailed from Hull, and he telephoned her from a box on the quayside. She sat at her desk in the silent and darkened hotel, just one light in the foyer and another above her head. She told him, 'Matt has gone to Spain. He left us a letter. You remember Helen Diaz, Sophie's friend? She has gone to be a nurse out there and he says he couldn't let her go alone.' It was a good line and she heard Jack groan. In the background there was the clatter of a winch working and the hooting of a distant siren. She thought, with an oddly detached part of her mind, that it might be the tug come to ease the packet from its berth.

Jack said, 'I'll get the next train home.'

'No!' Chrissie was firm about that. 'You have to go on.' They had to find a buyer for the tanker. Too many livelihoods hung on its sale. 'He said they weren't travelling by conventional routes but going underground, so it would be no good our trying to stop him or even find him.' Then she went on quickly before the inevitable explosion, 'But listen, Jack, don't get the wrong impression. He's not taunting or jeering. He says he's sorry, he loves us . . .' She scanned the letter again for those phrases that had given her some consolation. 'He says, "I had to go with Helen. I think if Dad was in my place, if you had set off for Spain, he would have been with you." You see what I mean, Jack?' Chrissie paused, listening. Another siren wailed on a different note, mournful, lost. She waited while the seconds dragged out.

Then Jack said, 'He has a point. I have to go – she's about to sail. Write to the Foreign Office and ask for their help. The first thing we have to do is find Matt and that girl.' The siren moaned again and he said, 'I've got to hang up.'

'Yes, go, my darling. And don't worry. Matt will be all right.' Then he was gone. She put down the telephone and thought miserably, Don't worry? The first light was showing through the cracks at the sides of the curtains. It was Sunday morning and she laid her head on her hands and prayed.

On Monday Tom returned to Newcastle, to his job and his new lodgings there. Sophie left with the Beaumont Band for a six-month-long tour of South Coast ballrooms, starting in Southampton. She went disbelieving her luck and delighted, but worried for Matt and Helen. Chrissie would not hear of either changing their lives because of Matt's leaving: 'There's nothing you can do.' Then she wondered what she herself could achieve. She wrote to the Foreign Office and they replied that they did not know the whereabouts of either Matt or Helen but they would institute a search. Chrissie waited . . .

Sarah still worked at the club. One night she was washing glasses in the room behind the bar and paused to rest, leaning on the sink. The door leading to the passage was an inch ajar and she heard the murmur of voices, but ignored them, her thoughts elsewhere with Tom Ballantyne. Then she caught the phrase: 'You'll get a fiver to fight him, double if you win

– same as before.' She hesitated then stole over to the door, set her eye to the crack and peered out into the passage.

Peter Robinson appeared to have just come in to train at the gym, shrugging out of his jacket, and found Fannon, grubby raincoat tight over his belly, waiting for him. The bookmaker's pudgy face was sweating and he smiled falsely. Now Peter asked, 'What's McNally getting?'

Fannon assured him, nodding and licking his lips, 'The same, just the same.'

Peter was tempted to refuse, sick of the bloody business, but driven to accept the challenge; he was out of a job and needed the money badly. His mother seemed stronger now from the diet of eggs and milk, and insisted on cooking and doing some light housework. But that diet had to be maintained and the dole would not pay for it. So far Peter had just about made ends meet by selling coal from the colliery tip or the sea shore, or by any other means that came to hand, but it was a precarious living. He said curtly, 'Usual place?'

Fannon shook his head, pendulous cheeks wobbling. 'No, we're changing it. I think we've been there too often and the pollis might get to hear of it. It'll be in Jackie's yard, ten o'clock Wednesday night.'

Peter said, 'Right,' then he pushed past Fannon and walked into the gym, the door slamming shut behind him.

Fannon stayed in the passage, watching him go, then the door of the bar opened and Gallagher came out, McNally on his heels, the pair of them still in dirty overalls. Gallagher asked, 'Did he bite?'

Fannon said unhappily, 'He swallowed it.'

McNally smacked a big fist into the palm of the other hand and gloated, 'Now I'll have him!'

Fannon said, 'Well, you won't want me any more . . .'

But Gallagher seized his arm as he turned to walk away. 'Not now, but you'll be there on the night.' His tone and expression were contemptuous. 'You'll not be much use but we're all in this together.'

They tramped away along the passage, boots drumming on the boards, and left the club. Sarah realised she had been breathing shallowly from fear and now let out a long sigh, but she was not relieved. She knew she had overheard the arrangements for a fight between Peter Robinson and McNally. She also suspected that all was not as it should be, or as Peter believed.

She tried to warn him, left the door to the passage open and intercepted him later when he came out of the gym. She told him what she had heard but Peter shrugged it off. 'Oh, aye, McNally wants his revenge. They're all in the business together; I worked that out after the fight when I beat him. But I can do it again. I'll fight him like I said.'

Sarah was still unhappy. She would have asked Tom for help but he was in Newcastle and she did not have his address there. She wondered, should she tell Mrs Ballantyne? But she was afraid Chrissie might go to the police and Peter would be arrested along with the others, because street-fighting was illegal.

A couple of days later Chrissie chanced to ask her, not for the first time, 'Will you slip your coat on and take these to the post, please, Sarah?' She handed over a sheaf of letters then added another: 'And this is for Sophie.' Sarah memorised the address and wrote to Sophie herself.

On the Monday evening before the fight Peter answered a knock on his kitchen door and found a ten-year-old boy standing there. The urchin, in a ragged jersey, shorts and worn plimsolls, was panting, having run all the way with his message. He asked, 'Are you Peter Robinson, mister?'

'Aye, that's me.'

'Mr Nolan says can you come up to the club for a minute? He says he has some good news for you.'

'Righto.' Peter fumbled for the few coppers in his pocket and gave the boy a halfpenny. 'There y'are. Good lad.'

'Ta, mister.' Then he pattered along the boards of the passage in his holed plimsolls and ran out into the street.

Peter pulled on his jacket and told his invalid mother, knitting in her chair before the fire, 'I'm just going up to the club. Won't be long.'

She smiled at him. 'You get away and enjoy yourself.'

Billy Hackett, nine years old now, sat on a cracket, a little stool, by his mother, his nose in an old comic he had got through a swop. Peter told him, 'You be in bed by the time I get back.'

Billy started to complain, 'Aw, Peter . . .' but he stopped when he caught Peter's eye and said resignedly, 'Aye, I will.'

At the club Peter found Joe Nolan in conversation with the ex-boxer he had talked with some weeks ago, a man in his fifties, his hair still thick but greying, hands gnarled and tattooed. Joe said, 'Aye, aye, Peter. This is Harry Latimer.' The two men shook hands. 'Harry was a handy lad in the ring in his time but he's been going to sea for the past thirty-odd years. He can put you in the way of a job.'

'Can he?' Peter turned to the old seaman eagerly.

Harry Latimer saw that eagerness and warned, 'I'm not offering a soft touch and I'm not recommending it, either. It's hard work and hard lying, but we – that's the ship I'm on now – we're short of a hand. The mate was going to get somebody from the shipping office but I thought o' you. D'ye want the job?'

Peter did not hesitate. 'I'll take it. When do I start?'

Harry said drily, 'I hope you don't regret it.' He warned, 'Just remember it was your choice. You'll be paid by the month and all found so you won't have to bring any grub with you. We're sailing with the tide early Thursday morning. Get yourself aboard some time on Wednesday night. I'll tell the mate you'll be turning out.'

Peter set out for home, happier than he had been for a long time. As he left the club he met Gallagher and McNally. The latter challenged, 'Are you goin' to turn up on Wednesday?' Peter hesitated, thinking that he no longer needed to fight because he had a job. Then he remembered that he would not be paid until the end of the month and he would have to leave some money for his mother and Billy to live on. McNally seized on that hesitation and taunted, 'Turning yellow, are ye?'

'I'll be there.' Peter shoved past so that McNally staggered, swore and lifted a fist. Gallagher grabbed his arm and muttered something and McNally lowered his hands.

That Wednesday started unseasonably warm, leaden clouds hanging low. As the sun set, the first thunder rolled. Peter packed a battered old suitcase he had bought secondhand for a few coppers. It gaped at the corners and was secured with a length of clothes line but it would serve his turn. When it was close to ten and Billy was in bed and asleep, Peter said to his mother, 'I'm just going out for a bit.'

Margaret Hackett sighed. 'I wish you wouldn't, son.'

Peter tried to reassure her. 'I'm only off for a walk.'

'I know all about the fighting.' His mother kept on knitting. 'Folks talk. And I've seen you after you've had a fight. I'm not blind.' Peter had hoped she had not noticed his bruises but now he knew he was wrong. Margaret Hackett pleaded, 'Don't do it, Peter. We'll manage till you get paid at the end o' the month.'

Peter hesitated as the needles click-clicked, not wanting to hurt her, but then he remembered how his mother and Billy would 'manage'. It would have to be by economising on food, because that was where their little money was spent after paying the rent. He said, 'I've got you a bit better. I'm not going to throw that away. You rest easy, Mam. I won't be long.' He kissed her and left.

When the tread of his boots had receded down the passage Margaret Hackett laid down the knitting, fumbled in the pocket of her pinny for her handkerchief and held it to her eyes.

Peter walked down to Jackie's yard, which lay not far from the river. A hawker kept his carts and stabled his horses there. A gate in a high wall stood open and the yard lay beyond. It was flanked by the blank gable ends of terraces of houses and backed by the blind windows of a deserted warehouse. Peter walked in through the gate and on towards where he could see a lamp shedding a pool of light. Halfway across the yard he heard the gate slam shut behind him.

*   *   *

Sophie had only received Sarah Tennant's letter that morning. She caught the first train she could from Southampton but it was past nine in the evening when she reached Sunderland. She took a taxi and rode across the bridge as the thunder rolled. Rain bounced off the road and filled the gutters so they ran like small rivers. 'Wait here!' She left the taxi and ran through the rain into the club as lightning cracked. She sought out Sarah Tennant and demanded, 'Tell me everything they said.' So she heard, word for word, the conversation Sarah had overheard between Fannon, Gallagher and McNally. This only increased the sense of foreboding that had sent her hurrying north and been with her all the way.

Sophie said, 'I don't like the sound of it.'

Sarah agreed simply, 'I think there's badness.'

Sophie remembered the man who had helped her before. 'Is Joe Nolan here tonight?'

'I saw him earlier on, going into the gym.' Then Sarah cried, 'But you can't go in there!'

She was too late. Sophie knew that women, particularly young girls, were barred from the gym but she didn't care. Tom was not with her to go in her stead so she pushed in through the door herself. Joe Nolan stood by the ring, leaning on a corner post and watching two young men sparring. Several others were punching bags or shadow boxing. A chorus of yells greeted her entry and Joe Nolan whirled around, outraged. 'You can't come in here!'

Sophie retorted defiantly, 'I'm already in. And I'm sorry, but I need your help. Will you come outside?'

He was only too willing. He gripped her arm and almost ran her out of the room. In the passage he let her go and complained, 'I don't know what's getting into young lasses these days.'

Sophie ignored that and asked, 'Will you take me to this fight?'

He stared at her, uncomprehending. 'What fight?'

'In Jackie's yard. Between Peter Robinson and McNally.' Then seeing his blank face, Sophie questioned, 'You don't know about it?'

Joe shook his head. 'Not a thing.'

Now Sophie took his arm and urged him towards the door to the street. 'You tell the driver where to find Jackie's yard.'

The taxi drove through streets emptied of people by the rain. The pubs were turning out but there were few customers on a wet midweek night, nearly everyone's money having been spent at the weekend. The scattering of people they saw were hastening home, caps pulled down and collars turned up against the deluge.

As the taxi turned into another street of terraced houses down by the river, Joe muttered, 'Funny. I'd ha' thought there'd ha' been look-outs, even if it is raining.' But no one stood on watch at the street corner. Then he shouted, 'Here it is!' The driver braked outside a closed gate and Joe was out of the taxi in a flash and shoving at the gate.

Sophie joined him and the taxi driver shouted, 'Here! What about my fare?'

Sophie called over her shoulder, 'Just wait there!'

Joe Nolan swore. 'The bloody thing's bolted!' He looked up at the high wall in which the gate was set and the other three blank walls that enclosed the yard. The rain ran down his face and he said uneasily, 'I don't like the look of this.'

Sophie stood back and blinked through the rain at the wall lifting above her. Its top had been sown with broken glass. The driver appeared at her side to argue, 'All very well saying "wait here", but I haven't seen a copper yet and you owe me—'

Sophie shoved her handbag at him. 'Hold that.' As she slipped out of her coat she said to Joe, 'Give me a lift up.' She pushed him so he stood with his back to the wall. 'Hands together.' He linked his fingers and she set her foot in the step thus formed, grabbed at his shoulders and heaved herself up, balanced precariously.

Now she could see over the wall. As she spread her folded coat over the ragged edges of glass she saw carts ranked along each side of the yard, forming an aisle that ran from the gate to a stable building at the back. An oil lamp hung on the wall there and by its dim light she saw an animal with a half-dozen legs, and arms that appeared as fists then disappeared again into the shapeless mass of the body. The animal uttered occasional grunts and snarls of rage, cries of pain, but mostly it was horribly silent but for sobbing breathing. Then she realised she was watching three men locked in close combat.

Sophie moaned softly, fearful, but now the coat was spread and she pulled herself up and over the wall. She lowered herself to the length of her arms and fell the last foot or so. She staggered but did not fall, shoved down her skirt that had worked up around her waist and ran to the gate. There were bolts at top and bottom where it was set into the wall. They were big, and stiff with rust, but she strained at them and drew first one then the other. The gate swung wide as she pulled at it and Joe Nolan set his shoulder to it outside. Then he ran past her and into the yard.

Sophie stumbled, a heel turning under her, but recovered and ran after him. The rain beat on her head and washed down her face into her mouth. A spray of dirty water and mud was kicked up by her running feet to splash up her legs and skirt. Lightning cracked again and in that second-long flash of light she saw Joe Nolan reach the fighting group and clamp his hands on one of them. The raincoated Fannon stood nearby, fat fist raised as if awaiting a chance to strike a blow. Then the light faded as the thunder rolled overhead.

The glow from the oil lamp showed Joe Nolan hauling Gallagher out of the group, and Fannon stepping up behind him. That was when Sophie raced out of the darkness and into Fannon. It was not a scientific attack. She simply ran into his back and he was thrown forward, arms flailing wildly as he tried to keep his balance. Then Sophie shoved him again and he fell.

She turned away from him and saw that Joe Nolan had his hands full with Gallagher, who was the bigger man and twenty years younger. Gallagher had hold of Joe at the length of one arm and was punching at him with the other while all Joe could do was block the blows. Sophie grabbed Gallagher's arm as he pulled his fist back. Startled, he half-turned and Joe broke his grip then got in two punches while Sophie still held that arm. Gallagher went down on one knee, head shaking dazedly. Sophie looked for Peter Robinson and saw him standing with his back to the stable wall. McNally lay at his feet, face down in the mud.

'Are you all right, bonny lass?' Joe Nolan took her arm

and she nodded, breathless. He grinned at her. 'We'll make a boxer out o' you yet. Or a steeplejack, the way you went ower that wall . . .' He shook his head in admiration and went with her as she crossed to Peter's side. His face was bloody and bruised, swollen. He still wore his jacket but that and his shirt were ripped so they hung on him. He was breathing deeply, head back.

Sophie said, 'You're hurt,' and her own hurt was in her voice.

Peter shook his head. 'Not bad. A few bumps, nothing serious, but it was a good job Joe turned up when he did.'

Joe said, 'Not me. Thank the lass here. She brought me and she climbed ower the wall to open the gate. I think if it hadn't been for her you'd ha' been crippled for life.'

Peter squinted at Sophie out of one half-closed eye then seized her arm, urged her aside so Joe could not hear and said bitterly, 'Thank you – Miss Ballantyne.' He saw her flinch as if he had struck her and went on, 'I got the sack from Ballantyne's – Gallagher fixed me – but I was down by the yard one day, pushing a barrow loaded wi' coal, when your father picked you up in the car. I saw you'd been having a bit o' fun wi' me while you waited for some rich feller to come along.'

'*No!*' Sophie tried to slap his face with her free hand. The move so surprised him that he grabbed her wrist only just in time to ward off the blow. He held her for a second, his fingers biting into her, then he saw her wince. The oil lamp's glow glittered on tears in her eyes.

Peter let Sophie go and said, 'Sorry.' And again, 'I'm sorry. I didn't mean to hurt you.'

The tears were not caused by the pain in Sophie's arms. She said, 'I wouldn't hurt you, either. It wasn't like that – what you said. I liked you but I didn't – don't want to be serious. I don't want to marry and I'm not waiting for "some rich feller". I told you once before, I want to be a singer. That first time we met, I couldn't use my real name in that talent contest and – and it just went on from there. I wasn't trying to fool you, just protecting myself.' Now the tears mingled with the rain on her face.

Peter reached out to touch her arm, but gently. 'All right. I got the wrong idea. But you can see how it looked to me.' Sophie nodded and wiped her eyes with the heel of her hand.

Now Joe called, 'Let's get outa here.' Gallagher was on his feet again but holding on to a cart with one hand clutching his middle where Joe had hit him. McNally was sitting up, his head in his hands.

Peter said, 'Just a minute.' He walked past them to where Fannon sat in the mud, wiping it from his face. Peter said, 'It was ten quid if I won.' He held out his hand. Fannon delved into his pocket and then counted the notes into Peter's hand. His fingers closed around them and he looked at Sophie and Joe. 'I'm ready.'

Sophie asked, 'Aren't you going to call for the police?'

Peter shook his head and jerked a thumb at Gallagher and McNally. 'They'll not get me again and I'll keep out o' their way. I've got a job on a ship and I want to get to it tonight. We won't tell the pollis anything.'

The taxi took Joe back to the club, then Sophie told its driver, 'Home, now.' She gave him the address in Ashbrooke

– there was nothing to hide now and he cheered up, confident he would get his fare at last.

Peter protested in whispers, aware of the driver's back in front of him, 'I want to go home!'

Sophie hissed, 'What would your mother think?'

'She knows I fight. She's seen me next day.'

'She hasn't seen you like this.' He had never been beaten so badly as this night. That silenced Peter for a moment and Sophie went on, 'Does she mind you fighting?'

'Aye.' His mother had confirmed her hatred of it less than an hour ago. If she saw him as he was now . . . He did not speak during the rest of the journey.

At the house Sophie paid off the taxi driver and took her overnight case as he handed it to her. 'He'll have something to talk about,' Sophie said drily as he drove away. He was rehearsing his tale already, practising phrases: 'Why, man, she went ower that wall like a monkey . . . been a hell of a fight . . . fellers lying about . . . clothes tore off his back . . . And they finished up in Ashbrooke!'

Peter said, 'I'll carry that,' and took the case.

The house was dark and silent, the staff gone home to bed. None of them lived in now. Sophie had her key and let them in. She found a note on the side table in the hall beside the telephone. Her mother had left it there for any of the staff who had to answer the phone: 'I will be working late at the hotel and staying there tonight, but I will be home for dinner, with Mr Ballantyne, tomorrow night.' Sophie thought that was convenient – and she wanted to talk to her father. She said, 'We have the place to ourselves, so you won't have to meet my mother.' She eyed his battered appearance and grinned. 'Probably just as well.'

She showed him to one of the bathrooms upstairs. 'You can have a bath. I am.' Then she saw his face and burst out laughing. 'Not in here!'

He grinned sheepishly.

Later, he wearing a robe of her father's, she in fresh clothing, Sophie cleaned his cuts and gave him a jacket and shirt. 'They're some of my brother Matt's old clothes. I've put your trousers in front of the kitchen stove to dry. You can have a pair of Matt's socks, too.' She wondered briefly where and how Matt and Helen were and prayed they were safe. She said, 'He wouldn't mind.'

Peter said, 'I didn't expect to see you tonight – or ever again.'

'I couldn't leave you to that.' She was intent on dabbing at a cut on his jaw. 'Can't you give it up?'

'I was going to. This was my last fight. I got the sack from the yard and I took on the fight for the money. My mother's poorly and there's my brother, he's only nine. But I've got a job now.'

Sophie said, 'Keep still. I can't do this while you're talking.' She was seeing him in a different light, but did that change anything?

Peter said, 'Sorry.' He could feel her breath on his cheek, smell her perfume. He felt awkward and rough.

Sophie went on with her task and finally lifted her hand from his face. 'There you are, all done.'

Peter said, 'Thanks for letting me get tidied up here. I wouldn't have wanted to go home as I was.' He hesitated, then explained, 'I don't want to upset my mother. The doctor says her heart is weak.'

Sophie laid a hand on his. 'I'm sorry.'

'Aye, well.' He read the time on the watch on her wrist, the watch that had impressed him. Now he knew how she had been able to afford it. He said, 'I've got to get away. I have to join a ship tonight.'

Sophie telephoned for another taxi while he dressed. When it arrived Peter objected, and she explained, 'Look, Peter, I'm getting the taxi so I can see you off, and I'm giving you a lift. I can afford it. The band pays me five pounds a week.' She admitted that a little guiltily because she knew roughly what he would earn in the yard or at sea.

He stared at her then grinned. 'I wonder if Joe Nolan could teach me to sing.'

So they went out laughing, she with relief.

The taxi took them from the big house in Ashbrooke to the two rooms that were his home, to collect his kit. His mother sat in her armchair by a fire that blazed in the blackleaded grate. The brass fire irons and fender around it all gleamed.

Peter introduced her: 'Mother, this is Sophie, a friend of mine. She's coming down to see me off.'

Margaret Hackett's eyes were on Peter as she started to get up from her chair, and she asked anxiously, 'You're not hurt?'

'No!' Peter laughed, but he was careful to keep his head turned so she would not see one of his eyes was almost shut. 'Some bumps and bruises, that's all. Here you are.' He pressed the roll of pound notes into her hand. 'That will keep you and Billy till I get paid.'

His mother, relieved that he was unhurt, now had time to smile at Sophie. 'That's a bonny lass you are. I'll just put the kettle on for a cup o' tea.'

'Not now, Mother, we haven't time.' Peter put his hands on her shoulders and gently seated her again. 'I've got to get aboard.' He brought his case from the other room and bent to kiss her.

She clung to him. 'I wish you weren't going. Look after yourself, son.'

'Aye, I will.' Peter released her and held open the door for Sophie.

Margaret Hackett wiped at her eyes and called, ''Bye, 'bye, bonny lass. You're always welcome,' and wondered why Peter had never mentioned her before.

Peter swung his suitcase into the waiting cab and said gruffly, 'She doesn't like me going to sea.'

Sophie said, 'Of course she doesn't.' They sat in silence, conscious of the driver as the taxi took them down to the dock. The rain had stopped and the sky was clear but there was a cold wind knifing in up the river from the sea. They left the taxi at the gate and walked down through the dark and deserted dock to where Peter's ship, the SS *Chatterton*, an old steam tramp, lay by the quay.

Sophie stood on the quayside as Peter carried his case up the gangway and then down the ladder into the fo'c'sle. One dim light burned in there showing the bunks set against the steel sides of the ship that glistened with condensation. The air was fetid with a smell of used breath, salt air, sweat and stale beer. All of the bunks seemed to be occupied by blanket-wrapped bodies, some snoring and all asleep bar one.

Harry Latimer lay reading but he looked up as Peter entered and set a finger on the book to mark his place. 'So you decided to take the job.'

'Aye.' Peter glanced round the bunks.

Harry said, 'Take that one.' He nodded towards one empty bunk. 'It belonged to the feller you're replacing.'

Peter dumped his case on the bunk. 'Has he got a better job?'

'Mebbe. He was lost overboard last trip.' Harry went back to his reading, but as Peter set his foot on the ladder again Harry called after him, 'You're a mug. Take the advice of another. You've seen what it's like in the fo'c'sle, so get your tickets to be a mate and get out of it.' Then as Peter stared back at him, Harry closed his book and turned on to his side to sleep.

Peter hurried back across the gangway and Sophie asked, 'Is everything all right?'

'Oh, aye, fine.' It was a job.

They walked back to the gate where the taxi waited. They halted then and there was an awkward silence as he watched her and she looked at the river and the ship, the dock . . . Then she returned his gaze and asked, 'Friends?'

'If you want.' He would settle for that, for now. 'We couldn't be anything else, you being who you are, me what I am.'

'Oh, Peter!' That hurt her. Sophie put her hands on his shoulders to kiss him, and he suffered it, standing straight with his fists, their knuckles skinned, hanging by his side. She released him when the taxi driver coughed ostentatiously. She whispered, 'Come home safe.' Her fingers brushed Peter's cheek lightly then she was in the cab and it was pulling away.

Peter walked back through the darkness of the dock and climbed into his bunk. He lay awake a long time, not because of his strange surroundings but thinking of what Harry Latimer had said. And of Sophie Ballantyne. When he finally slept his mind was made up.

Sophie lay awake a long time, unhappy. Peter had agreed that they would be friends, and that would be ideal, wouldn't it? That was what she had asked for and now she had got it . . .

Jack Ballantyne came home the next day. 'Did you have any luck?' Chrissie kissed him as he stepped off the train on his return from Holland, and guessed the answer before he shook his head.

'No.' Then he asked in his turn as they climbed the stairs from the platform to street level, 'Have you heard anything of Matt?'

'Nothing. Not from the Foreign Office or Matt himself. The post will be difficult, of course, and communications poor because of the war.' She made the excuses as much to reassure herself as for Jack. Then, to cheer him, 'Sophie is home so you'll see her. Just for a few hours, though, because she's going down south again tonight on the sleeper. I wrote and told you about the job she landed down there.'

Jack brightened at news of his daughter; he missed her. He asked, 'How is that working out?'

'She seems to be a success.' Her enthusiasm was assumed; Sophie's choice of career was still not Chrissie's. She was curious: 'I'm not sure why she came up. It was a flying visit. She tells me she arrived yesterday evening but I didn't see her until today. She came home late last night but I'd decided to work late and sleep at the hotel.' Chrissie smiled up at him. 'I get a bit lonely in there on my own. Sophie seemed happy when I saw her this morning but was a bit mysterious, said she would tell us all about it when you got back.'

Sophie did, telling them how she had met Peter, of his fighting to support himself and his family, how he had beaten McNally and the attempt at revenge by Fannon, Gallagher and McNally. Her voice was shaking when she finished, 'They would have beaten him senseless, probably crippled him, if Joe Nolan hadn't stopped them.' She didn't mention her own involvement in the struggle in Jackie's yard.

Sophie travelled south on the sleeper that night.

The following day Jack Ballantyne sacked Gallagher and McNally. He told them, 'You're getting off lightly. I understand the man you attacked does not want to press charges. If this had gone to the law you would have wound up with a jail sentence.'

Outside on the street and storming away from the yard, Gallagher fumed, 'We'll have to get out of this town because we'll get no work in any o' the yards on this river.'

McNally grumbled, 'That's a bloody fact. Where d'ye reckon we should go?'

'I don't know, but there's other places that build ships. Maybe we'll find jobs on the Tyne or the Clyde.' Then he glowered at McNally and asked, 'You know who told him?'

'Aye, that lass of his. The one we've seen with him at the yard. You said she was at the fight the other night.' McNally spat. 'Little bitch.'

Gallagher nodded. 'She's ruined the pair of us, but I'll get her for this. Not now, I'll wait my time, but I'll finish her one day.' And McNally knew he would; he was sworn to vengeance.

*   *   *

Saturday was a lovely early summer's day. Tom and Sarah walked out into the country behind the town, not for the first time. Sarah was laughing, happy. She was growing up, a young woman now. There had been several boys, transient *affaires*, but nothing like this. She had grown up with Tom always in the background, someone who always brought a smile to her face, whom she looked forward to seeing, but her feelings for him now were more intense.

They wandered through the lanes hand in hand, but not aimlessly. When they strolled into the woods they found the clearing they always came to and sat down there. And as the summer minutes ticked lazily by they ran out of conversation and soon were lying in the grass and kissing in the sunshine.

They became conscious of the laughter first of all. There was a track just beyond the trees and shrubs that hid them. The shrill cackling came from there. Then they heard the girls' voices, the words initially inaudible because of their distance, but becoming clearer as the unseen walkers came closer: 'Well, he's getting what he wants.'

The second voice said, 'She threw herself at him! It's one way of going up in the world.'

'On your back for some rich young feller!'

'The boss's son . . .'

The voices faded on their laughter.

For a long minute Sarah was frozen in shock. Then she slowly realised that she did not recognise the voices, had not seen their owners, and they had not recognised her. They had just been two girls out for a walk and gossiping about a third girl. It was nothing to do with her at all.

Was it?

She pushed Tom away and scrambled to her feet. He asked, bewildered, 'What's the matter?' Then he realised: 'You're not upset because of what they said? Sarah, that's rubbish! They weren't talking about us!'

'I know.' Sarah could not look at him, felt ashamed.

'Well, then?'

'It applies, just the same.' Sarah pulled on the cardigan she had carried this far, suddenly feeling cold. 'I just feel dirty. I want to go home.'

She hardly spoke another word until they parted, as usual and at her insistence, when they came in sight of the hotel. Tom said then, 'I'll see you next Saturday.'

'No.' Sarah faced him now, her mind made up. 'It won't work. We can't go out like anybody else, so it's all hole and corner, whispering and scheming. If we did go out like an ordinary couple they would talk behind my back like those two this afternoon.'

'Who would?'

'People.'

'What people?'

'Anyone who knows me – us. People I work with, went to school with.' Sarah was almost in tears.

Tom, exasperated, said, 'Oh, for God's sake!'

The argument wrangled on for another minute until Sarah ended it: 'Please don't speak to me again.' Tom grabbed at her arm but she pulled away and ran.

Tom found his father waiting for him when he got home. Jack Ballantyne grinned at him and asked, 'Remember I said I would send you to America for a few months to study working practices over there? Well, it's all come together.

The yard in Brooklyn will take you, your boss in Newcastle has agreed and I've got you a passage out of Southampton on Monday.'

So Tom spent the next twenty-four hours packing and putting his affairs in order, but the one affair he most desperately wanted to see to he had to leave undone. He tried several times to speak to Sarah but she was always working in a group and contrived not to be parted from it. He was still thinking of her when he sailed from Southampton on the Monday. Sarah wept at the same time but told herself it was all for the best.

A week later a letter arrived from Matt. Over the next four months there were three more. They bore no address but said he and Helen were safe and well and nowhere near the fighting. Chrissie and Jack heard this with relief and used it as evidence to console each other, but each privately wondered if Matt was telling the whole truth.

Early in October of 1938 Jack left again, this time for Greece, still seeking a buyer for the *White Elephant*. He was desperate now, because if no one purchased the tanker in the next few weeks he would have to lay off nearly all the men in the yard. Chrissie lay alone in her bed and worried over Jack – and Matt and Helen Diaz, her son and a girl she had virtually adopted over the past year. Helen had been a frequent visitor to the Ballantyne house. Chrissie told herself the two young people would come back to her, but she still cried.

She thought she had no reason to worry over Tom. The letters he wrote every week were full of his doings in America and what he was learning. In fact he was miserable. He wrote frequently to Sarah but she did not reply. Chrissie knew nothing of this, though she had noticed that Sarah was quieter now.

Matt and Helen filled Chrissie's mind and she wondered, where were they now?

She would soon have news.

And Sarah kept Tom's letters.

22

October 1938

Chrissie took note of the advertisement as she walked past the Havelock Cinema, because it was for 'A Tourville Film', and the director was shown as Phillip Massingham. She was glad to see that Phillip was doing so well, and wrily amused that Randolph Tourville, the oil multimillionaire, was also making money from his sideline, the financing of motion pictures. She remembered Tourville very well: he was a hard man to forget, though she had tried. She thought about him for a long time that afternoon as she sat at her desk in the hotel, and hesitated still longer.

At one point, restless and undecided, tempted but nervous, she left her office to walk around the hotel. Ostensibly she was carrying out a routine inspection, but in reality her thoughts were elsewhere. She became aware of a kindred spirit: Sarah Tennant stood by a window, staring out at a darkening sky that threatened rain and lost in thought. It was so unusual for the normally busy and energetic Sarah, that Chrissie paused and delayed further – with relief – the decision that was troubling her mind. She asked, 'Penny for them?'

Sarah started, turned to face her, and tried to smile, failing. 'Sorry. They're not worth a penny.'

Chrissie saw the girl was unhappy and probed, teasing, 'Dreaming about the boyfriend?' And if there wasn't a boyfriend the question might still bring the answer.

Sarah blushed and admitted in her confusion, 'Well . . .' She stopped there and Chrissie thought, So there is a boy. She had not known of one. Sarah went on, 'Not exactly.'

Chrissie smiled. 'What does that mean?'

Sarah said carefully, wanting to be truthful but yet give nothing away, 'I – was – going out with a chap but then I broke it off because it wasn't a good idea.'

'Oh?' Chrissie wondered, then asked, 'Was he married?'

'No!' Sarah shook her head, shocked. 'No, but—' She hesitated again.

A relieved Chrissie prompted, 'But?'

'Well, he's – his family are well off . . . very well off. So I don't think it would work.'

'Ah!' This was a situation Chrissie knew something about. She wondered who the young man might be. Probably a guest in the hotel? But his identity did not matter. Sarah was looking miserable, and Chrissie put her arm around the girl. 'I won't tell you that money and background don't make any difference because it wouldn't be true. But if love's there and you come to each other as equals in the eyes of both of you, then you can manage all the other problems.'

Sarah was not consoled. 'Oh, I know that, but it's what people would say.' And she quoted bitterly, mimicking, '"It's one way of going up in the world. On your back for some rich young feller."'

Chrissie realised that these were words Sarah had over-heard, and saw the girl's embarrassment as she repeated them. Chrissie said, 'There's an old saying, "Don't believe what you hear, only what you see!" Some people try to make mischief out of envy or just badness. But if he is the man for you, don't let those others spoil it for you. Just be sure of him. And let him be sure of you.'

Sarah was still for a moment, then she smiled and nodded. Chrissie gave her a squeeze and a pat. 'Go on now.' She watched the girl walk away and recited in her mind again, 'You've got to be sure of him.' Her mind made up, she walked quickly back to her office and as the first drops of rain tapped against the windows, she telephoned long distance to Randolph Tourville's London office.

She had to wait for the call to come through, of course, and changed her mind twice while waiting, but then his secretary told her, 'Mr Tourville has travelled north to carry out an engagement this evening.'

'When will he be back?'

'Not for some days, madam. He is going abroad, sailing from Newcastle.'

Newcastle? Chrissie asked, 'Can I get in touch with him there?'

'Well, madam, I'm afraid . . .'

'Of course, I understand, you have your instructions, but thank you for the help you have given me.' It was not difficult to find out which ships were to sail from the Tyne in the next twenty-four hours, and while there were several, only one was a passenger vessel. And there were only two or three hotels at which Tourville might stay. She rang one: 'I wish to speak to Mr Tourville, please.'

The clerk at the other end of the line answered, 'Mr Tourville has not yet booked in, madam, but we expect him on the next train from London. Can I give him a message?'

'No, I'll telephone later.' She had already decided not to wait for that.

She drove home through heavy rain and high winds, bathed and dressed carefully in an evening dress that left her shoulders bare. Jack was expected home from Greece that evening. She left a note for him, saying that she would not be home until late. She felt an awful sense of desertion but she got into the Ford and drove through the storm to Newcastle.

At the Newcastle hotel the clerk on reception told her Randolph Tourville had booked in and had gone out for the evening. Chrissie dined in the hotel but with little appetite. Afterwards she settled in the lounge with coffee, choosing a place from which she could see anyone entering the hotel. Then she waited with increasing nervousness.

It was close to ten when he came, pushing through the swing doors and shedding his overcoat, shaking the rain from it – the storm was still at its height. His dinner jacket fitted smoothly on his wide shoulders and deep chest, and the starched white shirt-front showed off his tan. As he sauntered across the foyer Chrissie rose from her chair and went slowly to meet him. When he turned from the desk with his key he found her in front of him. He blinked in surprise for a second but then said, 'Chrissie, isn't it?' His eyes raked her in one quick head-to-foot glance then returned to her face. He said approvingly, 'I'm very pleased to see you.'

Chrissie said huskily, 'And I, you.'

'A fortunate coincidence, meeting you here?' His raised brows made it a question and expressed his doubt.

'No, I came to see you,' Chrissie admitted. 'Can we talk? In private?'

'Of course.' He took her arm and steered her towards the lift. 'Talk all night if you like. I don't sail until midday.' Chrissie knew that but kept silent. Tourville told the boy in buttoned uniform operating the lift, 'First floor, please.' Then to Chrissie, 'I've been dining with a few local businessmen but tomorrow I'm going to Germany.' Chrissie knew that, too, as she had known the time of sailing of the only passenger vessel. He went on, 'I have a number of irons in the fire over there. The people in Hamburg want to sell me a tanker, but our fleet has enough ships for the time being.' Chrissie had not known that and her heart lurched.

As they stepped out of the lift he said, 'This way.' He put a hand on her waist to turn her towards his room. Chrissie felt its pressure through the thin dress. Then it was gone and he asked, 'How is the hotel business?'

'We're surviving.'

He agreed, 'Yes, and very well, in spite of the fire.'

'You heard about that?' Chrissie was surprised.

'And how quickly you opened up again. Incredible. But why haven't you rebuilt on the original site? The place you have now is fine as a stopgap, but not longterm. You need to purpose-build on the old site.' Now Chrissie wondered how much this man knew about her.

'Scotch?' They were in his suite and he was holding up the bottle for her to see. The connecting door was open and she could see the big double bed, the sheet turned down. Rain pattered on the window but the room was warm.

307

'Please.' It would give her courage. Chrissie sat down on the couch where he pointed and slid the stole from her shoulders, laid it aside.

Tourville brought the drinks over and set them on the low table, sat beside her on the couch. He lifted his glass and toasted, 'To us. Now . . .?' He waited.

Chrissie told him about the *White Elephant*, how Ballantyne's was desperate to find a buyer, that without a buyer the yard would close.

Tourville smiled showing strong, white teeth. 'I hope you aren't hoping to sell me a tanker. I told you on the way up here that the fleet needs no more ships at present.'

Chrissie pleaded passionately, 'But you would be giving work to your own countrymen if you bought from Ballantyne's!' Then she pointed out, 'And the last time I asked you for a favour it proved profitable to you. I'm talking about the films made by Phillip Massingham.' She knew that she was flushed, saw the admiration in his eyes and felt the heat in her face.

Tourville said softly, 'I am not persuaded.'

Chrissie sat still, not avoiding his gaze. As the silence dragged out they could hear the howl of the gale outside, the rattle of the rain on the windows, but they sat in a warm, quiet little world. Chrissie swallowed the last of the whisky in her glass and drew a breath . . .

Sophie Ballantyne waited on the quay at Sunderland as the gale lashed the town. She was one of a small group of women in raincoats or shawls, all looking out to the mouth of the river, their eyes blinking against the rain as the wind drove it into their faces. They were all waiting for one ship, the SS *Chatterton*, because their men were aboard her. One old woman, her grey hair sticking damply to her forehead where it escaped from under the rain-sodden shawl, said, 'My Joe's been a bad bugger, drunk his pay more times than I've seen it, but I wouldn't like to lose him at sea.'

Sophie stared out at the huge, wild, white-topped breakers bursting over the pier, and shivered.

The ship, an old steam tramp with one tall funnel, came in over the bar in a welter of foam. She tied up at the quay, and finally Peter Robinson walked down the gangway of the *Chatterton* with the rest of her crew. Sophie had not seen him for five months and she was breathless with excitement.

Peter stared at her in delighted surprise. 'Hullo!' He had thought of her all the time he was away but never expected to see her waiting on the quay. Then he remembered that she was still Jack Ballantyne's daughter. He went on in a more neutral tone, 'How did you know I was coming in tonight?'

'I came home for a day or two and just happened to hear.' In fact she studied Lloyd's list every day to follow the progress of his ship and had travelled north from Bournemouth when she saw the *Chatterton* was due to dock that night.

They took a tram to his home, talking in friendly fashion of ordinary things. As Peter pushed the door open and entered the kitchen his mother put her arms around him and young Billy Hackett grabbed his hand. They all laughed together and there were tears on Margaret Hackett's cheeks. Excitement and joy had given her a little colour, belying her fragile health. She held Peter out at arm's length and said happily, 'By, it's grand having you home! I got a ham shank and I've made some broth. Sit down, the pair o' you.'

So Sophie shared the meal and afterwards Peter went with her, hurrying, to catch the last tram. Sophie squeezed his hand. 'I was pleased to see you.'

Peter answered, 'It was lucky you were here. I won't be home for long. The *Chatterton* has paid off.'

Sophie laughed. 'So you'll be throwing your money around.' Sailors were notoriously open handed with their pay. Then she realised what his words also meant and said with dismay, 'You're out of a job, then?'

Peter shrugged. 'I'll have to look for another ship. And I won't be tossing my money away. I have to buy some books. One of the mates lent me his but I want my own for the next trip.'

'Books? What for?'

So he told her how Harry Latimer had urged him, 'Get your tickets to be a mate . . .'

Sophie had to jump on the tram then as the conductor yanked on the bell cord. She called down from the platform to Peter, 'I'll drop you a line with my address! Let me know what ship you get!' so leaving him no chance to argue or refuse. She waved to him as the tram pulled away and he lifted a hand in reply. But Peter, after that first moment of pleased surprise, had kept his distance – and kept her at a distance.

When Sophie arrived home she found only a note left by her mother for her father. She concluded that he must be coming home and was glad, but felt unhappy about Peter.

Jack arrived in a taxi at midnight, returning from a fruitless visit to Greece. He read the note that Chrissie had left for him, saying that she would not be home until late. He was disappointed but told himself there had to be a good reason. He mixed a stiff whisky and took it up to bed. Tomorrow he would continue the fight to save the Ballantyne yard. He was not finished yet.

Chrissie returned at one in the morning. The storm had passed and the night sky was clear and sprinkled with stars. She saw Jack's overcoat tossed over the back of a chair in the hall and the note she had left for him lying opened on the table. She kicked off her shoes and ran lightly upstairs. In the bedroom she undressed without putting on the light and slipped into bed with the sleeping Jack. Then she woke him.

Chrissie had asked Randolph Tourville, 'Did you hear Chamberlain's agreement with Hitler?'

He had, as had everyone. 'Promising "peace in our time".'

Chrissie shook her head. 'I don't believe it. Hitler won't stop now. He moved into the Rhineland, then Austria, now he has Czechoslovakia. He intends to rule Europe. There's a war coming and we'll need ships. Remember 1917 when the U-boats nearly starved us into surrender? Your oil won't be worth a penny if you haven't ships to move it.'

Tourville said drily, 'I know all this, and we have a programme to buy a new ship every year for the next five years. There's one building on the Tyne now.'

Chrissie said, 'I think Hitler has a programme, too – and you should speed up yours. Buy another tanker this year.' Then as he stared at her, impressed by her grasp of world politics, she pressed him, 'Suppose Hitler went to war in the next twelve months?'

Tourville said slowly, 'It is possible.' He was silent a long time, then said, 'I'm the boss but I have a board of directors representing a hell of a lot of shareholders. That board doesn't want to spend the money now.'

'Tell them if they don't spend it now they won't have it for long.'

Tourville had grinned at her then. 'I'll do it.' They had gone on to discuss details.

Tourville had also volunteered to put up the money for the rebuilding of the original Railway Hotel: 'I think you're a good investment, Mrs Ballantyne.' He went on wrily, 'This has not been the evening I expected. You're an honest woman and Jack is a lucky man.'

Chrissie had told him the simple truth that had given her the confidence to seek him out: 'Jack is the only man for me, always was and always will be.' As she had told young Sarah Tennant: 'Be sure of your man. And let him be sure of you.'

So that Saturday morning Chrissie and Jack shared a cheerful breakfast with a subdued Sophie. Jack was eager to go to the yard and break the news that the *White Elephant* was sold and work could start again, while Chrissie had similar good tidings for the hotel. Then the post arrived. One of the letters was in a buff envelope that bore the words: 'On His Majesty's Service'. All three guessed what it contained. Jack opened it, scanned its contents quickly then laughed at Chrissie and Sophie. 'They've found Matt and Helen!'

It was agreed reluctantly by both Chrissie and Jack that

he should stay to work in the yard now it was active again and also to handle the negotiations with Tourville. Chrissie would go to Spain.

When Jack dropped her from the Ford she almost ran into the hotel. During the drive into town she had planned what she had to do, so as she hastened across the foyer she called to Dinsdale Arkley: 'I need to see you now, please!'

He came limping into her office and Chrissie remembered how she had first taken him on when he came home from the war, invalided out of the Army after losing a leg. That had been twenty years ago and she congratulated herself now on a wise decision taken then, because she could leave the management of the hotel in safe hands. 'I have to go away for two or three weeks, maybe longer, and you'll be in charge . . .' Then she went into details of what she wanted done in her absence and Arkley wrote them down in his notebook.

They had been at it ten minutes when Mrs Featherstone, the housekeeper, tapped at the open door. Normally cheery and bustling, she was now tearful and explained, 'I have to give me notice in, Mrs Ballantyne.' Her husband had been given a better-paid job in the South and they were moving in a week's time. Chrissie consoled her and reassured her when she wailed, 'You've always been good to me, Mrs Ballantyne, and I don't like letting you down all of a sudden like this.'

Chrissie said, 'We don't want to lose you, but you and Mr Featherstone have to take this opportunity. We'll just have to manage.'

When Chrissie had finished with Arkley she spent the morning clearing her desk and planning her trip with a railway timetable and numerous telephone calls to shipping agents. Then, with all settled save one pleasurable duty, she ate a late lunch in the hotel dining-room, her mind still churning with details of times and routes.

Afterwards she sought out Sarah Tennant and told her, 'Mrs Featherstone is leaving and I want you to take over her job . . .' Sarah listened to her open mouthed, delighted and excited at the promotion, as Chrissie explained, 'I have to go to Spain. We've heard where Matt and Helen are.' Then she remembered another letter received that morning and mentioned its news as she turned away, her thoughts already running ahead to her trip. 'And Tom will be home in a week or so.'

Sarah said, 'Oh! That will be nice.' She tried to keep her voice neutral as Chrissie walked away, told herself it did not matter to her when Tom came home. But in truth she did not know if she was thrilled or frightened.

Sophie accompanied her mother as far as London. They parted there, Sophie to go back to the Beaumont Band on the South Coast, Chrissie to take the cross-Channel packet from Dover. Sophie hugged her mother. 'Take care, Mummy. Bring them back.'

'I will.' Chrissie prayed that she could.

And so they parted.

Tom Ballantyne came home a week later on the sleeper, and his father met him at the station. Even in his preoccupation, Tom noticed the change in his father: the worry lines smoothed out, the old familiar grin back on his face. Tom was glad to see him and to hear the news that had wrought the transformation, but after the first warmth of their meeting

Tom was impatient to be away. As the porter put his suitcases into the taxi Tom asked his father, 'Can I see you at home later? I have some . . . things to clear up.'

Jack mentally raised his eyebrows but only said, 'That's fine.'

Tom crossed the road to the Ballantyne Hotel and asked the receptionist, 'Where is Sarah Tennant, please?'

'Why, Mr Ballantyne! It's lovely to see you again. Your mother did say you were coming home.' The girl remembered his question and finished, 'I think she's on the first floor. I saw her go up—' But she stopped there because Tom was already taking the stairs three at a time. He found Sarah in the corridor, giving instruction to a pair of new chambermaids, girls a year older then herself. Because of them she did not try to evade Tom when she saw him coming, presuming he would pass her by in that company. She was wrong.

Tom smiled at the two girls and nodded. 'Excuse us.' He took Sarah's arm and she found herself steered through the open door of an empty room. Then the door closed behind them.

'Tom!' She knew the girls would be giggling, couldn't hear them but could picture it. Her anger rising, she demanded formally, 'What do you think you're doing, Mr Ballantyne?'

'I'm trying to talk to you because you didn't answer my letters. No!' As she started towards the door he stepped in front of it so that she almost walked into him. Then as she drew a breath he urged, 'What are you afraid of? Me?'

Faced with the direct question and with him hanging over her, Sarah could only admit, 'No. I . . .'

Tom went on quickly, 'So just listen for a minute. Hear me out because I won't let you go till you do.'

Sarah saw that he meant it, and realised they stood very close together. She took a half pace back so she could breathe. 'Well?'

Tom was tongue-tied at first, fumbling at how to start. 'I know what upset you that day, what you heard those girls say, but it wasn't – isn't true. I knew somebody like that. She wanted to marry the boss's son, though it was her mother who put her up to it. But it's not like that with you and you're not like her. I was talking to a friend – ' He paused on the word for a second. Dagger a friend? Well, he was now. Tom went on, 'This friend of mine was about to get married. He was having to leave home and go down south to find work but he was taking this girl with him and he said he was happy. He'd got all he wanted and he didn't care about anything else.' He stopped to draw breath, then asked, 'See?'

Sarah said hesitantly, 'You mean, no more hiding? Out in the open like ordinary people?'

'We *are* ordinary people and we ought to give ourselves a chance and never mind what anybody says.'

Sarah remembered that his mother had said something like that, but her gaze slid to the door, remembering the girls giggling outside. 'I don't think it will be as simple as that.'

Tom admitted, 'No, I don't suppose it will.'

'But you don't care.'

'No.'

So long as he got what he wanted. Now Sarah recalled that Chrissie had also said, 'Just be sure of him.'

Sarah took a half pace forward into his arms.

*   *   *

Sophie travelled north again. She had written Peter a short letter, to give him her address, that was friendly and only mildly affectionate. She tore up a half-dozen drafts before posting the final copy. He had read it over and over. When Sophie had returned to her lodgings one evening, after singing at a *thé dansant*, she found his letter awaiting her. He had found another ship. She was on a train early the next morning and at eight that night she went with him as he went to join the *Florrie Dawe*.

As the tram clanked and swayed across the bridge he said drily, 'She's not really new. In fact she's older than me by ten years, but she'll do.'

Harry Latimer had told him, as they stood in the shipping office in Tatham Street, 'It's her or nothing. We ship in her or we stay on the dole.' So Peter had signed on.

Sophie asked, 'Is she a good ship?'

'She was still afloat the last time I saw her.' Peter grinned at her. He did not tell her of Harry Latimer's doubts: 'She's been laid up for years and she's rusted to hell, had her hull repaired with cement.'

Peter had questioned, disbelieving, '*Cement?*'

'Aye.' Harry explained, 'It's a cheap way of curing leaky seams and rivets. You get a carpenter to make a wooden box to fit over that section of the hull then you fill it with cement.' While Peter digested this, Harry added, 'And her skipper is a wrong 'un. He's lucky he hasn't lost his ticket afore now. The mates aren't any better.' But as Harry had said, it was sign on in her or go on the dole.

Peter told Sophie now, 'She's a ship and she'll do.'

So when Sophie stood on the quayside, cold in a biting

wind, and watched him walk up the gangway she had no more worries than any woman seeing her man off to sea. Except that he had not kissed her. She took another tram to the sea front and watched his ship steam out between the piers and fade into the night.

As the sleeper took her back to the South Coast that night she prayed that he would come back safely – and for her mother and her mission.

23

Helen Diaz looked up from stooping over the wounded man in the cot. The rifle-fire seemed to rattle all around the big old house that was serving as a forward field hospital in this Catalonian village. She thought she caught the odour of the firing, a whiff of cordite mingling with the hospital smell of disinfectant and the pungent cigarette smoke of the patients. When she, Matt and the rest of the medical team first arrived at the house, the front line had been five miles away at Gandesa. It was closer now.

They had found the house without working electricity or running water. They had all – doctors, nurses, orderlies, ambulance drivers – laboured to turn it into a forward field hospital and succeeded. It was far from perfect but it worked. The operating theatre was below on the ground floor, in what had originally been the slaughter house, because it had a concrete floor which was easily washed down. The handbasins for washing, and the steriliser, stood in one corner with the water tank outside. The ambulance drivers, Matt among them, had to keep the tank filled. Water was brought up to the house in tanks on the backs of trucks. They had become used to hard conditions. Before they came to the house they had slept in the open and Helen had hated the scampering of the rats. Now she had a tiny cupboard of a room she shared with a Spanish nurse.

She had finished replacing the Spanish soldier's dressing and now she patted his shoulder, her smile crinkling the corners of her dark eyes. He looked up at her apathetically, exhausted. He was one of six men on the narrow cots crowded into the room. The few small, weak lightbulbs made the ward a place of shadows. Helen was the only nurse, in her white uniform and a white cap that covered what was left of the glossy, black hair she had cut short soon after arriving in Spain.

She washed her hands in a dented tin bowl, dried them on a scrap of towel then moved to the window and looked round the edge of the black-out curtain. The sun had set, and fat-bellied black clouds hung low overhead. She could just make out the village square below, its dirt surface churned into mud by soldiers' boots. The rain fell steadily, dripped from the eaves of the houses and the blackened branches of the trees. The road that ran through the village passed across the far end of the square and a constant stream of men trudged along it. Then, as she watched, the men scattered and a battery of guns galloped through. The horses tossed their heads, the men on their backs lashing them on with whips, while the guns bounced on their iron wheels and hurled up sprays of mud. When the fourth and last gun passed the men returned to the road and trudged on.

'That's very heavy firing.' Luis Zamora, the young doctor, spoke behind Helen. As she turned to face him he said, 'And those soldiers have been going through for the past hour. I'm going to find out what's happening. Are you all right here?'

'I can manage,' she said with confidence: Helen had learnt a lot in a very short time since she came to Spain.

Luis smiled. He had come to rely a great deal on this girl. He left her now and Helen heard him tramping down the stairs. She had a sense of unease born of her experience since she came to Spain. It had taught her that anything unusual might spell danger. In recent months she had seen enough of death and destruction, pain and grief. But duty called and she went to another man and started replacing the dressing applied hastily in the field.

Luis returned ten minutes later, breathless from running up the stairs. He panted, 'It's a retreat! I spoke to an officer. He wouldn't stop but he told me that Franco's men attacked under cover of an artillery barrage. The line held for an hour or two but then it broke. He said their troops were right behind him. You've got to get out. Grab what things you can but be ready to move in five minutes. I'm going to tell the others.' Then he was gone.

Helen ran to her little room, tore off the white uniform and pulled on the clothes she wore off-duty: a soldier's trousers, shirt and boots. With her short hair she looked like one of the troops now. She picked up her pack and threw some clothes into it. As she stepped into the corridor again she heard shouting in the hall below, echoing up the stairwell.

When she reached the head of the stairs she saw that the hall, lit by a single swinging bulb, was filled with soldiers, but they were strangers in strange uniforms. The little corporal who had sat at the table in the hall that was the reception area was being hustled out of the door into the street. Luis Zamora in his white coat stood with his back to the wall and a rifle muzzle was pointed at his chest.

One man, an officer from the insignia on his tunic, looked up the stairs and saw Helen. He shouted at her to come down and pointed his pistol at her. She descended the stairs, realising that she was now a prisoner, but in her shock and fear her first thought was for Matt. It seemed he had rarely left her side since they had sailed for Spain. He was always there, remonstrating, arguing, outraged or admiring, repairing the ambulance, making her a bed, putting up her tent, cleaning her shoes, teaching her how to drive. She made sure that he ate, and drove while he slept, looked for him when her nursing duties were done, delighted in arguing with him. They were a smooth-working, mostly happy team. Now she worried: was he safe?

Matthew Ballantyne, his tall body folded into the bucket seat, clung to the wheel of the ambulance as it rocked slowly along the rutted road. The night was dark, the sky overcast and rain washed across the windscreen as the wipers flapped. He rubbed a hand over his sandy hair, cropped to a rusty stubble now, and blinked tired eyes as he strained to pierce the gloom. The hooded headlamps of the ambulance shed barely enough light to illumine the road for a few yards ahead. It was no more than an elderly Fiat van, roughly converted to carry stretchers and kept running only by Matt's constant attention.

He nursed the van now, well aware of its age and fragility. He was eager to return to the forward hospital which was both home and base for himself and Helen. He had left it that morning to carry some wounded to a base hospital far in the rear. Helen Diaz had been safe and well when he left her but he was worried about her now. He had worried about her since they crossed the border into Spain and shells had fallen close to their hospital in the past few days.

The ambulance bounced into and out of a pothole and he twisted the wheel to hold it on course as it tried to swerve off the road. For a second it snaked back and forth, skidding across the muddy surface, taking up all of the road. As it straightened under his steering he breathed thanks that the road was empty.

Earlier he had passed a stream of men trudging in the opposite direction. He had thought they were returning from the front line. They had stared up at him, eyes glitteri~ pale smudges of faces as they were caught in the light all looked startled by his sudden appearance and gap the ambulance swayed past. Once he had to pull o. road to let a battery of guns canter by, the drivers flog 3 the weary horses that pulled the guns. Afterwards the road had been empty for a half-hour or so as the ambulance crept on, but just a few minutes ago he had passed a group who seemed to be digging a trench by the side of the road. They had scattered when he drove down on them, looming out of the rain and darkness. One of them had fired on him as he rolled on down the road, and automatically he ducked and cursed them but without surprise. Men became jumpy and trigger happy when close to the front line. That was another thing he had learned in this Spanish war.

He was almost there now and could see what had once been the outlying buildings of the village. The place had been fought over before and shelling had reduced a lot of it to heaps of rubble. There were people on the road again, soldiers of course because the villagers had left to escape the fighting. Matt could understand that. He had seen what the fighting did to combatants and neutrals, innocent bystanders alike. He had pictures burnt into his mind that he would never expunge.

Now he turned into the little square, and there stood the house in the corner that had belonged to some big landowner but was now the hospital. He was looking for Helen Diaz already as he extinguished the lights of the ambulance, braked it to a halt in front of the house and switched off the ignition. It was only then that he saw the flag hanging above the door. It had not hung there when he left that morning. It was the banner of Franco's Fascist army.

He sat frozen by shock in the seat of the ambulance. Now he remembered that his fellow Republican soldiers he had left in the village that morning had looked different, although they had worn the usual mixture of khaki uniforms with miscellaneous items of civilian clothing such as leather or sheepskin jackets, or blankets serving as capes. Those in the village now wore different helmets, the coal-scuttle type like those of the German army. Now he understood why the earlier traffic on the road had all been one way and why the men had been startled by his appearance. They had thought he was mad to be heading in that direction because they knew he was driving into the arms of the enemy.

Where was Helen? He had last seen her in the hospital. Was she still there? He decided that was the first place to look. He swallowed. There was no sentry posted at the door though there might be one inside. Soldiers occasionally came out or went in, each time letting out a blink of light as they pushed aside the black-out curtain hung inside the doors. The darkness was on his side.

He got down from the ambulance and walked steadily to the street that ran down the side of the building. He was tensed, ready for the first shout if someone challenged him as an enemy, ready to run, though he did not know where. But no one yelled at him to stop, and here was the side gate. The house was built in a square and this gate opened on to a passage which ran through the ground floor of the house to the courtyard within. The gate was wrought iron and he could see through its ornate twinings. The passage inside was empty.

He pushed open the gate and walked through the passage, his boot heels clicking on the paving, echoing under the arched roof of the passage. The courtyard was also paved, with tall shrubs standing like sentries in the darkness. Matt walked around the courtyard, peeping through cracks at the sides of windows where the black-out curtains did not quite cover, looking into the wards on the ground floor. He did not see Helen.

He stopped at a door that led to the front of the house and the stairs to the upper floor. Beyond that door would be light, no darkness to hide him. Only his tunic with its Red Cross armband would immediately identify him as serving in the Republican Army, so he pulled it off and looked for somewhere to hide it. Then he saw the box standing to one side of the door. It was a crate about a cubic foot in size with a rope carrying-handle on each of two sides. He folded the tunic so only its inside showed, laid it on the top of the crate then picked that up by its handles, lifting it to chest height. He jammed his jaw down on the tunic to hold it in place, and that also served to hide his face to some extent. He had soon learned that his pale blue eyes were an oddity in Spain, bound to make him noticeable, and he could not afford that. The door opened outwards. He pulled it towards him with one finger, still holding the box, then eased it open with his foot and walked in. He wondered if he would get out again.

He crossed the hall, heading towards the stairs. This was the reception area for the hospital. When there was a battle it would be filled with stretchers bearing wounded men. Matt knew there would soon be many. The breaking of the line, the Republican retreat and Nationalist advance, had all happened too swiftly for the wounded to be brought in. But they would be. There were a half-dozen now, and one clerk moving among them, questioning them, reading the labels tied to them, writing down their details in a book. He was one of the enemy and glanced around as Matt crossed the hall but saw nothing suspicious in some soldier in fatigues carrying a box, and went back to his work.

There were two sentries on duty at the front door but they stood leaning on their rifles and smoking, and did not challenge Matt. He realised one of them was supposed to be guarding the door by which he had entered but had gone to while away the weary hours in talk with his comrade. They were surely only there to prevent prisoners escaping – why should anyone break into the hospital?

Matt climbed the stairs and started his search of the wards up there. The wards were just rooms with five or six narrow iron cots crammed into them. Their doors stood open so the air could circulate, held there by wedges jammed under them, so Matt did not have to enter each room, could peer in from the corridor outside. He was three quarters of the way round when he saw Helen.

She stooped beside a cot assisting a doctor working on a wounded man. Instead of her white uniform and cap she wore the soldier's clothes she kept for off-duty hours. She stroked the man's brow and held his hand. Matt saw the young doctor was Luis Zamora, one of the Republican staff, now a prisoner with Helen. As Matt clumped down the ward between the close-packed cots she looked around and her lips parted in shock. Matt stopped at her side and said softly, 'We've got to get out of here.'

The doctor looked at Matt, a sideways glance of startled recognition. Then he said, 'Take her, Matthew. God knows what they will do to us.'

The next cot was occupied, the soldier's greatcoat hanging above it at its head, but he was just a still shape under the grey blanket that was pulled up to cover his face. Matt took the greatcoat and thrust it at Helen: 'Put that on.' A cap hung on another cot, its owner snoring, mouth open. Matt shoved the cap on to Helen's head and she grimaced but settled it there. It covered her short, dark hair.

Helen struggled into the coat that was damp and stiff with mud. She hissed, 'You shouldn't have come! How will we get out? They won't do anything to me!'

Matt was not so sure, because he had heard stories of the executions carried out by both sides. He was afraid for himself and for her. 'Just do as I say.' He led the way, pausing to stoop and yank the wedge from under the door of the room, then picked up his crate again and headed for the stairs. Behind him the door swung, creaking, on a draught of air and then slammed shut. The two sentries at the front door looked up.

Matt started his descent, crate held two-handed before him and slightly to one side so he could see the stairs, but so that it half-hid his face. He muttered to Helen, 'Through the courtyard to the gate on the left. The van is in the square.' He realised he should have moved it to the side gate and left it with its engine running, but that might have aroused suspicion. He thrust the argument from his mind as useless now and concentrated on the present.

The light was not good in the hall, with just the one bulb hanging from its flex. Helen was covered by the over-large coat from neck to ankles and the cap shadowed her face, but Matt wondered if the disguise would pass a close inspection. The guards were watching them descend, and had to be distracted. Matt seemed to slip on the last treads and the crate clattered and skidded across the floor of the hall with Matt shambling in pursuit, bent double as if trying to catch it, but in fact still hiding his eyes.

The guards were guffawing, one of them pointing a finger at Matt, both watching him. He seized the crate and hoisted it again, pushing his tunic under his chin, still holding the wedge in one hand. Now was the time . . . He turned away from the guards and strode towards the rear door. Helen was ahead of him, had got off the stairs unnoticed by the guards and now she brushed the black-out curtain aside and pushed the door open. One of the guards shouted behind Matt on a rising note of enquiry. He did not understand a word and bawled back, *'Buenas noches!'* Then he went through the door. As he turned he saw the guards starting towards him and lifting their rifles. He threw the crate into the passage and slammed the door, jamming the wedge under it with a kick of his boot, and ran.

Helen was a shadow flitting across the courtyard, the skirts of the greatcoat flapping like wings. Matt galloped after her, through the gate and up the street to the square.

As she climbed in one side of the ambulance, he leaned in the other and switched on the ignition. Then he ran round to the front, seized the starting handle and whirled it furiously, his eyes on the front door of the house. The engine fired and ran. He swung up into his seat, shoving his tunic on to the floor out of the way, and reversed the ambulance in a tight half-circle, skidding on the mud.

That was when he saw the guards again, not at the front door but in the street by the side door. They had somehow smashed open the door to the courtyard against the restraining wedge and now ran towards the sound of the gunned engine.

'Get down!' he shouted at Helen.

She slid down in her seat and shouted back, 'You get down!'

The ambulance snaked and slid across the square, mud squirting up from under its wheels, then turned out on to the road. The rifles *crack-crack!*ed behind them and something struck the ambulance with a *clang!* like a blacksmith's hammer. Matt winced and shrank down in his seat still further so his knees were against the dash. Then he told himself that the back of the seat would not stop a bullet anyway.

At last they were on the road, the village left behind them, and there was no more shooting. Slowly they eased themselves up until they were sitting upright again. After some minutes during which their breathing returned to normal and their nerves quietened, Matt asked, 'What happened? When I left this morning we were nearly two miles behind the line!'

Helen took off the cap and ran her fingers through her hair. 'Some guns went through the village, teams of horses pulling them, all galloping and sweating . . .' She told how she and the other staff were captured and rounded up. 'Then their officer talked to Dr Zamora and he said they were going to let us carry on looking after the wounded because none of their own medical staff had come up yet. That's where you found us.' Helen paused, then said, 'Their forward troops must be ahead of us now.'

Matt nodded agreement, peering through the rain. He had slowed from the wild pace he had set escaping from the village. Speed was impossible on that road and in those conditions of darkness and muddy, pot-holed surface. 'We might have to leave the ambulance and try to sneak past them on foot, because they'll be on the road.' He remembered the group he had passed who had appeared to be digging a trench.

They had no chance to abandon the ambulance. The group of soldiers showed suddenly as one man standing in the middle of the road, hand raised, with others at the side. Matt pressed his foot to the floor and held on. The old ambulance responded, though sluggishly, and the man on the road jumped aside. Then he and the others were no more than thin yells fading in the night. Matt and Helen slumped with relief. They covered another half-mile and then the engine hammered madly and died. Matt threw out the clutch and the ambulance coasted to a halt.

Helen asked, 'What's wrong?'

Matt said wearily, 'Old age at bottom, but it's just seized up, I think. Anyhow, we can't stop here. God knows who might come along. We'd better walk on.'

He shrugged into his tunic. Helen stood small in the flapping greatcoat under the rain, her wet face turned up to him. He said, 'I'm sorry.'

'Sorry? Oh, Matt!' She reached up to pull his head down and kissed him. After a while they set off, walking hand in hand. They walked all through the night. Sometimes they talked but mostly they just trudged along happily. After two hours they caught up with the last and slowest of the stragglers on the retreat. An hour after that they passed the point where the Republicans were trying to establish another defensive line. They went through among the stragglers in the night and no one took any notice. Matt said reluctantly, 'We'll have to find another medical unit and report to them.'

Helen answered without enthusiasm, 'There must be one somewhere.' They did not find it but did not care greatly.

As the sun rose they came to a small town. They had been walking for eight hours, and that after a long day, but they were laughing as they entered the town. They found a pension down a narrow side street and Helen bargained with the old woman, pausing to say, 'I haven't any money, Matt. How much have you got?' When he had counted his pesetas Helen went back to her haggling. The bargain was struck and the old woman fed them bread and sausage and thin, black coffee. Then she showed them to a small room with a double bed that almost filled the floor, and closed the door behind them.

Matt asked, 'Whose is this?'

Helen avoided his eyes. 'Ours. Look, Matt, the money you have will just pay for one room and our board for a couple of days. If we had a room each we'd be out of here tomorrow. I told her we were married.' She held up her hand to show the ring. It had been her mother's, worn on the index finger of her left hand. It was now on the third. 'I changed it over behind my back.'

Matt took her in his arms.

It was morning of the next day when the soldiers came for them.

24

November 1938

'Tell him they weren't *hiding*!' Chrissie Ballantyne ran long fingers through her dark hair and pleaded with Jefferies, the young man who had come with her from the British Consulate in Barcelona, but her eyes were on the Spanish officer behind the desk. 'They'd got away when their unit was overrun and just found a place to rest!' She waited while Jefferies rattled away in his fluent Catalan.

It was two weeks since she had left home, two weeks of travelling and waiting for permits. She had lived out of her small suitcase and slept where she happened to be, in a wooden seated railway carriage or on a station bench, in a pension or a hut abandoned by some peasant. Chrissie had taken it all with a shrug because she had lived in spartan conditions in her youth, but she was weary now.

She had spent the whole of one long day trudging the narrow streets of this little town, seeking out one officer after another. One after the other they all told her that Matt and Helen had been reported missing and then found hiding in a backstreet pension. They had with them the cap and greatcoat of an enemy soldier, which could mean that they were spies. The punishment for either spying or desertion was execution by firing squad. Jefferies had told her unhappily, 'I'm afraid thère have been a lot of executions.'

Chrissie shivered. Matt was her baby, her firstborn, and Helen was a girl she had taken to her heart. The town was in chaos, close to the front line now, the streets full of weary men coming back from the line or going up to it, guns pulled by skinny horses, small tanks clanking and grinding over the cobbles. This office was in some sort of headquarters, with officers, clerks and signallers crammed into every room, messengers continually entering and leaving. Night had fallen and the windows were shuttered and blacked out. The rooms were hot and smelt of sweat and leather, cigarette smoke and cordite. Even in the bustle of this place she could hear the rumble of the guns.

Now this last officer was shaking his head. Chrissie felt the tears coming, but then . . . He was nodding, slowly.

Chrissie did not take her eyes from him, but asked Jefferies, 'What did he say?'

He wiped his sweating face with his handkerchief. 'I've threatened him with all the power of the British Empire and he says that he will release your son as he is a British subject, but he is to leave the country at once. The woman he says is Spanish and so must face the consequences of her actions. He cannot do more.'

'He must! Helen Diaz is the daughter of a Spaniard but of an English mother and she was born in England!' Chrissie's weariness and fear conspired together and now the tears came. 'I have known her since she was a child!' She held out her hand at thigh level. 'She is a schoolfriend of my daughter, she lives in my house, she and my son are lovers!' She broke off there, surprised at those last words but accepting that they were probably true. Why else was Matt there?

Jefferies had translated the outburst as she spoke and finished with her now. The officer behind the desk – it was no more than a trestle table covered with a blanket – stared as the tears ran down her face then looked down at the file in front of him. Then he said something in a low voice and Jefferies matched his quiet tone so Chrissie barely heard the words. 'He says there has been enough killing. Take your children and go.'

The officer was scribbling on a sheet of paper. He signed it with a flourish, banged a rubber stamp on its foot and stood to hand it to Jefferies. He passed it to Chrissie. 'An order for their release.' As she took it the officer bellowed and a soldier entered, listened to the orders barked at him by the officer and saluted, then held the door open.

Chrissie said, 'Thank you.' The officer gave a stiff little bow and she walked out followed by Jefferies. Fifteen minutes later she held Matt and Helen in her arms.

It was on a Wednesday that Sophie, now in Brighton, received a telegram from her father saying: MOTHER MATT AND HELEN DUE HOME FRIDAY. She travelled north that night by sleeper, arriving on Thursday morning. She decided to visit her father in the yard before going home, but as she walked down Church Street, blonde hair blowing in the wind, she turned aside to look in on Margaret Hackett, Peter's mother. The house was quiet as she walked along the passage and she concluded the upstairs neighbours were at work. She tapped at the kitchen door, then called, 'Mrs Hackett?' She received no reply. Suddenly uneasy, she turned the handle, pushed the door open and paused again to call, 'Mrs Hackett?' Then she was still, hardly breathing.

A small fire, burned down to ash and embers, glowed in the black- leaded grate and reflected from the brass fender and the fire irons on the hearth. Peter's mother sat near it in her armchair. Her hands, holding her knitting, lay in her lap and her head bent forward as if she dozed. She was very small, seemed to have shrunk in on herself, and she was very still. Sophie held tight to the door for a full minute in the silence of the empty house. She could hear, distantly, the hammer and clangour from Ballantyne's yard where the men were at work again.

Finally she moved slowly to kneel by the old woman and touch her hand, feeling for a pulse and looking up into her face. The hand was cold and the eyes stared at her unseeing. When the doctor came he said she had been dead for several hours.

Chrissie and Helen whiled away the journey home with plans for a wedding. When they stepped down from the train they were met by Jack – and Sophie, in black. By her side was a short and sturdy boy of nine or ten in a new suit of navy blue jacket and shorts. There was a joyful reunion and later, in the house, Sophie took her mother aside and explained, 'The little lad is Billy Hackett, Peter's half-brother. I found his mother dead.'

Chrissie said softly, 'Oh, Sophie!' She knew this was her daughter's first experience of death. She listened to Sophie's account of her doings, how she had contacted some distant relatives in Yorkshire by telegram. 'They replied saying they left it to me. "We parted for good when she married again!"

I suppose that was when she married Billy's father. Well, I've organised the funeral, but then there's Billy. Peter will look after him when he gets home but that won't be for a week or more.'

Chrissie said, 'Peter can't care for him while he is at sea. That won't do . . .'

After the funeral Sophie paid the rent on Peter's home for two weeks ahead. Billy went to live with Chrissie and the pair of them saw Sophie off at the station, on her way back to Brighton on a day of storm. Chrissie asked Sophie as the guard's whistle shrilled, 'Where is Peter now?'

'He's on board a ship called the *Florrie Dawe*. She was reported as passing through the Straits of Gibraltar over a week ago.' Sophie grinned wryly. 'So he's somewhere between there and here!' They looked up to the roof of the station where the rain pounded, listened to the howl of the wind outside. Sophie said, 'I hope he's all right.'

Peter had seen bad weather in the Bay of Biscay and coming through the Channel but now, in the North Sea, it was growing worse. The seas pounded the *Florrie Dawe* and the wind piled them in over her bow. She butted into the big, green seas all that day and into the night. In the early hours of the morning the second mate called all hands out of the fo'c'sle. Peter, in oilskins and sou'wester, stumbled after Harry Latimer and shouted above the storm, 'What is it?'

As he spoke the ship rolled. She had rolled for days now but never so badly as this and now she did not recover. They clawed their way out of the fo'c'sle to find the deck tilted so that they looked over one bulwark at the dark and cloud-wracked sky, and over the other down into the raging sea. Harry shouted, 'Her steering's gone and she's broadside to wind and sea! We've got to rig some sort of steering or she's finished!'

Peter fought his way aft along the canted deck with Harry and the others, sometimes up to their waists in water as the seas broke over the *Florrie Dawe*. He saw that the sea had smashed in the covers of numbers one and two holds. Harry pointed and shouted, 'She's filling up!' With every sea that burst inboard the ship was taking in tons of water. They fought to save her, working on the exposed stern, trying to rig chains from winches to the swinging, useless rudder. The *Florrie Dawe* was a single screw ship and so could not be manoeuvred by her engines. The steering had to be restored.

However, the sea was too strong and the ship was too old. Every time Peter looked up from his labour he could see she lay lower in the sea, had listed further.

'Abandon ship!' The cry came down from the bridge, passed from mouth to mouth, shouted against the wind. Peter traversed the deck, that now stood like a cliff, clinging to a safety line in order to reach the superstructure amidships and the boats there. He helped to launch one of them and saw the men crammed into her pull away. He started working at a davit trying to lower another into the sea that was only a few feet below him. Then the churned-white surface boiled up towards him and over him. As it closed over his head he knew the *Florrie Dawe* was sinking and she was taking him with her.

Sophie cried out and started up in her bed in the Brighton hotel. The sheets were torn off her by her wild thrashing, her blonde hair was tangled and sweat stood on her brow. She was frightened, shaking, but did not know why, could not remember the dream that had wracked her. Her window was open and a breeze blew out the curtains so they fluttered like pale wings in the darkness. She wondered if that had woken her. She got out of bed and closed the window then stood with her brow against the coolness of the glass, staring out at the sea. She wondered where Peter was and shivered, feared for him.

He surfaced gasping, borne up by the air in his oilskins. Something smashed against his shoulder and he yelled in pain, then realised it was a floating oar. He seized it and held to it at arm's length. That gave him some support while he kicked off his seaboots and shrugged out of the oilskins. He saw the *Florrie Dawe* standing on her head, only her stern and the propeller showing above the sea. He struck out desperately, striving to avoid being sucked down as the ship dived under. He glimpsed a boat – the one he had tried to lower at the end? He did not know, but made for it. He was close when he saw another man clinging to a hatch cover and recognised Harry Latimer. As he passed he shouted, 'Hold on, Harry!' The face Harry turned to him was pale in the night, open mouthed and with staring eyes. Peter knew Harry would not last long in this sea.

He reached the boat and found it empty when he clambered in over the stern. He shipped the oars and rowed the boat, bouncing and pitching, towards Harry. Twice he lost him in the night as Harry and the boat were tossed on the huge seas, now up on a high crest then down in a dark valley. He closed on him at last, held out an oar for him to grab and then hauled the exhausted man aboard.

He made Harry take an oar and try to pull, partly to help in keeping the boat's head to sea but mainly to keep Harry alive: if he had been left to fall asleep in the bottom of the boat he would never have woken. They were still pulling wearily at the oars when the dawn came and brought with it a big, new freighter. She stopped to make a lee as she drifted down on them, then took them aboard. They collapsed when they were hauled up to her deck.

Michael Beaumont looked up from the telegram sent by Chrissie Ballantyne, exasperated. 'I know it's not your fault, Sophie, but this is a *business*. I contract to supply a band and singers, a standard of entertainment. If I don't do that, if one of my singers is always missing, then people won't want to *pay* me. Now you're good, darling, *very* good, but that's no use if you're always away! I would be better off with somebody who is around all the time! So make your mind up. This tour round the South Coast finishes in another couple of weeks but then we're contracted for a winter season of four months up north. Do you want to work for me? Because if you do, you'll stay with me now. After all, this . . .' and he waved the buff form '. . . says: "Peter safe in hospital Newcastle. Ship sunk." It doesn't say he is at death's door. He could be out of hospital by the time you get up there.'

'And maybe he won't.' Sophie was still shaken from seeing the newspaper reports of the loss of the *Florrie Dawe* with only a few survivors. She took the telegram from him. 'I see your point of view – and thank you for the time I've had with you and the boys. I'm sorry.'

Beaumont sighed. 'So am I. That Peter must be quite a man. Good luck, Sophie.'

She blushed then and wept after she left him, tears for lost opportunities. She had not shown him the other telegram from Solly Rosenberg, telling her he had got her an audition the next day with Leslie Taylor, who had a big London band that broadcast across the country. Sophie sent two telegrams herself: one to her mother to say she was returning home, the other to Solly, telling him she had left Michael Beaumont and she would not be able to attend the audition for the Leslie Taylor band.

Chrissie drove to Newcastle in the Ford, met Sophie there and told her, 'I've been to see Peter twice, took him some books and fruit.' It was the first time Chrissie had met Peter, and she had gone to the hospital with some foreboding, wondering about this 'friend' – as Sophie insisted on calling him – who eked out a meagre living by prize fighting. She found him a likeable, open-faced young man, ready to smile when he had got over the first shock of her introduction: 'Hello! I'm Chrissie Ballantyne, Sophie's mother.' Now Chrissie went on, 'He's had a bad time but he's getting over it. I think he may well be out in a few days.'

Sophie said brightly, 'Oh, I'm sure he's fine.'

Chrissie did not ask why, if that was the case, Sophie had travelled over three hundred miles to see Peter. She drove her daughter to the hospital, dropped her at the door and said, 'I'll go and park. See you inside in five minutes.'

Her tact was wasted. Sophie found Peter in a ward with

nineteen other men who watched her with interest and
approval as she tap-tapped, blonde and slender and long
legged, between the beds to where Peter lay. They both
said, 'Hello,' conscious of the spectators. Sophie sat on
a straight-backed chair some two feet from the bed and
asked, 'How are you?'

Peter grinned at her. 'They had to hang me up for a bit
to dry out but I'm all right now.' Then he became serious.
'Thank you for all you did. Mrs Ballantyne told me about
my mother, how you looked after things – and took care
of Billy.'

Sophie, embarrassed, said, 'He's a good little lad. I'm just
sorry you came home to such bad news.'

They talked on politely until Chrissie appeared. She smiled
around her at the other patients, who were as admiring of
her as they had been of Sophie. Chrissie had thought that
as a woman turned forty she was too old to blush, but she
was wrong.

She came in on a strained pause in the conversation,
which Sophie broke: 'He says he's going back to sea as
soon as he's fit. Tell him he's mad.'

Peter said flatly, 'I've no chance of a job ashore.
I've been through all that. I bought some books out
of my pay from that first voyage. They went down
with the *Florrie Dawe* but I'll buy some more. Harry
Latimer, a shipmate of mine, told me I might be able
to pass my certificates for mate and work my way up.
I'd be somebody. So as soon as I can get a ship I'll
be off.'

Sophie challenged, 'What about Billy?'

Peter was unmoved. 'I'll find somebody to look after him

while I'm away. He'll be better off that way than he would with me at home and on the dole.'

Sophie appealed, 'Mother?'

But Chrissie shook her head. 'I could never keep your father ashore when he wanted to go, but I don't like the idea of Billy being passed around from one home to another. There's a garage behind the hotel with a little flat over it. Both are empty. You can have the flat for when you come home and I can find some light work for you until you're ready to go back to sea. And when you're away Billy can stay with us.' She did not think Peter would stick at a job in the hotel for long, but it would give him an occupation until he was ready to go to sea again and a home for him and his brother.

Peter said stiffly, 'I don't want charity.'

Sophie exclaimed, 'Oh, for God's sake! Don't be such a pompous—' She was stopped by her mother's hand gripping her arm.

Chrissie said icily, 'I don't waste my time on young men who are well able to look after themselves. I'm thinking of the boy.'

Peter was silent a while, thinking it over. Then he said grudgingly, 'All right, so long as I can pay you a fair rent for the flat – and I'll pay you for putting up Billy while I'm at sea.'

Chrissie agreed because it was what she had expected. 'Of course.'

Peter looked from her to Sophie and said, 'I'm lucky to have such good friends. Thank you.'

Driving home in the Ford, Chrissie said, 'I'll bring you through again tomorrow.'

'No.' The corners of Sophie's mouth were down. 'I know he's safe. That's enough. I can't live wondering where he is and whether he's all right.' She remembered the old woman waiting on the quay for the ship to come in. The wall was still between her and Peter. They had put it up together over six months ago when he sailed on the *Chatterton*. Sophie had proposed, 'Friends?' and he had replied that they couldn't be anything else. Sophie had gone to the hospital today hoping the wall lay in ruins – but it still stood.

Chrissie wondered . . . She said, 'He's a determined young man, means to get on.' She had seen him looking at Sophie and thought she knew the cause of that determination.

Now Sophie said ruefully, 'So do I, but I've been making things hard for myself.' She told her mother how she had given up her job with the Beaumont Band. 'That was one big chance thrown away. And Solly handed me another and I've missed that.' She explained how she had failed to go for the audition with the Leslie Taylor band.

Chrissie was silent for a while, eyes on the road as they passed the old windmill at Fulwell and drove on into the town. The doubt that she had harboured for some time, that she might have been wrong in her opposition to Sophie trying to make a living as a singer, now hardened into near certainty. The fear that Sophie might turn out like her own mother, Vesta Nightingale, was no longer there. 'I was going back to the hotel anyway. I'll leave the car there and walk across to the station with you. There's a train in about ten minutes that will connect with the London express at Durham.'

So the next morning Sophie stood outside the brand new palais that was plastered with big posters announcing 'The

Leslie Taylor Band'. She wore a new costume she had bought just ten minutes before for close on five pounds. She told herself, 'All or nothing, lass.' She had rehearsed what she would say but she went over it again one last time: the apology for not turning up for the audition, the request to be given another chance and: 'I don't think you'll regret it, Mr Taylor. Ask Michael Beaumont.'

Then she walked in with a long-legged, swinging stride, her head up and smiling.

25

April 1939

'You're looking bonny,' said Jack Ballantyne, stooping to kiss his wife. His hand caressed her shoulder through the green silk of her day dress and she read the message in his eyes and laughed breathlessly. She sat at the foot of the long table and now he straightened to stand tall above her, then strode to take his seat at the head of the table and smile at her.

Chrissie thought of it afterwards as a breathing space, that Easter Sunday lunch when she was able to gather all of her family around her. There was a chill stillness in the air but bright sunshine poured through the tall windows of the Ballantyne Hotel and laid contrasting strips of light and shade across the carpeted floor of the dining-room. It reflected, dazzling, from the glasses and silver on the table and cast light like a blessing on the people seated along each side of it.

Jack was happy because the Ballantyne yard was busy. A week ago the headlines of the Foreign pages of the newspapers had shouted of the scandal in France. Angélique, the widow of Jean-François, had, with the lawyer Dupuis and two of his clerks, been charged with forging what purported to be Jean-François' will leaving all to her. Dupuis had confessed and admitted that he and Angélique had been lovers. Jack had already spoken to Benoit, Jean-François' manager, who was leading the management team now running the French company and they wanted to talk to him about buying another ship. They, like Randolph Tourville, were preparing for a war.

Chrissie was glad for Jack and the yard but hid her own fears of the threat of war. She saw Matt, who seemed to add more muscle to his tall frame every day, in conversation with his father. Matt was working in the yard now but he had joined the Territorials, and told his parents with certainty, 'Hitler and Mussolini will have to be stopped. I've seen what they did in Spain.'

She smiled at Ursula Whittle, who had been nervous and uncertain in enforcing discipline as Sophie's teacher, but had grown in confidence over the years, and a warm friendship had grown between herself and Chrissie. Ursula was still a little severe, still on her guard, but she was smiling now, the sun glinting on her spectacles, as she talked to another of her former pupils, Helen Ballantyne, formerly Diaz. Helen's black hair had grown lustrous and long again. Chrissie heard her daughter-in-law say, 'So I will be able to go to medical school after I have had my baby,' and enjoyed a glow of happiness and pride.

It was good to see Helen's happiness. Soon after her return from Spain she had received a letter from the officer commanding the regiment in which her father and brother had fought. He said that they had both been killed in action at a time and place near where Helen had been nursing. She had wept bitterly and turned to Chrissie for solace, who held the girl to her breast.

The war in Spain was over, but now . . . Tom was in the Royal Air Force Volunteer Reserve. He was an inch or two shorter than Jack, but more like him, with his dark hair, than the sandy Matt. Now Tom called from halfway down the table, 'I hear the Railway Hotel will be open again about August, Mother.'

'That's right.' Chrissie knew where he had got his information. Sarah Tennant sat by his side. While seemingly little changed, still slight and shy, she had matured. She was more assured, though she was young for the responsibility she carried now – and there would be more before long. She worked closely with Chrissie. It was the culmination of a decision Chrissie had taken two years before, when she had promoted the girl out of the kitchen to be a chambermaid, to train Sarah as an assistant manager, a job she would have when the Railway Hotel, being rebuilt with the loan from Randolph Tourville, reopened. Chrissie, Sarah and Dinsdale Arkley would run the two hotels between them. Sarah was too young, just past her eighteenth birthday, to be a manager, though she would be ready when it came to her in time. Chrissie looked at Sarah and Tom and could foresee another wedding there. But as to her own daughter?

Sophie saw her mother's gaze fixed on her and smiled. Peter Robinson, home between voyages, sat at Sophie's side. The double-breasted suit he had saved for fitted his muscular body snugly. His hands resting on the white cloth were rough and calloused, the knuckles scarred. He was still uneasy in this company and would be for a long time to come, but while he was only uneasy, Sophie was screwing up her courage. She was slender in a linen tweed suit with a short jacket, and laughing to hide her nervousness. The talk was going on around them and leaving them in a little backwater of their own. She said, 'I told Mother six months ago that I was finished with you, that I wasn't going to spend my life waiting to see if you would live to come home, but here we are.'

Peter shook his head. 'You were right for the wrong reasons. There's more sailors die in retirement ashore than ever drown at sea. But you said you only wanted to be friends and that's all we are. There's no call for you to worry about being tied to me.'

Sophie had known it would not be easy. She kept her smile in place and went on, 'Is that still what you want?'

Peter said grimly, 'It's what I can afford. I've seen chaps that married lasses with money. I'm not going to trot around after you like a bloody poodle.'

Sophie winced inside. Peter was a seaman, paying his way and owing to nobody, but far from wealthy, while she was now a name in the entertainment world, vocalist with the Leslie Taylor Band, broadcasting, recording, even appearing in a film. She knew that if she wanted Peter there was only one way. She said, 'That won't happen to you because I'm not going to marry.' Sophie turned her head to face him and thought, Now for it! 'I still want my own life. No rings, no wedding. Just you – and me.' She knew she was pink cheeked and thought, A fine scarlet woman you are!

He stared at her, shocked. 'We couldn't do that! What would folks say?'

'I don't care what they say. Do you?'

'Aye. And I'd flatten any man that called you a bad name!' Peter glared at her.

'I don't want that.' Sophie felt she was winning and laid a soothing hand on his sleeve but grinned at him wickedly. 'So I'll have to be careful.' She decided she had gone almost far enough now. She challenged huskily, 'Can you tell me you don't love me? Honestly?'

Peter's glare faded and after a time he said, 'I can't do that. But it won't make any diff—' She stopped him then with her finger on his lips.

That night Peter's half-brother Billy Hackett was away at an Easter Cubs camp and Peter sat in his flat above the garage behind the Ballantyne Hotel, over his books at the table in the sitting-room. He was studying for his 'ticket', his certificate as 'mate', but that would lie in the distant future because first he had to be rated able seaman. He found this a good time to study, after the pubs had shut and the streets outside were silent. He did not hear the tap of heels that broke that silence but looked up when a key was inserted in the lock on the front door at the foot of the stairs. Frowning, he shoved back his chair and was at the head of the stairs when Sophie climbed them.

He stared at her, surprised. 'I didn't know you had a key.'

'Nobody else knows,' she answered softly. 'I told you I would be careful.'

Chrissie, with Jack sleeping by her side, lay wakeful, and looked back over the day with only partial contentment. All her family around her . . . She remembered the promise she had made nearly twenty years ago, that she would hold them together. She had done it and that was cause for congratulation, but she felt that the worst test was yet to come.

Gallagher stumbled out into the night from a Liverpool pub, McNally lurching drunkenly at his side. Gallagher was cursing under his breath, harping on the subject that always upset him when the drink hit him, mouthing obscenities.

'That little cow. She cost us our jobs. I'll never get a foreman's billet again.' He staggered and fell against a sagging wooden fence, shoved himself upright and vented his rage and lust for vengeance on the insensate timber. He kicked the fence down, smashed it under his stamping feet, all the time seeing it as Sophie Ballantyne.

26

September 1942

'We only know that she was brought in by an ambulance that found her lying in the road.' The nursing sister lifted her hands helplessly. 'We presume she had been run down by a car in the black-out. It's not uncommon.'

Chrissie and Sophie knew it was not. They had lived through three years of war and black-outs now. Chrissie asked, 'Can we see her?'

The sister guessed that they had come a long way. Both had North Country accents, though the older woman's was more marked. And she looked tired – from travelling? Her smart two-piece suit was wrinkled. They were both attractive and the younger woman – girl, really – the sister summed up as 'like a film star': blonde, slender, blue eyed.

'Of course.' The sister got up from her chair. 'This way.' She led Chrissie and her daughter down the long ward between the lines of beds. The hospital was in South London, and its outside walls bore the signs of bombing and the marks of shell fragments from anti-aircraft barrages, holes and long scars in the red brickwork. The sister stopped by one bed and stooped over the patient there for a moment. Then she straightened and indicated two straight-backed chairs: 'Would you like to sit with her for a while? I'm afraid there's no sign of a recovery,' she said, and after a moment's hesitation, added, low voiced, 'I think she might go at any time.'

'Thank you.' Chrissie sank down on to one of the chairs. 'We'll stay.' Sophie took the other, with a smile for the sister who turned away and went back to her work. Chrissie stared at her mother and whispered, 'My God! She's skin and bone!'

Martha Tate's arms, lying on the sheet, were skeletal, her head like a skull with sunken cheeks and eye sockets. She seemed quite still. It was only when they watched her carefully that they saw the faintest of breaths fluttering her bloodless lips. They had nowhere to go so they sat and waited.

When Martha Tate was admitted to the hospital the staff had found only one address in her bag and that was of Solly Rosenberg. They had sent a telegram to him and he had telephoned Chrissie. Sophie had chanced to be at home and accompanied her mother on the journey south through the night. They had spent twelve hours sitting in railway carriages, dimly lit and with their windows blacked, crowded with servicemen, their rifles and kitbags. Then they had gone straight to the hospital.

Chrissie felt bedraggled and guessed that her bolero suit looked as if she had slept in it – which she had. It was made from a pre-war edge-to-edge coat she had cut down and converted. Her new raincoat was one of the wartime 'utility' models, cut to economise on cloth. It had used fourteen of her sixty-six clothing coupons for the year. She had used it as a blanket in the train and now it hung over the back of an empty chair.

They waited all through that long day, taking turns to go out to a nearby café in the afternoon for a cup of tea and a sandwich of bread thinly spread with margarine and jam. They waited into the evening, and as the day died, so Martha Tate breathed her last. She never woke.

Chrissie found she was weeping as she stood and watched the screens being closed around the bed. Sophie put her arm around her mother but Chrissie wiped the tears away angrily. 'I don't know why I'm crying. She handed me over to strangers, never gave me love or a word of kindness or anything else. She only came to me when she wanted something.'

It had been Chrissie's adoptive mother, Mary Carter, who had given her affection and guidance. And it was Mary's example that Chrissie followed when bringing up her own children.

Chrissie went with Sophie and collected the few belongings of Martha Tate. As they waited by the desk a tired-looking, middle-aged man entered the ward. He carried a shabby raincoat over one arm and held a trilby hat in the other hand. He paused to ask the sister. 'What's the news on Vesta Nightingale?'

Chrissie glanced at him, startled at his use of her mother's stage name. The sister shot him a warning look and said, 'This is Mrs Tate's daughter and granddaughter.'

'Oh?' He looked from Sophie to Chrissie, then back to Sophie, his brow wrinkling, puzzled.

The sister said, 'Mrs Tate died not long ago.'

'I see. Well, that settles that.' He still looked at Sophie

but Chrissie asked him, 'What did you want with my mother?'

Now he turned to her. 'I'm Detective Sergeant Gurney. If you could spare me a minute or two outside?' He waited until Chrissie had signed for the surprisingly large parcel of Martha's belongings, then led them out to a corner in the corridor where they had a little privacy. There Gurney explained, awkwardly, 'Sorry if I looked surprised in there when the sister said who you were. Fact is, you're not what I would have expected.' He went on disjointedly as the thoughts popped into his head: 'See, down at the station we all knew Vesta – Mrs Tate – mind, she usually called herself Vesta Nightingale. Sang in the pubs and clubs around here. She was a –' he hesitated, then finished diplomatically – 'a character. Mind you, she was a heroine when the worst of the blitz was on. Singing her heart out in the shelters when the rest of us were shi—were scared we weren't going to get out again.' He grimaced. 'There were a lot killed and we thought we were next. The floor lifting under your feet and bits o' the roof falling down on your head but she sang through it all. Should ha' had a medal.' He was looking past them, his eyes unfocused, remembering. Then he grinned wrily and admitted, 'O' course, she was probably pie eyed.' Then he recalled who he was talking to and apologised. 'Sorry. But she did take a drink, now and again.'

Chrissie said wearily, 'I know all about her drinking and a lot of other things, Sergeant. You can be frank with me. What did you want with her?'

Gurney cleared his throat. 'Well, if you want it straight, we knew she wasn't being paid anything for singing. To tell the truth, she was probably good in her day, but that was years ago. All the time I've known her, that's three or four years now, she's been singing for her booze and that's all. So she used to make a few bob for the rent – ' he hesitated again, then finished awkwardly, 'In other ways.' Chrissie remembered the men she had seen with her mother and Sophie recalled those Martha Tate had brought back to the rooms she shared with Sophie in Newcastle. Gurney looked away, embarrassed, and hurried on. 'But lately we reckon she's been involved with the black market. Nothing big, but acting as somebody's go-between. Of course, we'll not be pursuing that line of enquiry any further now.'

At Chrissie's request he showed them where Martha Tate had lived, in one rented, damp basement room. Chrissie found there were four weeks' rent owing and she paid that to the landlady, who lived upstairs. There was nothing in the room that she wanted, little in fact but a bed and a chair, some old playbills from bygone variety theatres showing Vesta Nightingale near the top of the bill, and a handful of bills of another kind – unpaid. There were a few old clothes and a small box of jewellery, all imitation. Chrissie wrote cheques to settle the bills and told the landlady that anyone who wanted the clothes and jewellery could have them.

She and Sophie found a room in a small hotel and there they opened the brown paper parcel brought from the hospital. It held the clothes Martha Tate was wearing when she was picked up by the ambulance, and a brown paper carrier bag. This seemed to hold clothing, but when Chrissie pulled out the much darned cardigan stuffed on top and the folded skirt below she found the bottom of the bag lined with packets of tea.

Sophie said drily, 'Well, it could be her ration for months.'

However, they both knew Gurney had been right and Martha had been selling tea on the black market. Chrissie remembered his talk of Martha drinking and finding the rent by making money 'in other ways'. Her mother had died as she had lived.

Chrissie organised the funeral and stood dry eyed with Sophie as her mother's body was interred. Then she and her daughter went home.

'Tack! Tack! Tack! Tack! Tack!' Chrissie looked up from her desk, at first refusing to believe what she had heard.

Sophie had accompanied Chrissie home but only stayed for one night. She had left to make a tour of army camps and airfields before going back to work for the Leslie Taylor Band in London. Chrissie went back to running the rebuilt Railway Hotel. The Ballantyne had been requisitioned by the government in January 1940, soon after the outbreak of war, and was now a hostel for workers directed into the town. Dinsdale Arkley managed the hostel and Chrissie the Railway Hotel. Sarah – Ballantyne since her marriage to Tom in 1940 – worked for and with both of them. The two women had become very close.

It was on a morning in early October that Chrissie sat in her office in the Railway Hotel, working through the correspondence that had arrived that morning, and listened in disbelief. Then the dry rattle came again: *'Tack! Tack! Tack! Tack! Tack!'*

Chrissie had never heard one before but knew it was a machine-gun. She swung out of her chair and around the desk and ran. She shouted to the girl in reception, '*Air Raid! Sound the alarm!*' then dashed on along the corridor leading to the rear of the building. The jangle of the fire alarm filled the corridor as she reached the door at the end of it and passed through into the yard. Then she heard the belated banshee wailing of the air-raid warning sirens.

Billy Hackett was in the yard. Thirteen years old now and home from school for a half-term holiday, he was looking after the two toddlers as they played. Chrissie snatched up Jean, Tom and Sarah's one-year-old, and grabbed the arm of three-year-old Robert, Matt and Helen's son. She tugged him along, his short legs barely touching the ground so that he skipped, making for the brick-built surface air-raid shelter that took up a quarter of the yard.

She heard a whistling, and knew what caused it, had heard it too often. She shouted, 'In the shelter, Billy!' and herded him before her, seeing his frightened face turned to her, to push him in at the door of the shelter. The whistle became a scream as they stumbled in the cold, concrete darkness of the shelter. Then the floor of solid concrete shuddered under them, the blast blew open the door behind them and snatched at their clothing. The *boom!* of the explosion deafened them and dust boiled in at the open door.

Chrissie realised young Robert was clinging to her leg and she released his arm then used that free hand to search for the shelf and the torch standing on it. She found it and flicked the switch. The beam was feeble and she made a mental note to get another battery for it, though that would be difficult since they were in short supply. Nevertheless, the light cut through the swirling dust cloud and showed Billy comforting little Robert, though he was scared himself but trying to hide it. Jean, the baby, in the crook of Chrissie's arm, had her face scrunched up, eyes shut and mouth wide open. It was a second or two before Chrissie realised she had been deafened by the bomb and could not hear the child wailing.

There were three benches, one along each wall of the shelter except that pierced by the door. They served as bunks or seats. Chrissie sank down on one, feeling her legs give loosely under her. Billy sat beside her, holding Robert on his knee. All of them were covered in the dust that still hung in the air. Chrissie and Billy tried to soothe the young children and waited tensely for another bomb. It did not come. The dust settled and their hearing returned, their breathing slowed to normal. Then the door was pushed open again and Sarah cried frantically, 'Mother! Are you there?' Then as she saw the little group huddled together in the light of the torch: 'Oh, thank God!'

She said she had been working on the top floor of the hotel, had been halfway down the stairs when the bomb exploded, and had feared for them. Chrissie surrendered Jean and Sarah clutched her baby. So they waited together until the sirens sounded the all-clear.

They found every window in the hotel shattered and the yard where the children had played full of broken glass. They learned that the aircraft had been a lone raider which had sneaked in past the defences. It had dropped one big bomb – a landmine – that had fallen two streets away, flattening two buildings and killing several people.

Chrissie looked at the damage to the hotel and said, 'We'll have to find somewhere inside for the bairns to play, then we'll clear up this lot.'

They faced an awesome task, but before they had been at work an hour Peter Robinson walked in at the front door of the hotel. He stared around at the dirt and broken glass and said grimly, 'I don't have to ask. A porter told me about it when I got off the train five minutes ago.'

Chrissie wiped a dirty hand across her brow, smearing it. 'Peter! By lad, it's lovely to see you!'

He smiled at her. 'Nice to be here. We berthed in the Tyne this morning.' Peter had his second mate's 'ticket' now, earned by his hard work and courage, and the quicker promotion to meet the demands of wartime. His ship was a coaster on the East Coast convoy run, from the North East down to London and back again. He had seen a lot of ships sunk by U-boats and E-boats but wore no uniform, just a small badge in the lapel of his jacket bearing the letters 'MN' for Merchant Navy. He said, 'I have to go back tomorrow night but I'll give you a hand here.'

Chrissie protested, 'You're entitled to a rest while you're between convoys!' but he insisted, and by nightfall the broken windows were boarded up and the hotel was trading as usual.

His ship sailed the following night, and just twelve hours later, on a Saturday morning, Matt Ballantyne walked into Chrissie's office in the Railway Hotel. She looked up and saw him, tall and broad as his father now and in the khaki serge battledress of the Royal Army Medical Corps, the three stripes of a sergeant on his sleeve. He held his beret in his hand and his once unruly sandy hair was clipped short and neatly combed. Chrissie clapped her hands in delight and ran from her desk to kiss him. 'Matt! How long have you got?'

He grimaced at the question then grinned good naturedly. 'People always ask the same thing when you come on leave: "How long have you got?" Or "When do you go back?"'

'Only because we want to make the most of the time while you're here.' Chrissie hung on to him happily, feeling the solid strength of him. Then she saw his attention had strayed and she pulled away. 'But you want to see the bairn!' and Matt stepped past her to where Robert and little Jean played before the fire.

Matt squatted on his heels in front of his son, who looked at him shyly because he had only seen his father for a few days at a time when Matt had leave, and was still uncertain of this big stranger. But he relaxed with the innocent confidence of a child as Matt played with the children, helping to build a house with a box of blocks.

Chrissie brought Sarah to see Matt and he smiled up at her and asked, 'How's Tom?'

She smiled brightly. 'He's fine. I get a letter three or four times a week. I don't know what he's doing – except flying, of course.' Tom was in Bomber Command.

When it was time for the children's midday meal Matt said, 'I'll go up to the hospital and see Helen.'

He met her outside a ward where she had just finished rounds. She was a medical student, in white coat with a stethoscope around her neck that dug into his chest as she hugged him. They walked in the grounds and talked of Robert. Then Matt said, 'Now I know what I want to do with my life.' He had been at Dieppe and seen too many men die, knew how precious life was and was conscious of his own mortality.

That night before they slept Chrissie said, 'It was good to see Matt home again.'

Jack grunted happy agreement. 'I'm looking forward to having him back in the yard.'

But Matt would never return to the yard.

'It will be a challenge, of course.' Ursula Whittle, spruce in a Scotch tweed suit, smiled brightly at Chrissie but blinked behind her spectacles. 'No doubt the boys will try to take advantage of me but I'll be ready for them.' She had been given a post at the local grammar school, which was short of teachers because so many of its young men had gone to the war. The smile hid uncertainty. Ursula had grown in confidence over the years but now she would be breaking new ground. She had come for reassurance.

Chrissie gave it: 'Just start as you mean to go on. Jump on the first one who disobeys or gives you cheek. They'll soon settle down when they know how they stand. I'm sure you'll be a success.'

Ursula would give heed to the words later but it was the underlying reassurance coming from Chrissie that she took in. Her smile became less brittle as she relaxed. 'Where's Sophie? And Tom?'

Now Chrissie could have done with some reassurance. She laughed ruefully, 'Tom is at the same airfield in Lincolnshire but I don't know about Sophie.'

In fact, at that moment Sophie stood on a makeshift stage fashioned from oildrums and planks on a desert airstrip. A solitary piano accompanied her as she sang song after song for a thousand men sitting on the sand under a blazing sun. A press photographer was there and took a picture. It appeared in a newspaper some weeks later, and in a shipyard on the Clyde McNally passed a copy to the man who sat beside him as they ate their sandwiches. Gallagher glared at the photograph then crumpled the paper in his big fist. 'We'll get even with the bitch one o' these days!'

Then one morning the telegraph boy in his pillbox cap pedalled his bicycle up to the Railway Hotel and took a telegram from the pouch on his belt. It was for Sarah, and Chrissie opened it for her. 'Regret to inform you Flight-Lieutenant Thomas Ballantyne missing . . .' Sarah held Jean in her arms, all she had left of Tom.

27

May 1945

Almost three years after that telegram, Peter Robinson stood duffel-coated on the bridge of his ship in the last of the night and looked out at the lights. There were the red and green navigation lights of other vessels in the middle distance and further still to westward lay a line of white radiance that marked the coast of Norfolk. The lights were still strange after six years of war, blacked-out countryside and cities, darkened ships.

The war in Europe was over. He no longer had to be prepared to meet attacks by submarines or E-boats. He had passed his examinations for his first mate's 'ticket' a year ago and now was studying for a master's. The owners of the shipping line which employed him had told him he could expect a command of his own before too long. He watched the sun rise with hope in his heart.

Gallagher woke when the sun was high with hatred in his heart. He got out of Fannon's bed and sat at the kitchen table. He gulped tea made for him by the fat bookmaker, who was dishevelled and worn after spending the night in an armchair with his fear.

Gallagher said thickly, 'You say there's a ladder?'

Fannon answered nervously, 'Aye. In the garage under the flat.'

Gallagher nodded. 'So now we want a gallon o' paraffin and a bottle o' gin.'

McNally sat up on the settee, yawning. 'I could do wi' some beer.'

'I'll fetch some. And the gin.' Fannon licked his loose lips. 'What d'ye want the paraffin for?'

Gallagher glared at him out of cold little eyes. 'Just get it.'

Fannon left without a word.

That same evening Chrissie and Jack sat in the stalls at the Empire Theatre. They watched and listened as their daughter Sophie, top of the bill as 'the broadcasting and recording star', wound up the show to a roar of applause and several curtains. Jack sniffed and blinked while Chrissie wept openly and dabbed at her eyes with her handkerchief.

In Sophie's dressing-room Jack said gruffly, 'Well done, lass.' Chrissie kissed Sophie, who laughed at her parents out of sheer happiness. Topping the bill in this theatre was a dream come true, all her hopes realised – well, almost.

She told them, 'I'm expecting Peter home tonight and I want to make some supper for him. So I'll just clean this make-up off and change then get along there.'

Sophie had told them when she arrived at the start of the week for this engagement at the Empire, 'I'm going to live in the flat.' It was empty while Peter was at sea – Billy Hackett lived with Chrissie and Jack. 'It will be handy for the theatre and I expect it could do with a dusting.'

Jack had wanted to ask questions but Chrissie had caught his eye and he refrained. Later he said to her, worried about his daughter, 'What's going on?'

Chrissie answered tranquilly, 'I trust Sophie and I trust Peter, so we don't need to ask.'

Sophie left the theatre at her usual time, only ten minutes after her parents. She knew Peter's ship was due to dock about one in the morning and he would be at his flat behind the old Ballantyne Hotel by two. All the streets were lit now, though the narrow lane that led down past the side of the Ballantyne Hotel had only one lamp. That was sufficient to show Sophie, high heels tapping on the cobbles, the way into the yard through the double gates that stood open. The hotel itself, still government property but no longer a hostel, stood empty and dark. Rain was beginning to fall as she turned her key in the lock of the door to the flat, locked it behind her and climbed the stairs. There was no light on the stairs but a red glow in the sitting-room above that came from the embers of a fire in the grate. She thought that first she should put some coal on the fire. As she came to the head of the stairs she saw the furniture in the shadowed room, the table with its spread cloth and the vase of flowers she had set there. Then as she stepped into the room the hand went across her mouth, and arms wrapped around her.

For a moment she was frozen in shock, only her eyes shifting frantically, taking in that the curtains were drawn. She thought that she should have seen them from outside and remembered she had left them open. She saw it was the burly Gallagher standing on her left, whose hand was over her mouth, and big McNally on her right whose apelike arms pinned her own to her sides. Both wore dark suits.

Stepping out from the shadows, old raincoat tight over his belly, reluctant and frightened, came Josh Fannon.

Shock gave way to panic then and Sophie fought. She twisted and wriggled, threw herself from side to side to try to break free. McNally only laughed and held her easily. She could smell the drink on his breath. Then she kicked out, hacking with the high heels and now she brought grunts of pain and curses from the two men holding her. Gallagher snarled at Fannon, 'Get hold of her legs! We want her on the bed!'

Fannon obeyed, bending to catch Sophie's legs, yelping with pain as she kicked him, but persevering as Gallagher cursed him. He held her ankles, pulled off the shoes and with the others dragged her to the bed in the corner, threw her on to it. Gallagher knelt on top of her, his knees grinding painfully into her upper arms, his hand still clamped over her mouth after she had tried to bite him and failed. He panted, 'One o' you get those bottles opened and bring the gin here.' Then he glared down at Sophie. 'You'll be bloody sorry you crossed me. You got us kicked out of our jobs and put me back on the shop floor in a strange town wi' a lot o' bloody Jocks. I'll make you pay for that . . .' He went on, mouthing obscenities.

Meanwhile McNally held Sophie's legs, grinning at her drunkenly. Her eyes rolling, Sophie watched Fannon fetch a canvas shopping bag from the shadows and take from it a pint-sized bottle and a gallon can. He opened both and called shakily, 'Do you want me to toss the paraffin around?'

'No! Not yet!' Gallagher twisted his head to snarl at the fat man. 'Bring the gin over here! I *told* you! We'll pour that down her, strip the clothes off her and leave her in the bed. When they find her it'll look like a coal fell out o' the fire and she never woke up!' He showed his teeth when he saw the horror in Sophie's eyes. He took the bottle from Fannon and released her mouth only to seize her nose. Sophie screamed once, emptying her lungs, then choked as the neck of the bottle was thrust between her teeth and the raw spirit flooded into her mouth.

Peter Robinson came up the stairs and into the room at a run. He swept Fannon out of his way with a back-handed swing of his clubbed fist that took the fat man in the face and sent him staggering into the table. It overturned and he fell with it. The gallon can of paraffin went flying and landed on its side on the fender, its contents pouring out.

McNally had released his grip on Sophie's legs and was trying to turn to face this threat. He was too late. Peter seized him by the lapels of his jacket, swung him aside and McNally's legs tangled. Then Peter threw him after Fannon. They sprawled in a heap, Fannon wheezing and McNally cursing. Then both of them yelled as the paraffin, gurgling out of the can in the fireplace, ignited with a *whoosh*!

Gallagher lashed out with the gin bottle he held but Peter caught his wrist and used Gallagher's own momentum to pull him off the bed. He fell awkwardly, face down, with a crash that shook the floor. The bottle broke but he still held the neck, ready to use it as a weapon. He pulled his hands under him to shove himself up but Sophie, released from his weight, rolled over, choking and retching, then fell off the bed. Peter caught her by the shoulders, but her legs and all her weight behind them smashed down on the back of Gallagher's neck. He was slammed face down on the floor again and the fragment of broken bottle he held was driven into his throat.

Sophie tried to scramble away and Peter lifted her to her feet and ran her to the head of the stairs. McNally rolled wildly over the floor with flailing arms, trying to extinguish the flames licking from his jacket. Fannon was struggling to stand and pulling off his smouldering raincoat. The room was filling with smoke and all of them were coughing. Peter shoved Sophie ahead of him down the stairs: 'Get out of here!' At the bottom she yanked the door towards her and staggered out into the cool night air.

Peter followed her and made sure the door swung shut behind him. He took Sophie's arm and led her clear of the building, into the lane, and only then let her stop and rest. But he still watched the door of the flat to see if they were being pursued.

Fannon, who had been sent by Gallagher the night before to reconnoitre, had found the ladder in the garage below. They had climbed it to reach the window they broke to get in. Fannon did not think of the ladder now, and instead ran for the stairs. The others followed him in their panic.

Fannon was first to blunder through the smoke and flames to the head of the stairs but McNally was close on his heels. Gallagher followed, with a hand trying to staunch the flow of blood from the awful wound that was draining his life away. McNally tried to shove Fannon aside but only succeeded in thrusting him head first down the stairs. Fannon fell, rolling. His skull crashed against the door at the bottom and he lay still. McNally followed him, wild to get away from the room with its mounting flames and throttling smoke. He stood on Fannon's body to get at the door but then found he could not open it because of Fannon's loose bulk jammed against it. He attempted to step back and haul the obstruction clear, but found Gallagher in his way. Gallagher was on his knees, dying, sliding down to join Fannon. McNally cried for help but nothing came from his open mouth because the smoke filled it and choked him.

Peter and Sophie stood under the rain that was now a deluge, uncaring. Sophie leaned against the wall, head back, feeling the downpour sluicing blessedly clean and cold over her face. She breathed deeply, glad to be alive.

Peter saw flames spurting through the roof of the flat and licking up the curtains at the windows. The inside was lit red like a furnace. He looked away, took Sophie into his arms and held her against him. She mumbled, shuddering, 'They said they were going to kill me. I thought your ship wasn't due in till one in the morning. It's not midnight yet.'

Peter answered absently, stroking her hair, 'We developed engine trouble and had to put into Hull. She'll be there for a few days so I came on by train. I'd just put my key in the lock when I heard you scream.' His grip on her tightened. 'It was just luck I was here. Just luck. If it wasn't for that . . .' But he could not bear to think what would have happened if he had not come to the flat when he had. He could not face the thought of losing her.

He held her, the pair of them standing in the rain as the fire burnt through the roof. It lit them and the alley with a rippling tiger's skin of light and black shadows as the wind fanned the flames. Then they heard above its roaring the clanging of bells and the fire engines braked at the mouth of the alley.

Peter walked Sophie away then, still holding her, and

now he spoke from the heart: 'Listen, I've got a decent job and a chance of a better one, but it wouldn't matter if I was out of work and back getting coal off the tip. I want you. I don't care how much money you've got. And you can sing all you like, but I want you. Now. Not tomorrow or next year – now.'

Sophie turned up her face, reached up to lock her fingers in his wet hair and pulled his head down to kiss him.

One morning a week later Sarah smiled at the girl on reception in the Railway Hotel and told her, 'You get away for a break now. I'll look after the desk.' She stood behind it, slender in a simple 'utility' cotton dress, glancing through the register to confirm who was leaving that day and who was expected. Dinsdale Arkley had retired at the end of the war in Europe and Sarah was virtually manager of the hotel now, sharing the duties with Chrissie. They shared the care of Sarah's three-year-old daughter, Jean, too. Sarah had been grateful for the work, to be able to immerse herself in it. She had never given up hope that Tom might have survived, but as the weeks dragged by into months and years without word, that hope was worn thin. She told herself that she had a career and Jean, and that was enough, but she still grieved.

She did not look up when she heard the flap of the swing doors opening, her slim finger halfway down one page, but when she reached its end she raised her eyes and her heart lurched. Tom Ballantyne stood on the other side of the desk in a well-worn Royal Air Force uniform, his cap in his hand.

Later he was to tell her, 'We came down in Czechoslovakia.

I was picked up and hidden by a Resistance group but they had no escape network, no way I could get word out that I was OK. The Yanks liberated us the day before yesterday and flew us home.'

Sarah only knew that, incredibly, he was alive and come back to her. She took no note of the ill-fitting uniform lent to him by a brother officer but she saw there was a lean hardness about him now. He had been living in the open and on the run for the past three years and it showed. He was weathered by sun, wind and cold so that his teeth showed white against the tan. He came around the desk and she fell into his open arms.

At the end of that week Helen stood on the station platform in a raincoat sodden from drizzling rain as low-clouded, early dusk turned into dark night. A bomb had blown the roof from the station in 1940 and it had not been replaced, so the rain came in. The trains were running late and one by one they pulled in, discharged their passengers and clanked on. The temporary shelters built on the platforms kept off the worst of the rain but the wind drove it in, slanting, and Helen could feel her feet squelching cold in her shoes as darkness and her spirits fell.

Another train ground past her, slowing, and stopped with a hiss of steam and a clatter of couplings. She peered into the crowd that poured from its doors and swept around the slight figure of the solemn-faced girl. Then suddenly Matt towered above her. He was Lieutenant Ballantyne now, commissioned in the field, and his decorations made a block of colour on the left breast of his khaki tunic. The breath was crushed out of Helen and the khaki serge was rough against her skin. She protested and laughed and cried and held on to him.

28

September 1945

'Tea?' Jack put his head around the door to peer into the kitchen of the Ballantyne house, brows raised as he asked the question of the women in there.

'Just coming.' Chrissie, wearing a flowered apron over a pre-war silk dress, looked up from spreading the carefully hoarded butter thinly on the bread. Then voicing the thought she had cherished all afternoon, 'Do you realise this is the first time for more than six years that we've all been together?'

Jack nodded slowly. 'I thought about it this morning. It's been a long time.' Chrissie thought he looked older, that the war had aged him, and she knew it had put more than six years on her.

That Sunday was a clear, hot, Indian summer day, with no bitter north-east wind coming in off the sea. A few minutes later Chrissie came out of the kitchen door into the back garden, the apron discarded, her eyes slanted against the sunlight. She carried a tray loaded with plates, cups and saucers and put it down on the table set out for the purpose. Her favourite chair was there with the others grouped around the table and she sank into its creaking comfort of cushioned wickerwork.

The men were talking of ships, inevitably, and playing cricket. Robert, Matt's six-year-old, was at the crease, and Billy Hackett, Peter's grinning half-brother, kept wicket. There were no uniforms now, except that all were in their shirtsleeves and grey worsted trousers, though Tom was still in the RAF, Matt in the Army and Peter a ship's officer. Tom was eager to join his father in the yard and Matt had been accepted for medical school as soon as he was demobilised.

Now the girls in their cotton dresses came out of the kitchen carrying the cakes and bread and butter, pots of tea, milk and sugar, all scraped together from their rations. Sophie, married for three months now and expecting her first child, was looking for Peter as she chatted with Helen, a qualified doctor and due to return to her duties at the hospital in an hour or so. Sarah followed them, slowly because of her daughter, Jean, dawdling by her side. Ursula Whittle, now a head teacher, came with her.

Chrissie called, 'Tea!' and the cricketers wandered over, still talking, to gather around her and the table, sink into chairs. Little Robert bumped himself down cross-legged at her feet while Billy sat on the grass by her side and leaned against her legs and Jean clambered up into her lap. Jack watched her from across the table, content.

Chrissie looked around at them, all of them her children or her grandchildren, though she had only borne two. All the others – Tom, whom she and Jack had adopted, Peter, Sarah, Helen, Ursula and Billy – were as much her children as Sophie or Matt. She recalled how she had sworn over twenty years ago that she would hold this family of hers together for the sake of the children. There had turned out to be more children than she had bargained for but she had done it, and now she swore anew that she would go on doing it. She smiled at Jack and into the sunlight.